1: Mothers

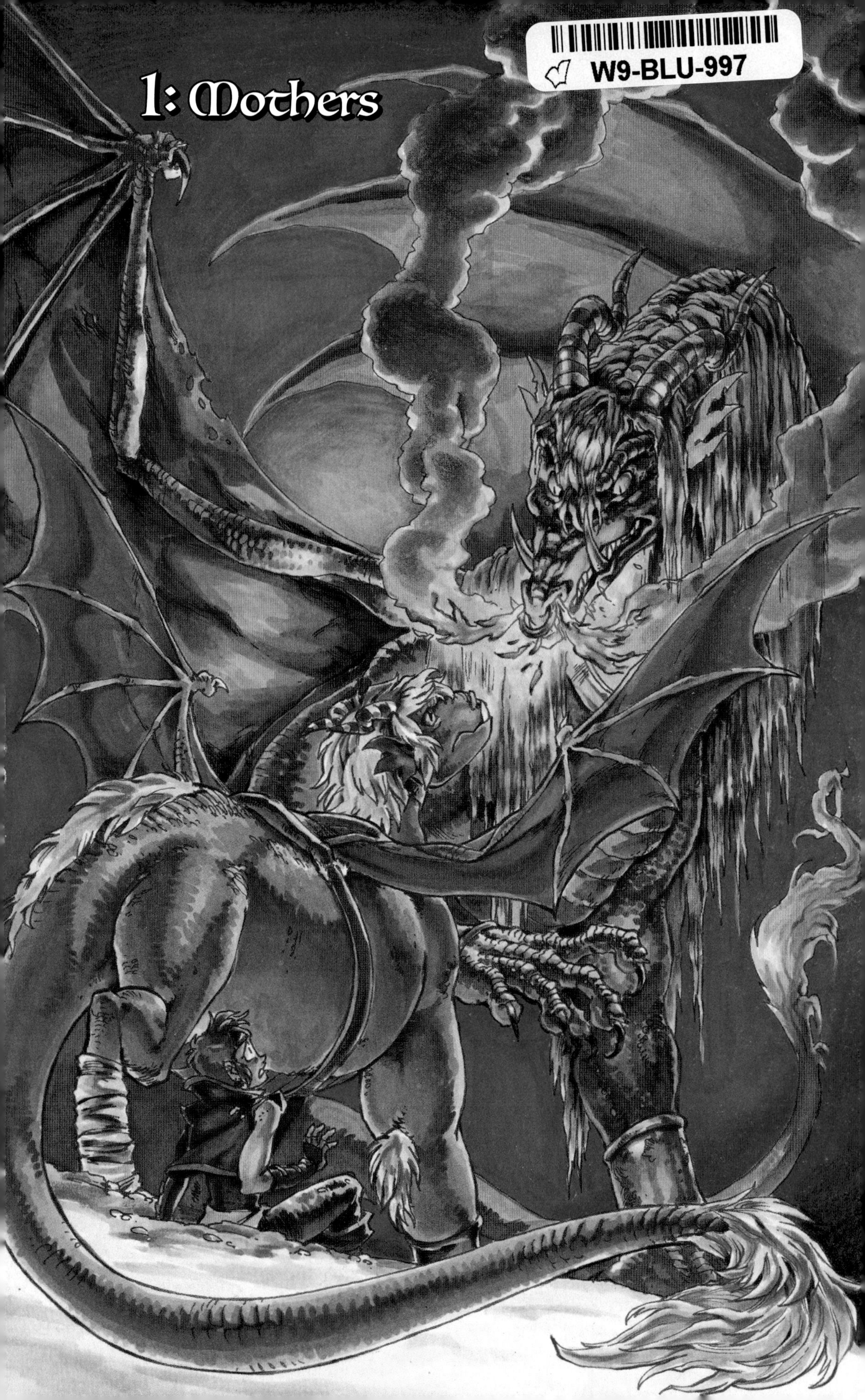

STORY:
Jeremy Whitley

ART:
Emily Martin

COLORS & LETTERS:
Brett Grunig

EDITORS:
Alicia Whitley (script)
Nicole D'Andria (comic)

Bryan Seaton: Publisher/ CEO • Shawn Gabborin: Editor In Chief
Jason Martin: Publisher-Danger Zone • Nicole D'Andria: Marketing Director/Editor
Jim Dietz: Social Media Manager • Danielle Davison: Executive Administrator
Chad Cicconi: Still Waiting For His Princess • Shawn Pryor: President of Creator Relations

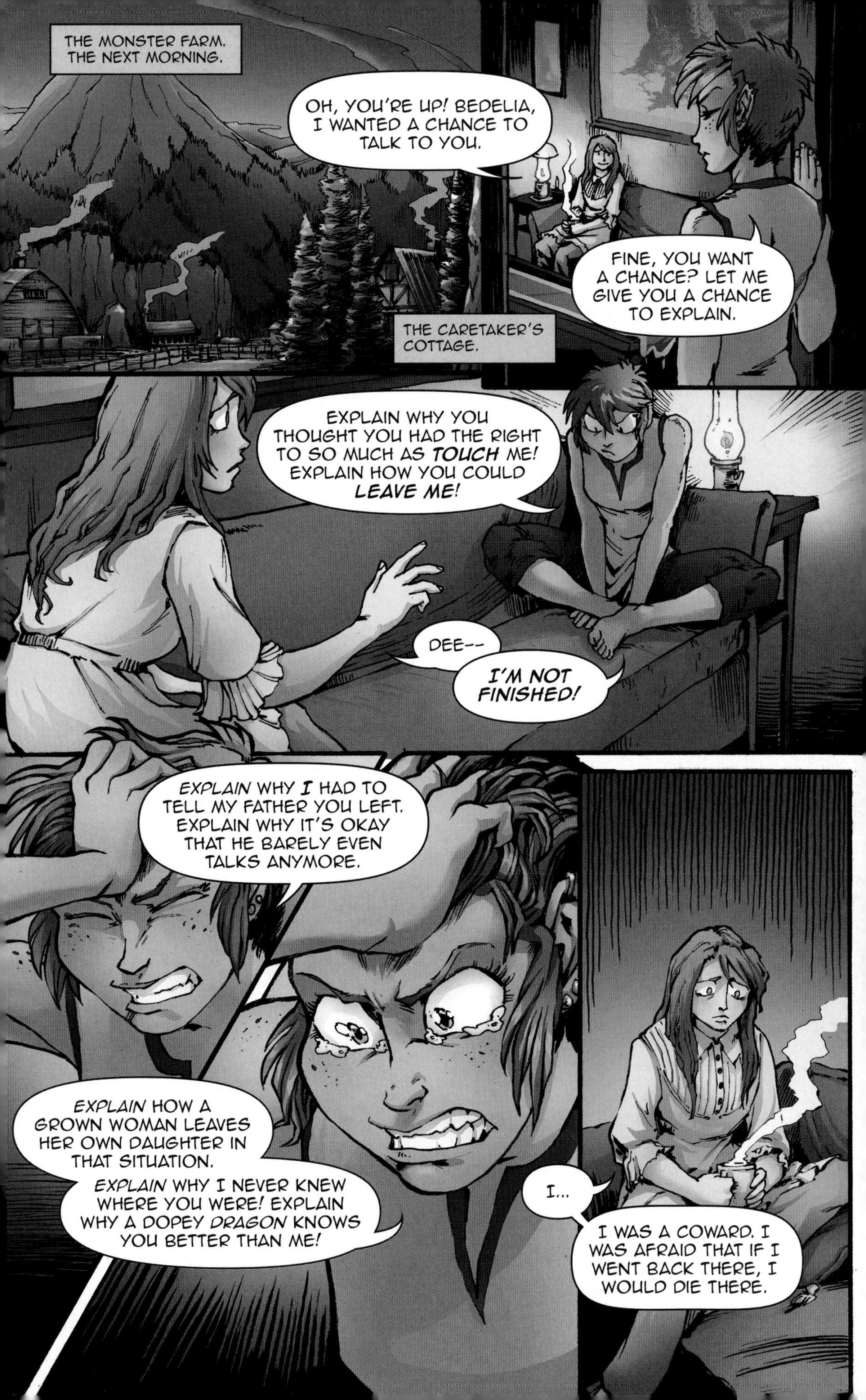
THE MONSTER FARM. THE NEXT MORNING.
OH, YOU'RE UP! BEDELIA, I WANTED A CHANCE TO TALK TO YOU.
FINE, YOU WANT A CHANCE? LET ME GIVE YOU A CHANCE TO EXPLAIN.
THE CARETAKER'S COTTAGE.
EXPLAIN WHY YOU THOUGHT YOU HAD THE RIGHT TO SO MUCH AS TOUCH ME! EXPLAIN HOW YOU COULD LEAVE ME!
DEE--
I'M NOT FINISHED!
EXPLAIN WHY I HAD TO TELL MY FATHER YOU LEFT. EXPLAIN WHY IT'S OKAY THAT HE BARELY EVEN TALKS ANYMORE.
EXPLAIN HOW A GROWN WOMAN LEAVES HER OWN DAUGHTER IN THAT SITUATION.
EXPLAIN WHY I NEVER KNEW WHERE YOU WERE! EXPLAIN WHY A DOPEY DRAGON KNOWS YOU BETTER THAN ME!
I...
I WAS A COWARD. I WAS AFRAID THAT IF I WENT BACK THERE, I WOULD DIE THERE.

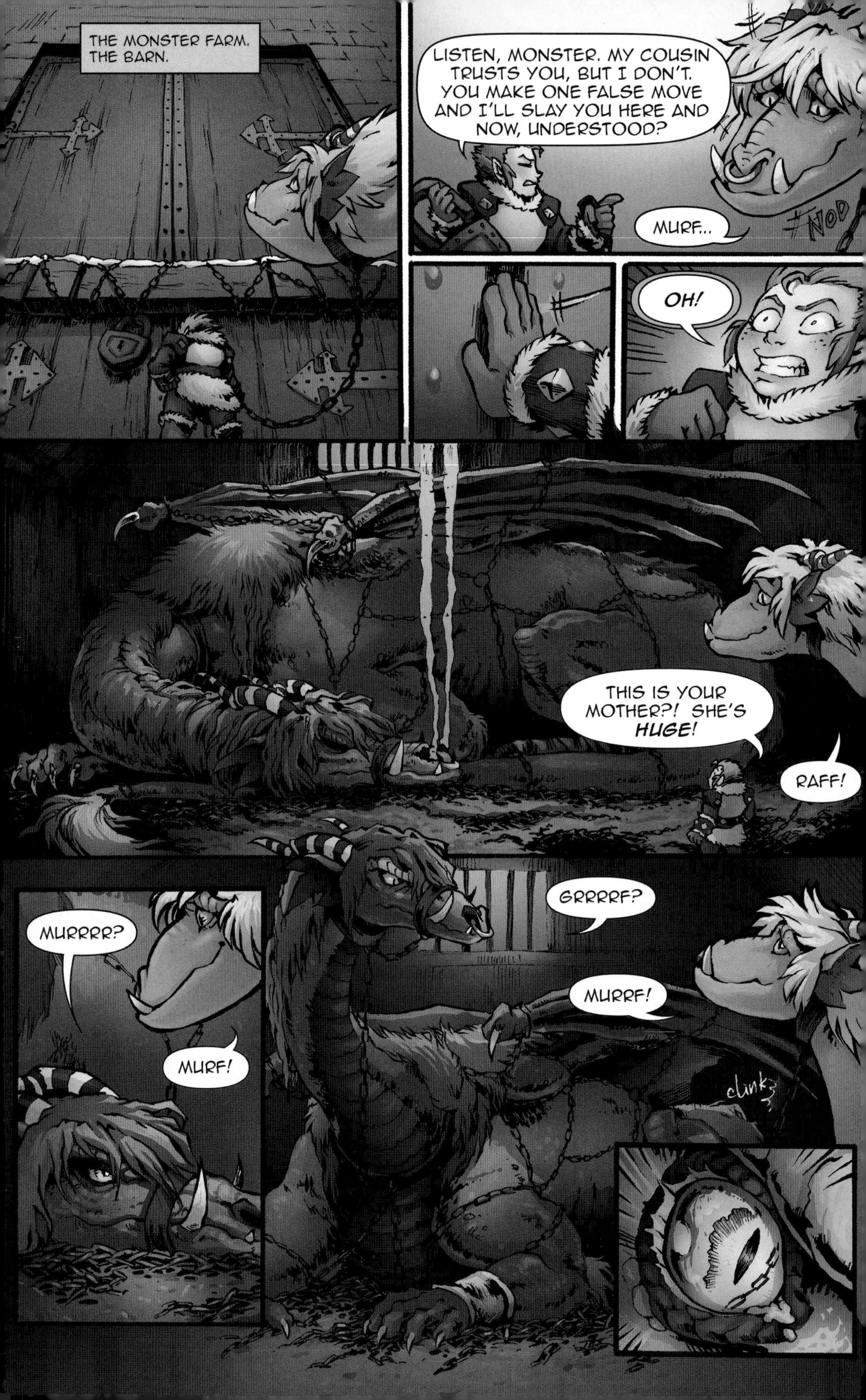
THE MONSTER FARM.
THE BARN.
LISTEN, MONSTER. MY COUSIN TRUSTS YOU, BUT I DON'T. YOU MAKE ONE FALSE MOVE AND I'LL SLAY YOU HERE AND NOW, UNDERSTOOD?
MURF...
NOD
OH!
THIS IS YOUR MOTHER?! SHE'S HUGE!
RAFF!
MURRRR?
MURF!
GRRRRF?
MURRF!
clink

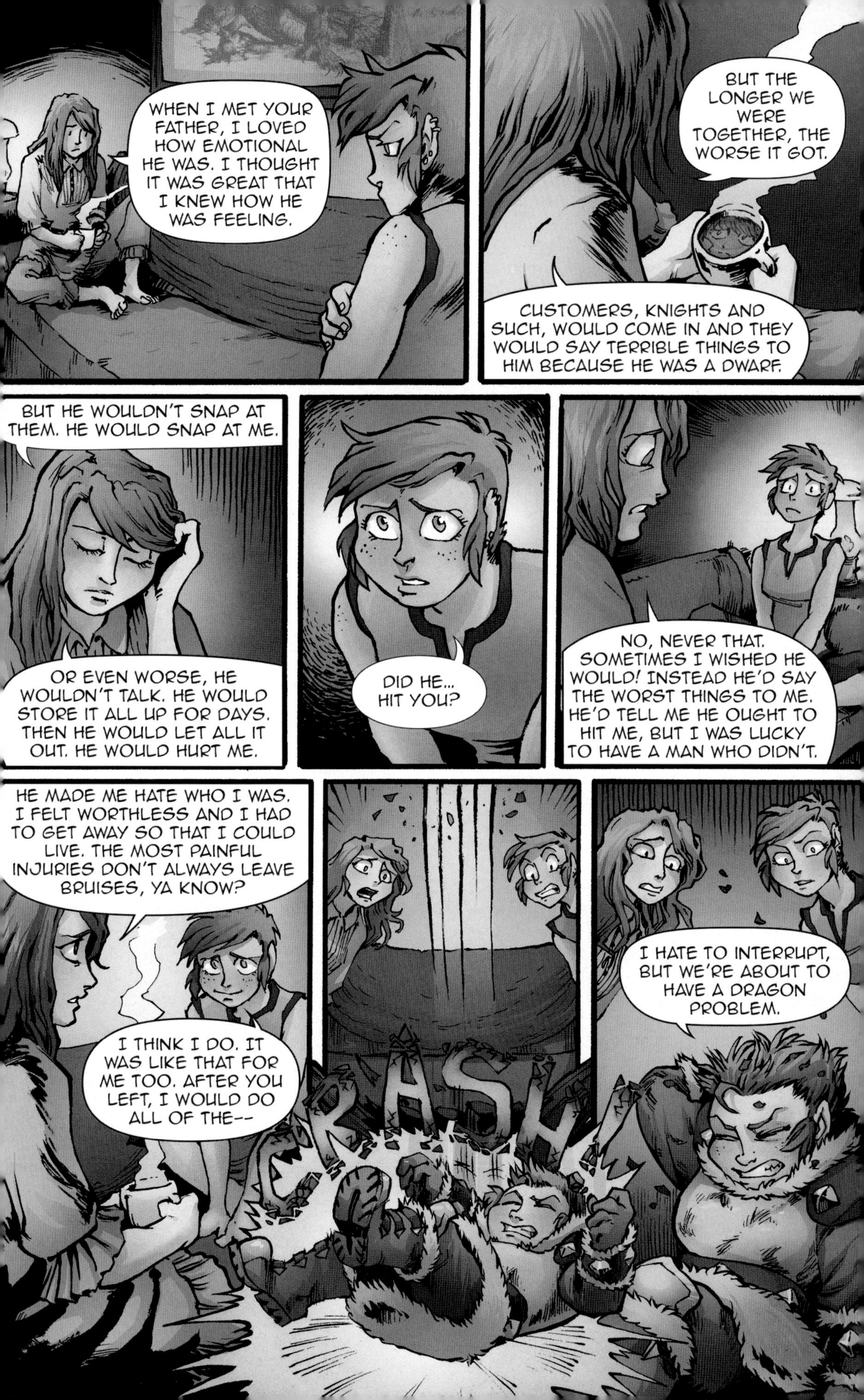
WHEN I MET YOUR FATHER, I LOVED HOW EMOTIONAL HE WAS. I THOUGHT IT WAS GREAT THAT I KNEW HOW HE WAS FEELING.
BUT THE LONGER WE WERE TOGETHER, THE WORSE IT GOT.
CUSTOMERS, KNIGHTS AND SUCH, WOULD COME IN AND THEY WOULD SAY TERRIBLE THINGS TO HIM BECAUSE HE WAS A DWARF.
BUT HE WOULDN'T SNAP AT THEM. HE WOULD SNAP AT ME.
OR EVEN WORSE, HE WOULDN'T TALK. HE WOULD STORE IT ALL UP FOR DAYS. THEN HE WOULD LET ALL IT OUT. HE WOULD HURT ME.
DID HE... HIT YOU?
NO, NEVER THAT. SOMETIMES I WISHED HE WOULD! INSTEAD HE'D SAY THE WORST THINGS TO ME. HE'D TELL ME HE OUGHT TO HIT ME, BUT I WAS LUCKY TO HAVE A MAN WHO DIDN'T.
HE MADE ME HATE WHO I WAS. I FELT WORTHLESS AND I HAD TO GET AWAY SO THAT I COULD LIVE. THE MOST PAINFUL INJURIES DON'T ALWAYS LEAVE BRUISES, YA KNOW?
I THINK I DO. IT WAS LIKE THAT FOR ME TOO. AFTER YOU LEFT, I WOULD DO ALL OF THE--
RASH
I HATE TO INTERRUPT, BUT WE'RE ABOUT TO HAVE A DRAGON PROBLEM.

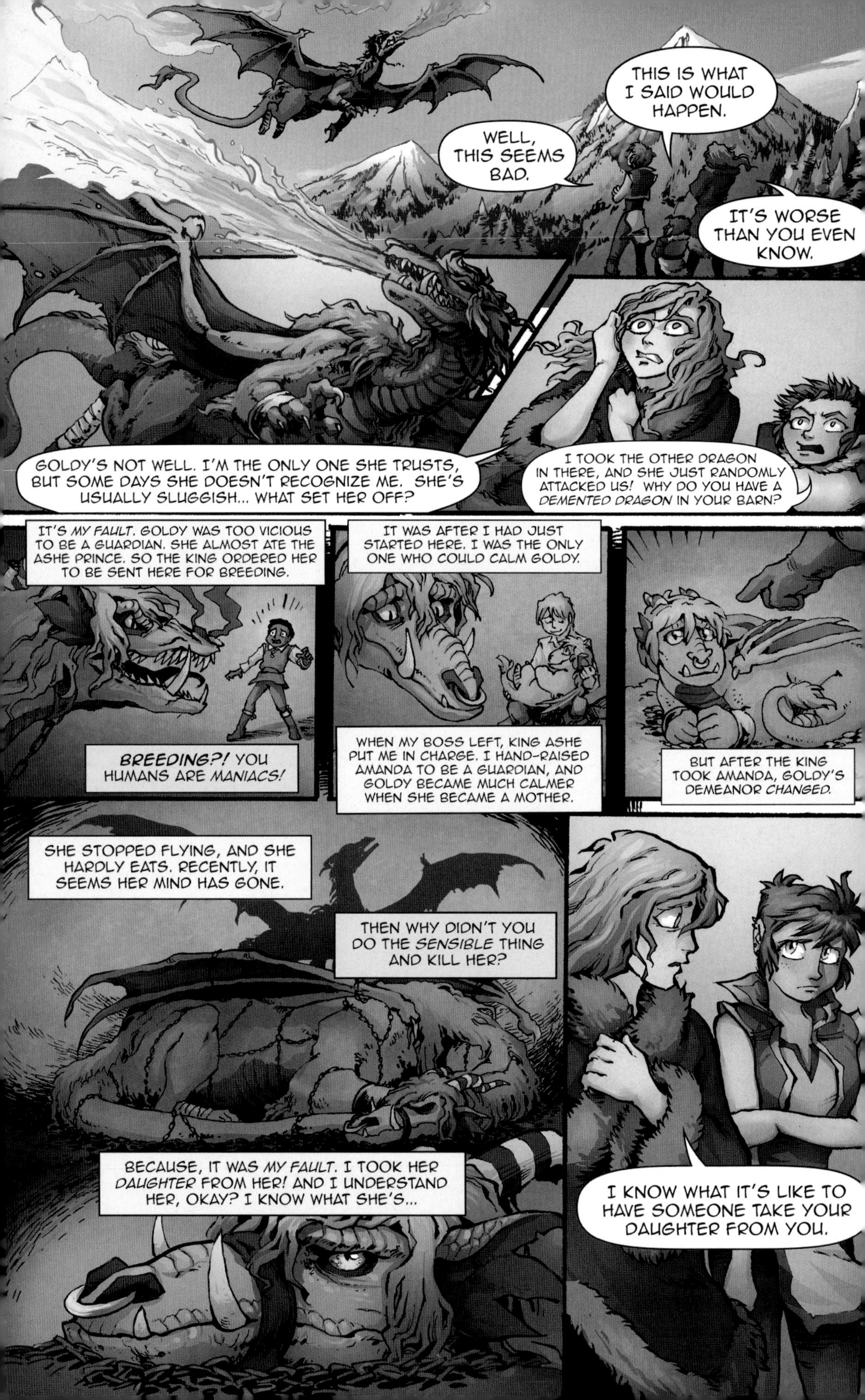

WELL, THIS SEEMS BAD.
THIS IS WHAT I SAID WOULD HAPPEN.
IT'S WORSE THAN YOU EVEN KNOW.
GOLDY'S NOT WELL. I'M THE ONLY ONE SHE TRUSTS, BUT SOME DAYS SHE DOESN'T RECOGNIZE ME. SHE'S USUALLY SLUGGISH... WHAT SET HER OFF?
I TOOK THE OTHER DRAGON IN THERE, AND SHE JUST RANDOMLY ATTACKED US! WHY DO YOU HAVE A *DEMENTED DRAGON* IN YOUR BARN?
IT'S *MY FAULT*. GOLDY WAS TOO VICIOUS TO BE A GUARDIAN. SHE ALMOST ATE THE ASHE PRINCE. SO THE KING ORDERED HER TO BE SENT HERE FOR BREEDING.
BREEDING?! YOU HUMANS ARE *MANIACS!*
IT WAS AFTER I HAD JUST STARTED HERE. I WAS THE ONLY ONE WHO COULD CALM GOLDY.
WHEN MY BOSS LEFT, KING ASHE PUT ME IN CHARGE. I HAND-RAISED AMANDA TO BE A GUARDIAN, AND GOLDY BECAME MUCH CALMER WHEN SHE BECAME A MOTHER.
BUT AFTER THE KING TOOK AMANDA, GOLDY'S DEMEANOR *CHANGED*.
SHE STOPPED FLYING, AND SHE HARDLY EATS. RECENTLY, IT SEEMS HER MIND HAS GONE.
THEN WHY DIDN'T YOU DO THE *SENSIBLE* THING AND KILL HER?
BECAUSE, IT WAS *MY FAULT*. I TOOK HER *DAUGHTER* FROM HER! AND I UNDERSTAND HER, OKAY? I KNOW WHAT SHE'S...
I KNOW WHAT IT'S LIKE TO HAVE SOMEONE TAKE YOUR DAUGHTER FROM YOU.

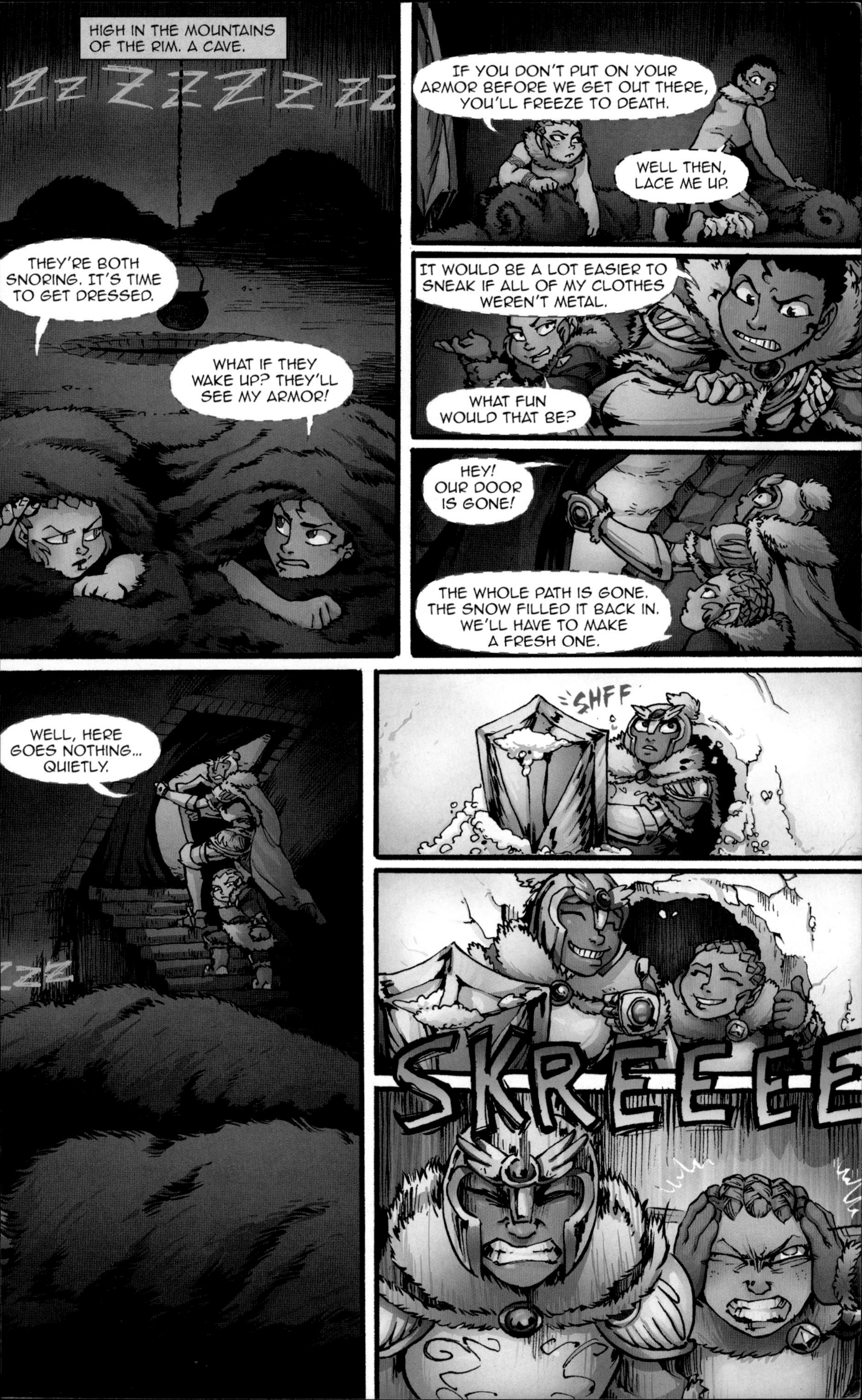
HIGH IN THE MOUNTAINS OF THE RIM. A CAVE.
zzZZZZZzz
THEY'RE BOTH SNORING. IT'S TIME TO GET DRESSED.
WHAT IF THEY WAKE UP? THEY'LL SEE MY ARMOR!
IF YOU DON'T PUT ON YOUR ARMOR BEFORE WE GET OUT THERE, YOU'LL FREEZE TO DEATH.
WELL THEN, LACE ME UP.
IT WOULD BE A LOT EASIER TO SNEAK IF ALL OF MY CLOTHES WEREN'T METAL.
WHAT FUN WOULD THAT BE?
HEY! OUR DOOR IS GONE!
THE WHOLE PATH IS GONE. THE SNOW FILLED IT BACK IN. WE'LL HAVE TO MAKE A FRESH ONE.
WELL, HERE GOES NOTHING... QUIETLY.
ZZZ
SHFF
SKREEEE

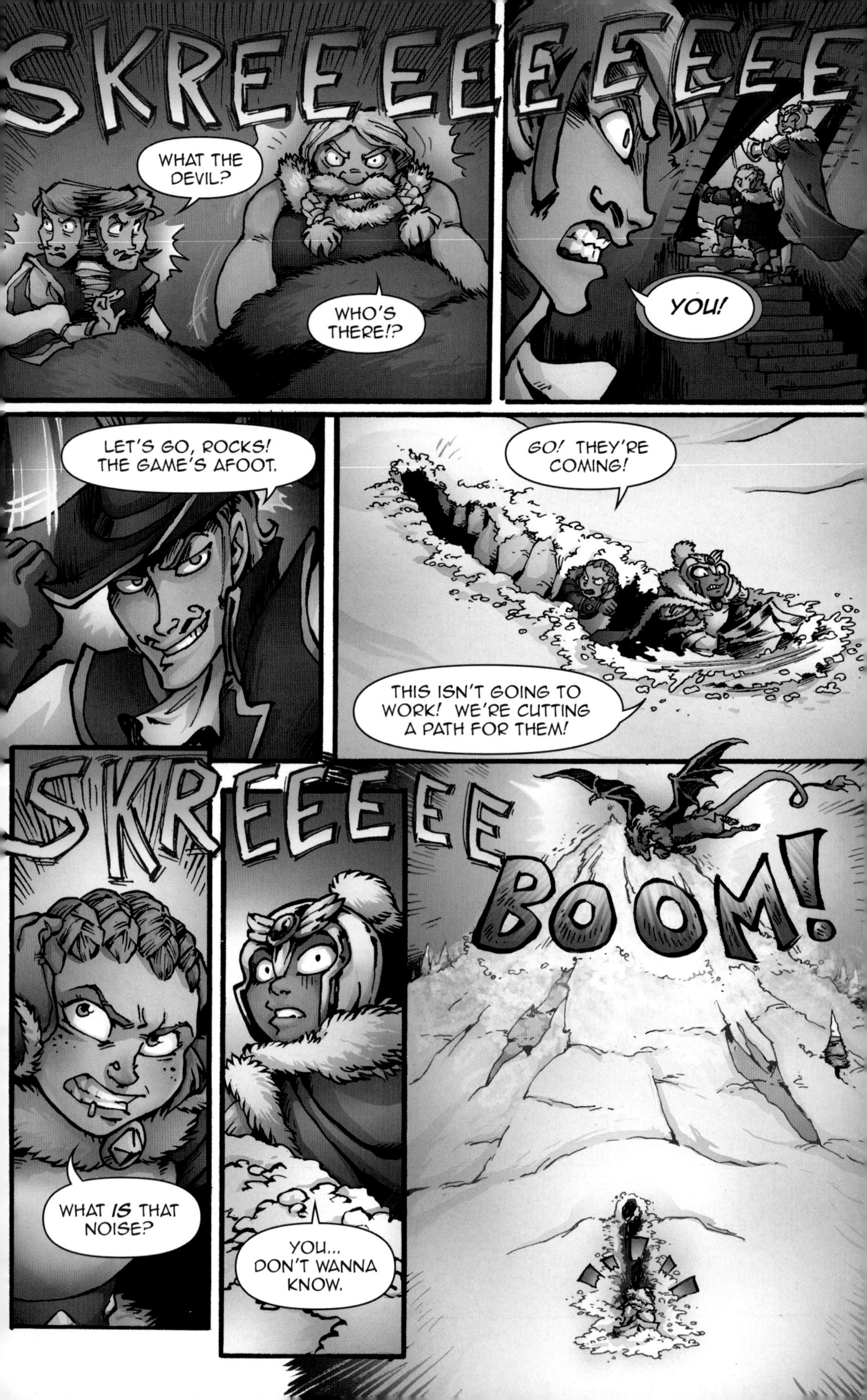
SKREEEEEEEEE
WHAT THE DEVIL?
WHO'S THERE!?
YOU!
LET'S GO, ROCKS! THE GAME'S AFOOT.
GO! THEY'RE COMING!
THIS ISN'T GOING TO WORK! WE'RE CUTTING A PATH FOR THEM!
SKREEEEE
WHAT *IS* THAT NOISE?
YOU... DON'T WANNA KNOW.
BOOM!

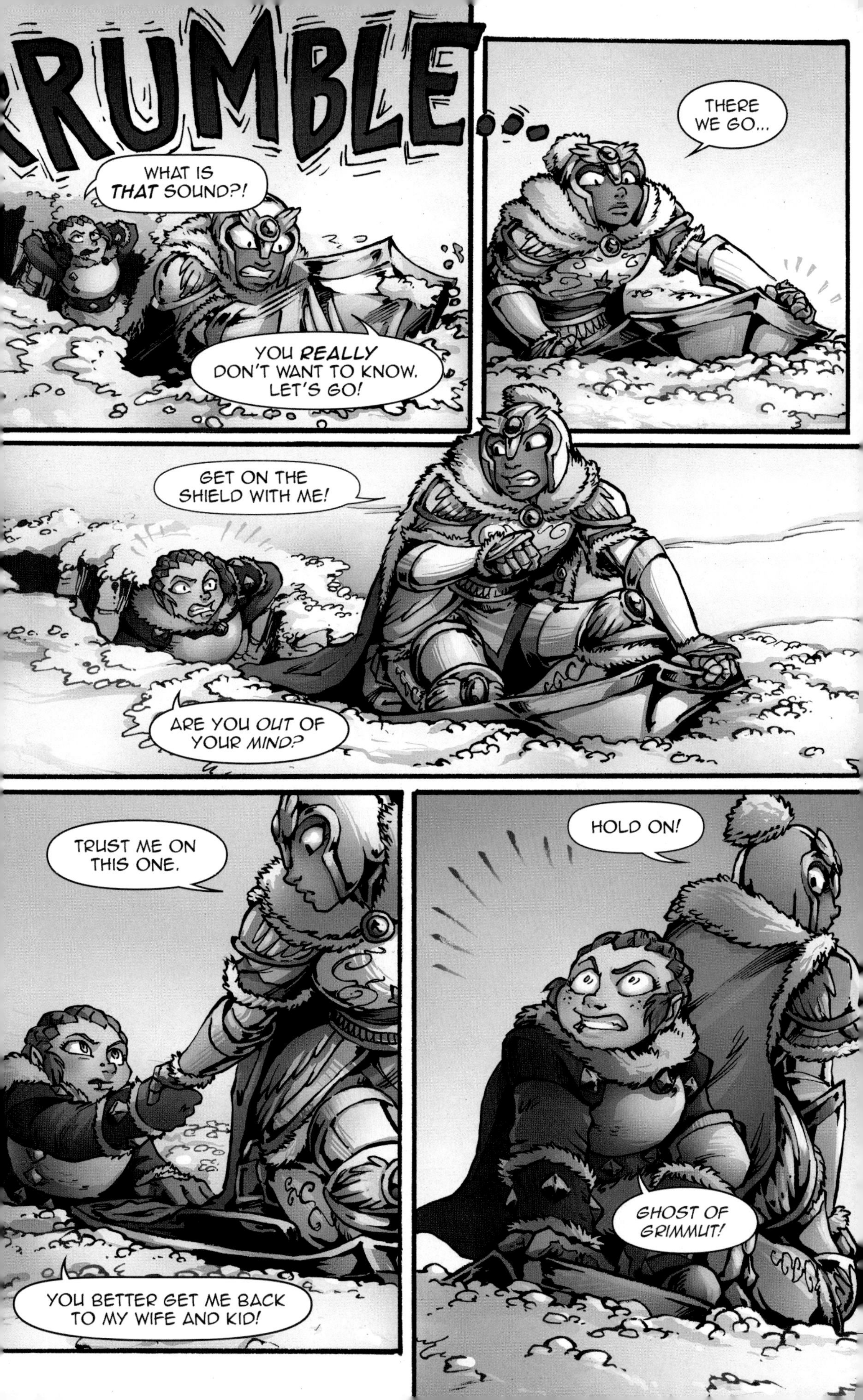
RUMBLE...
WHAT IS THAT SOUND?!
YOU REALLY DON'T WANT TO KNOW. LET'S GO!
THERE WE GO...
GET ON THE SHIELD WITH ME!
ARE YOU OUT OF YOUR MIND?
TRUST ME ON THIS ONE.
YOU BETTER GET ME BACK TO MY WIFE AND KID!
HOLD ON!
GHOST OF GRIMMUT!

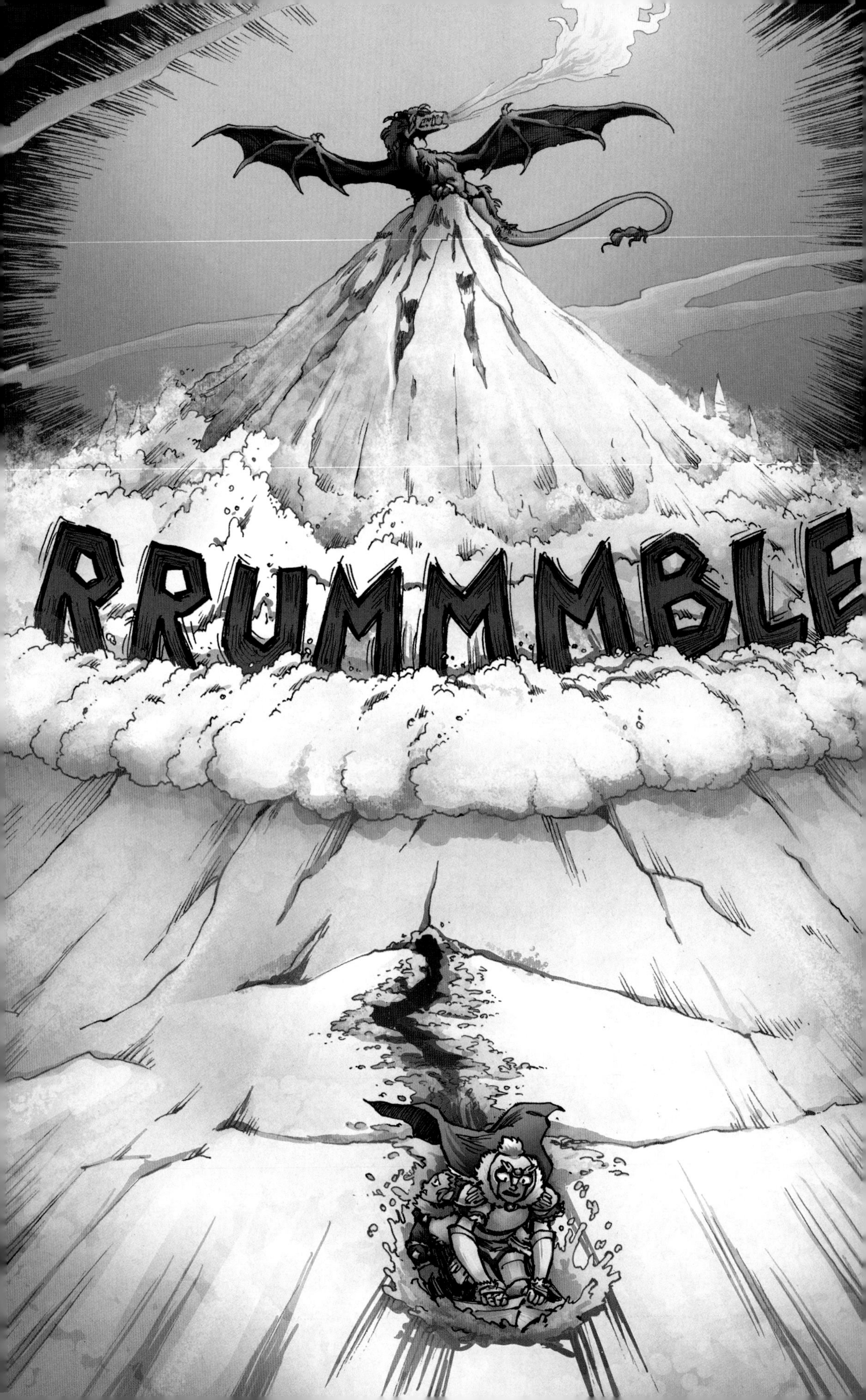
RRUMMMBLE

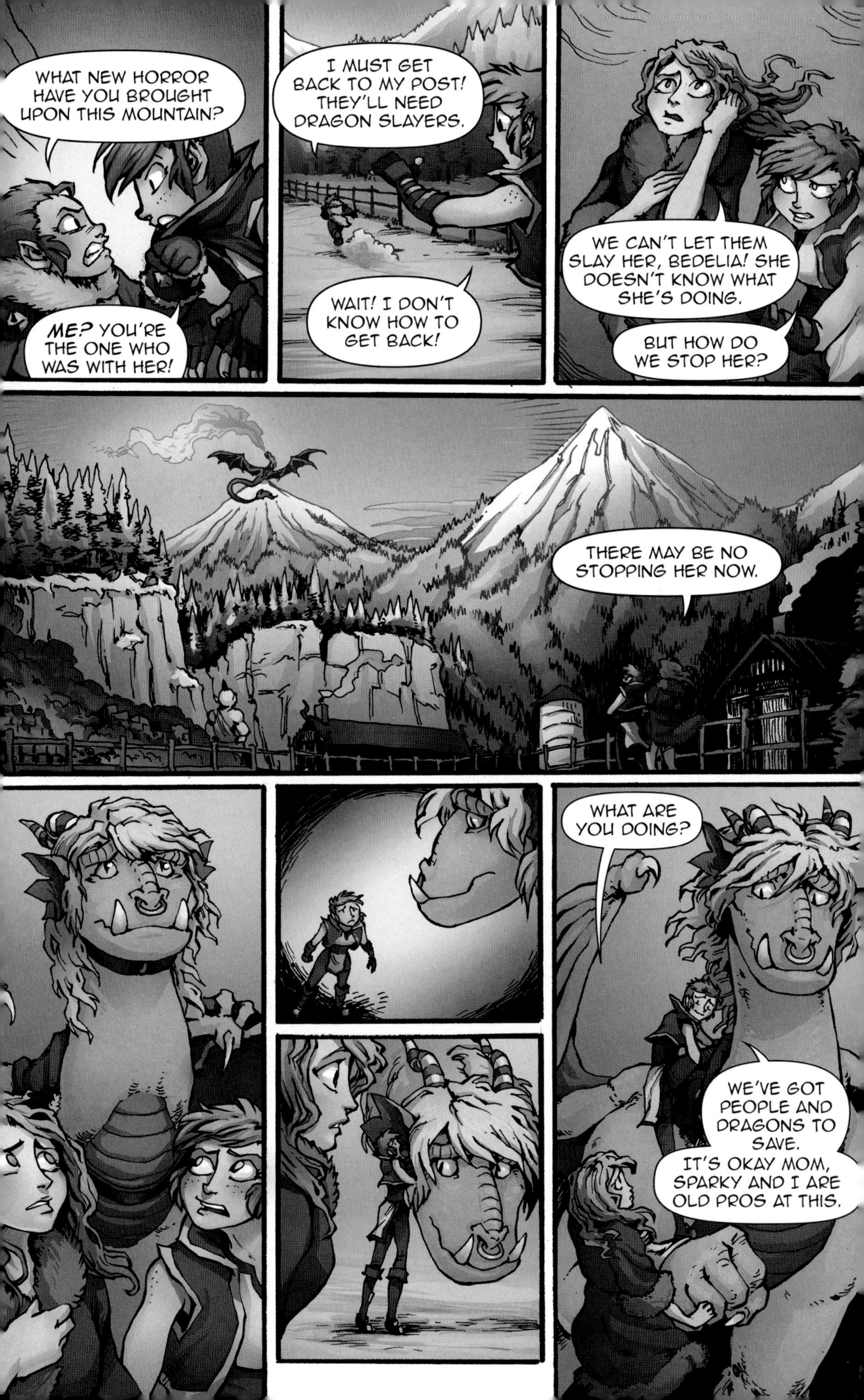
WHAT NEW HORROR HAVE YOU BROUGHT UPON THIS MOUNTAIN?
ME? YOU'RE THE ONE WHO WAS WITH HER!
I MUST GET BACK TO MY POST! THEY'LL NEED DRAGON SLAYERS.
WAIT! I DON'T KNOW HOW TO GET BACK!
WE CAN'T LET THEM SLAY HER, BEDELIA! SHE DOESN'T KNOW WHAT SHE'S DOING.
BUT HOW DO WE STOP HER?
THERE MAY BE NO STOPPING HER NOW.
WHAT ARE YOU DOING?
WE'VE GOT PEOPLE AND DRAGONS TO SAVE.
IT'S OKAY MOM, SPARKY AND I ARE OLD PROS AT THIS.

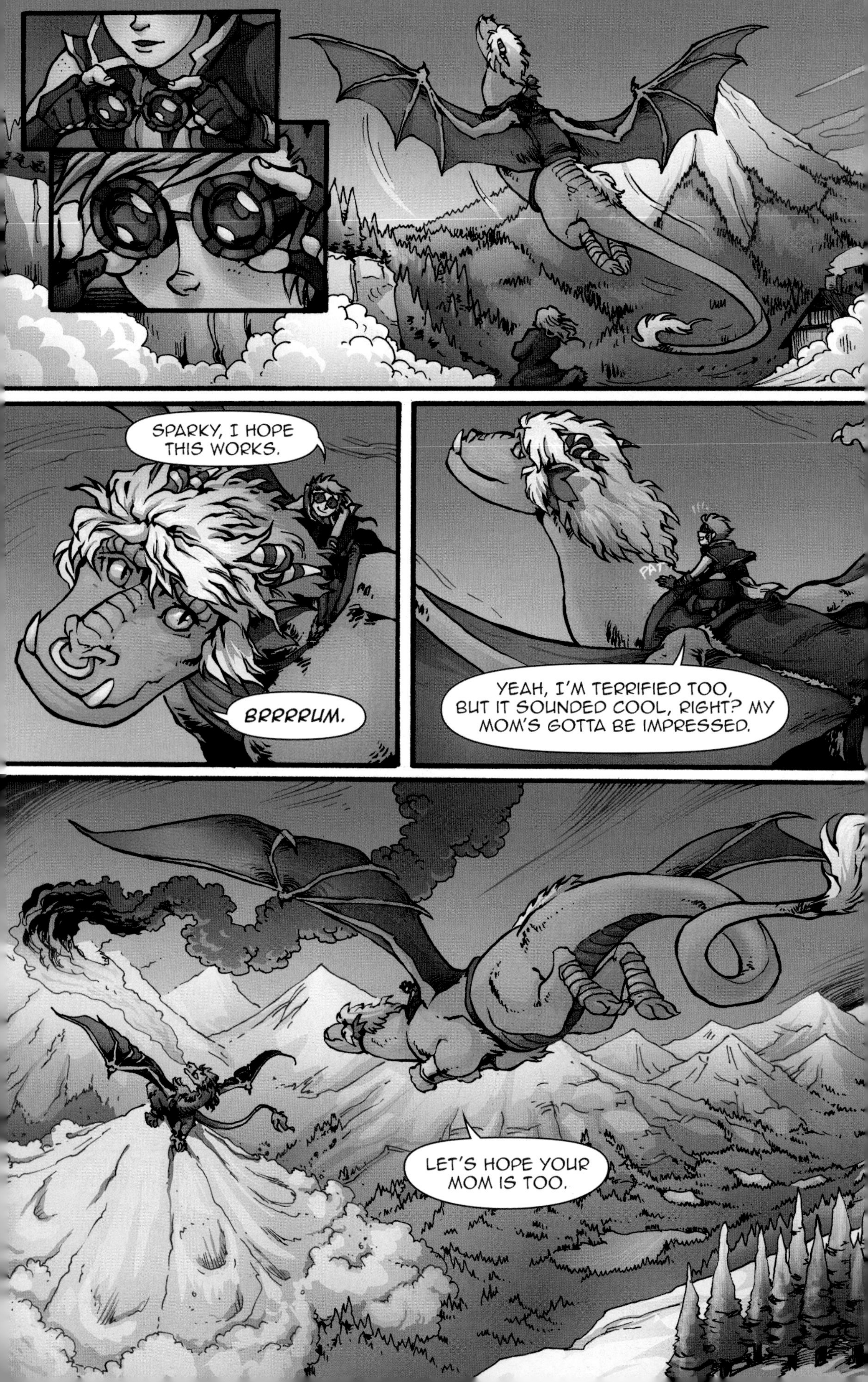
SPARKY, I HOPE THIS WORKS.
BRRRRUM.
PAT
YEAH, I'M TERRIFIED TOO, BUT IT SOUNDED COOL, RIGHT? MY MOM'S GOTTA BE IMPRESSED.
LET'S HOPE YOUR MOM IS TOO.

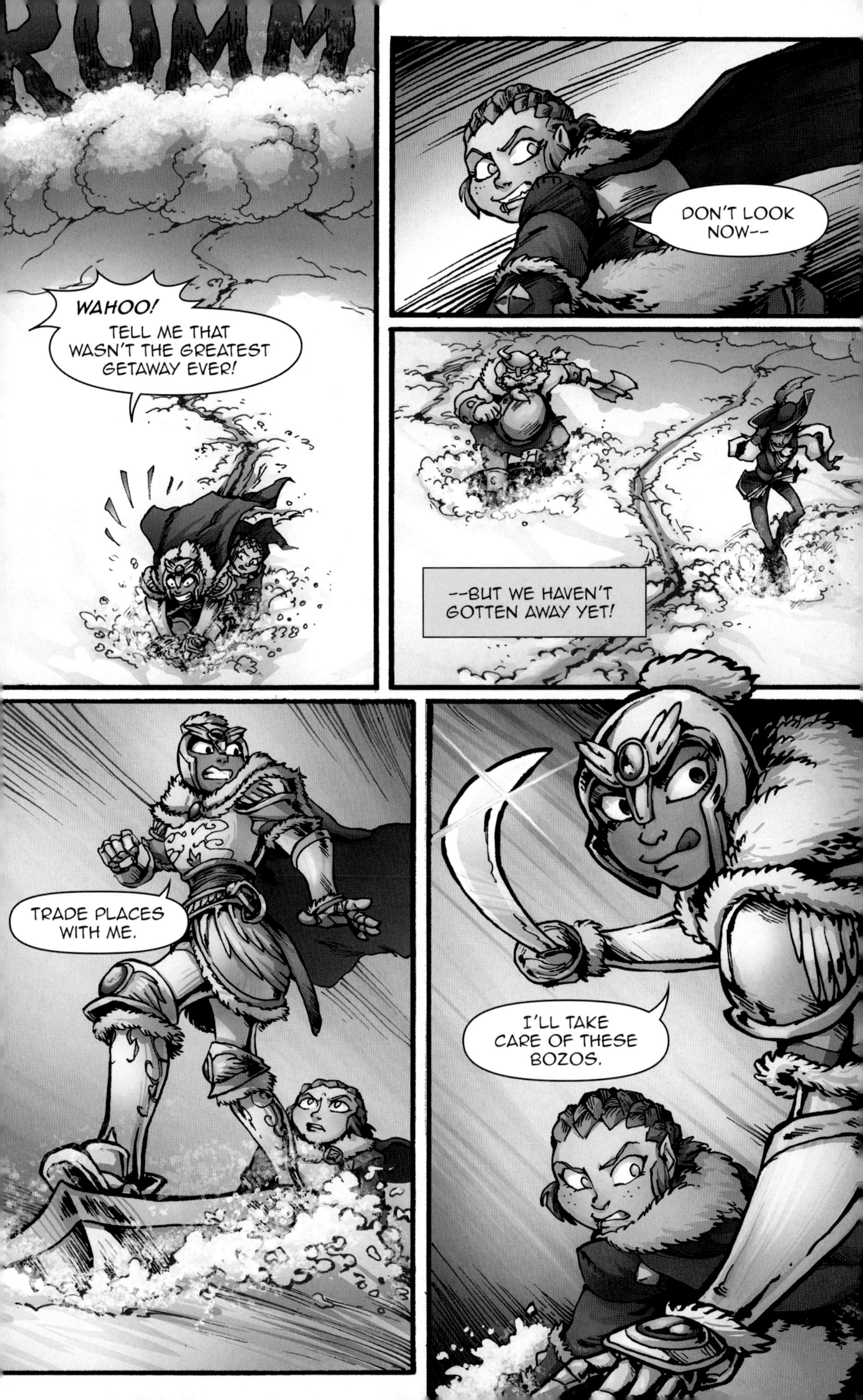
RUMM
WAHOO! TELL ME THAT WASN'T THE GREATEST GETAWAY EVER!
DON'T LOOK NOW--
--BUT WE HAVEN'T GOTTEN AWAY YET!
TRADE PLACES WITH ME.
I'LL TAKE CARE OF THESE BOZOS.

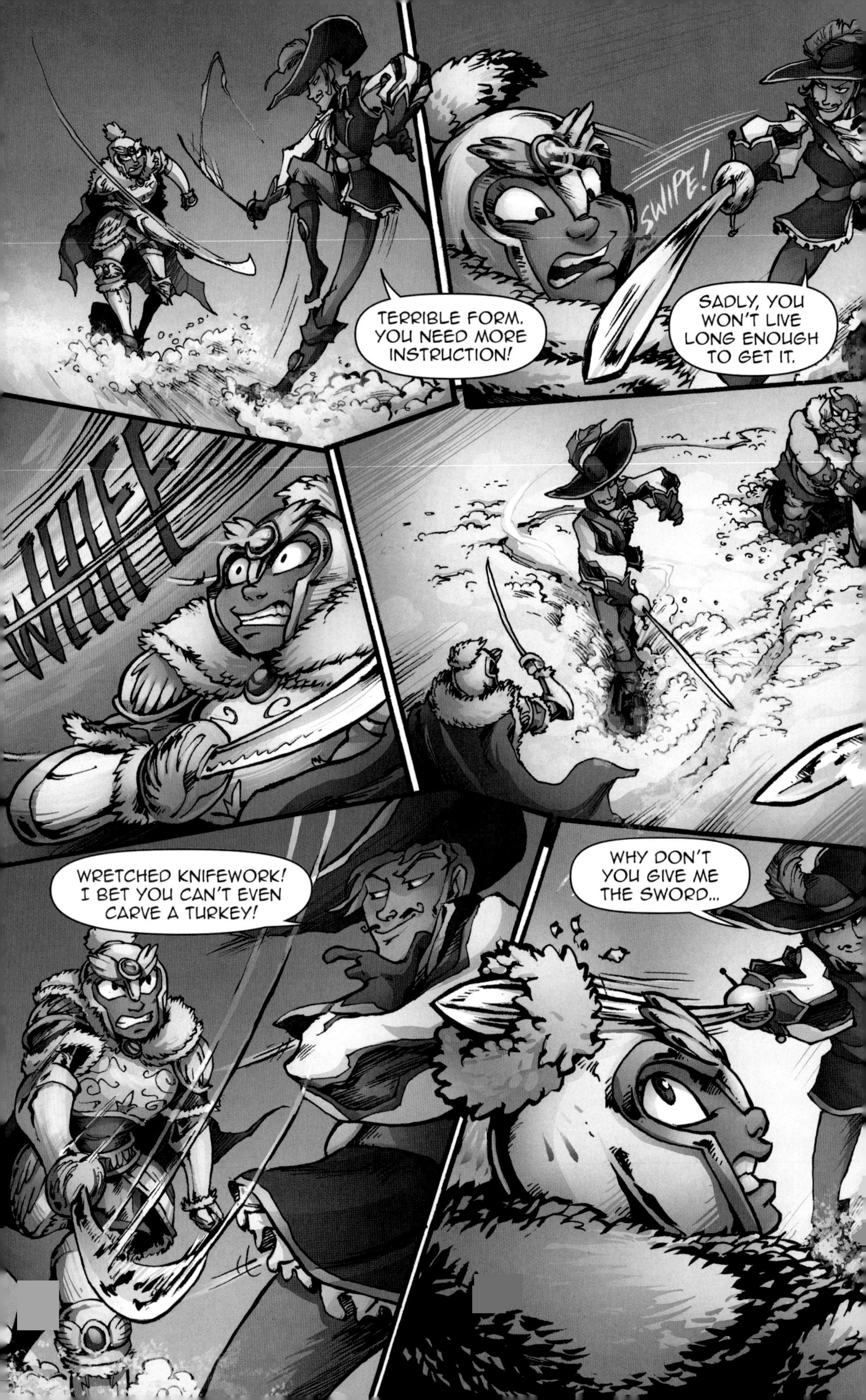
TERRIBLE FORM.
YOU NEED MORE
INSTRUCTION!
SWIPE!
SADLY, YOU
WON'T LIVE
LONG ENOUGH
TO GET IT.
WHIFF
WRETCHED KNIFEWORK!
I BET YOU CAN'T EVEN
CARVE A TURKEY!
WHY DON'T
YOU GIVE ME
THE SWORD...

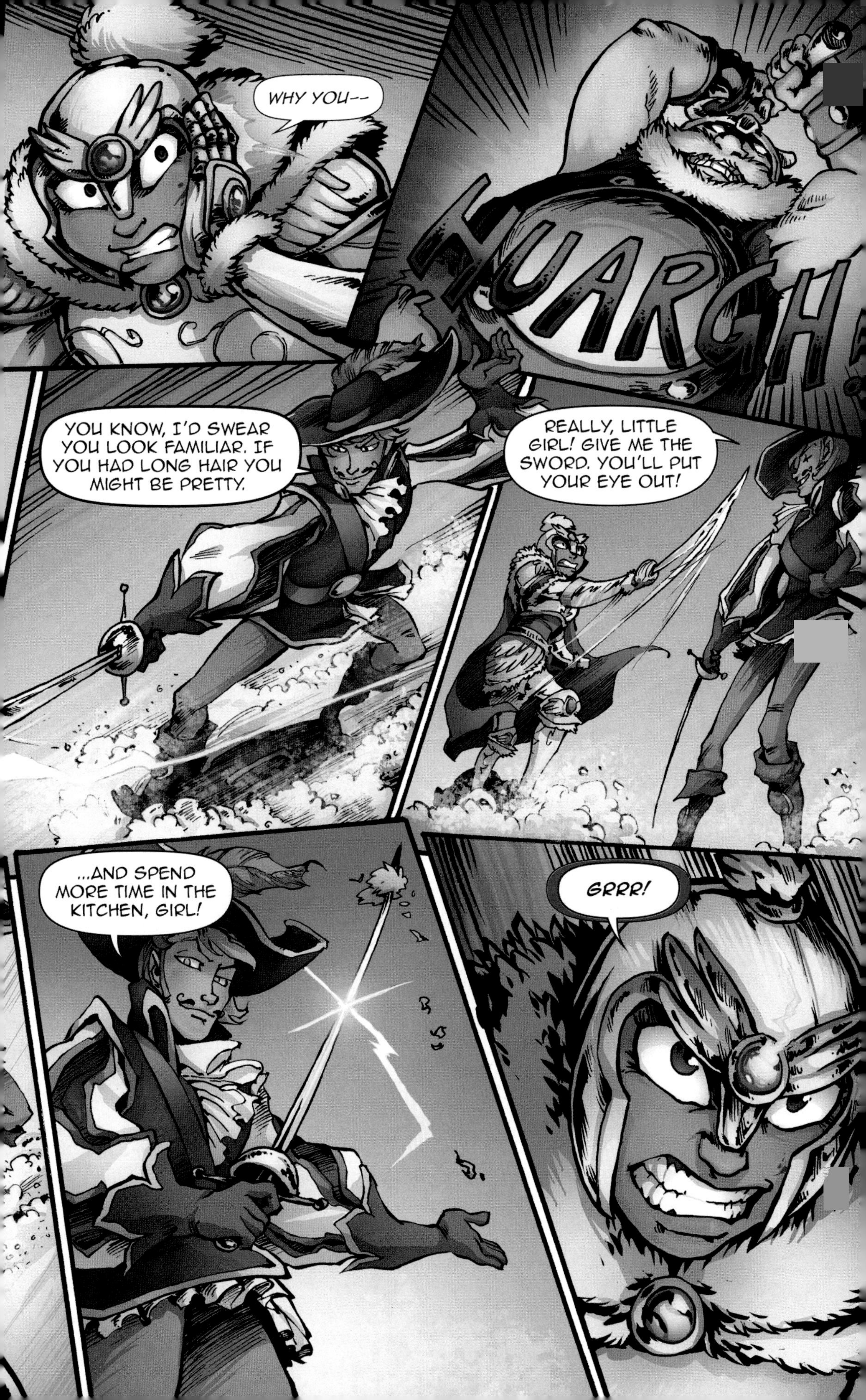
WHY YOU--
HUARGH!
YOU KNOW, I'D SWEAR YOU LOOK FAMILIAR. IF YOU HAD LONG HAIR YOU MIGHT BE PRETTY.
REALLY, LITTLE GIRL! GIVE ME THE SWORD. YOU'LL PUT YOUR EYE OUT!
...AND SPEND MORE TIME IN THE KITCHEN, GIRL!
GRRR!

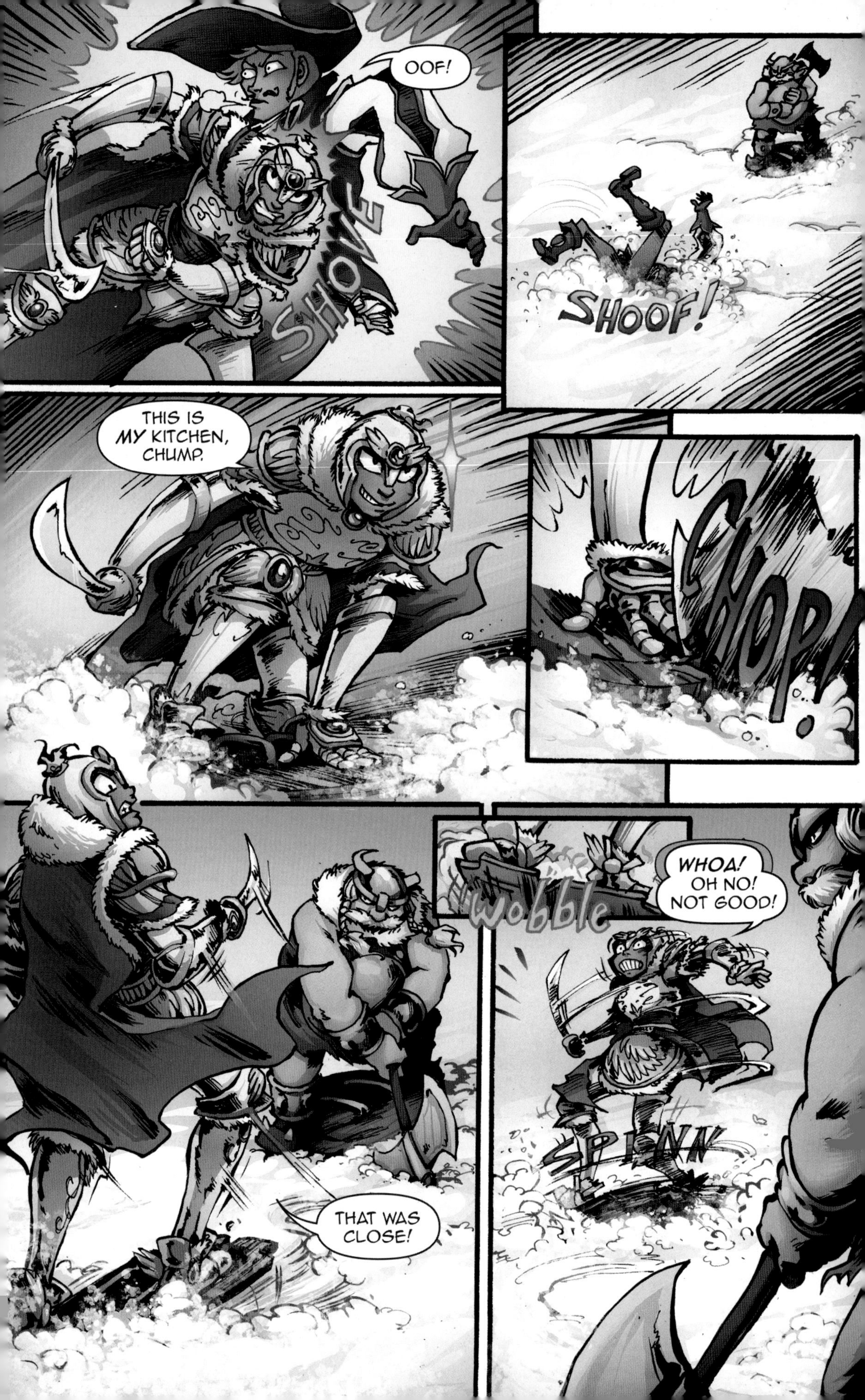
OOF!
SHOVE
SHOOF!
THIS IS MY KITCHEN, CHUMP.
CHOP!
THAT WAS CLOSE!
wobble
WHOA! OH NO! NOT GOOD!
SPINN

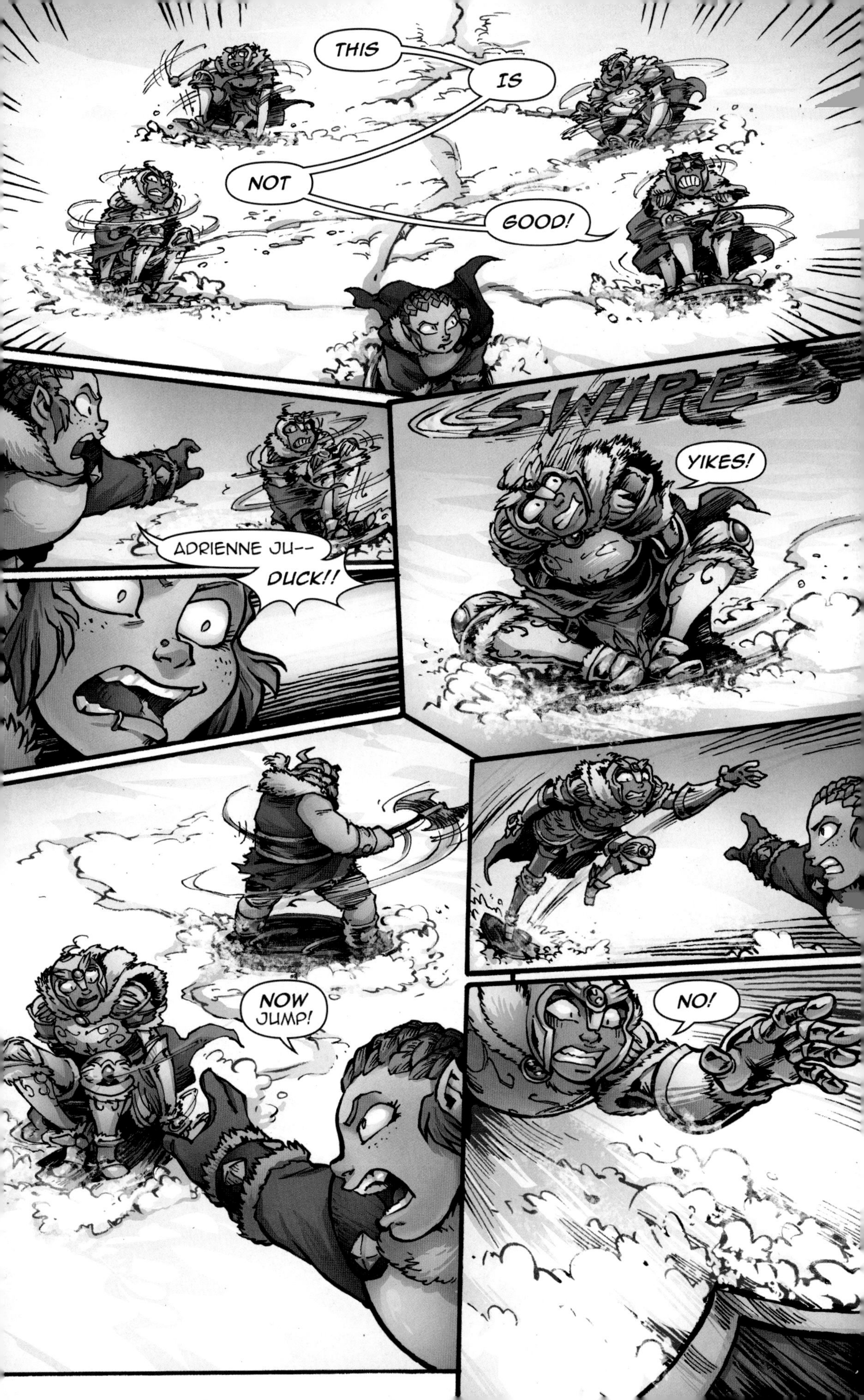
THIS
IS
NOT
GOOD!
SWIPE
YIKES!
ADRIENNE JU--
DUCK!!
NOW JUMP!
NO!

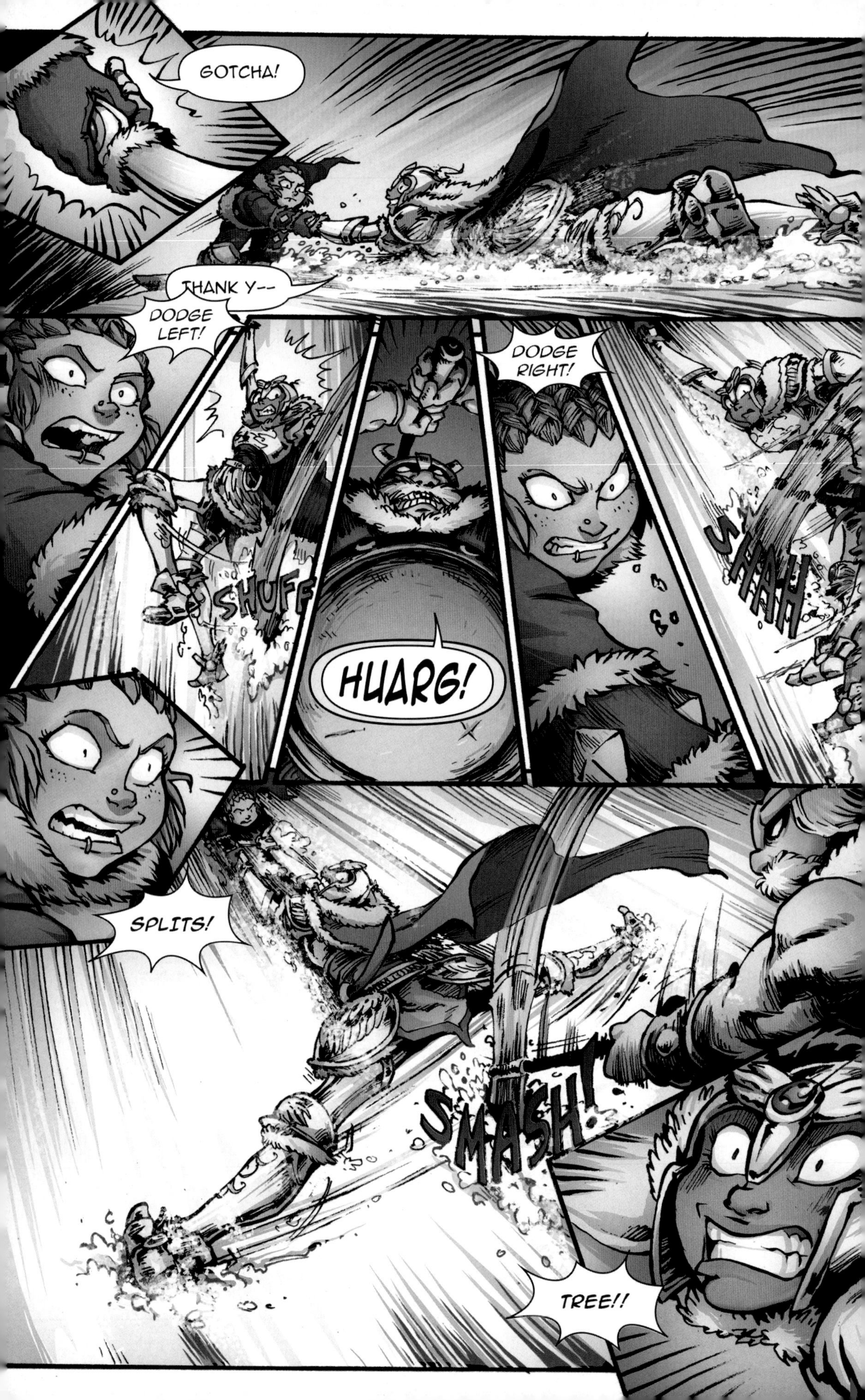
GOTCHA!
THANK Y--
DODGE LEFT!
SHUFF
HUARG!
DODGE RIGHT!
SHAH
SPLITS!
SMASH!
TREE!!

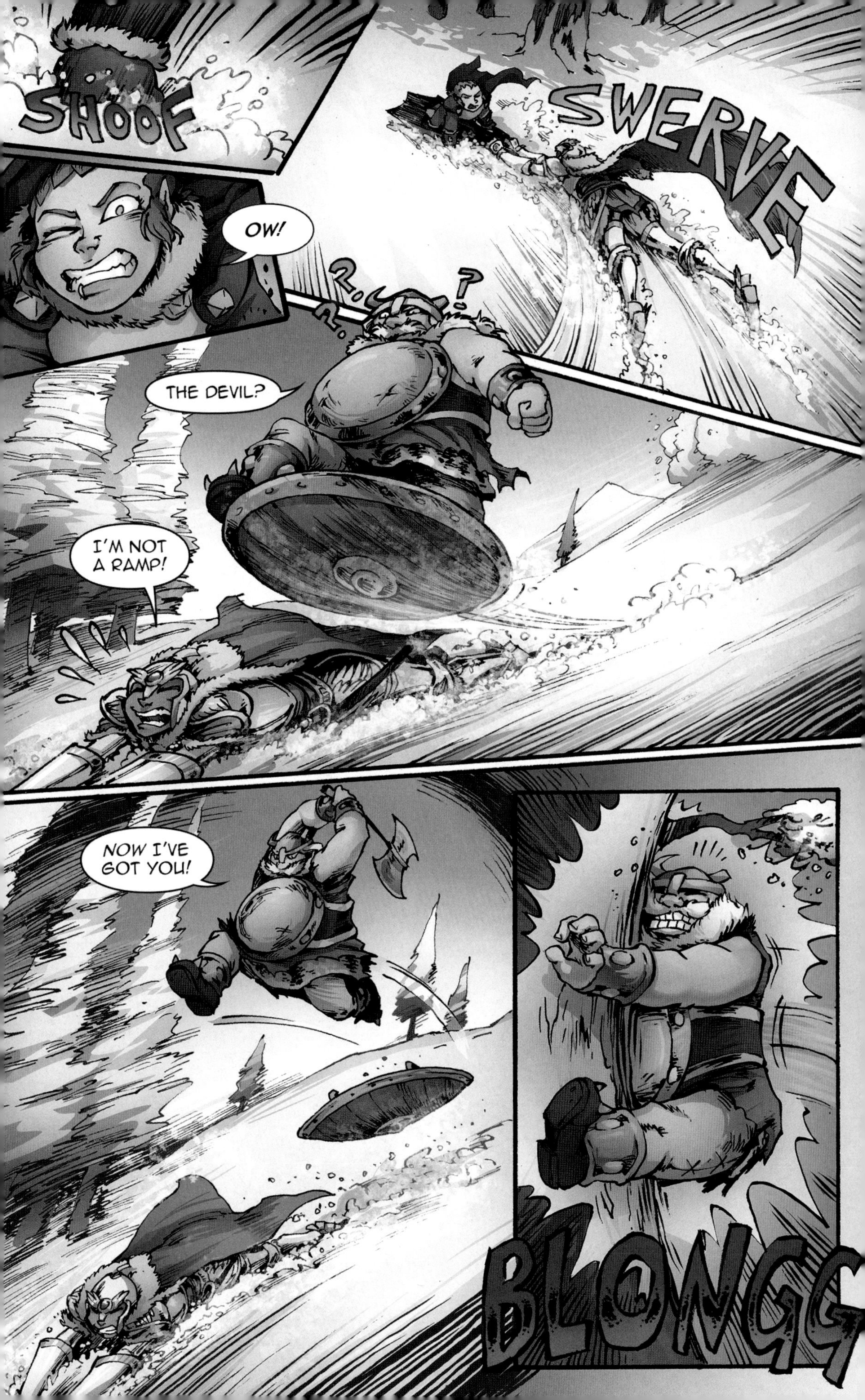
SHOOF
SWERVE
OW!
?
THE DEVIL?
I'M NOT
A RAMP!
NOW I'VE
GOT YOU!
BLONGG

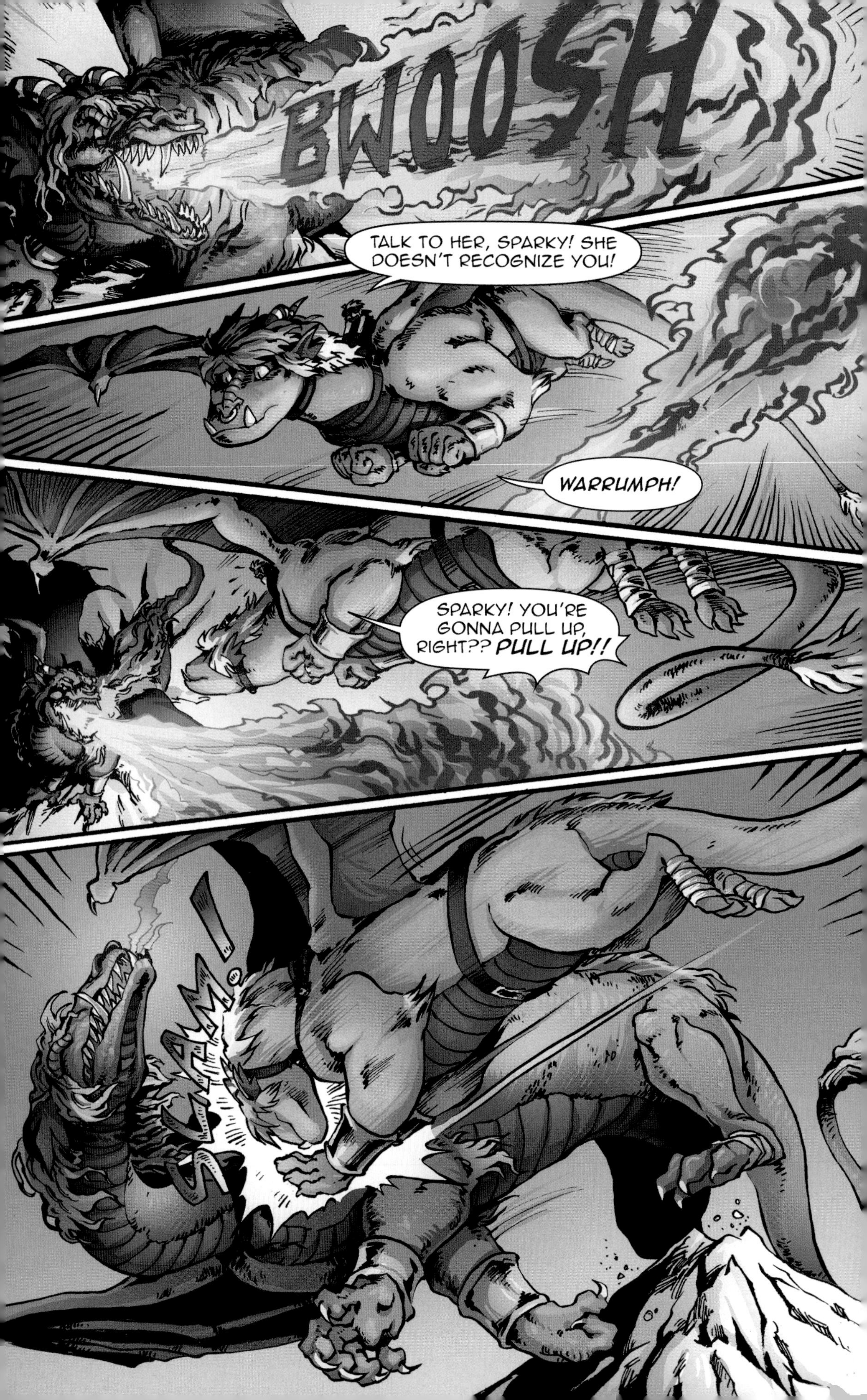
BWOOSH
TALK TO HER, SPARKY! SHE DOESN'T RECOGNIZE YOU!
WARRUMPH!
SPARKY! YOU'RE GONNA PULL UP, RIGHT?? PULL UP!!
!

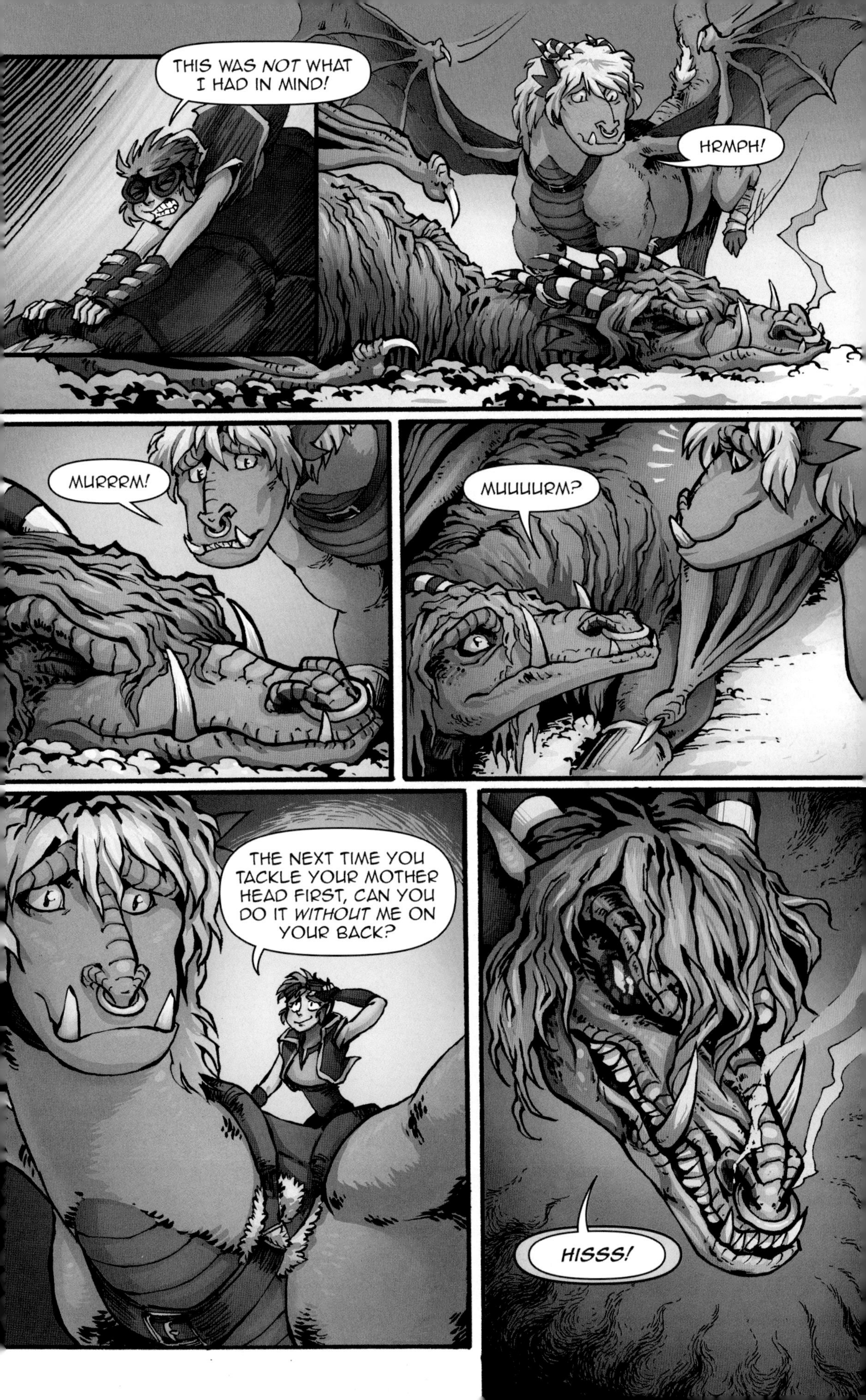
THIS WAS *NOT* WHAT I HAD IN MIND!
HRMPH!
MURRRM!
MUUUURM?
THE NEXT TIME YOU TACKLE YOUR MOTHER HEAD FIRST, CAN YOU DO IT *WITHOUT* ME ON YOUR BACK?
HISSS!

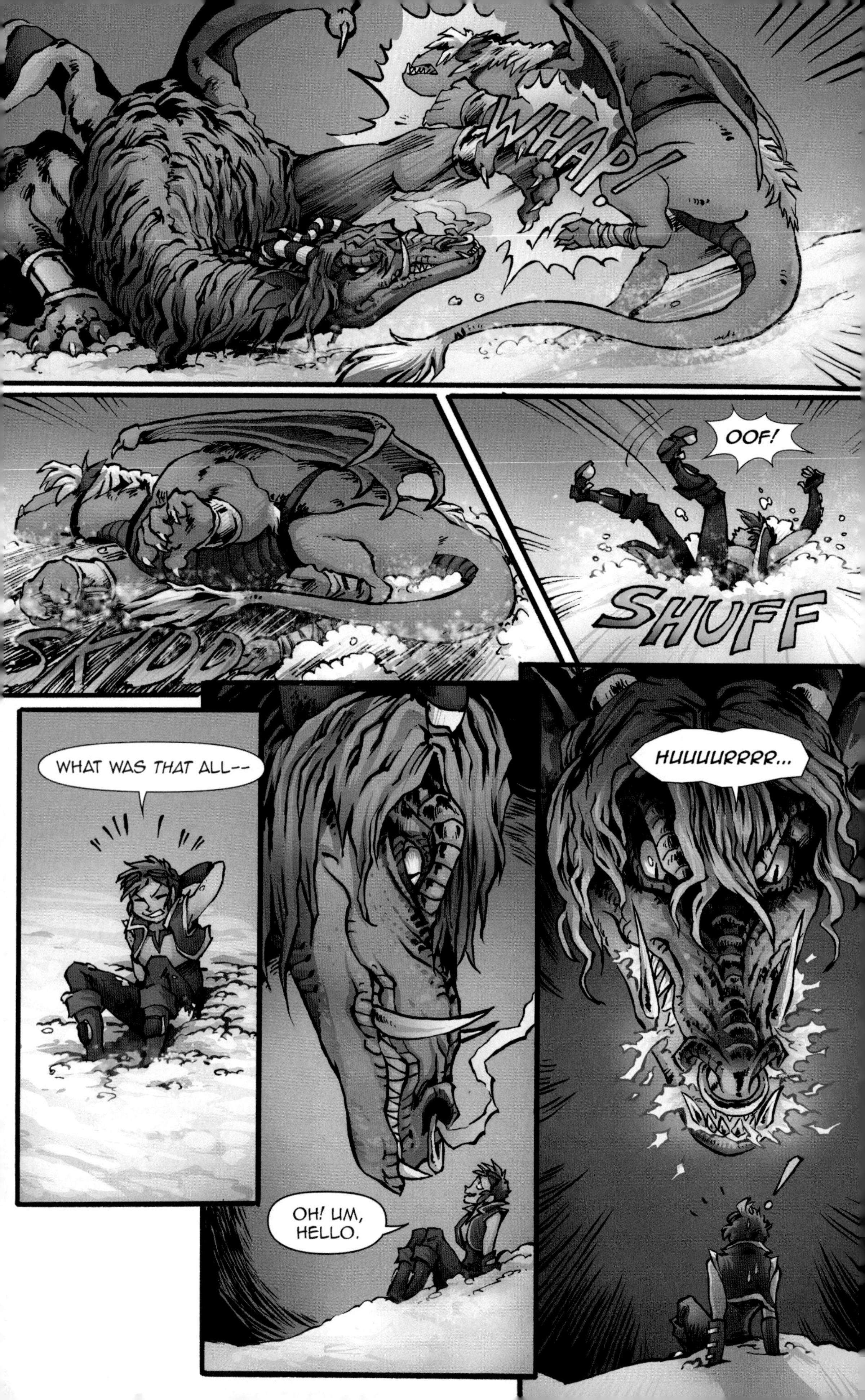
WHAP!
SKIDD
OOF!
SHUFF
WHAT WAS THAT ALL--
OH! UM, HELLO.
HUUUURRRR...

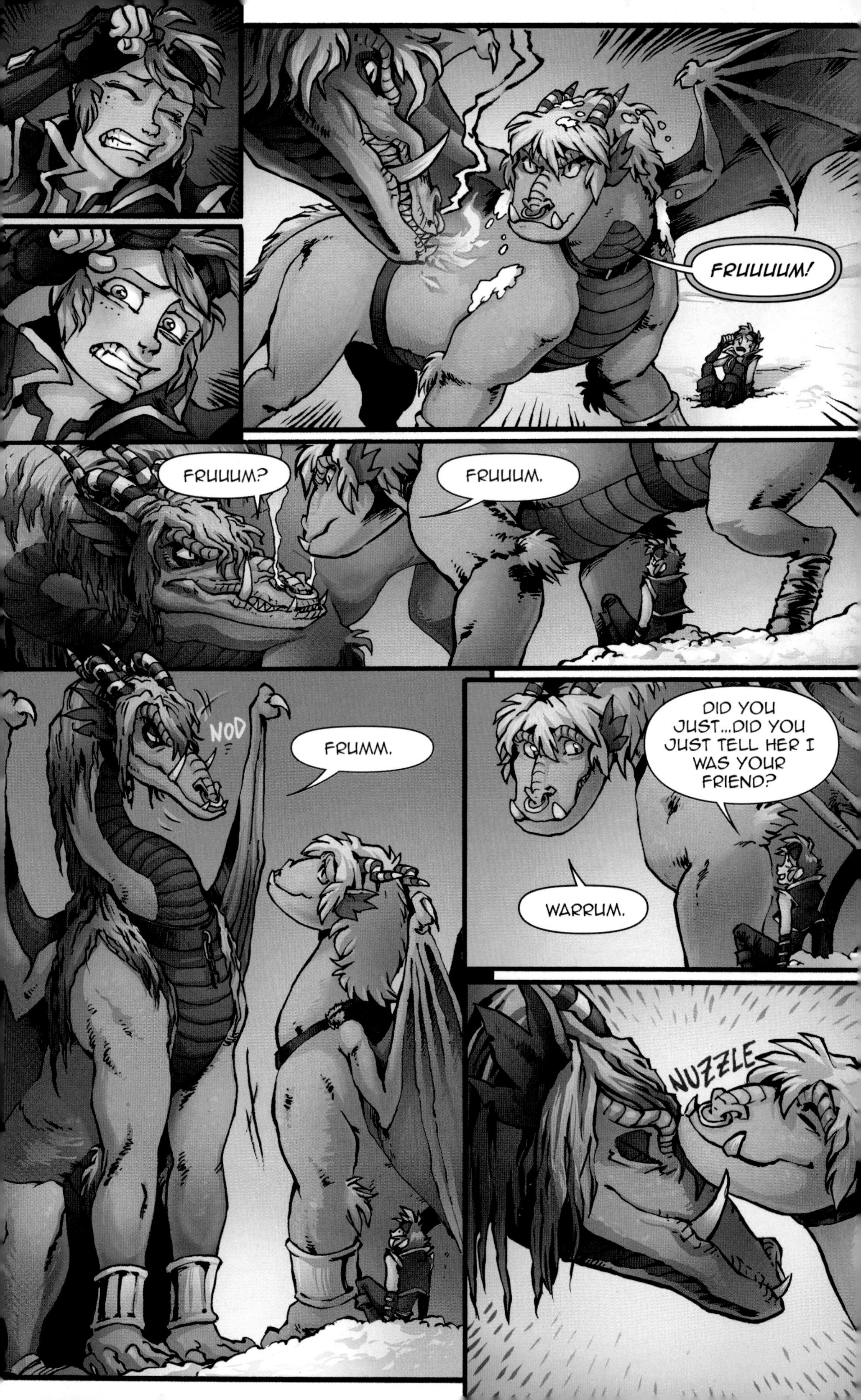
FRUUUUM!
FRUUUM?
FRUUUM.
NOD
FRUMM.
DID YOU JUST...DID YOU JUST TELL HER I WAS YOUR FRIEND?
WARRUM.
NUZZLE

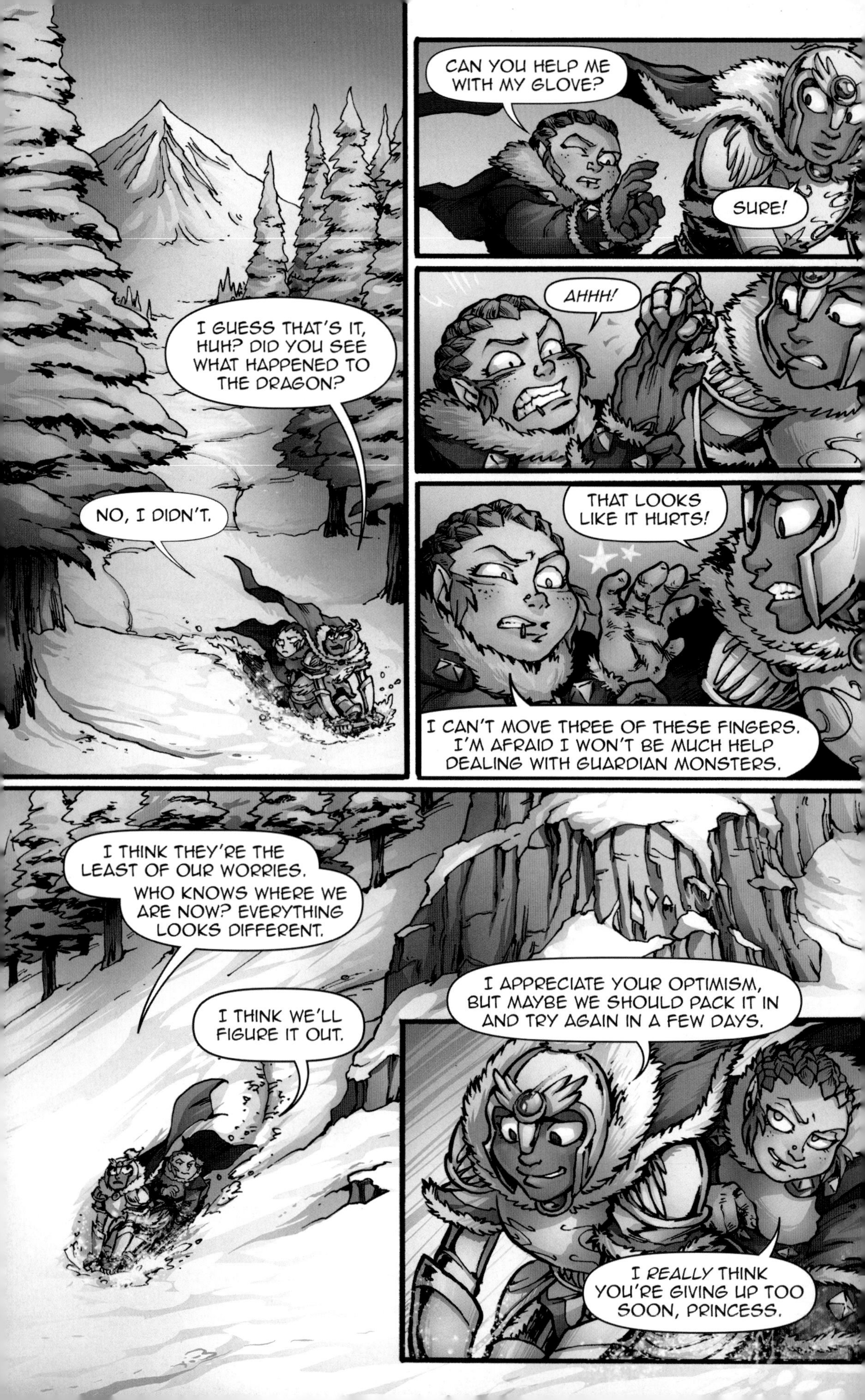
I GUESS THAT'S IT, HUH? DID YOU SEE WHAT HAPPENED TO THE DRAGON?
NO, I DIDN'T.
CAN YOU HELP ME WITH MY GLOVE?
SURE!
AHHH!
THAT LOOKS LIKE IT HURTS!
I CAN'T MOVE THREE OF THESE FINGERS. I'M AFRAID I WON'T BE MUCH HELP DEALING WITH GUARDIAN MONSTERS.
I THINK THEY'RE THE LEAST OF OUR WORRIES.
WHO KNOWS WHERE WE ARE NOW? EVERYTHING LOOKS DIFFERENT.
I THINK WE'LL FIGURE IT OUT.
I APPRECIATE YOUR OPTIMISM, BUT MAYBE WE SHOULD PACK IT IN AND TRY AGAIN IN A FEW DAYS.
I REALLY THINK YOU'RE GIVING UP TOO SOON, PRINCESS.

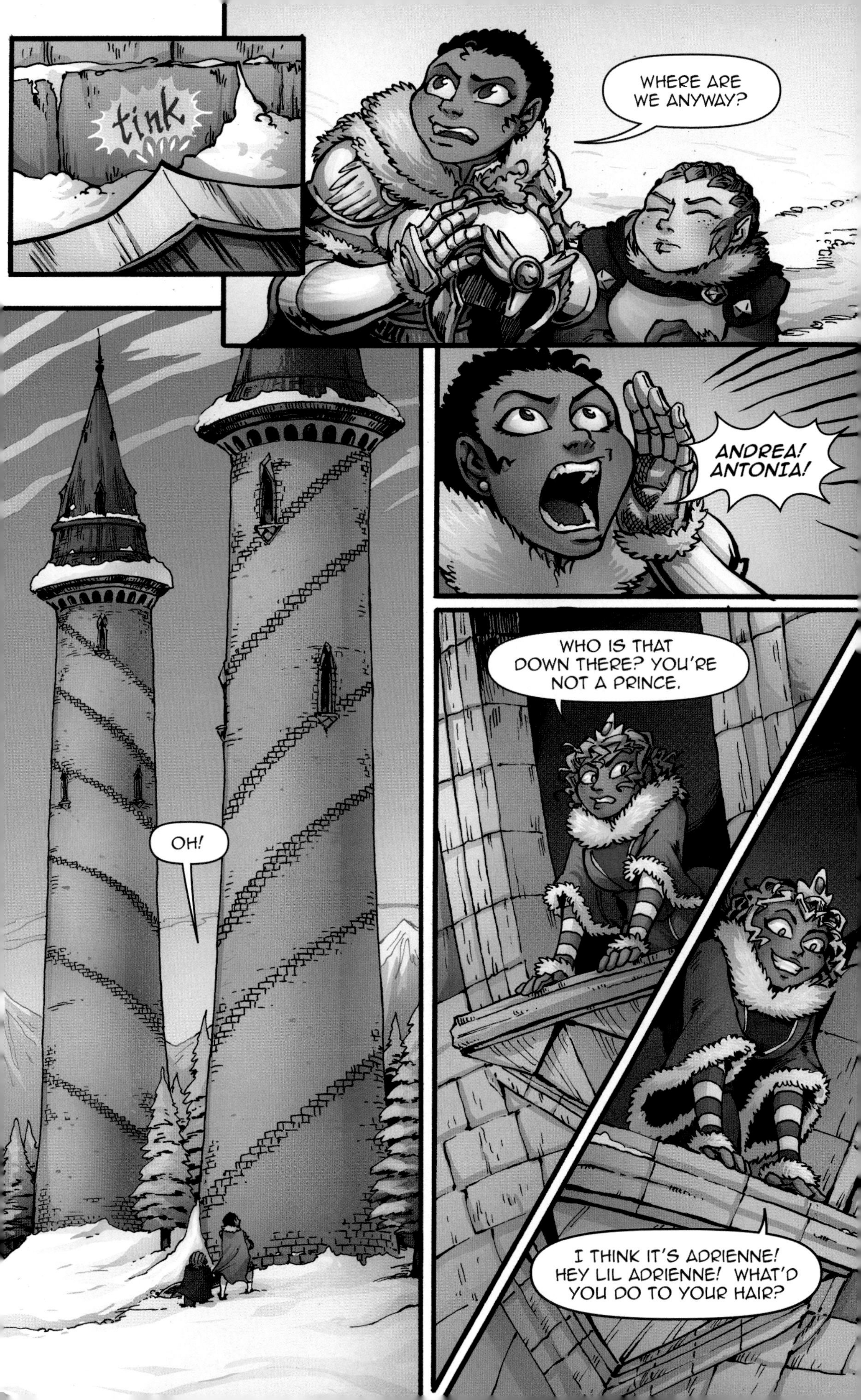
tink
WHERE ARE WE ANYWAY?
OH!
ANDREA! ANTONIA!
WHO IS THAT DOWN THERE? YOU'RE NOT A PRINCE.
I THINK IT'S ADRIENNE! HEY LIL ADRIENNE! WHAT'D YOU DO TO YOUR HAIR?

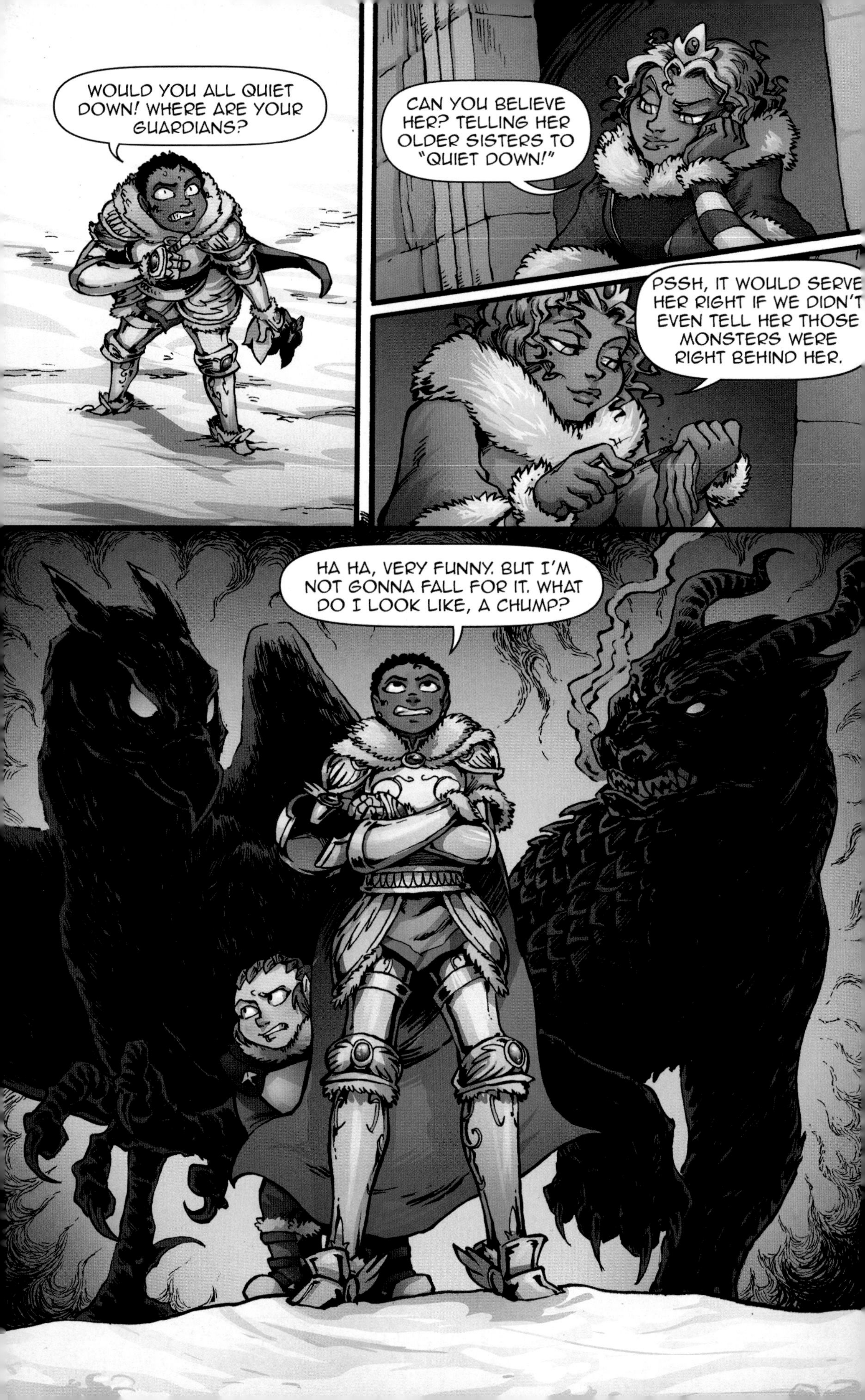
WOULD YOU ALL QUIET DOWN! WHERE ARE YOUR GUARDIANS?
CAN YOU BELIEVE HER? TELLING HER OLDER SISTERS TO "QUIET DOWN!"
PSSH, IT WOULD SERVE HER RIGHT IF WE DIDN'T EVEN TELL HER THOSE MONSTERS WERE RIGHT BEHIND HER.
HA HA, VERY FUNNY. BUT I'M NOT GONNA FALL FOR IT. WHAT DO I LOOK LIKE, A CHUMP?

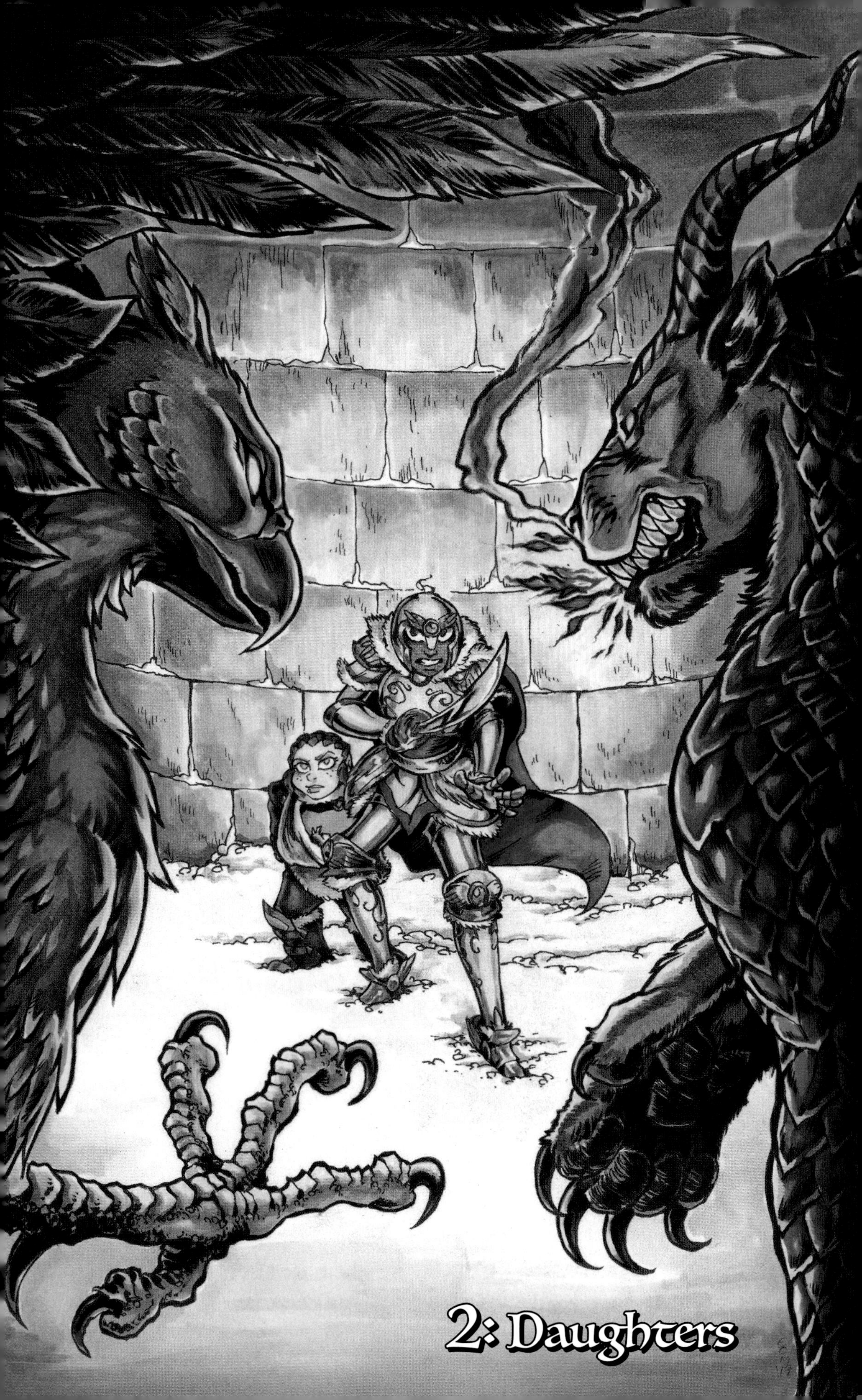

2: Daughters

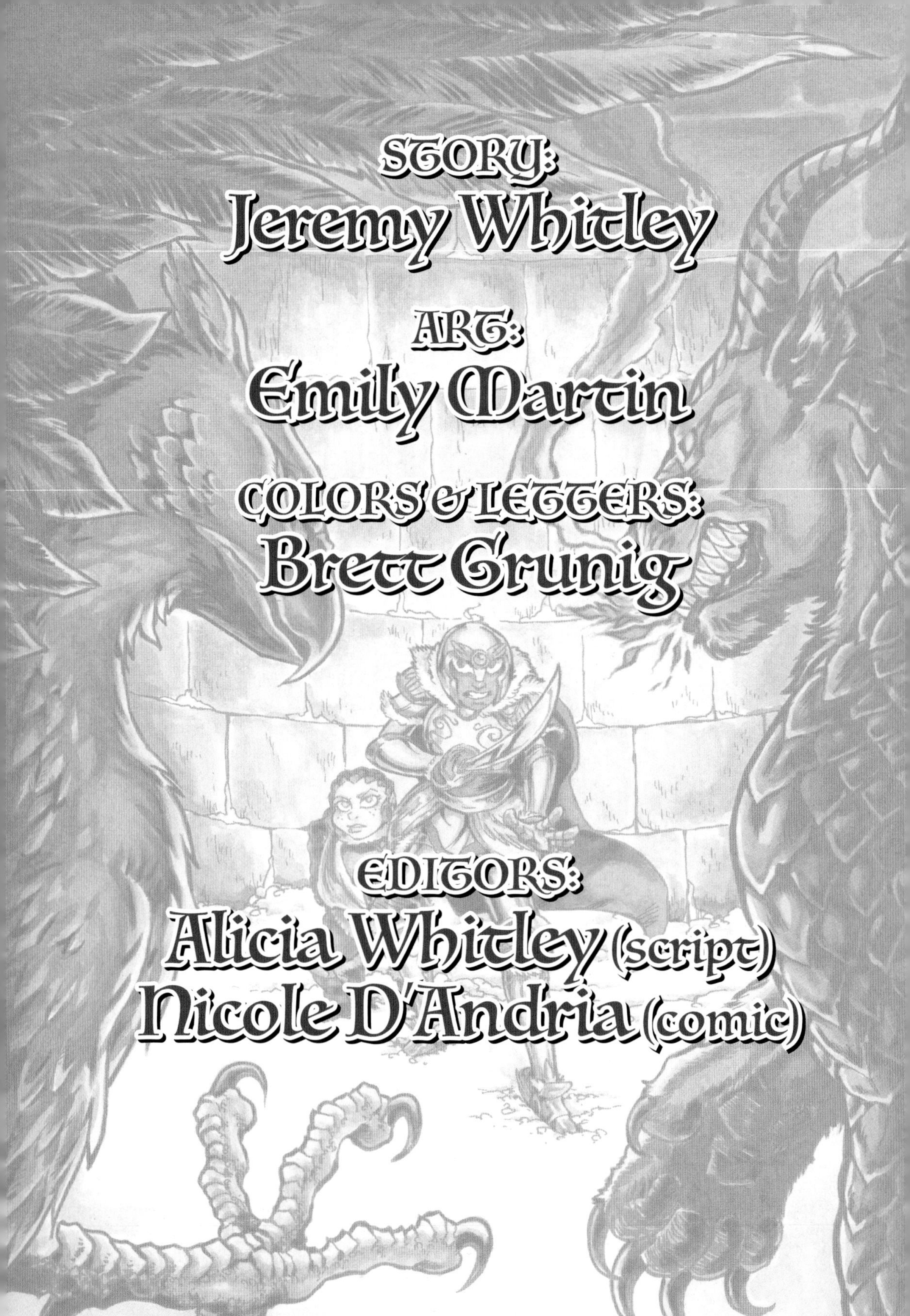

STORY:
Jeremy Whitley

ART:
Emily Martin

COLORS & LETTERS:
Brett Grunig

EDITORS:
Alicia Whitley (script)
Nicole D'Andria (comic)

Bryan Seaton: Publisher/ CEO • Shawn Gabborin: Editor In Chief
Jason Martin: Publisher-Danger Zone • Nicole D'Andria: Marketing Director/Editor
Jim Dietz: Social Media Manager • Danielle Davison: Executive Administrator
Chad Cicconi: Still Waiting For His Princess • Shawn Pryor: President of Creator Relations

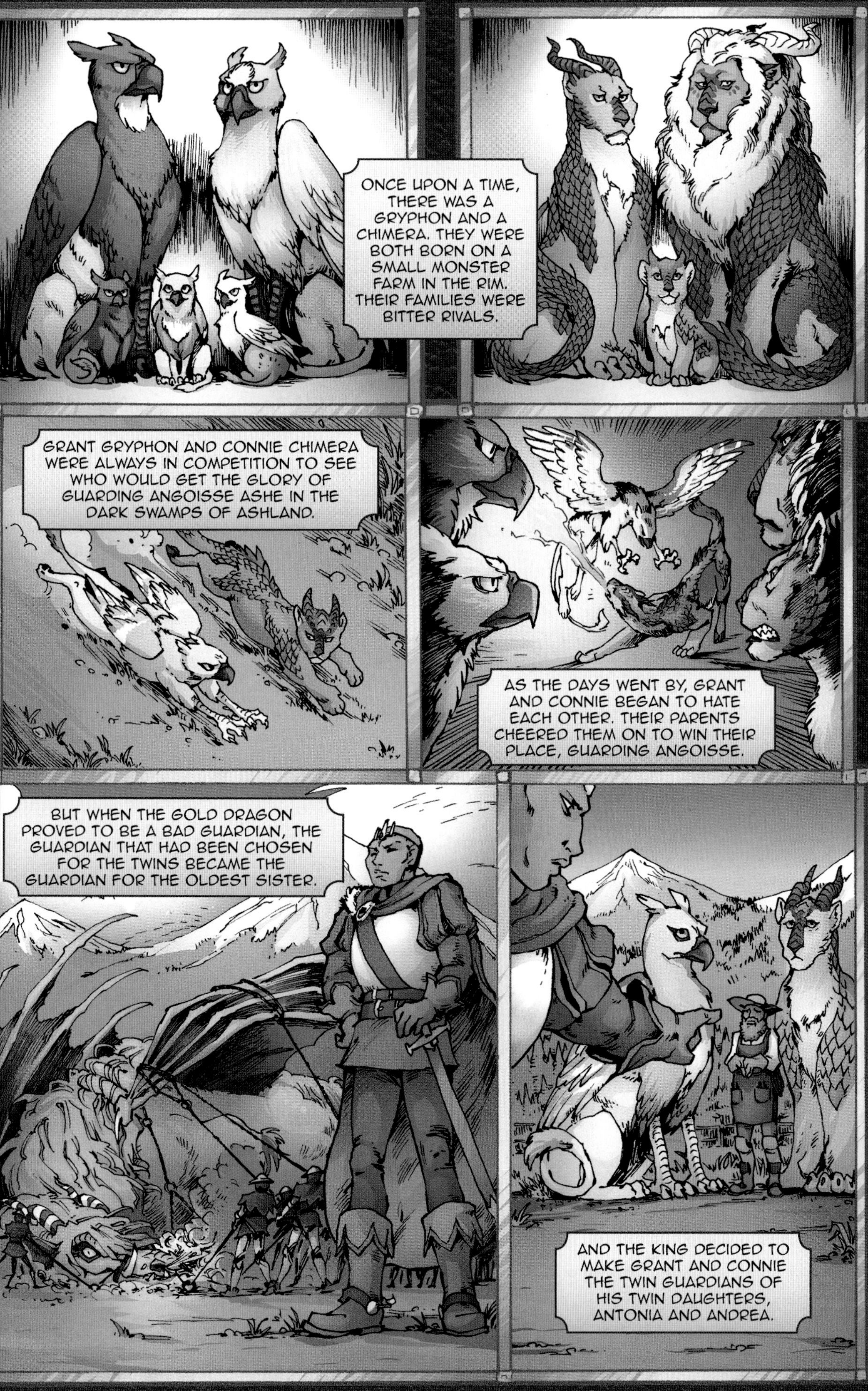
ONCE UPON A TIME, THERE WAS A GRYPHON AND A CHIMERA. THEY WERE BOTH BORN ON A SMALL MONSTER FARM IN THE RIM. THEIR FAMILIES WERE BITTER RIVALS.
GRANT GRYPHON AND CONNIE CHIMERA WERE ALWAYS IN COMPETITION TO SEE WHO WOULD GET THE GLORY OF GUARDING ANGOISSE ASHE IN THE DARK SWAMPS OF ASHLAND.
AS THE DAYS WENT BY, GRANT AND CONNIE BEGAN TO HATE EACH OTHER. THEIR PARENTS CHEERED THEM ON TO WIN THEIR PLACE, GUARDING ANGOISSE.
BUT WHEN THE GOLD DRAGON PROVED TO BE A BAD GUARDIAN, THE GUARDIAN THAT HAD BEEN CHOSEN FOR THE TWINS BECAME THE GUARDIAN FOR THE OLDEST SISTER.
AND THE KING DECIDED TO MAKE GRANT AND CONNIE THE TWIN GUARDIANS OF HIS TWIN DAUGHTERS, ANTONIA AND ANDREA.

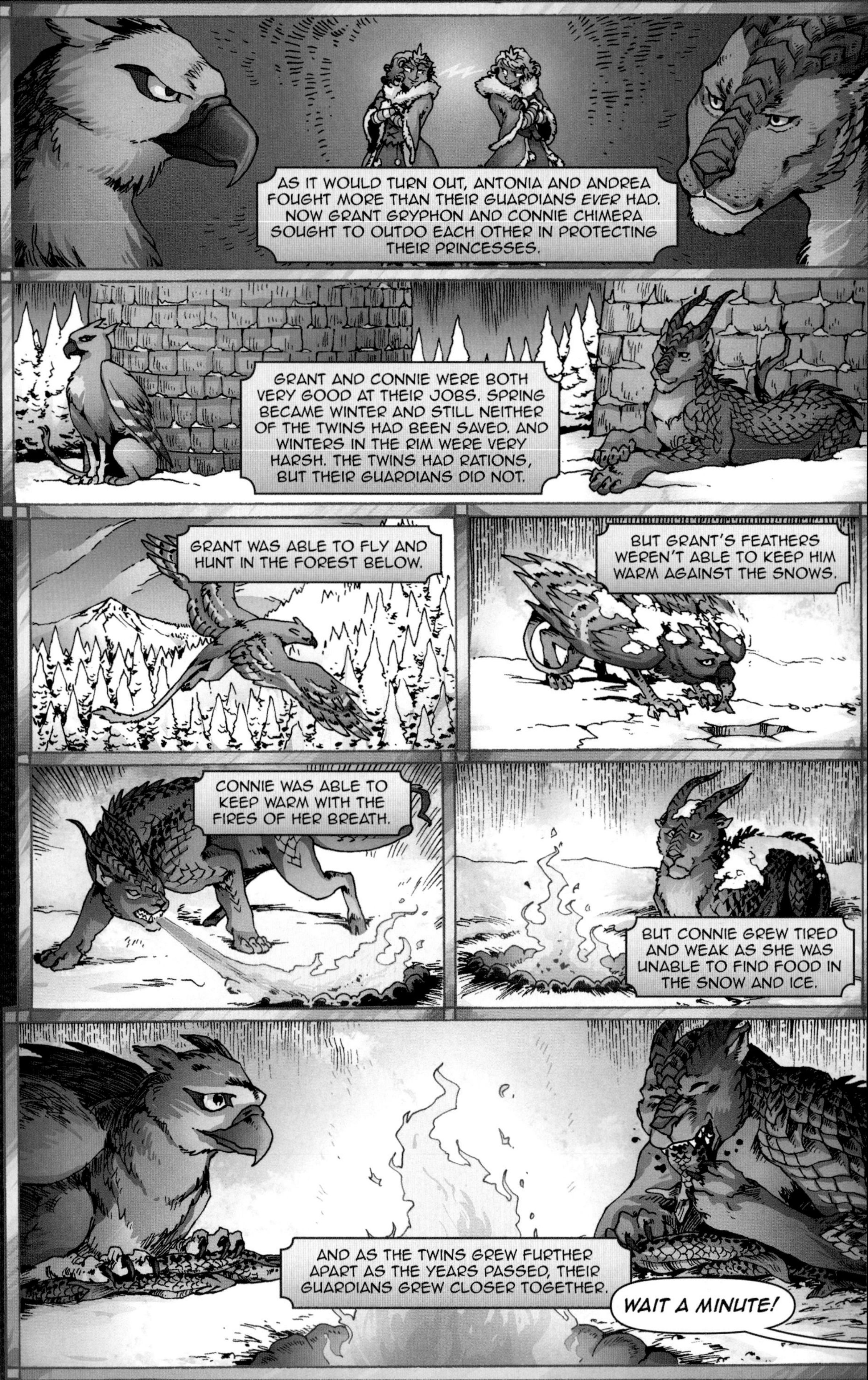
AS IT WOULD TURN OUT, ANTONIA AND ANDREA FOUGHT MORE THAN THEIR GUARDIANS *EVER* HAD. NOW GRANT GRYPHON AND CONNIE CHIMERA SOUGHT TO OUTDO EACH OTHER IN PROTECTING THEIR PRINCESSES.
GRANT AND CONNIE WERE BOTH VERY GOOD AT THEIR JOBS. SPRING BECAME WINTER AND STILL NEITHER OF THE TWINS HAD BEEN SAVED. AND WINTERS IN THE RIM WERE VERY HARSH. THE TWINS HAD RATIONS, BUT THEIR GUARDIANS DID NOT.
GRANT WAS ABLE TO FLY AND HUNT IN THE FOREST BELOW.
BUT GRANT'S FEATHERS WEREN'T ABLE TO KEEP HIM WARM AGAINST THE SNOWS.
CONNIE WAS ABLE TO KEEP WARM WITH THE FIRES OF HER BREATH.
BUT CONNIE GREW TIRED AND WEAK AS SHE WAS UNABLE TO FIND FOOD IN THE SNOW AND ICE.
AND AS THE TWINS GREW FURTHER APART AS THE YEARS PASSED, THEIR GUARDIANS GREW CLOSER TOGETHER.
WAIT A MINUTE!

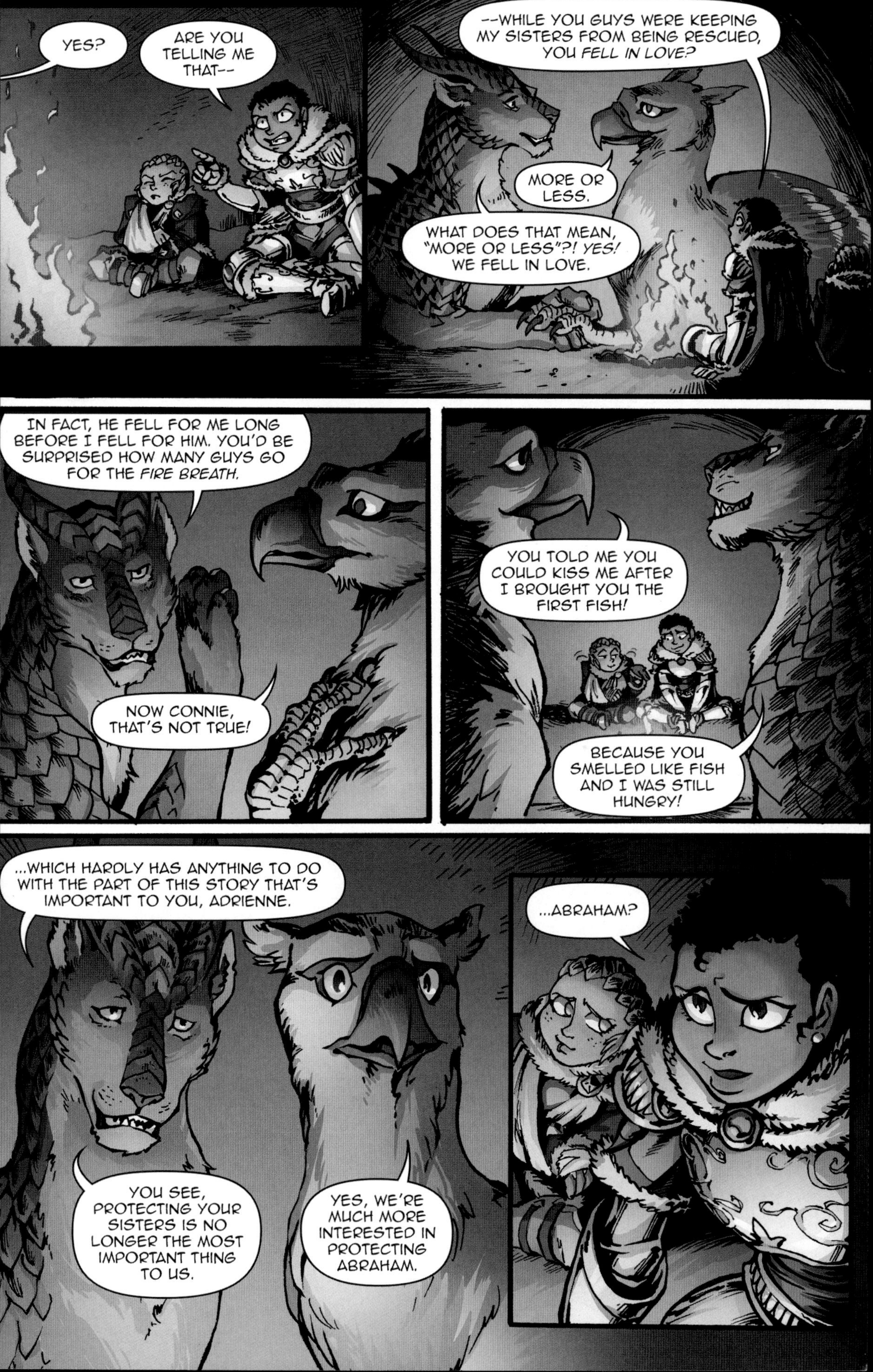
YES?
ARE YOU TELLING ME THAT--
--WHILE YOU GUYS WERE KEEPING MY SISTERS FROM BEING RESCUED, YOU FELL IN LOVE?
MORE OR LESS.
WHAT DOES THAT MEAN, "MORE OR LESS"?! YES! WE FELL IN LOVE.
IN FACT, HE FELL FOR ME LONG BEFORE I FELL FOR HIM. YOU'D BE SURPRISED HOW MANY GUYS GO FOR THE FIRE BREATH.
NOW CONNIE, THAT'S NOT TRUE!
YOU TOLD ME YOU COULD KISS ME AFTER I BROUGHT YOU THE FIRST FISH!
BECAUSE YOU SMELLED LIKE FISH AND I WAS STILL HUNGRY!
...WHICH HARDLY HAS ANYTHING TO DO WITH THE PART OF THIS STORY THAT'S IMPORTANT TO YOU, ADRIENNE.
YOU SEE, PROTECTING YOUR SISTERS IS NO LONGER THE MOST IMPORTANT THING TO US.
YES, WE'RE MUCH MORE INTERESTED IN PROTECTING ABRAHAM.
...ABRAHAM?

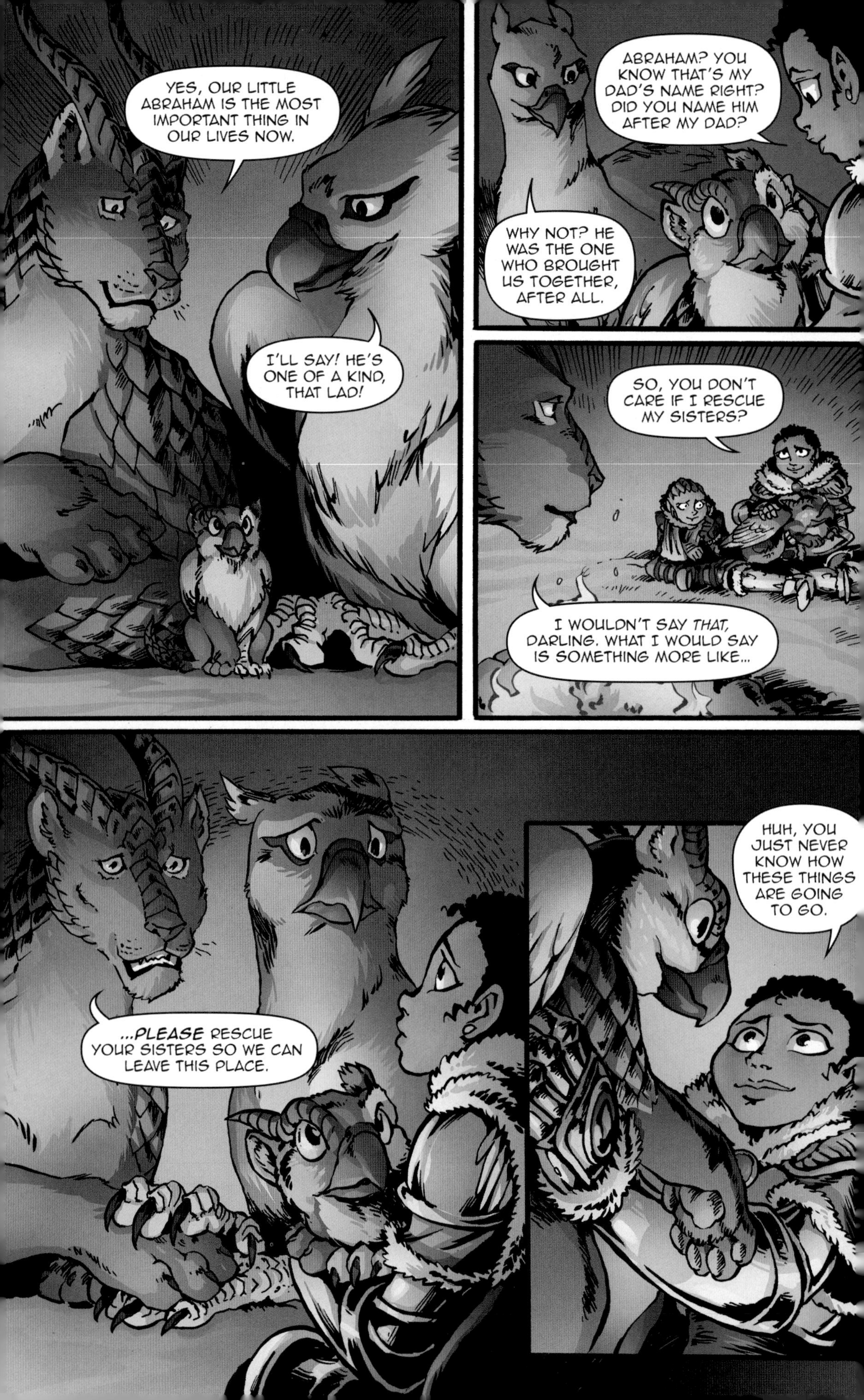
YES, OUR LITTLE ABRAHAM IS THE MOST IMPORTANT THING IN OUR LIVES NOW.
I'LL SAY! HE'S ONE OF A KIND, THAT LAD!
ABRAHAM? YOU KNOW THAT'S MY DAD'S NAME RIGHT? DID YOU NAME HIM AFTER MY DAD?
WHY NOT? HE WAS THE ONE WHO BROUGHT US TOGETHER, AFTER ALL.
SO, YOU DON'T CARE IF I RESCUE MY SISTERS?
I WOULDN'T SAY *THAT*, DARLING. WHAT I WOULD SAY IS SOMETHING MORE LIKE...
...**PLEASE** RESCUE YOUR SISTERS SO WE CAN LEAVE THIS PLACE.
HUH, YOU JUST NEVER KNOW HOW THESE THINGS ARE GOING TO GO.

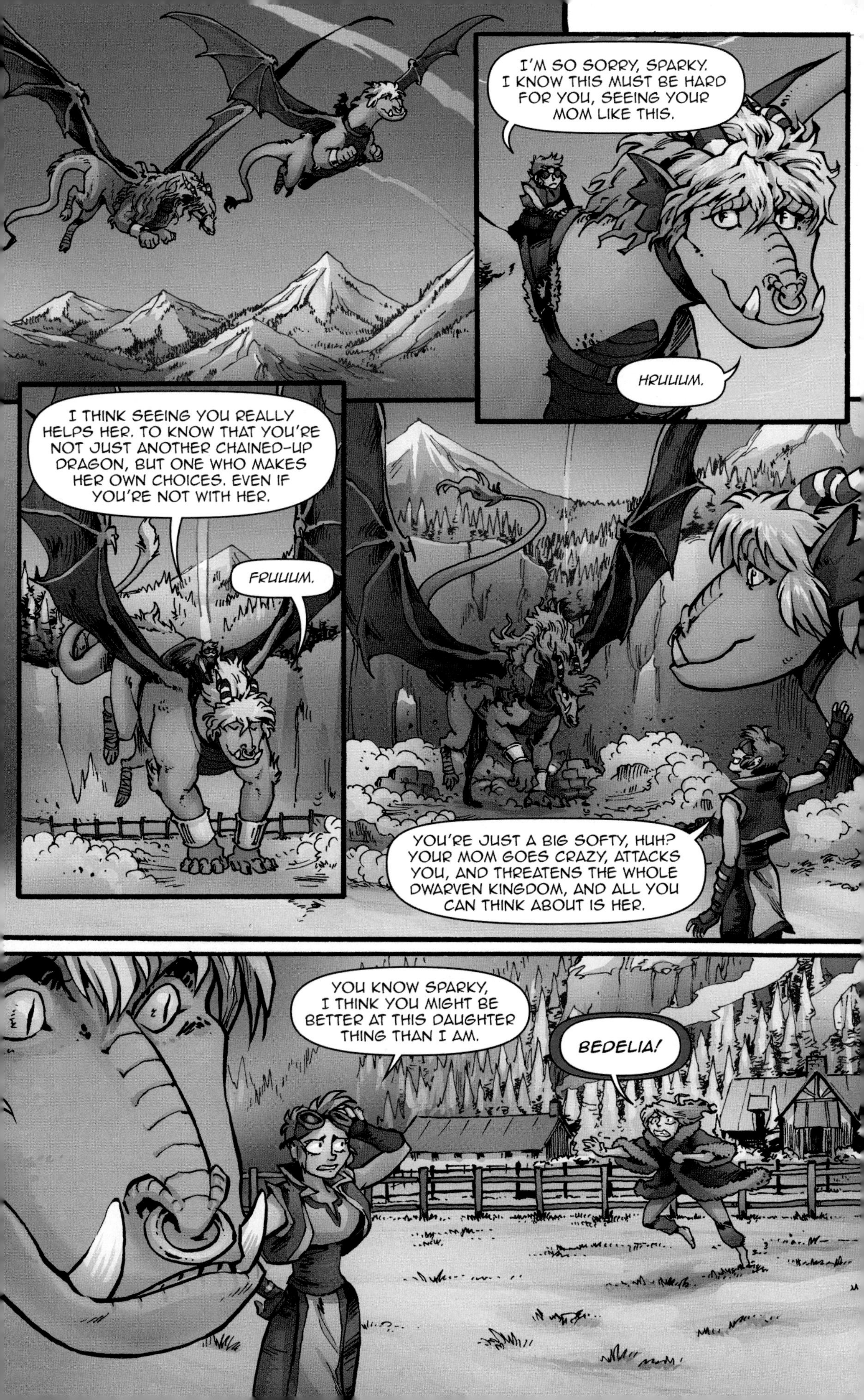
I'M SO SORRY, SPARKY. I KNOW THIS MUST BE HARD FOR YOU, SEEING YOUR MOM LIKE THIS.
HRUUUM.
I THINK SEEING YOU REALLY HELPS HER. TO KNOW THAT YOU'RE NOT JUST ANOTHER CHAINED-UP DRAGON, BUT ONE WHO MAKES HER OWN CHOICES. EVEN IF YOU'RE NOT WITH HER.
FRUUUM.
YOU'RE JUST A BIG SOFTY, HUH? YOUR MOM GOES CRAZY, ATTACKS YOU, AND THREATENS THE WHOLE DWARVEN KINGDOM, AND ALL YOU CAN THINK ABOUT IS HER.
YOU KNOW SPARKY, I THINK YOU MIGHT BE BETTER AT THIS DAUGHTER THING THAN I AM.
BEDELIA!

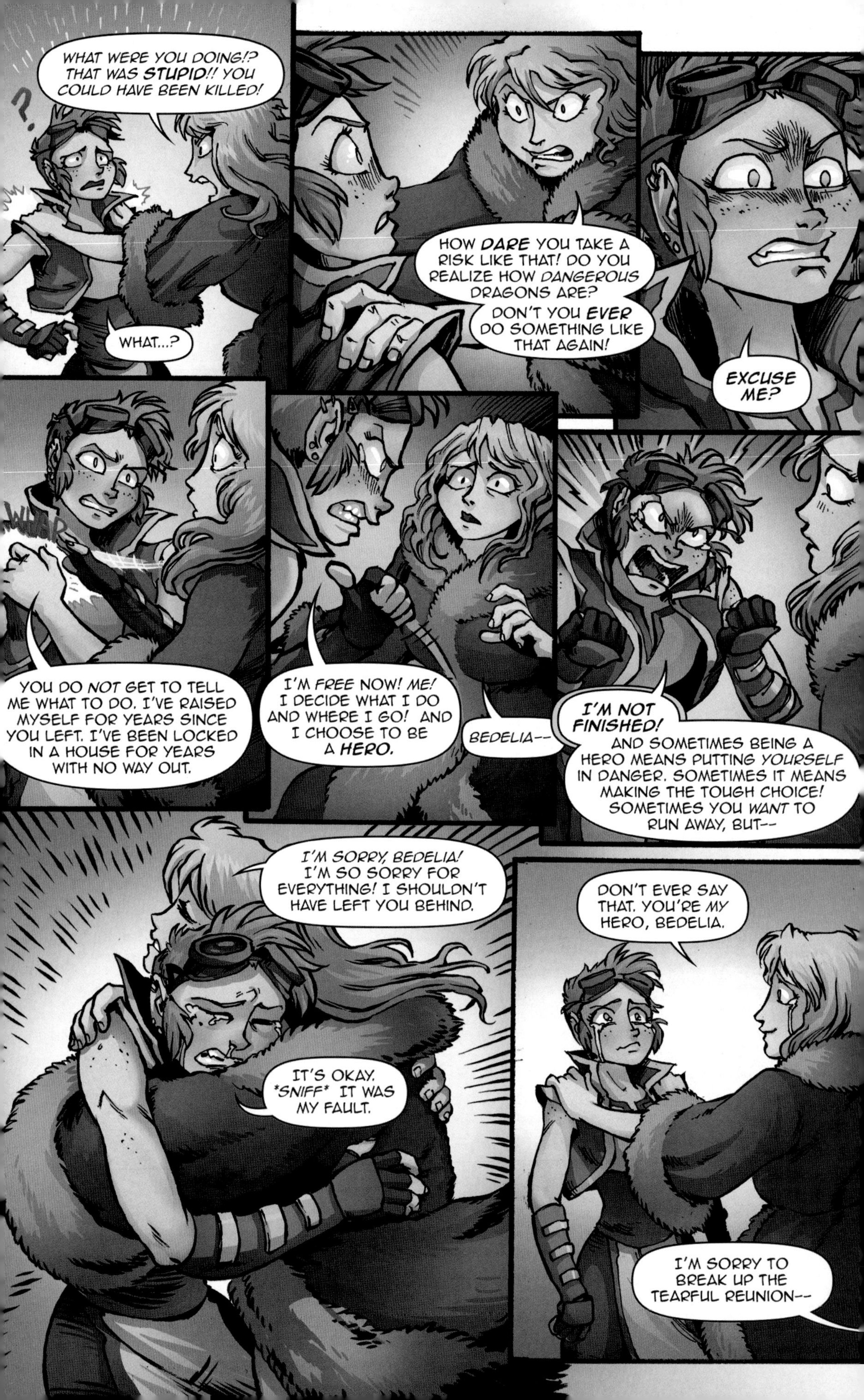
WHAT WERE YOU DOING!? THAT WAS STUPID!! YOU COULD HAVE BEEN KILLED!
?
WHAT...?
HOW DARE YOU TAKE A RISK LIKE THAT! DO YOU REALIZE HOW DANGEROUS DRAGONS ARE?
DON'T YOU EVER DO SOMETHING LIKE THAT AGAIN!
EXCUSE ME?
YOU DO NOT GET TO TELL ME WHAT TO DO. I'VE RAISED MYSELF FOR YEARS SINCE YOU LEFT. I'VE BEEN LOCKED IN A HOUSE FOR YEARS WITH NO WAY OUT.
I'M FREE NOW! ME! I DECIDE WHAT I DO AND WHERE I GO! AND I CHOOSE TO BE A HERO.
BEDELIA--
I'M NOT FINISHED!
AND SOMETIMES BEING A HERO MEANS PUTTING YOURSELF IN DANGER. SOMETIMES IT MEANS MAKING THE TOUGH CHOICE! SOMETIMES YOU WANT TO RUN AWAY, BUT--
I'M SORRY, BEDELIA! I'M SO SORRY FOR EVERYTHING! I SHOULDN'T HAVE LEFT YOU BEHIND.
IT'S OKAY. *SNIFF* IT WAS MY FAULT.
DON'T EVER SAY THAT. YOU'RE MY HERO, BEDELIA.
I'M SORRY TO BREAK UP THE TEARFUL REUNION--

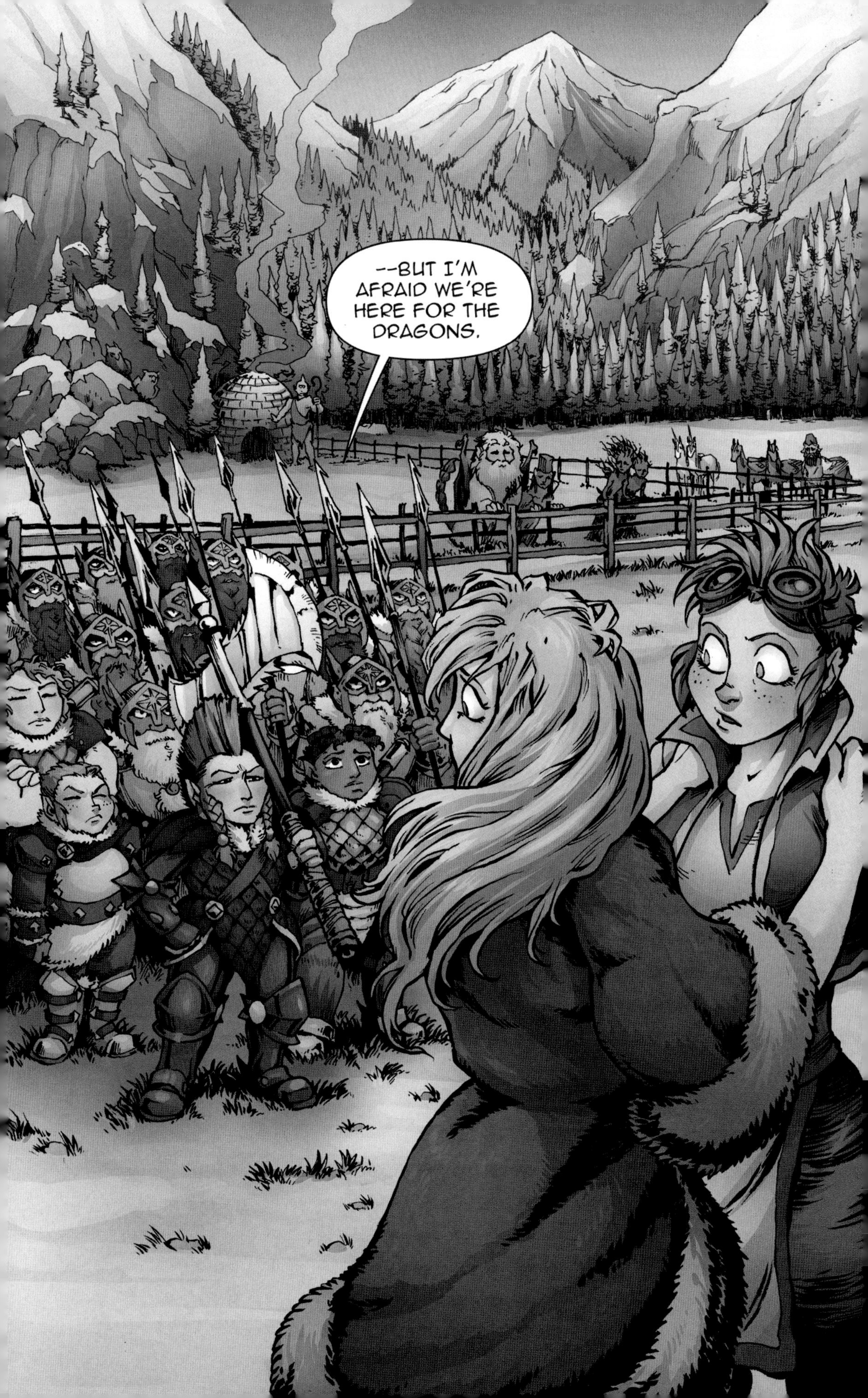
--BUT I'M AFRAID WE'RE HERE FOR THE DRAGONS.

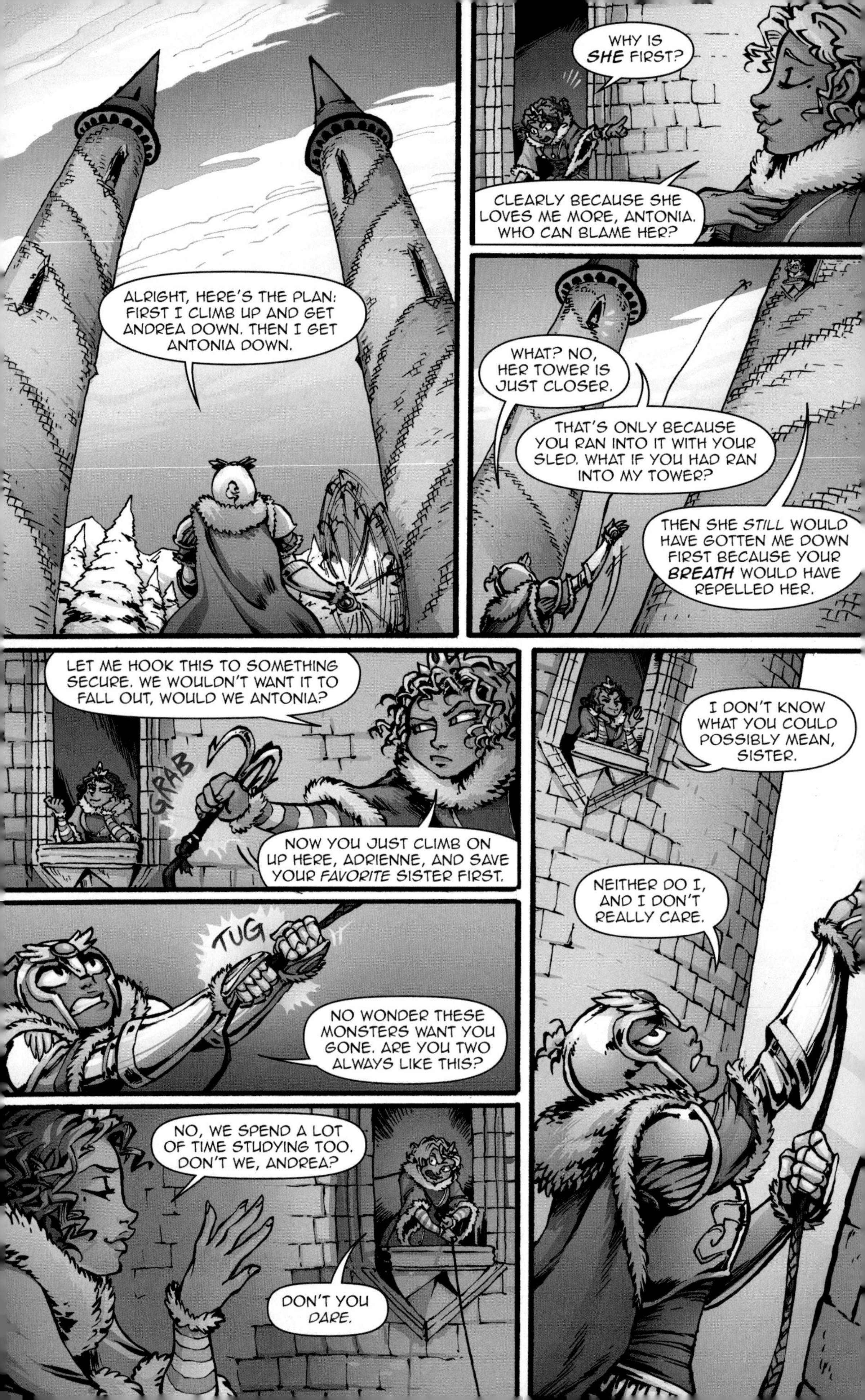
ALRIGHT, HERE'S THE PLAN: FIRST I CLIMB UP AND GET ANDREA DOWN. THEN I GET ANTONIA DOWN.
WHY IS SHE FIRST?
CLEARLY BECAUSE SHE LOVES ME MORE, ANTONIA. WHO CAN BLAME HER?
WHAT? NO, HER TOWER IS JUST CLOSER.
THAT'S ONLY BECAUSE YOU RAN INTO IT WITH YOUR SLED. WHAT IF YOU HAD RAN INTO MY TOWER?
THEN SHE STILL WOULD HAVE GOTTEN ME DOWN FIRST BECAUSE YOUR BREATH WOULD HAVE REPELLED HER.
LET ME HOOK THIS TO SOMETHING SECURE. WE WOULDN'T WANT IT TO FALL OUT, WOULD WE ANTONIA?
GRAB
NOW YOU JUST CLIMB ON UP HERE, ADRIENNE, AND SAVE YOUR FAVORITE SISTER FIRST.
TUG
NO WONDER THESE MONSTERS WANT YOU GONE. ARE YOU TWO ALWAYS LIKE THIS?
NO, WE SPEND A LOT OF TIME STUDYING TOO. DON'T WE, ANDREA?
DON'T YOU DARE.
I DON'T KNOW WHAT YOU COULD POSSIBLY MEAN, SISTER.
NEITHER DO I, AND I DON'T REALLY CARE.

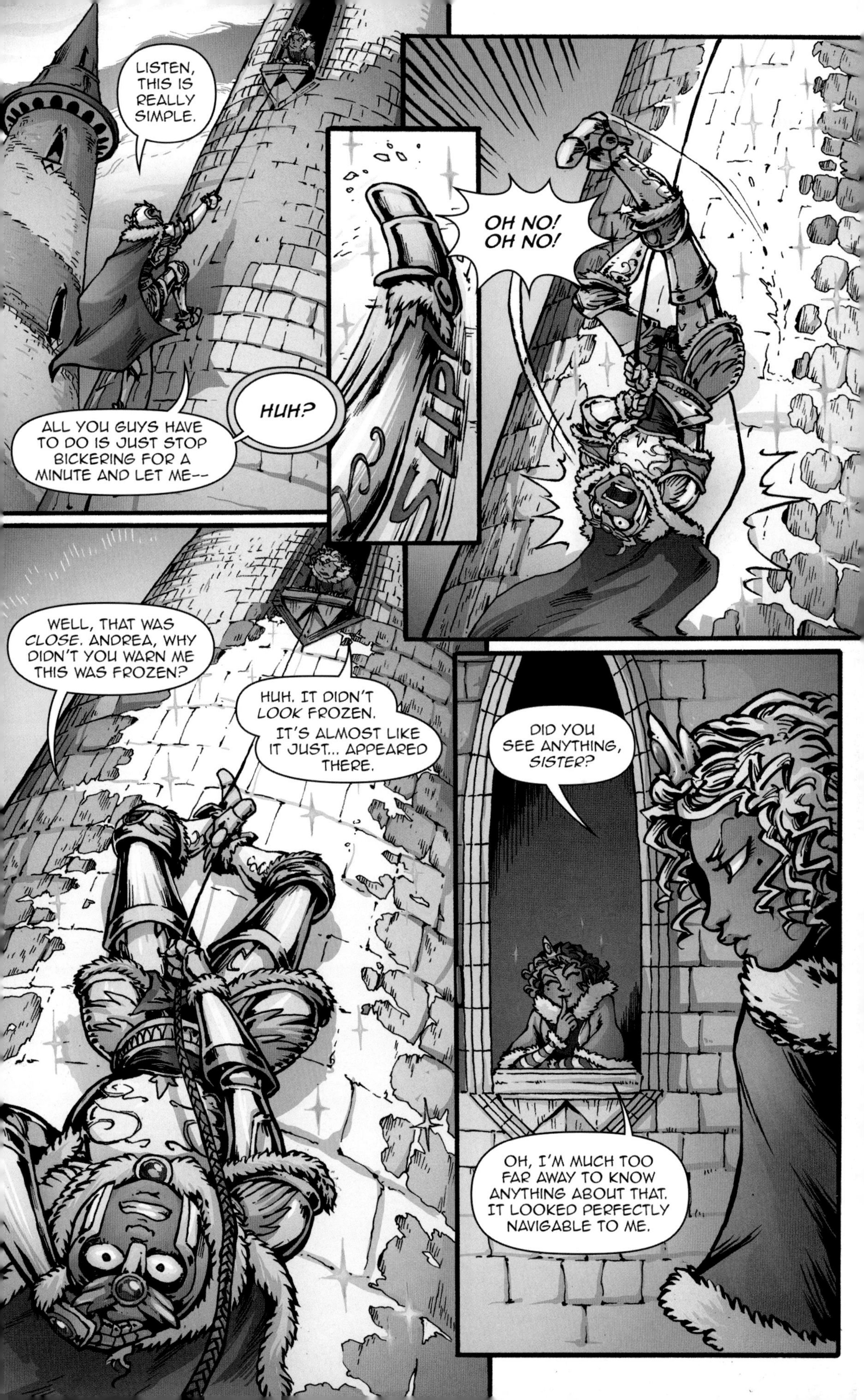
LISTEN, THIS IS REALLY SIMPLE.
ALL YOU GUYS HAVE TO DO IS JUST STOP BICKERING FOR A MINUTE AND LET ME--
HUH?
SLIP!
OH NO! OH NO!
WELL, THAT WAS CLOSE. ANDREA, WHY DIDN'T YOU WARN ME THIS WAS FROZEN?
HUH. IT DIDN'T LOOK FROZEN.
IT'S ALMOST LIKE IT JUST... APPEARED THERE.
DID YOU SEE ANYTHING, SISTER?
OH, I'M MUCH TOO FAR AWAY TO KNOW ANYTHING ABOUT THAT. IT LOOKED PERFECTLY NAVIGABLE TO ME.

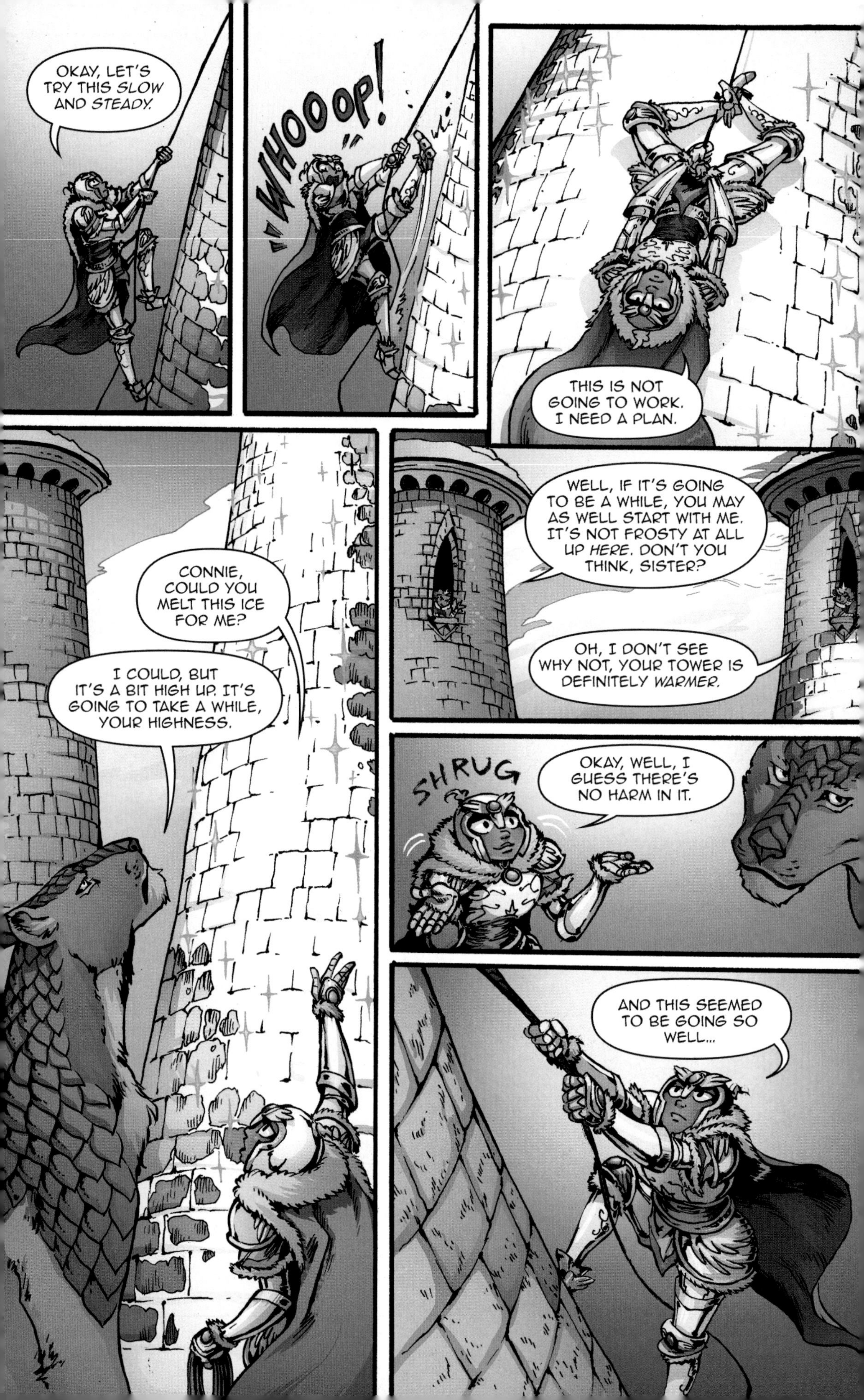
OKAY, LET'S TRY THIS SLOW AND STEADY.
WHOOOP!
THIS IS NOT GOING TO WORK. I NEED A PLAN.
CONNIE, COULD YOU MELT THIS ICE FOR ME?
I COULD, BUT IT'S A BIT HIGH UP. IT'S GOING TO TAKE A WHILE, YOUR HIGHNESS.
WELL, IF IT'S GOING TO BE A WHILE, YOU MAY AS WELL START WITH ME. IT'S NOT FROSTY AT ALL UP HERE. DON'T YOU THINK, SISTER?
OH, I DON'T SEE WHY NOT, YOUR TOWER IS DEFINITELY WARMER.
SHRUG
OKAY, WELL, I GUESS THERE'S NO HARM IN IT.
AND THIS SEEMED TO BE GOING SO WELL...

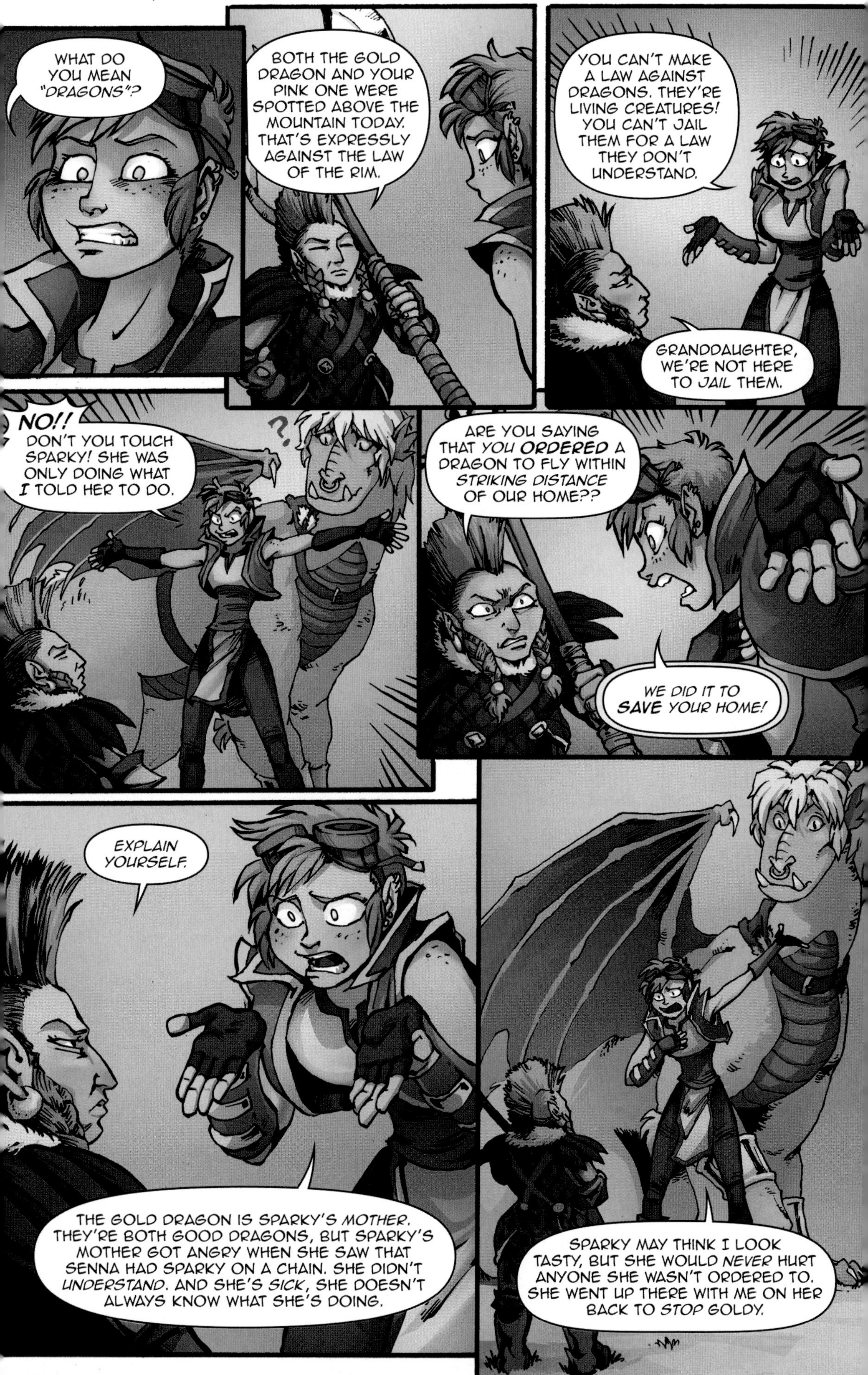
WHAT DO YOU MEAN "DRAGONS"?
BOTH THE GOLD DRAGON AND YOUR PINK ONE WERE SPOTTED ABOVE THE MOUNTAIN TODAY. THAT'S EXPRESSLY AGAINST THE LAW OF THE RIM.
YOU CAN'T MAKE A LAW AGAINST DRAGONS. THEY'RE LIVING CREATURES! YOU CAN'T JAIL THEM FOR A LAW THEY DON'T UNDERSTAND.
GRANDDAUGHTER, WE'RE NOT HERE TO JAIL THEM.
NO!! DON'T YOU TOUCH SPARKY! SHE WAS ONLY DOING WHAT I TOLD HER TO DO.
?
ARE YOU SAYING THAT YOU ORDERED A DRAGON TO FLY WITHIN STRIKING DISTANCE OF OUR HOME??
WE DID IT TO SAVE YOUR HOME!
EXPLAIN YOURSELF.
THE GOLD DRAGON IS SPARKY'S MOTHER. THEY'RE BOTH GOOD DRAGONS, BUT SPARKY'S MOTHER GOT ANGRY WHEN SHE SAW THAT SENNA HAD SPARKY ON A CHAIN. SHE DIDN'T UNDERSTAND. AND SHE'S SICK, SHE DOESN'T ALWAYS KNOW WHAT SHE'S DOING.
SPARKY MAY THINK I LOOK TASTY, BUT SHE WOULD NEVER HURT ANYONE SHE WASN'T ORDERED TO. SHE WENT UP THERE WITH ME ON HER BACK TO STOP GOLDY.

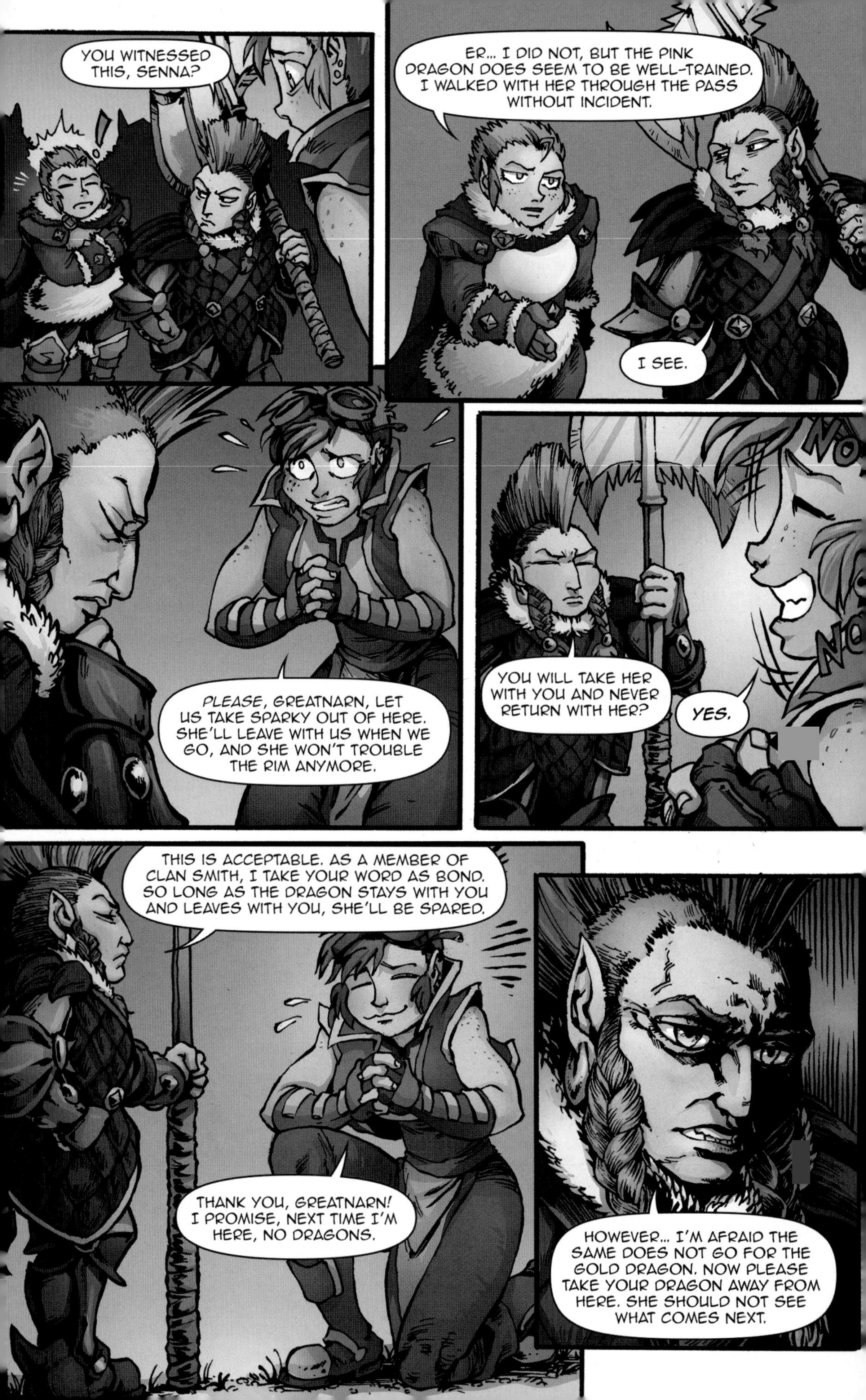
YOU WITNESSED THIS, SENNA?
ER... I DID NOT, BUT THE PINK DRAGON DOES SEEM TO BE WELL-TRAINED. I WALKED WITH HER THROUGH THE PASS WITHOUT INCIDENT.
I SEE.
PLEASE, GREATNARN, LET US TAKE SPARKY OUT OF HERE. SHE'LL LEAVE WITH US WHEN WE GO, AND SHE WON'T TROUBLE THE RIM ANYMORE.
YOU WILL TAKE HER WITH YOU AND NEVER RETURN WITH HER?
YES.
NO
NO
THIS IS ACCEPTABLE. AS A MEMBER OF CLAN SMITH, I TAKE YOUR WORD AS BOND. SO LONG AS THE DRAGON STAYS WITH YOU AND LEAVES WITH YOU, SHE'LL BE SPARED.
THANK YOU, GREATNARN! I PROMISE, NEXT TIME I'M HERE, NO DRAGONS.
HOWEVER... I'M AFRAID THE SAME DOES NOT GO FOR THE GOLD DRAGON. NOW PLEASE TAKE YOUR DRAGON AWAY FROM HERE. SHE SHOULD NOT SEE WHAT COMES NEXT.

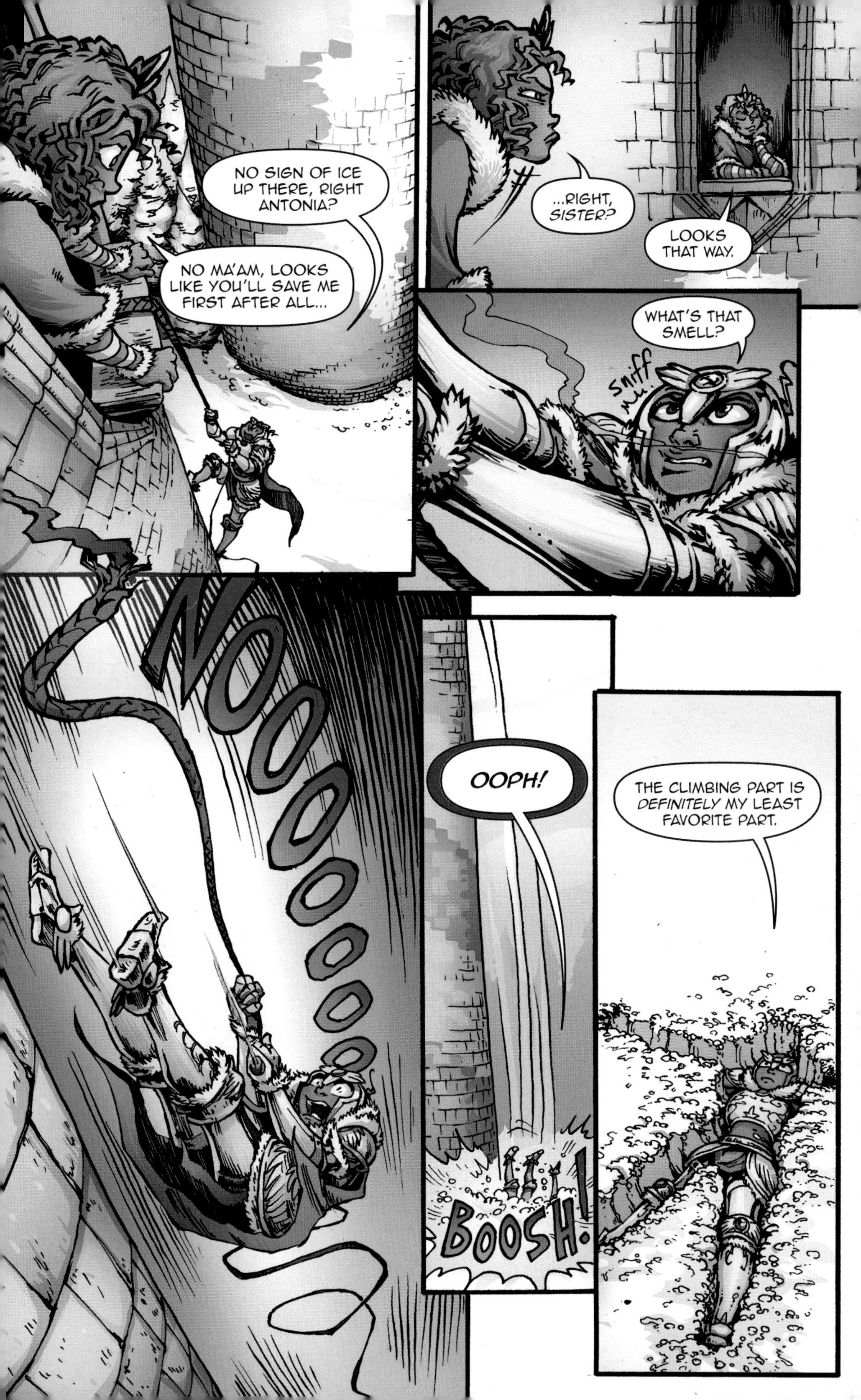
NO SIGN OF ICE UP THERE, RIGHT ANTONIA?
NO MA'AM, LOOKS LIKE YOU'LL SAVE ME FIRST AFTER ALL...
...RIGHT, SISTER?
LOOKS THAT WAY.
WHAT'S THAT SMELL?
Sniff
NOOOOOOOOO
OOPH!
BOOSH!
THE CLIMBING PART IS *DEFINITELY* MY LEAST FAVORITE PART.

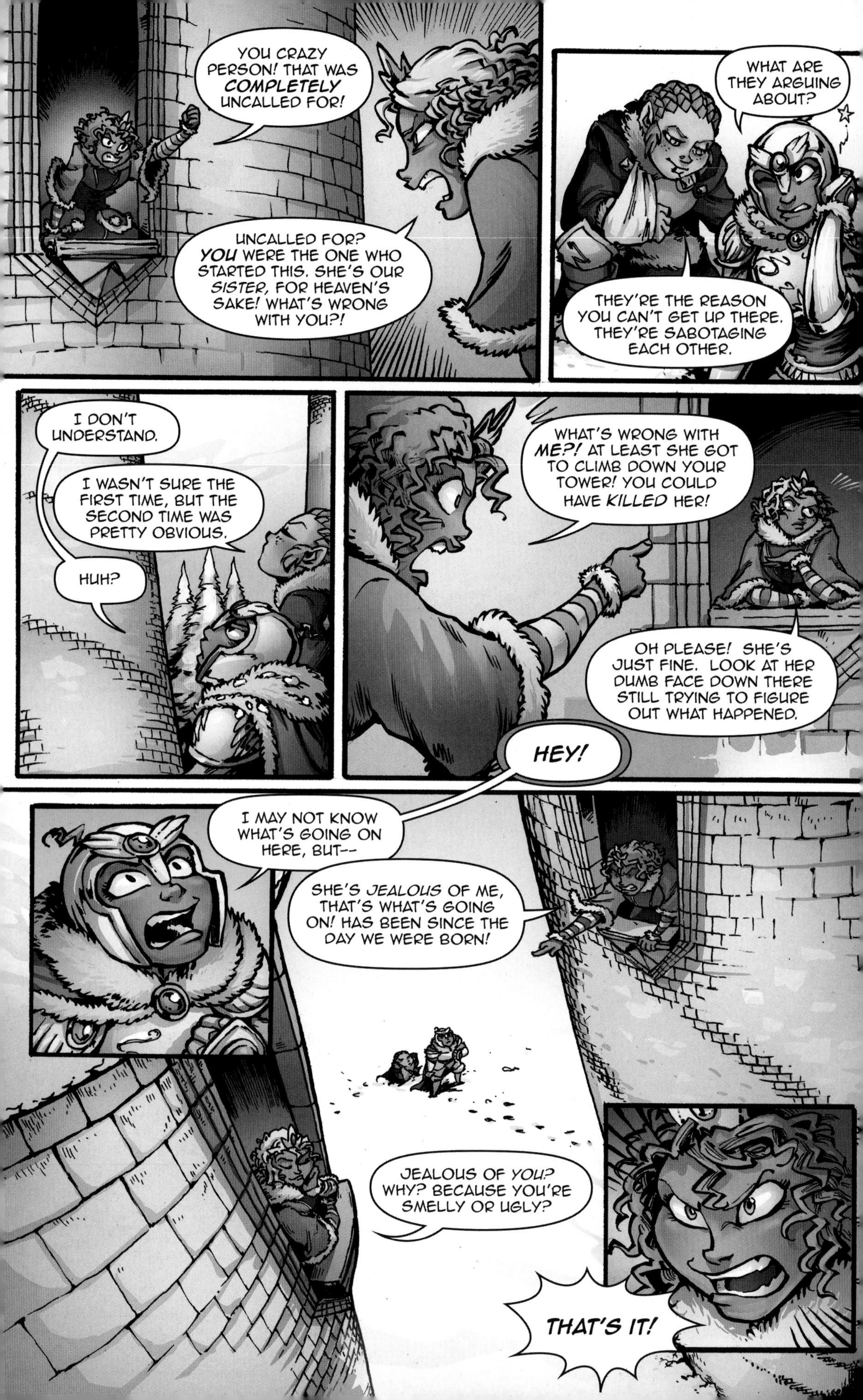
YOU CRAZY PERSON! THAT WAS *COMPLETELY* UNCALLED FOR!
UNCALLED FOR? ***YOU*** WERE THE ONE WHO STARTED THIS. SHE'S OUR *SISTER*, FOR HEAVEN'S SAKE! WHAT'S WRONG WITH YOU?!
WHAT ARE THEY ARGUING ABOUT?
THEY'RE THE REASON YOU CAN'T GET UP THERE. THEY'RE SABOTAGING EACH OTHER.
I DON'T UNDERSTAND.
I WASN'T SURE THE FIRST TIME, BUT THE SECOND TIME WAS PRETTY OBVIOUS.
HUH?
WHAT'S WRONG WITH *ME?!* AT LEAST SHE GOT TO CLIMB DOWN YOUR TOWER! YOU COULD HAVE *KILLED* HER!
OH PLEASE! SHE'S JUST FINE. LOOK AT HER DUMB FACE DOWN THERE STILL TRYING TO FIGURE OUT WHAT HAPPENED.
HEY!
I MAY NOT KNOW WHAT'S GOING ON HERE, BUT--
SHE'S *JEALOUS* OF ME, THAT'S WHAT'S GOING ON! HAS BEEN SINCE THE DAY WE WERE BORN!
JEALOUS OF *YOU?* WHY? BECAUSE YOU'RE SMELLY OR UGLY?
THAT'S IT!

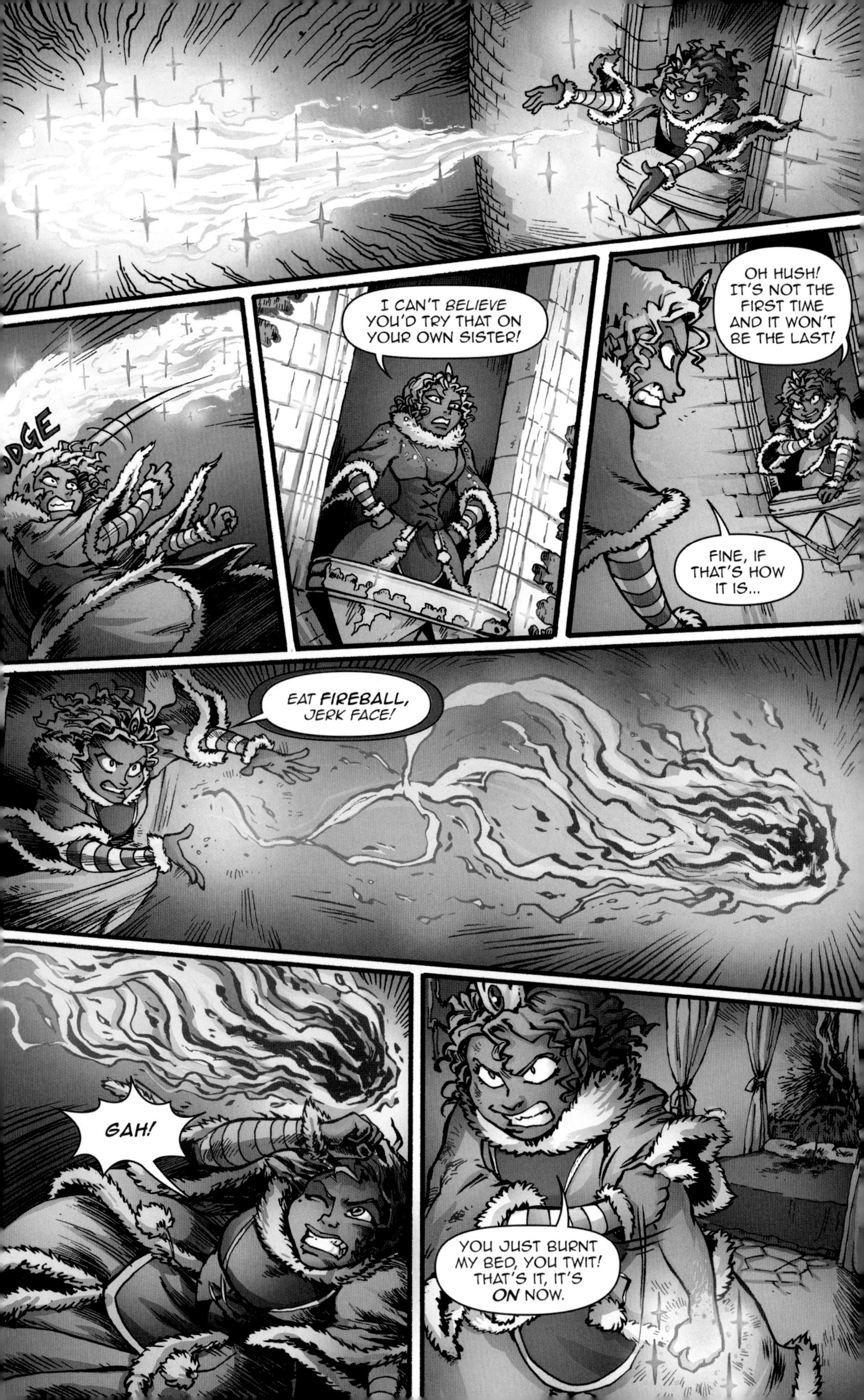
DGE
I CAN'T BELIEVE YOU'D TRY THAT ON YOUR OWN SISTER!
OH HUSH! IT'S NOT THE FIRST TIME AND IT WON'T BE THE LAST!
FINE, IF THAT'S HOW IT IS...
EAT FIREBALL, JERK FACE!
GAH!
YOU JUST BURNT MY BED, YOU TWIT! THAT'S IT, IT'S ON NOW.

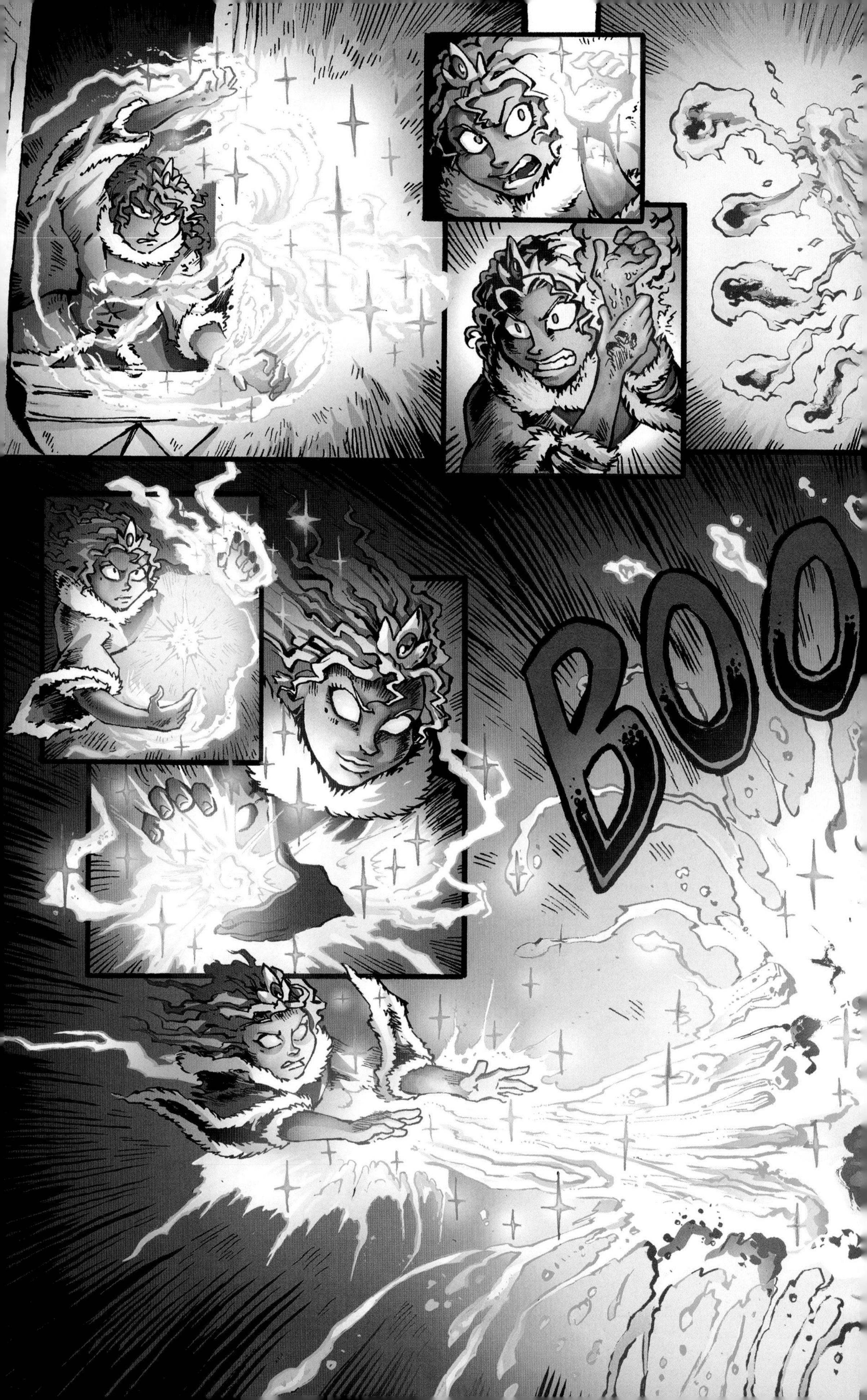
BOO

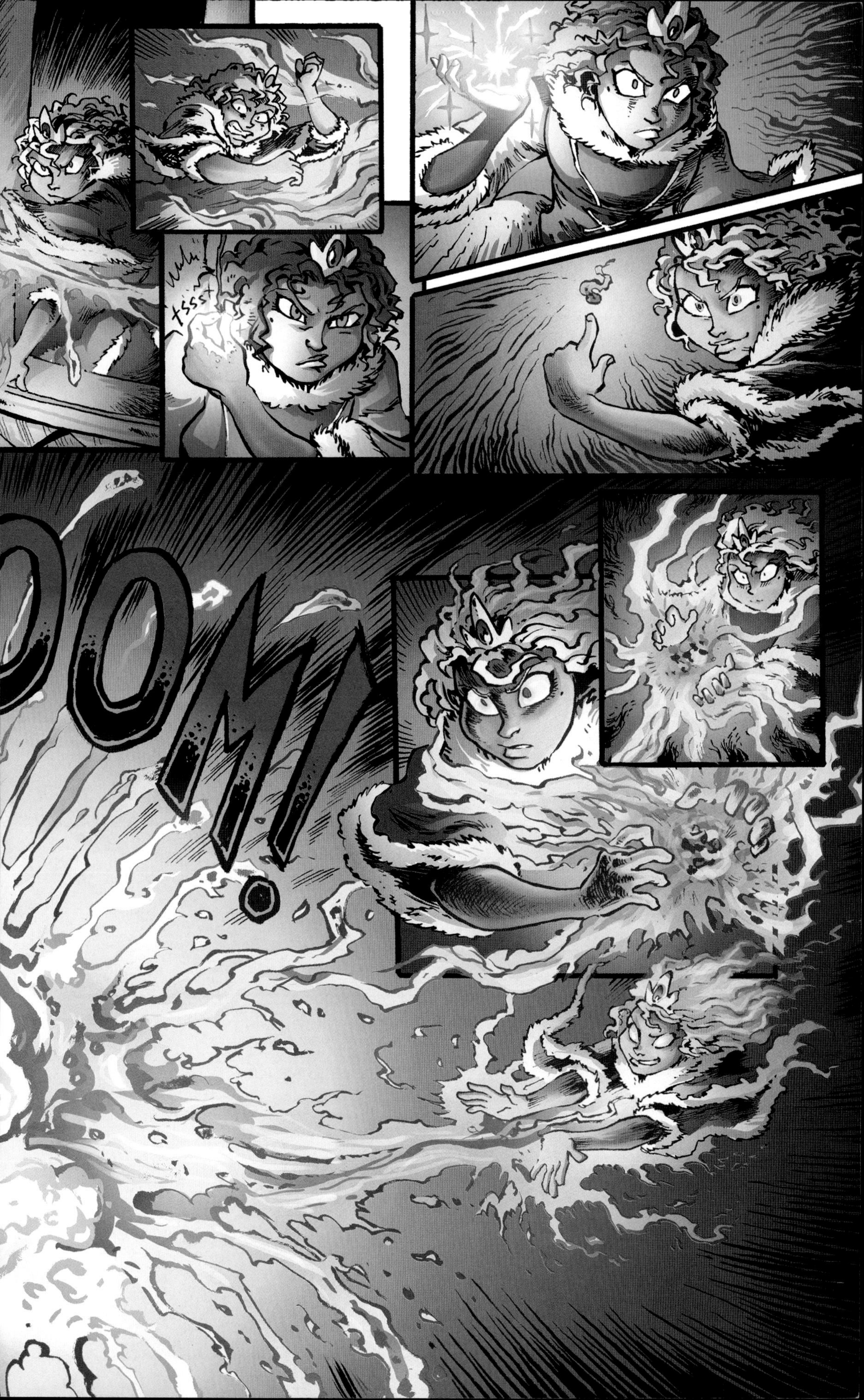
tssst
OOM!

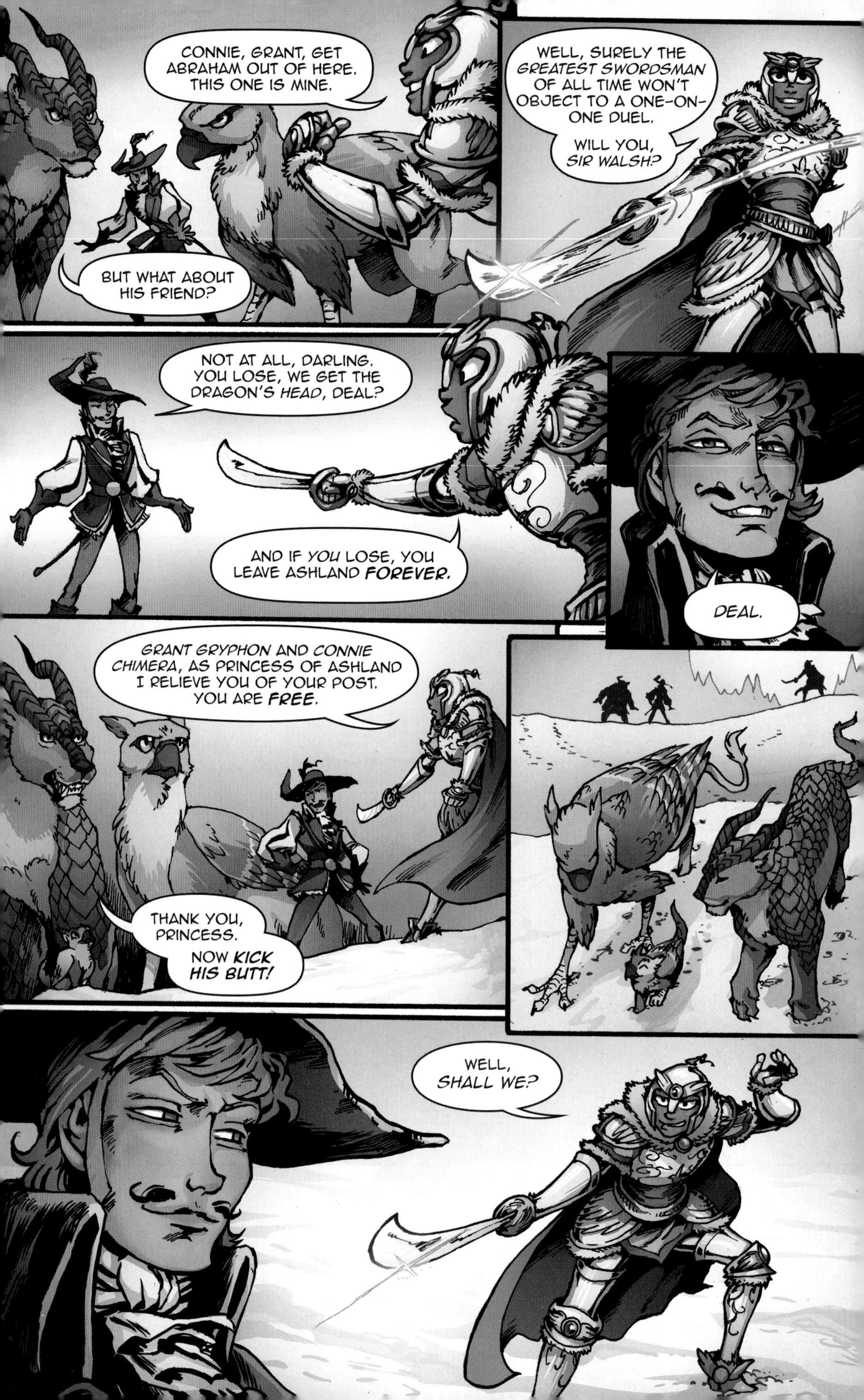
CONNIE, GRANT, GET ABRAHAM OUT OF HERE. THIS ONE IS MINE.
BUT WHAT ABOUT HIS FRIEND?
WELL, SURELY THE GREATEST SWORDSMAN OF ALL TIME WON'T OBJECT TO A ONE-ON-ONE DUEL.
WILL YOU, SIR WALSH?
NOT AT ALL, DARLING. YOU LOSE, WE GET THE DRAGON'S HEAD, DEAL?
AND IF YOU LOSE, YOU LEAVE ASHLAND FOREVER.
DEAL.
GRANT GRYPHON AND CONNIE CHIMERA, AS PRINCESS OF ASHLAND I RELIEVE YOU OF YOUR POST. YOU ARE FREE.
THANK YOU, PRINCESS.
NOW KICK HIS BUTT!
WELL, SHALL WE?

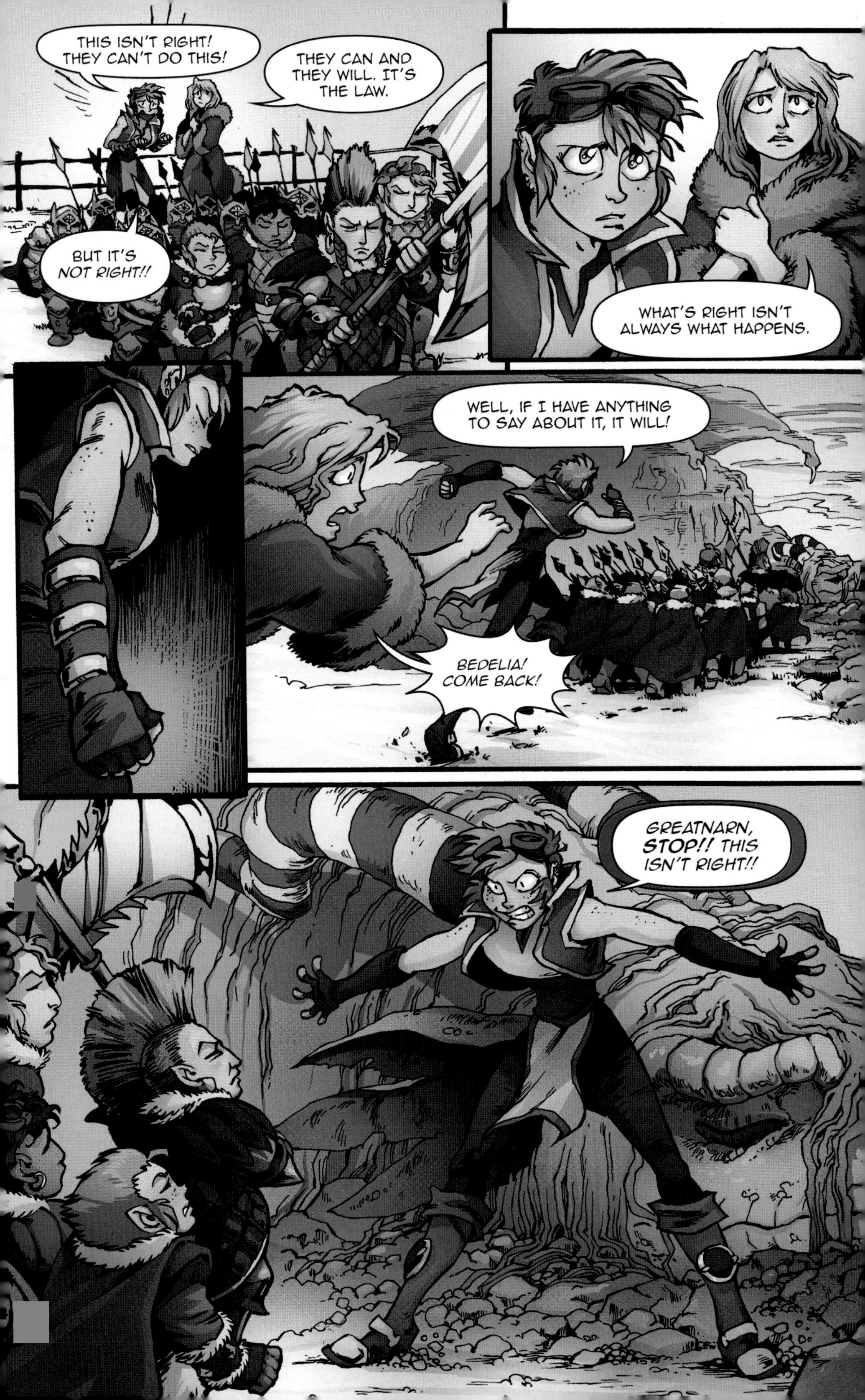
THIS ISN'T RIGHT! THEY CAN'T DO THIS!
THEY CAN AND THEY WILL. IT'S THE LAW.
BUT IT'S NOT RIGHT!!
WHAT'S RIGHT ISN'T ALWAYS WHAT HAPPENS.
WELL, IF I HAVE ANYTHING TO SAY ABOUT IT, IT WILL!
BEDELIA! COME BACK!
GREATNARN, STOP!! THIS ISN'T RIGHT!!

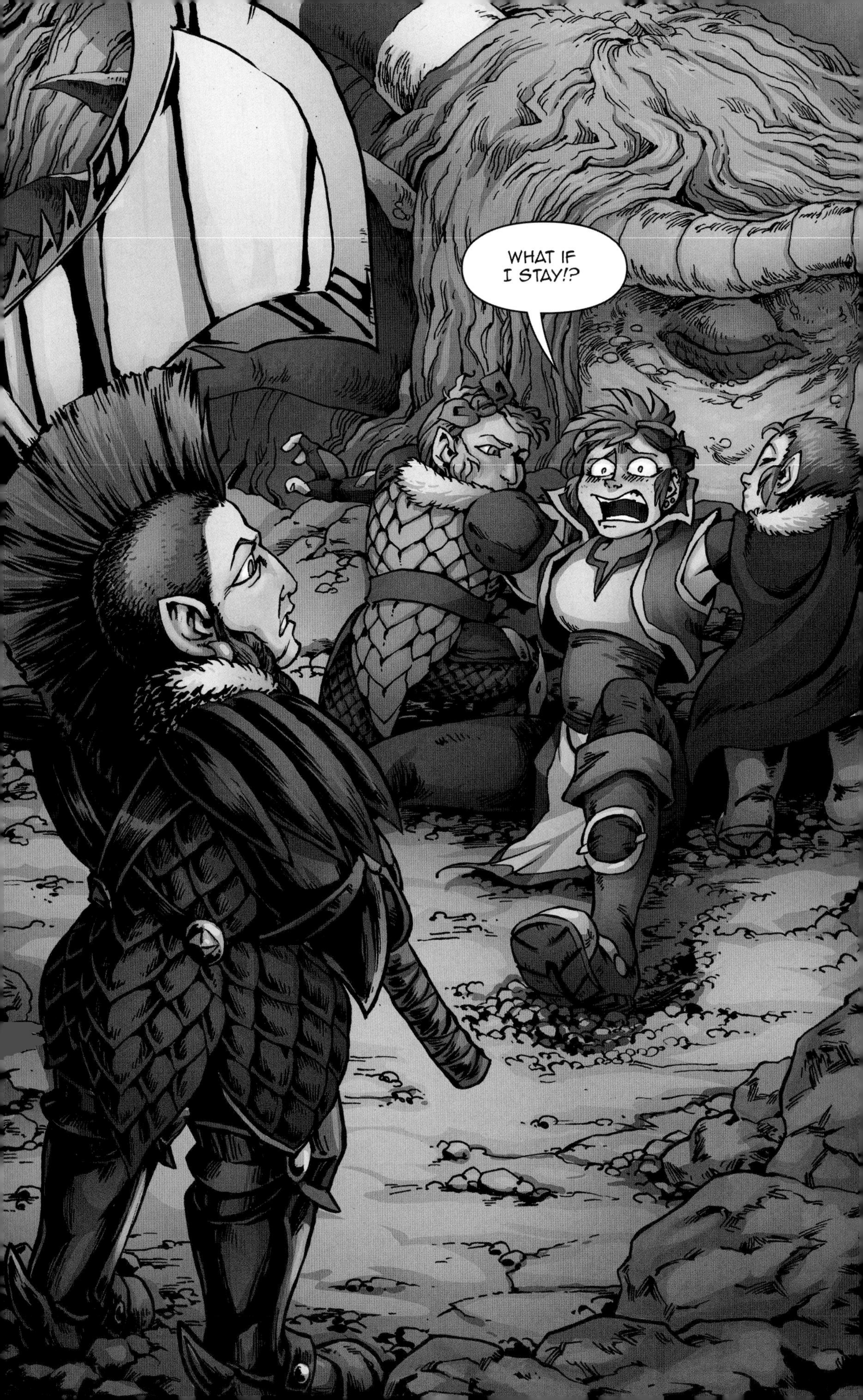
WHAT IF I STAY!?

3: Sisters

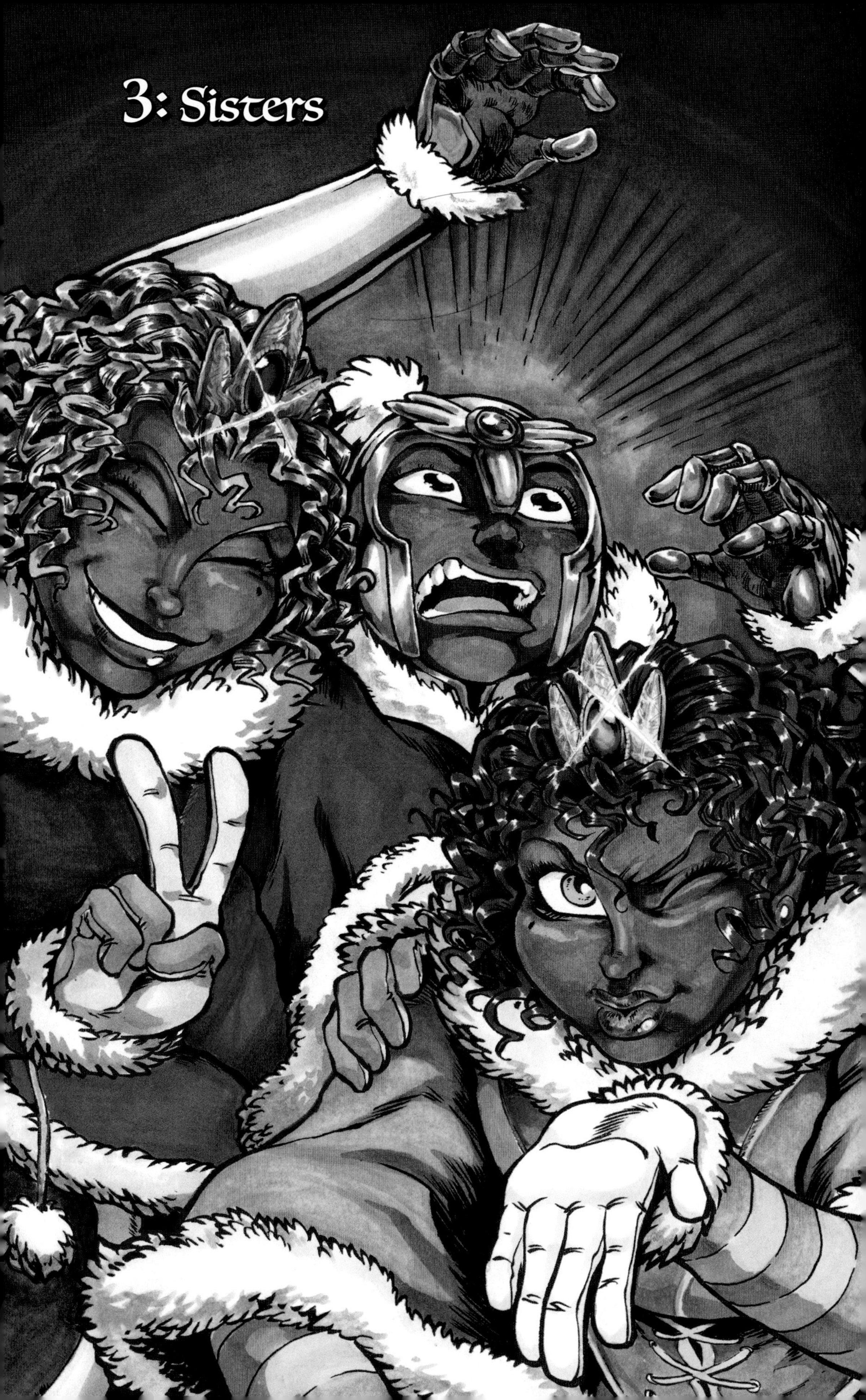

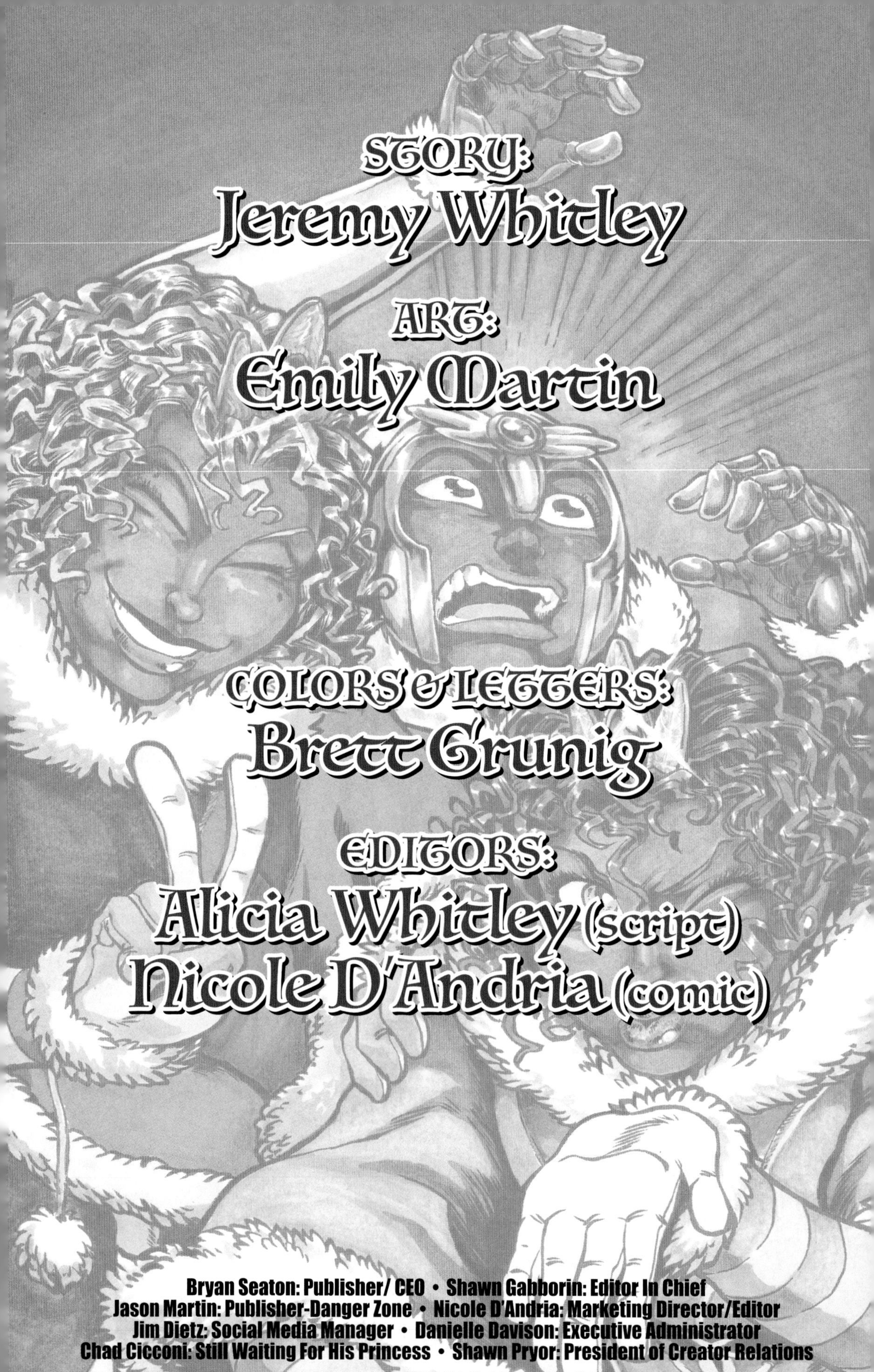

STORY:
Jeremy Whitley

ART:
Emily Martin

COLORS & LETTERS:
Brett Grunig

EDITORS:
Alicia Whitley (script)
Nicole D'Andria (comic)

Bryan Seaton: Publisher/ CEO • Shawn Gabborin: Editor In Chief
Jason Martin: Publisher-Danger Zone • Nicole D'Andria: Marketing Director/Editor
Jim Dietz: Social Media Manager • Danielle Davison: Executive Administrator
Chad Cicconi: Still Waiting For His Princess • Shawn Pryor: President of Creator Relations

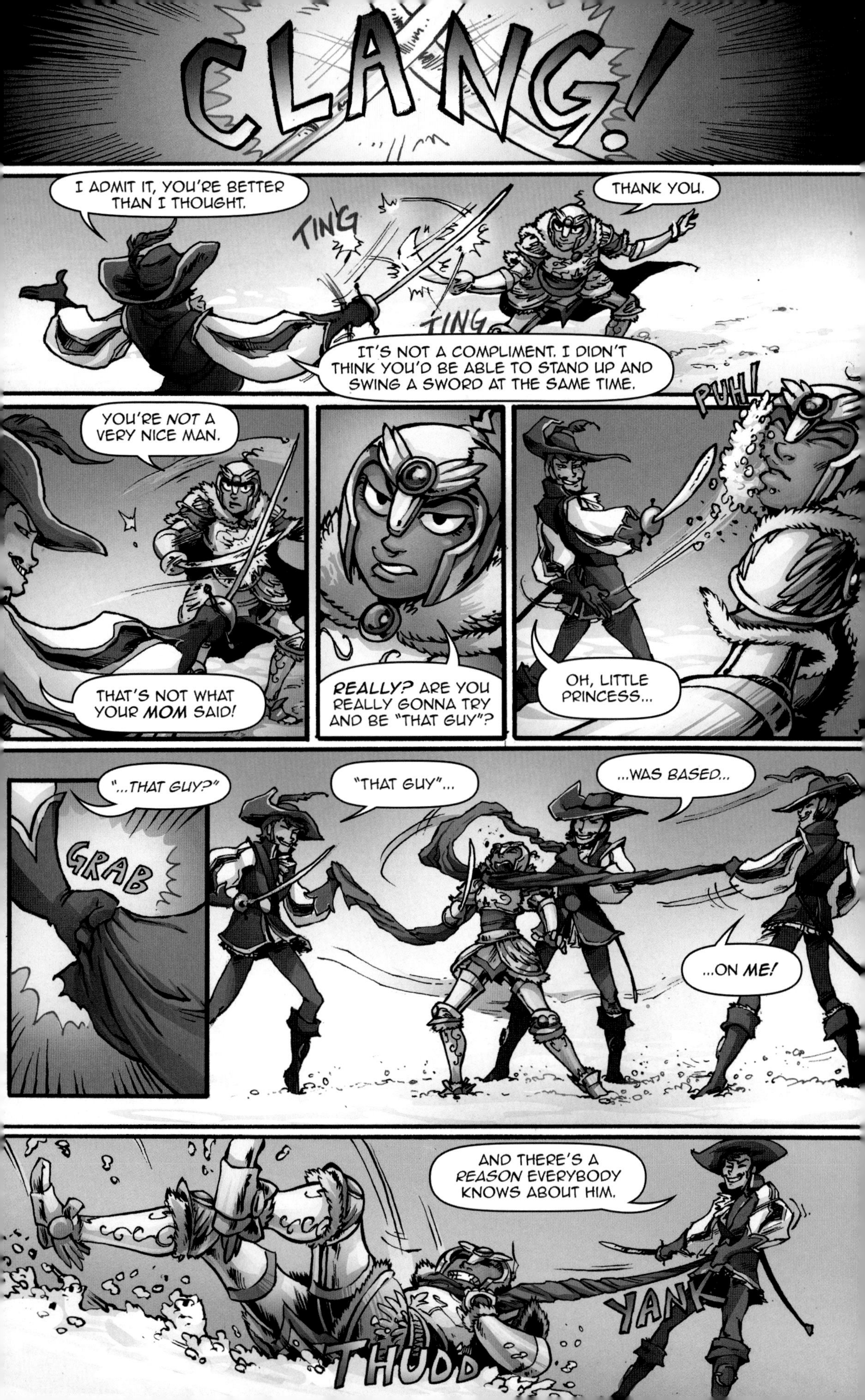
CLANG!
I ADMIT IT, YOU'RE BETTER THAN I THOUGHT.
TING
THANK YOU.
TING
IT'S NOT A COMPLIMENT. I DIDN'T THINK YOU'D BE ABLE TO STAND UP AND SWING A SWORD AT THE SAME TIME.
YOU'RE NOT A VERY NICE MAN.
THAT'S NOT WHAT YOUR MOM SAID!
REALLY? ARE YOU REALLY GONNA TRY AND BE "THAT GUY"?
PUH!
OH, LITTLE PRINCESS...
"...THAT GUY?"
GRAB
"THAT GUY"...
...WAS BASED...
...ON ME!
AND THERE'S A REASON EVERYBODY KNOWS ABOUT HIM.
YANK
THUDD

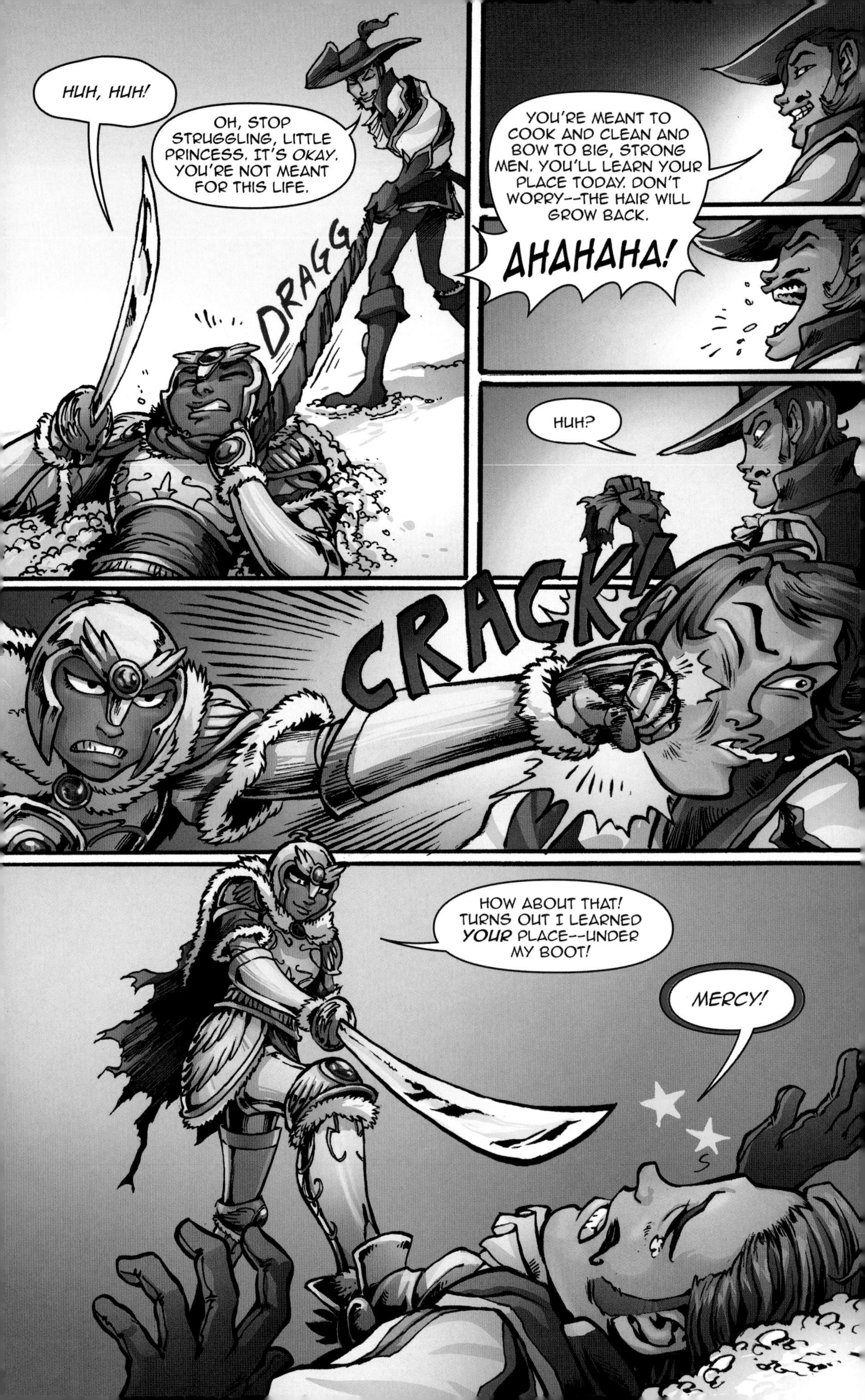
HUH, HUH!
OH, STOP STRUGGLING, LITTLE PRINCESS. IT'S OKAY. YOU'RE NOT MEANT FOR THIS LIFE.
DRAGG
YOU'RE MEANT TO COOK AND CLEAN AND BOW TO BIG, STRONG MEN. YOU'LL LEARN YOUR PLACE TODAY. DON'T WORRY--THE HAIR WILL GROW BACK.
AHAHAHA!
HUH?
CRACK!
HOW ABOUT THAT! TURNS OUT I LEARNED YOUR PLACE--UNDER MY BOOT!
MERCY!

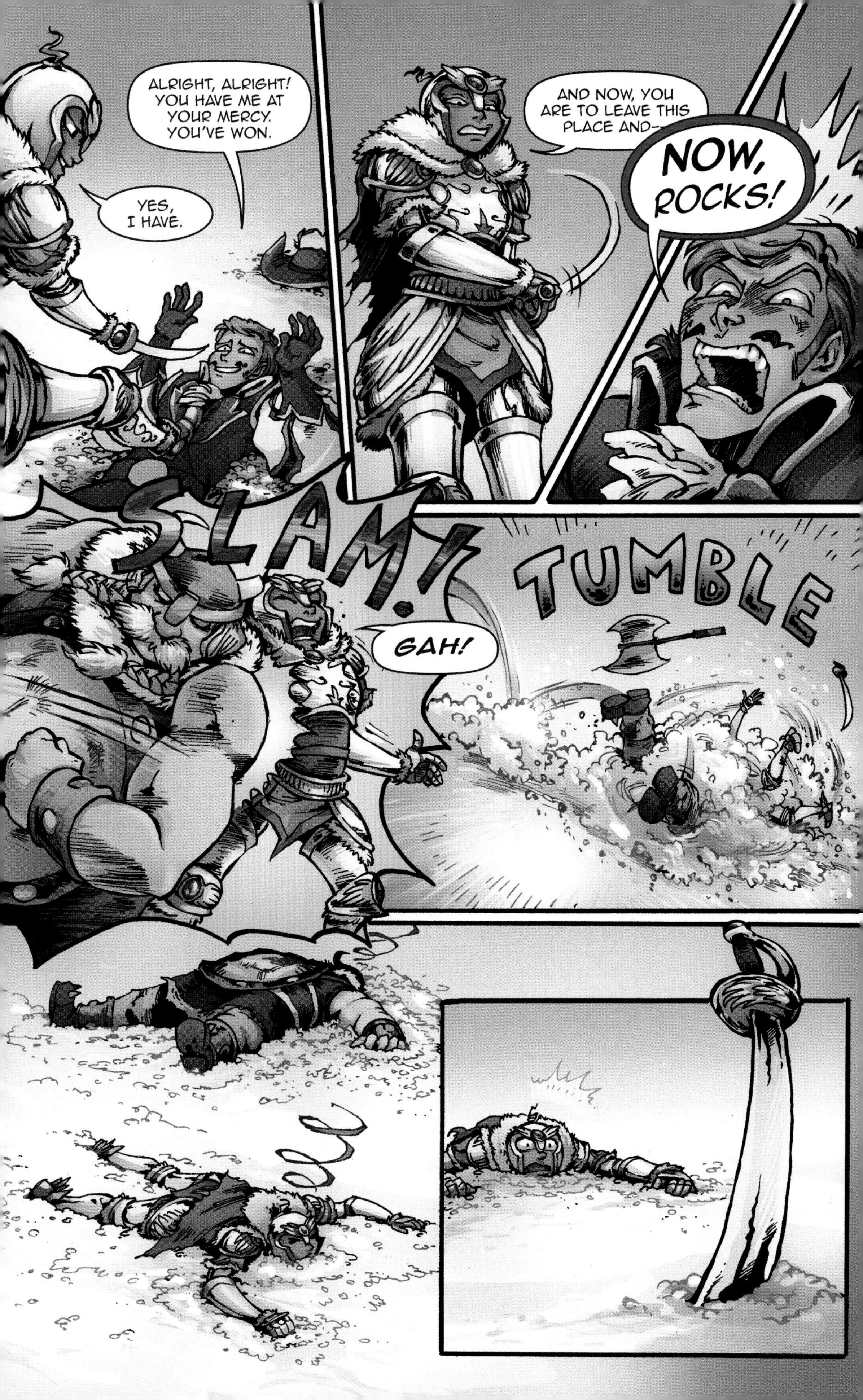
ALRIGHT, ALRIGHT! YOU HAVE ME AT YOUR MERCY. YOU'VE WON.
YES, I HAVE.
AND NOW, YOU ARE TO LEAVE THIS PLACE AND--
NOW, ROCKS!
SLAM!
GAH!
TUMBLE

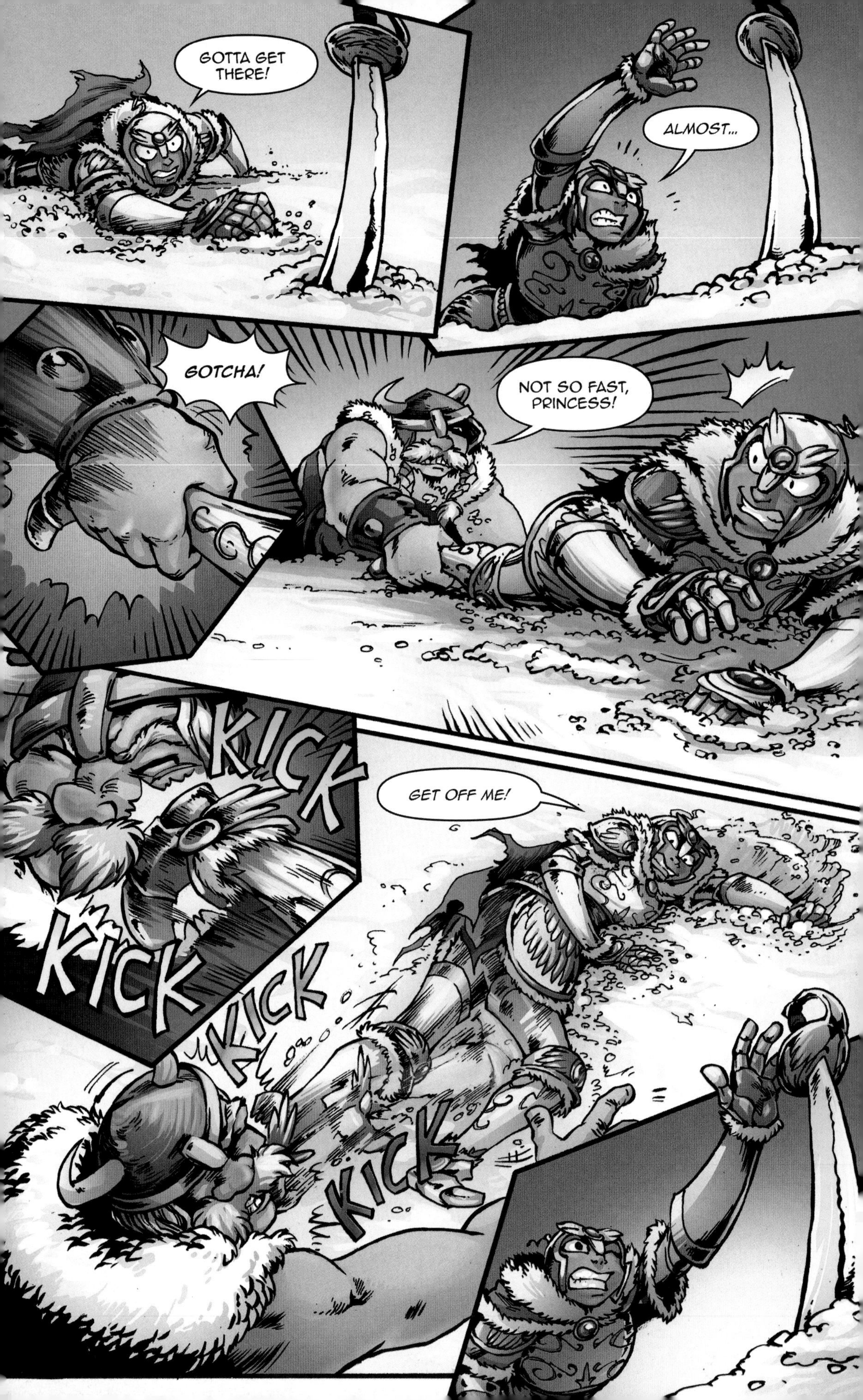
GOTTA GET THERE!
ALMOST...
GOTCHA!
NOT SO FAST, PRINCESS!
GET OFF ME!
KICK
KICK
KICK
KICK

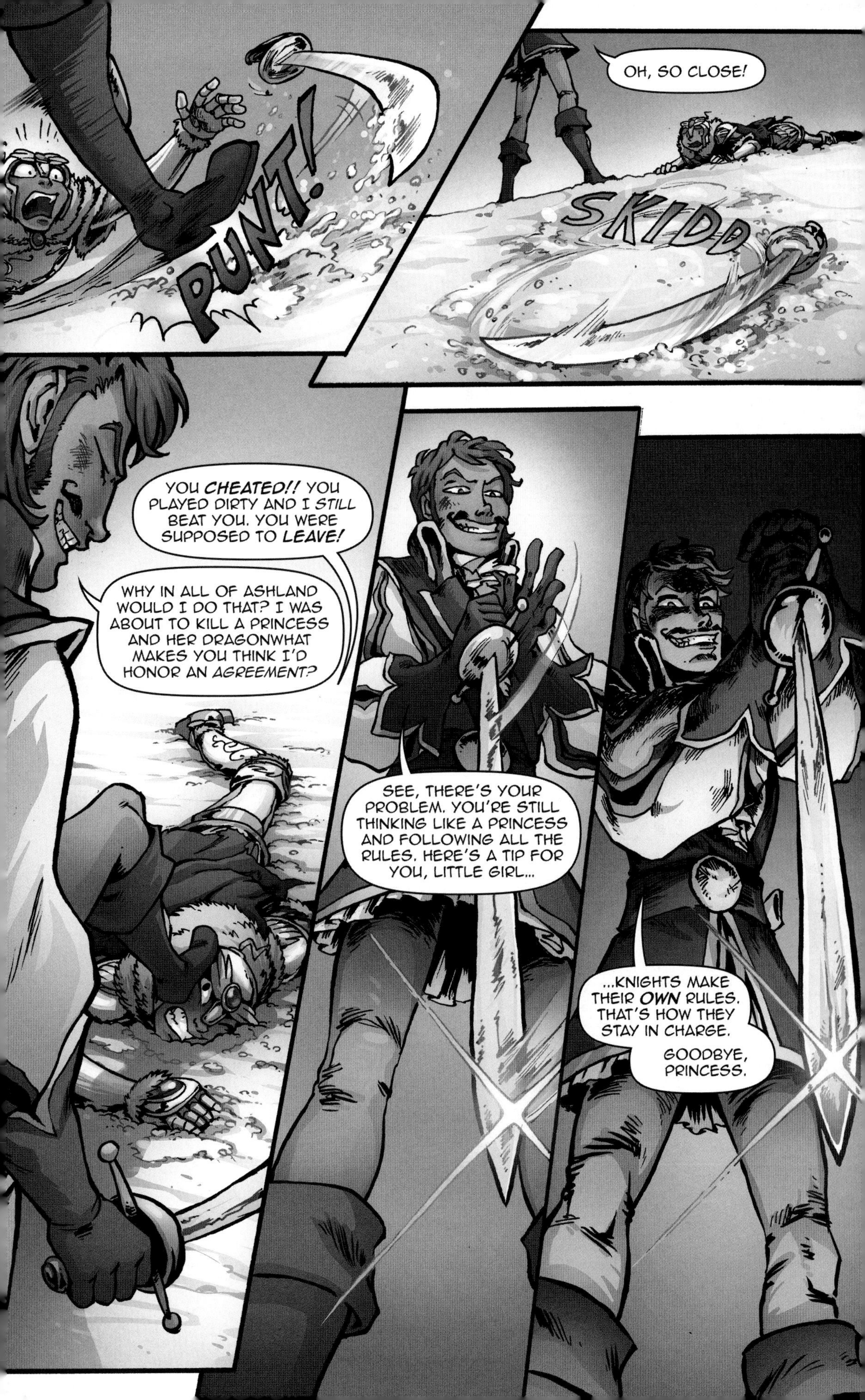
PUNT!
OH, SO CLOSE!
SKIDD
YOU CHEATED!! YOU PLAYED DIRTY AND I STILL BEAT YOU. YOU WERE SUPPOSED TO LEAVE!
WHY IN ALL OF ASHLAND WOULD I DO THAT? I WAS ABOUT TO KILL A PRINCESS AND HER DRAGONWHAT MAKES YOU THINK I'D HONOR AN AGREEMENT?
SEE, THERE'S YOUR PROBLEM. YOU'RE STILL THINKING LIKE A PRINCESS AND FOLLOWING ALL THE RULES. HERE'S A TIP FOR YOU, LITTLE GIRL...
...KNIGHTS MAKE THEIR OWN RULES. THAT'S HOW THEY STAY IN CHARGE.
GOODBYE, PRINCESS.

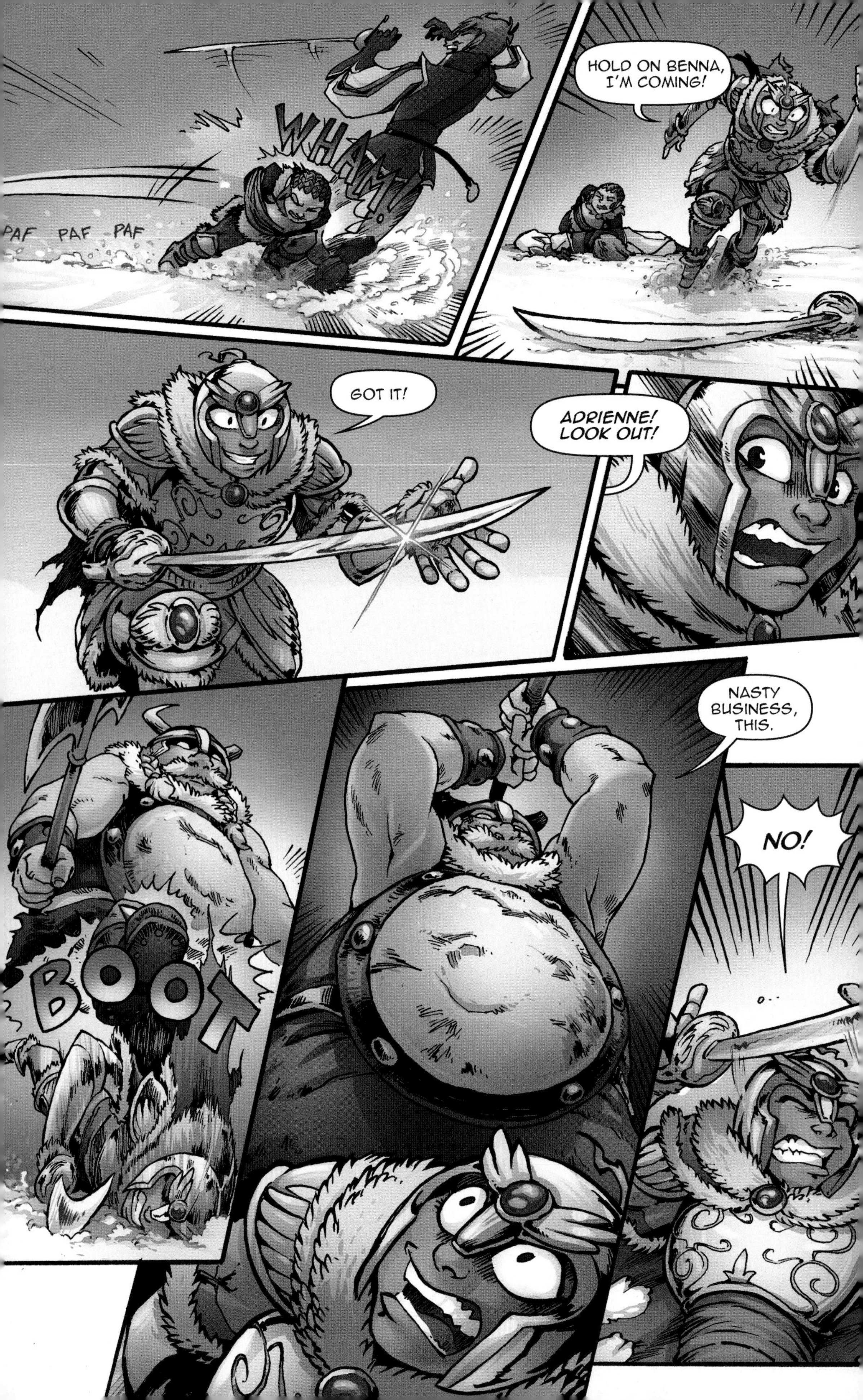
WHAM!
PAF PAF PAF
HOLD ON BENNA, I'M COMING!
GOT IT!
ADRIENNE! LOOK OUT!
BOOT
NASTY BUSINESS, THIS.
NO!
O..

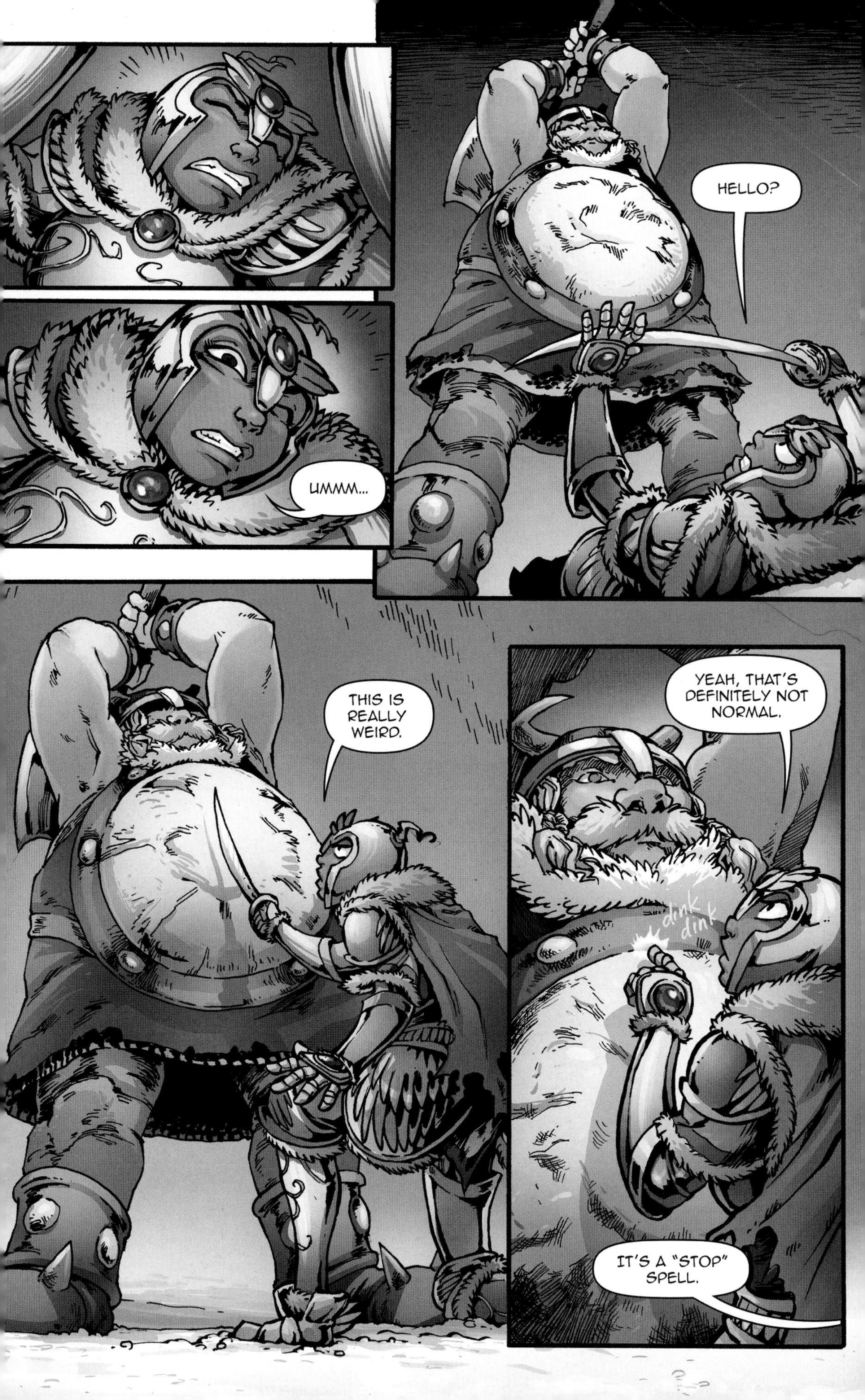
UMMM...
HELLO?
THIS IS REALLY WEIRD.
YEAH, THAT'S DEFINITELY NOT NORMAL.
dink dink
IT'S A "STOP" SPELL.

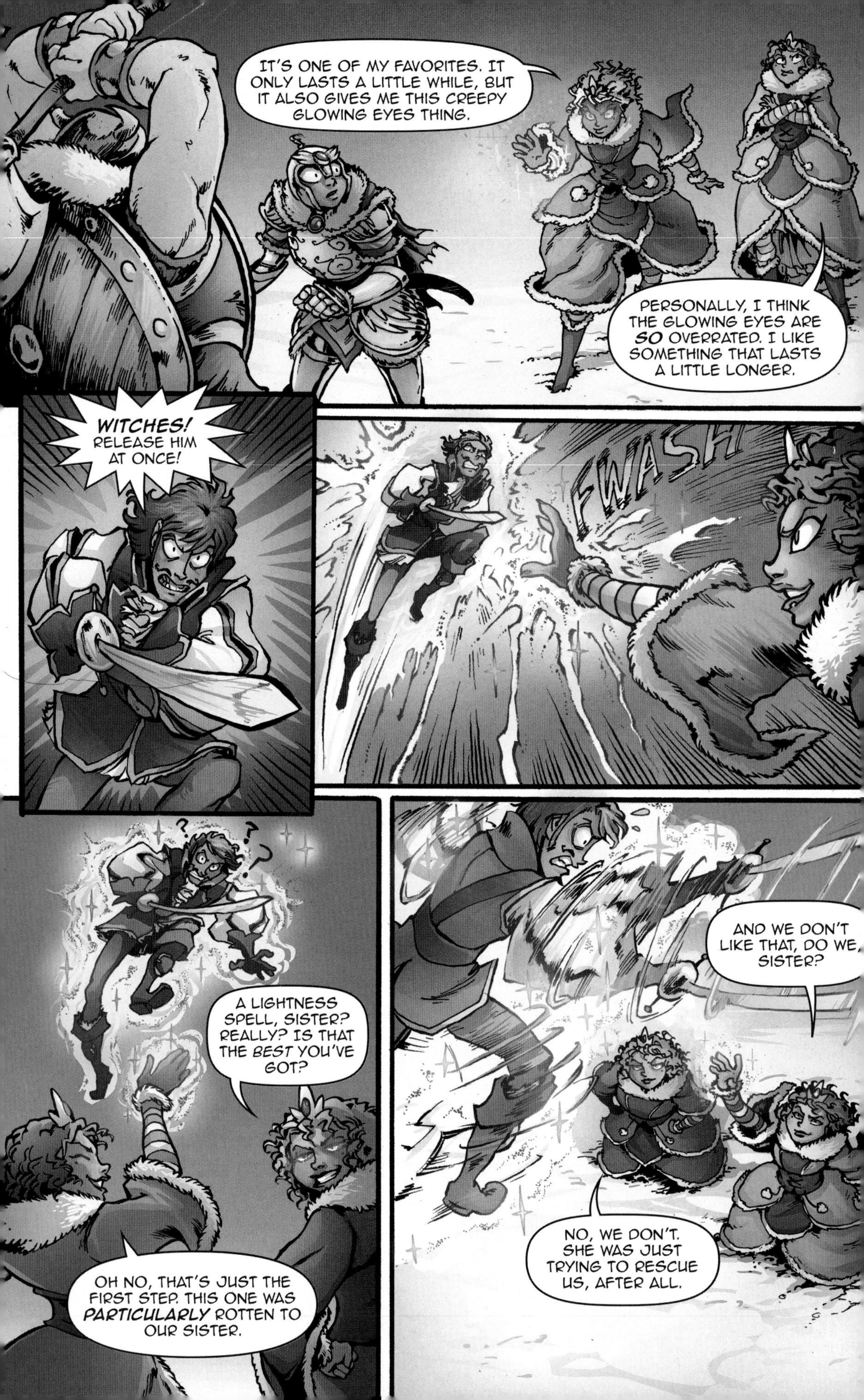
IT'S ONE OF MY FAVORITES. IT ONLY LASTS A LITTLE WHILE, BUT IT ALSO GIVES ME THIS CREEPY GLOWING EYES THING.
PERSONALLY, I THINK THE GLOWING EYES ARE *SO* OVERRATED. I LIKE SOMETHING THAT LASTS A LITTLE LONGER.
WITCHES! RELEASE HIM AT ONCE!
FWASH
A LIGHTNESS SPELL, SISTER? REALLY? IS THAT THE *BEST* YOU'VE GOT?
OH NO, THAT'S JUST THE FIRST STEP. THIS ONE WAS ***PARTICULARLY*** ROTTEN TO OUR SISTER.
AND WE DON'T LIKE THAT, DO WE, SISTER?
NO, WE DON'T. SHE WAS JUST TRYING TO RESCUE US, AFTER ALL.

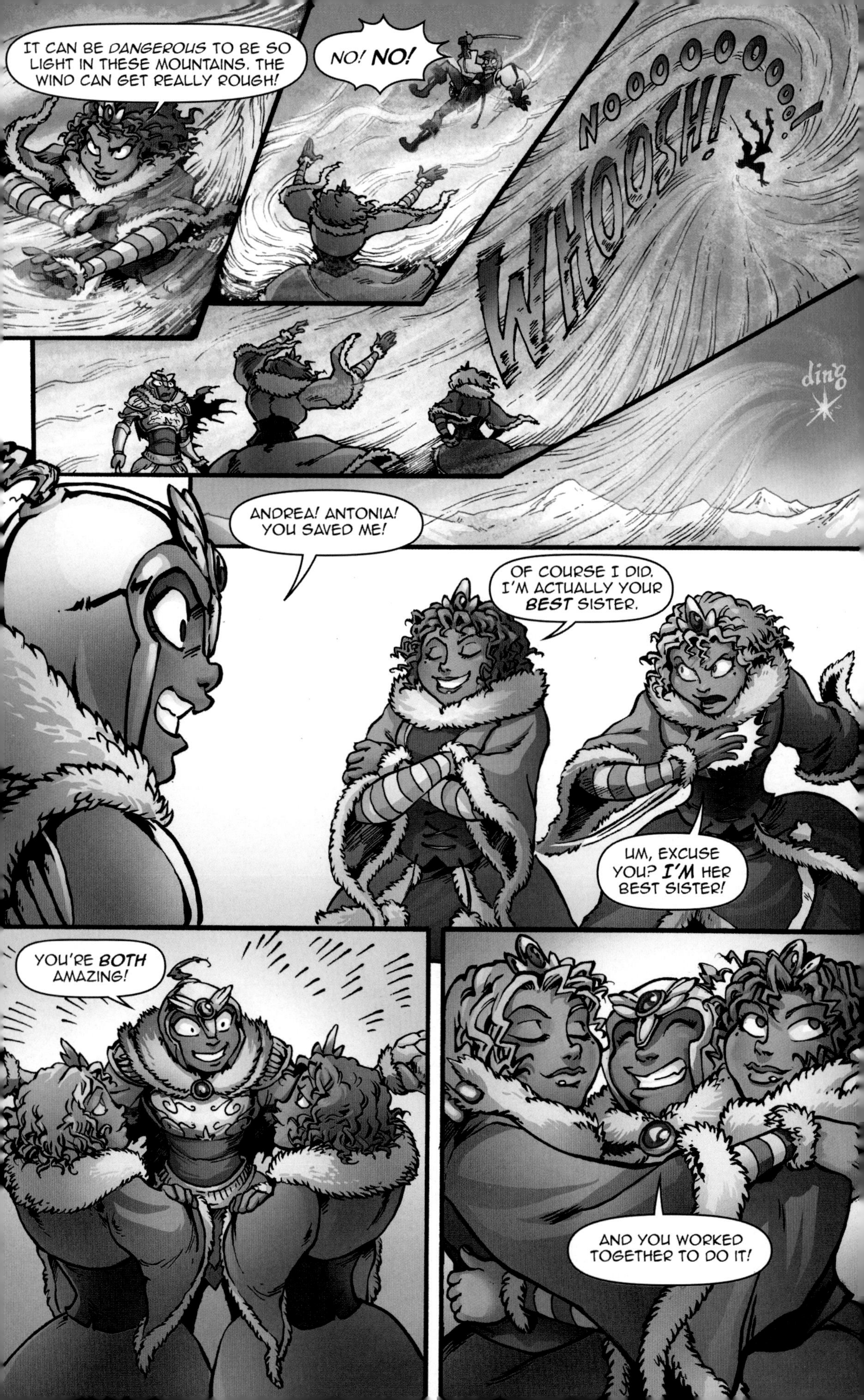
IT CAN BE DANGEROUS TO BE SO LIGHT IN THESE MOUNTAINS. THE WIND CAN GET REALLY ROUGH!
NO! NO!
NOOOOOOOOOOOO!
WHOOSH!
ding
ANDREA! ANTONIA! YOU SAVED ME!
OF COURSE I DID. I'M ACTUALLY YOUR BEST SISTER.
UM, EXCUSE YOU? I'M HER BEST SISTER!
YOU'RE BOTH AMAZING!
AND YOU WORKED TOGETHER TO DO IT!

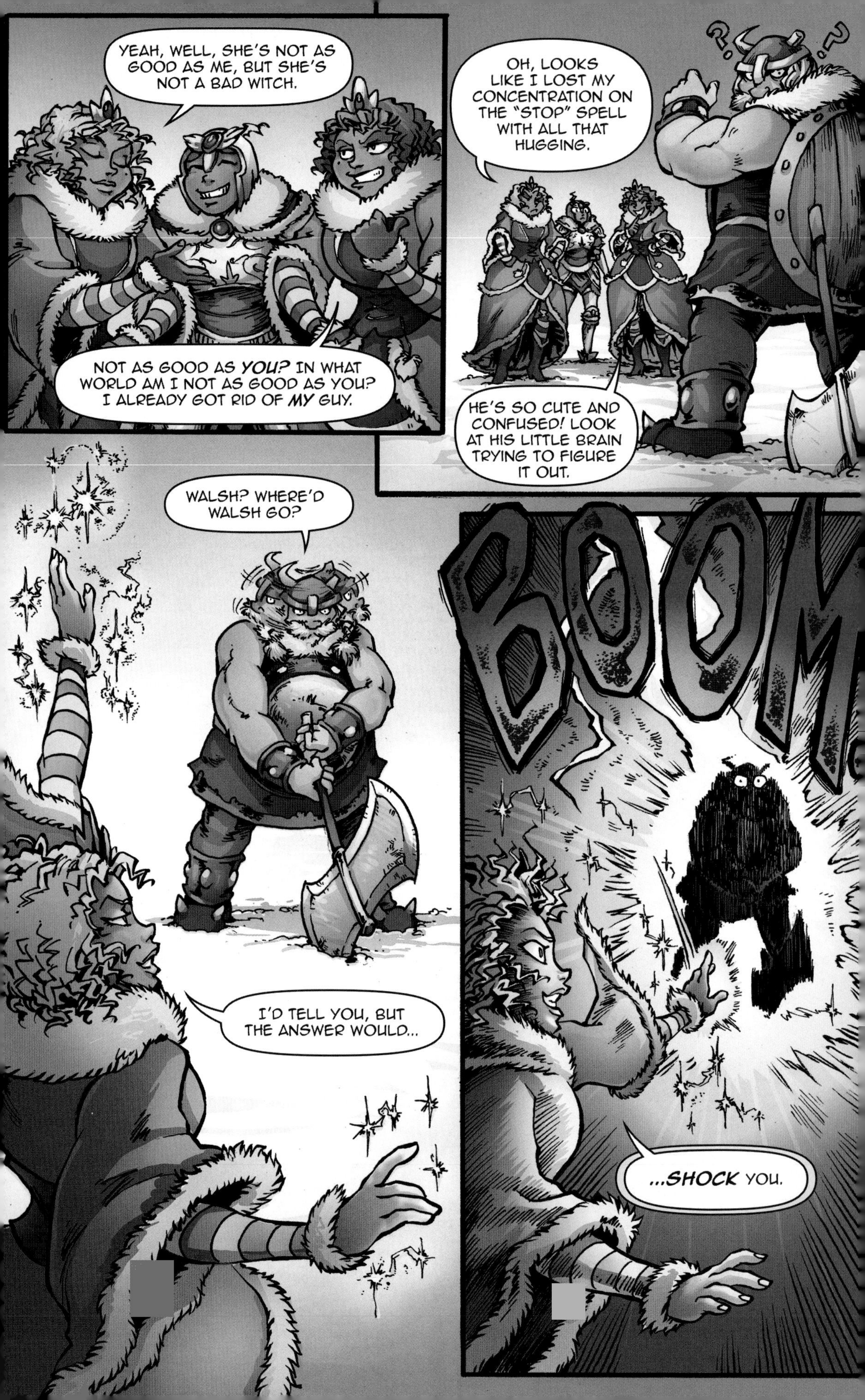
YEAH, WELL, SHE'S NOT AS GOOD AS ME, BUT SHE'S NOT A BAD WITCH.
NOT AS GOOD AS *YOU?* IN WHAT WORLD AM I NOT AS GOOD AS YOU? I ALREADY GOT RID OF *MY* GUY.
OH, LOOKS LIKE I LOST MY CONCENTRATION ON THE "STOP" SPELL WITH ALL THAT HUGGING.
HE'S SO CUTE AND CONFUSED! LOOK AT HIS LITTLE BRAIN TRYING TO FIGURE IT OUT.
WALSH? WHERE'D WALSH GO?
I'D TELL YOU, BUT THE ANSWER WOULD...
BOOM!
...*SHOCK* YOU.

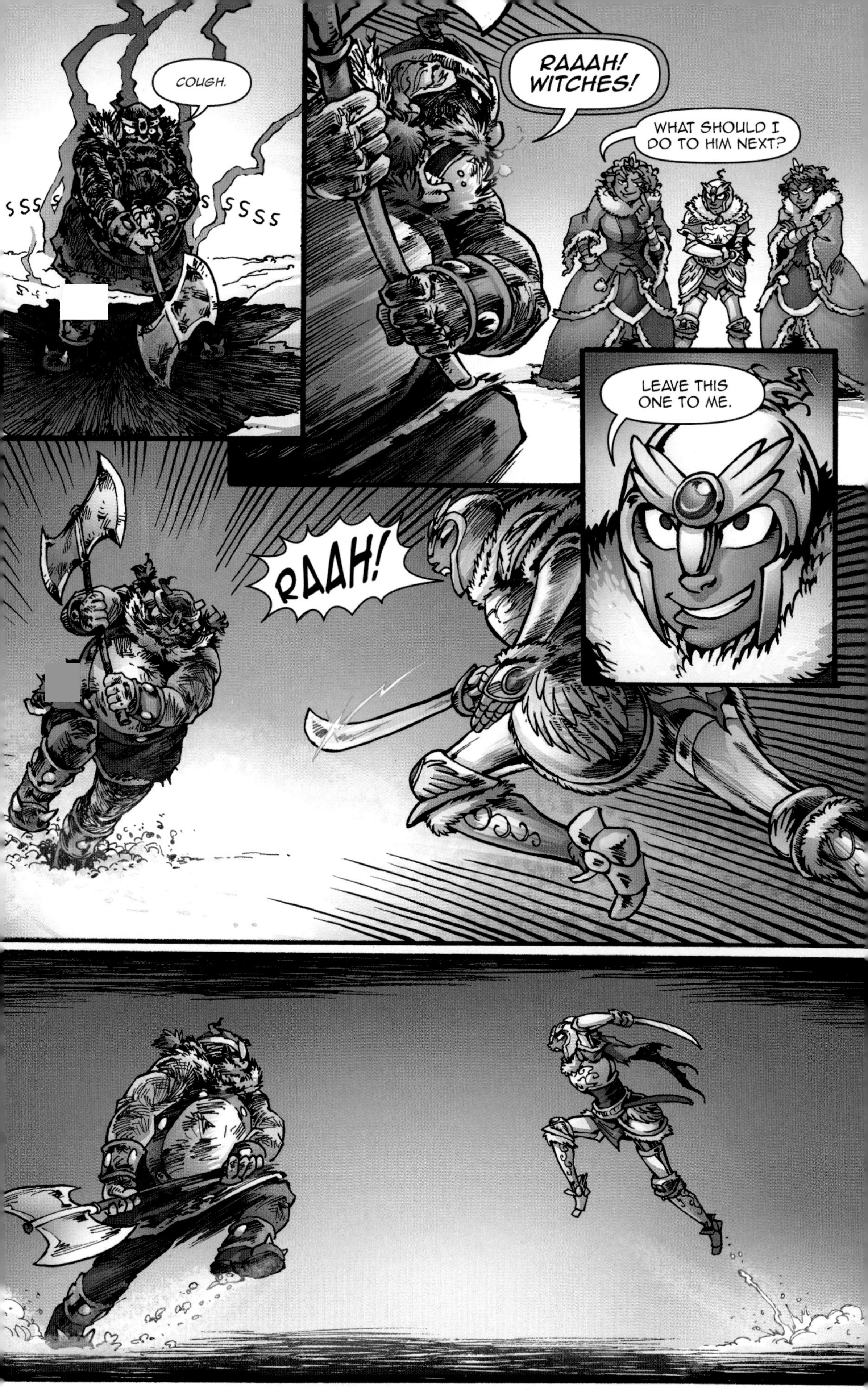
COUGH.
SSSS
SSSSS
RAAAH! WITCHES!
WHAT SHOULD I DO TO HIM NEXT?
LEAVE THIS ONE TO ME.
RAAH!

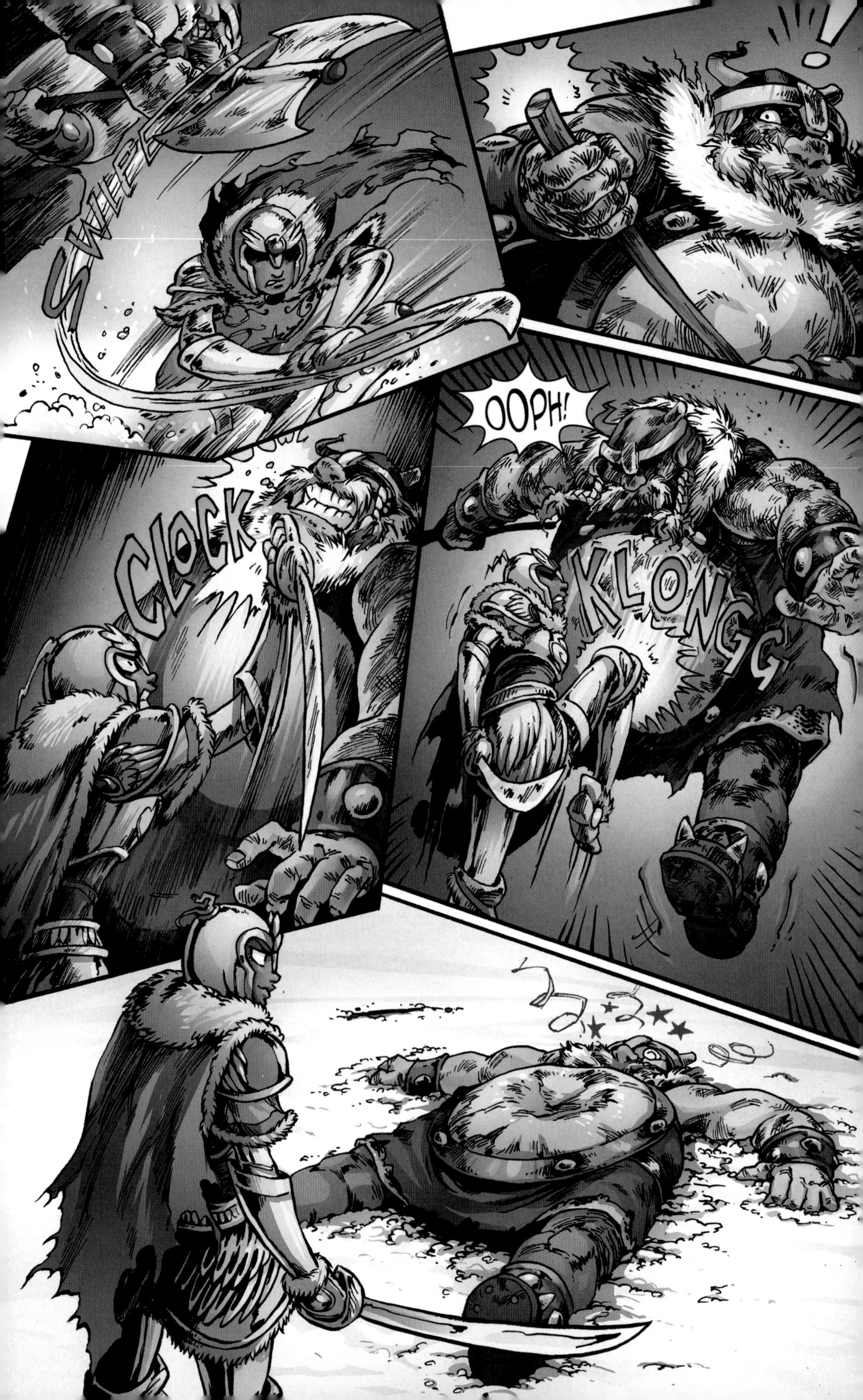
SWIPE
!
OOPH!
CLOCK
KLONGG

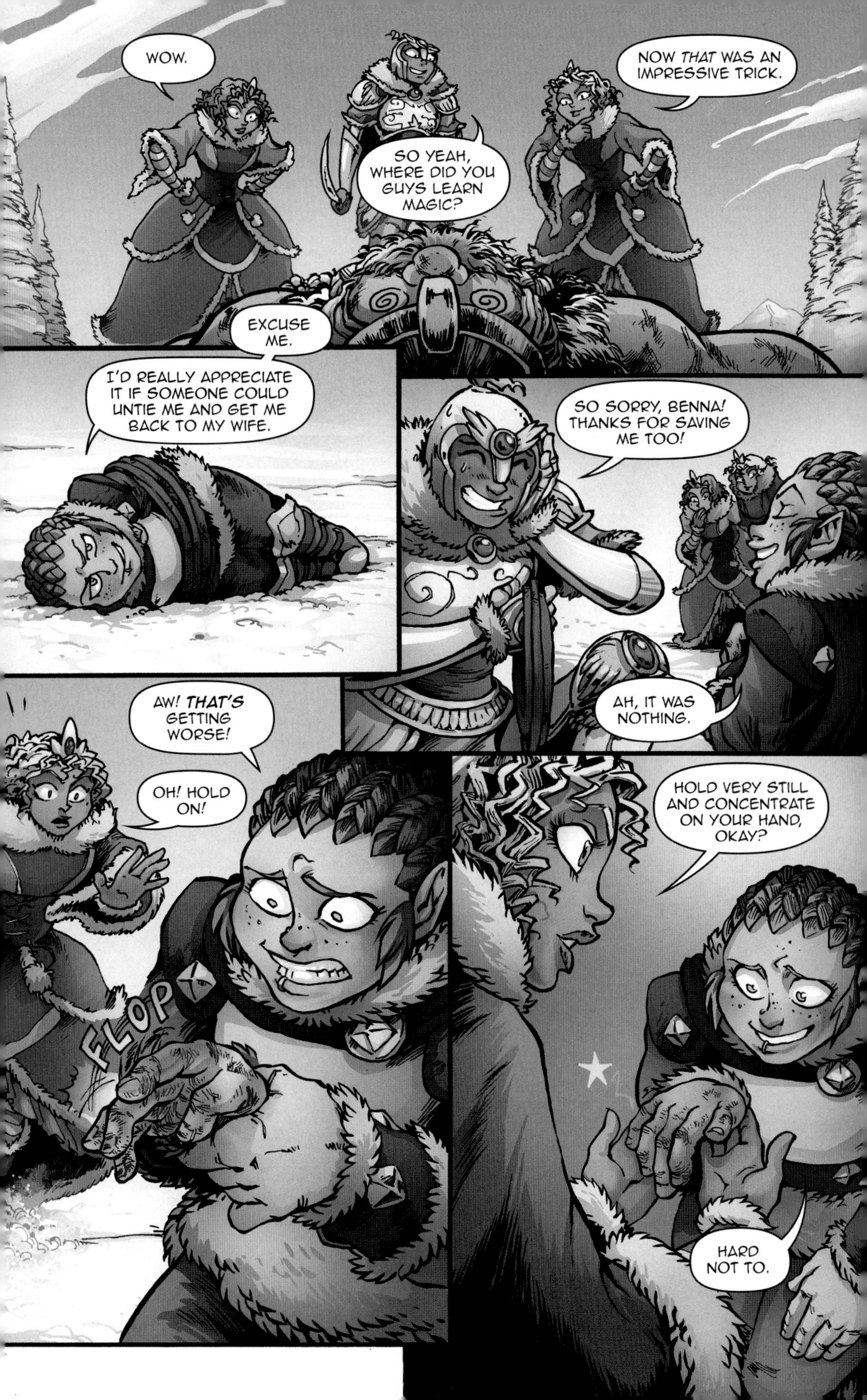
WOW.
NOW THAT WAS AN IMPRESSIVE TRICK.
SO YEAH, WHERE DID YOU GUYS LEARN MAGIC?
EXCUSE ME.
I'D REALLY APPRECIATE IT IF SOMEONE COULD UNTIE ME AND GET ME BACK TO MY WIFE.
SO SORRY, BENNA! THANKS FOR SAVING ME TOO!
AH, IT WAS NOTHING.
AW! THAT'S GETTING WORSE!
OH! HOLD ON!
FLOP
HOLD VERY STILL AND CONCENTRATE ON YOUR HAND, OKAY?
HARD NOT TO.

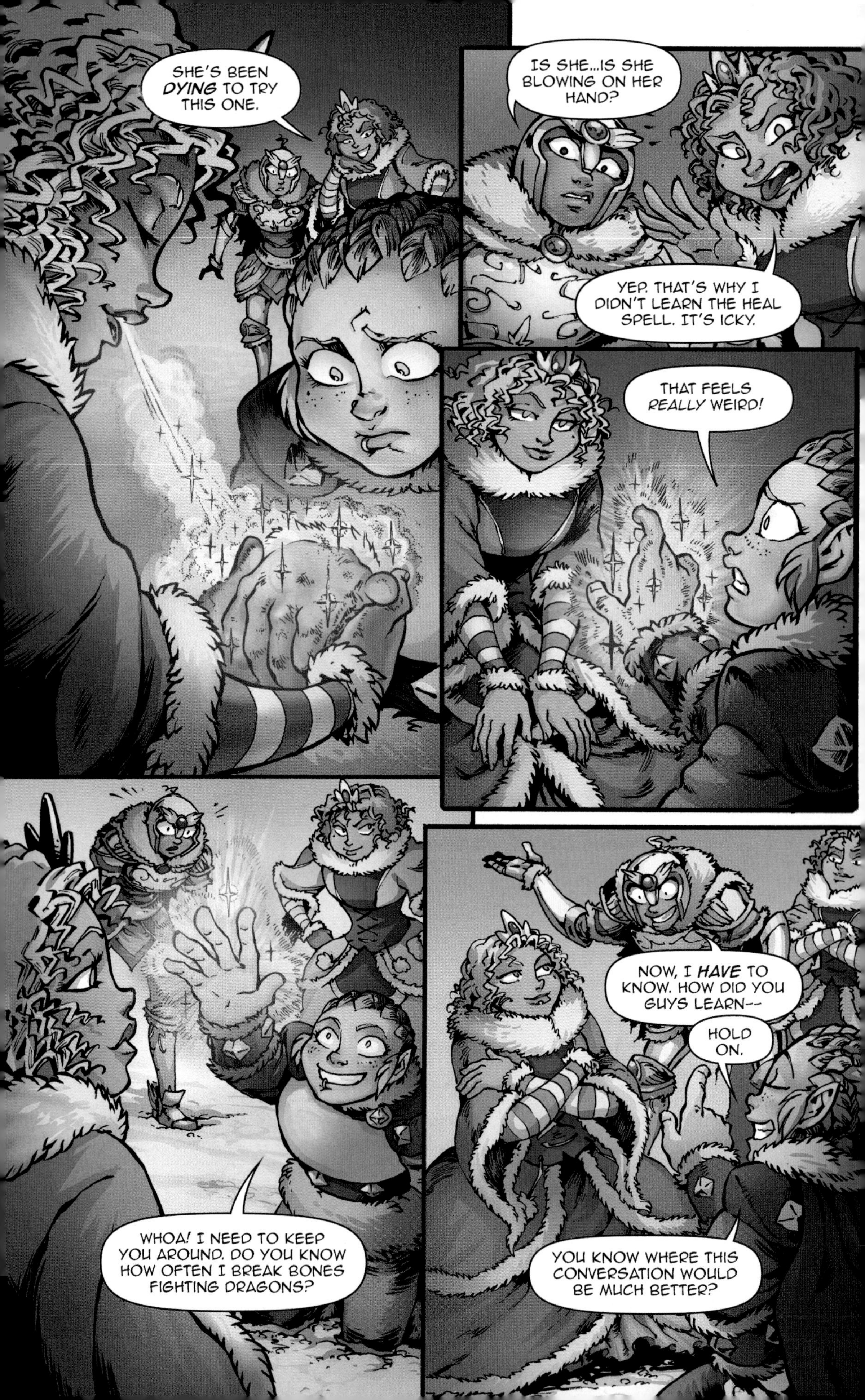

SHE'S BEEN *DYING* TO TRY THIS ONE.
IS SHE...IS SHE BLOWING ON HER HAND?
YEP. THAT'S WHY I DIDN'T LEARN THE HEAL SPELL. IT'S ICKY.
THAT FEELS *REALLY* WEIRD!
WHOA! I NEED TO KEEP YOU AROUND. DO YOU KNOW HOW OFTEN I BREAK BONES FIGHTING DRAGONS?
NOW, I ***HAVE*** TO KNOW. HOW DID YOU GUYS LEARN--
HOLD ON.
YOU KNOW WHERE THIS CONVERSATION WOULD BE MUCH BETTER?

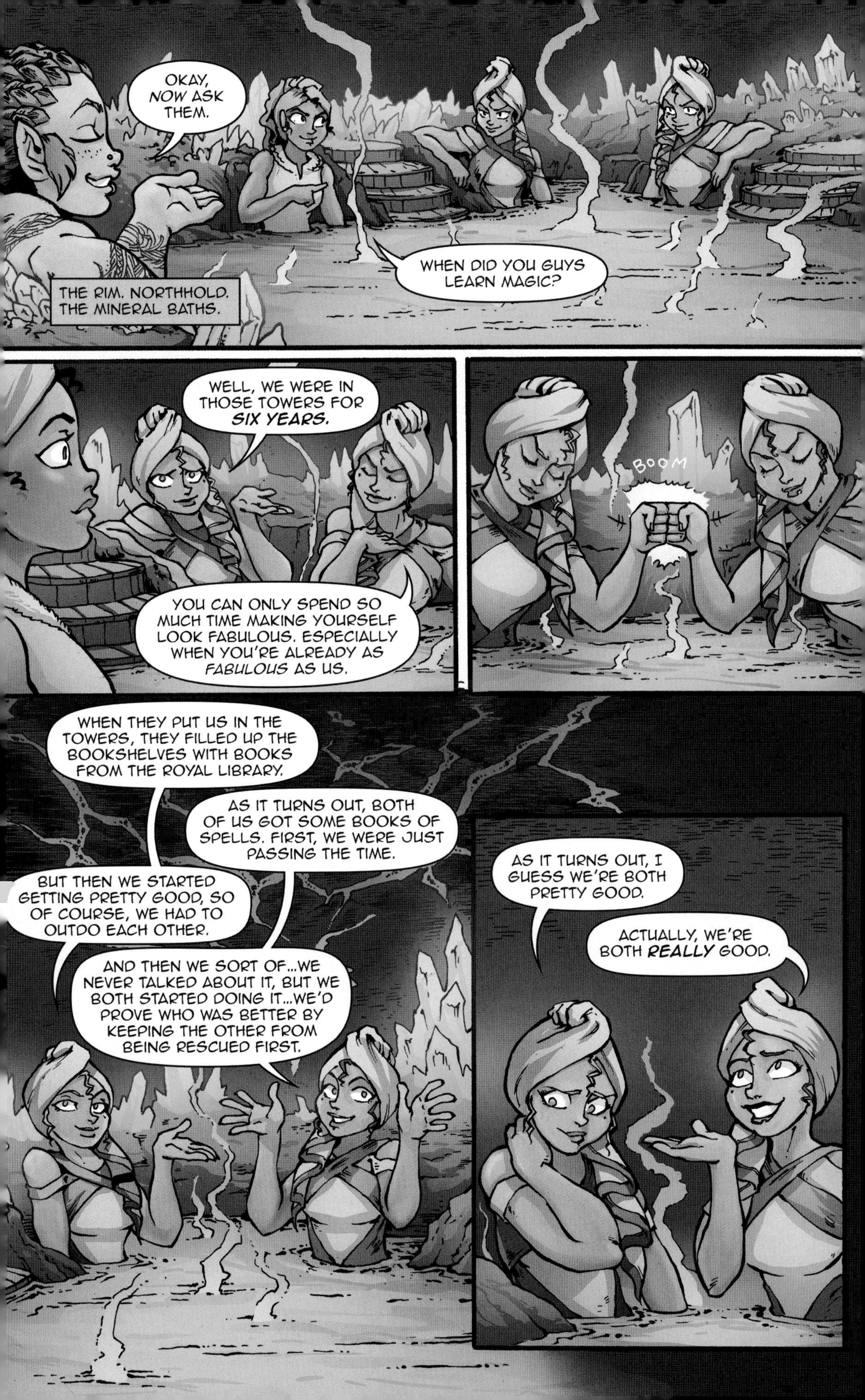
OKAY, NOW ASK THEM.
THE RIM. NORTHHOLD. THE MINERAL BATHS.
WHEN DID YOU GUYS LEARN MAGIC?
WELL, WE WERE IN THOSE TOWERS FOR SIX YEARS.
YOU CAN ONLY SPEND SO MUCH TIME MAKING YOURSELF LOOK FABULOUS. ESPECIALLY WHEN YOU'RE ALREADY AS FABULOUS AS US.
BOOM
WHEN THEY PUT US IN THE TOWERS, THEY FILLED UP THE BOOKSHELVES WITH BOOKS FROM THE ROYAL LIBRARY.
AS IT TURNS OUT, BOTH OF US GOT SOME BOOKS OF SPELLS. FIRST, WE WERE JUST PASSING THE TIME.
BUT THEN WE STARTED GETTING PRETTY GOOD, SO OF COURSE, WE HAD TO OUTDO EACH OTHER.
AND THEN WE SORT OF...WE NEVER TALKED ABOUT IT, BUT WE BOTH STARTED DOING IT...WE'D PROVE WHO WAS BETTER BY KEEPING THE OTHER FROM BEING RESCUED FIRST.
AS IT TURNS OUT, I GUESS WE'RE BOTH PRETTY GOOD.
ACTUALLY, WE'RE BOTH REALLY GOOD.

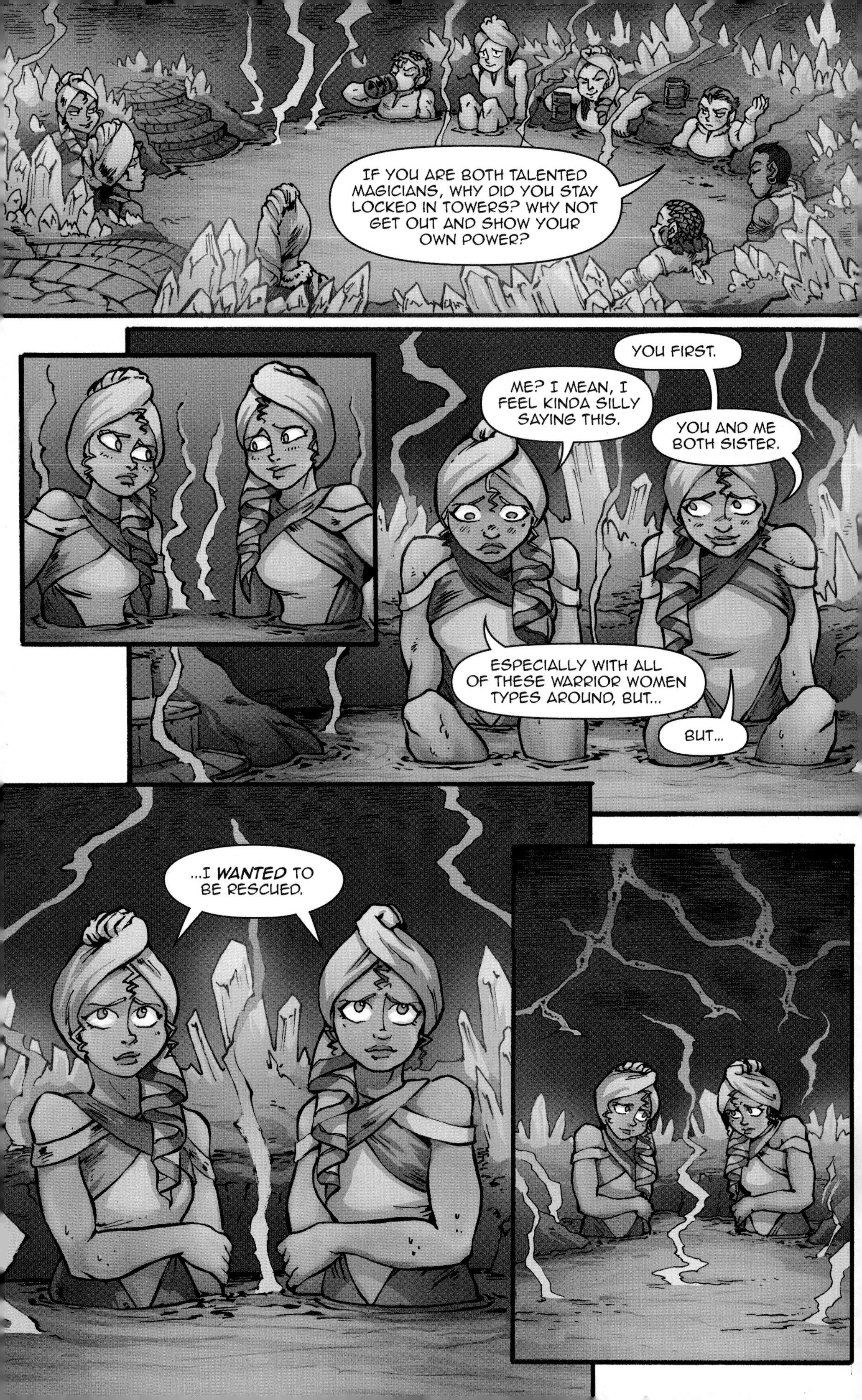
IF YOU ARE BOTH TALENTED MAGICIANS, WHY DID YOU STAY LOCKED IN TOWERS? WHY NOT GET OUT AND SHOW YOUR OWN POWER?
YOU FIRST.
ME? I MEAN, I FEEL KINDA SILLY SAYING THIS.
YOU AND ME BOTH SISTER.
ESPECIALLY WITH ALL OF THESE WARRIOR WOMEN TYPES AROUND, BUT...
BUT...
...I *WANTED* TO BE RESCUED.

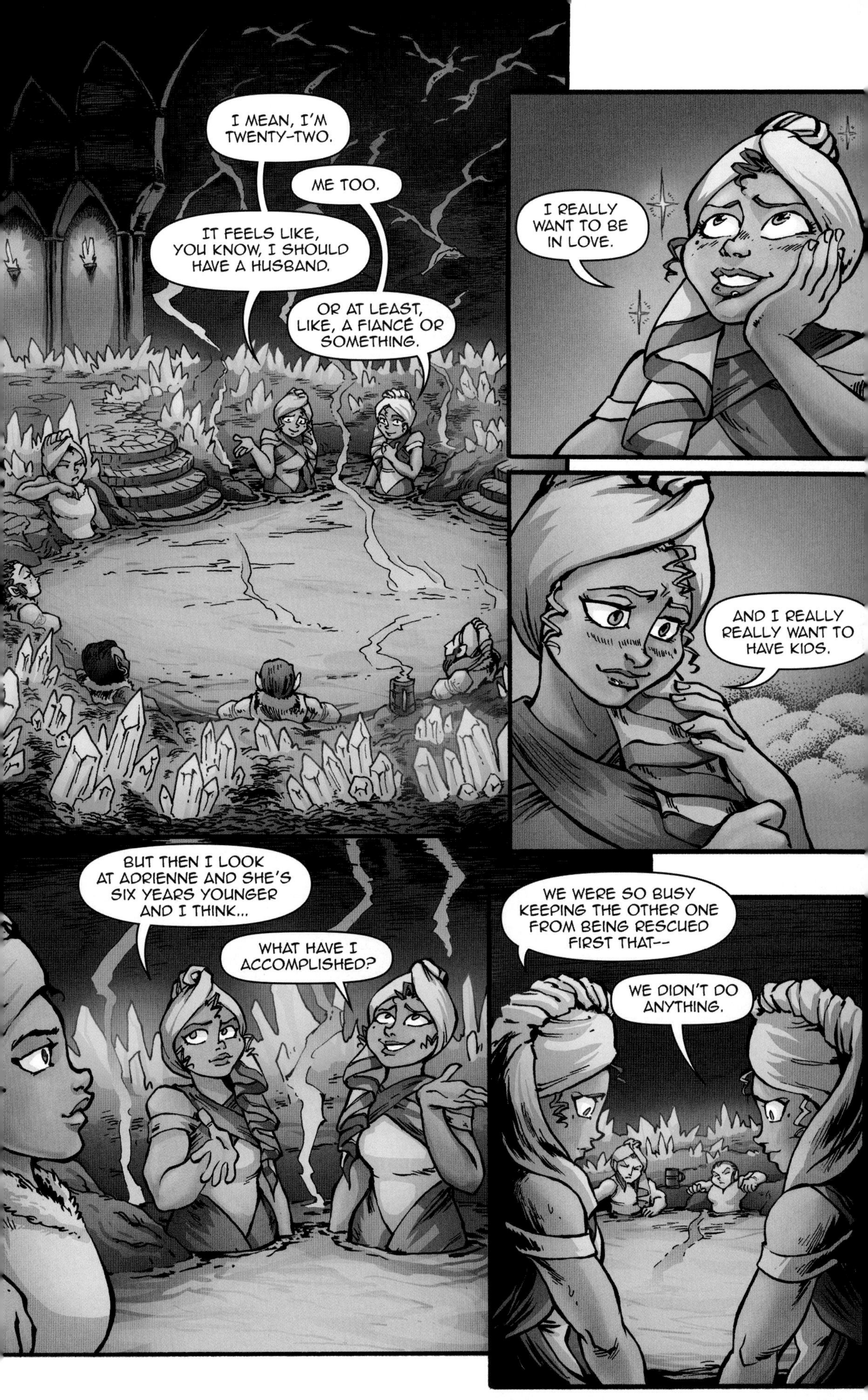
I MEAN, I'M TWENTY-TWO.
ME TOO.
IT FEELS LIKE, YOU KNOW, I SHOULD HAVE A HUSBAND.
OR AT LEAST, LIKE, A FIANCÉ OR SOMETHING.
I REALLY WANT TO BE IN LOVE.
AND I REALLY REALLY WANT TO HAVE KIDS.
BUT THEN I LOOK AT ADRIENNE AND SHE'S SIX YEARS YOUNGER AND I THINK...
WHAT HAVE I ACCOMPLISHED?
WE WERE SO BUSY KEEPING THE OTHER ONE FROM BEING RESCUED FIRST THAT--
WE DIDN'T DO ANYTHING.

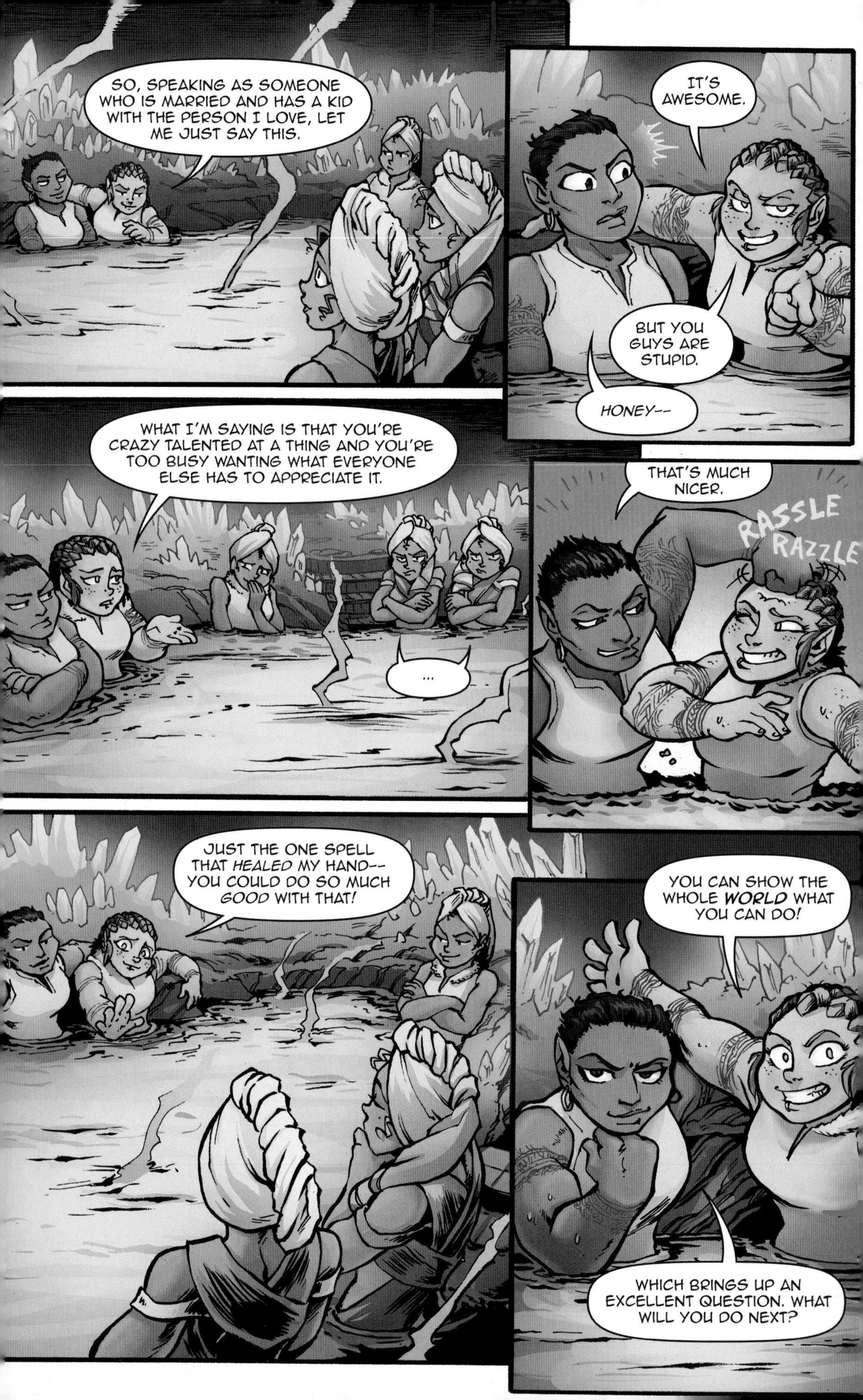
SO, SPEAKING AS SOMEONE WHO IS MARRIED AND HAS A KID WITH THE PERSON I LOVE, LET ME JUST SAY THIS.
IT'S AWESOME.
BUT YOU GUYS ARE STUPID.
HONEY--
WHAT I'M SAYING IS THAT YOU'RE CRAZY TALENTED AT A THING AND YOU'RE TOO BUSY WANTING WHAT EVERYONE ELSE HAS TO APPRECIATE IT.
...
THAT'S MUCH NICER.
RASSLE RAZZLE
JUST THE ONE SPELL THAT HEALED MY HAND-- YOU COULD DO SO MUCH GOOD WITH THAT!
YOU CAN SHOW THE WHOLE WORLD WHAT YOU CAN DO!
WHICH BRINGS UP AN EXCELLENT QUESTION. WHAT WILL YOU DO NEXT?

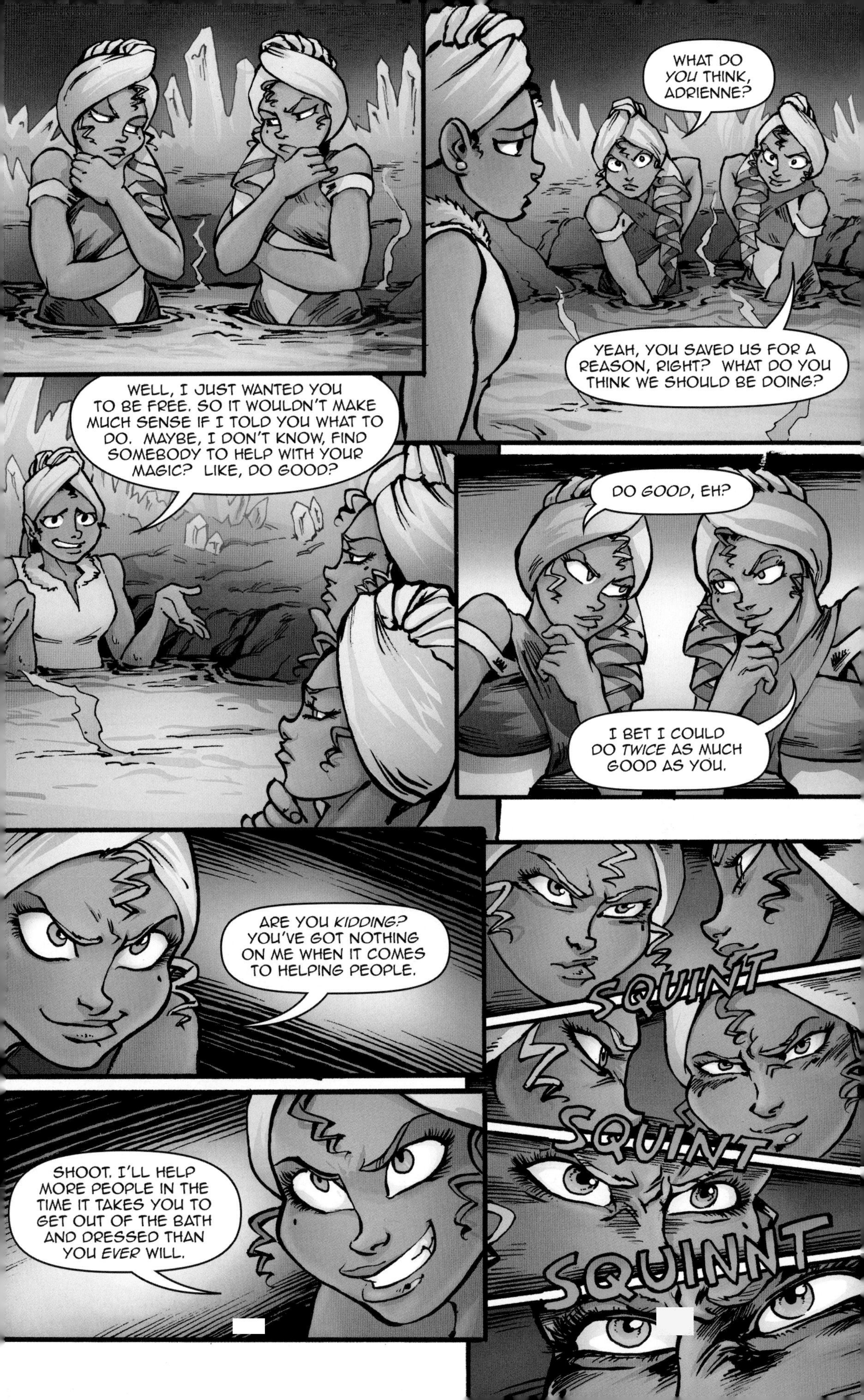
WHAT DO *YOU* THINK, ADRIENNE?
YEAH, YOU SAVED US FOR A REASON, RIGHT? WHAT DO YOU THINK WE SHOULD BE DOING?
WELL, I JUST WANTED YOU TO BE FREE. SO IT WOULDN'T MAKE MUCH SENSE IF I TOLD YOU WHAT TO DO. MAYBE, I DON'T KNOW, FIND SOMEBODY TO HELP WITH YOUR MAGIC? LIKE, DO GOOD?
DO *GOOD*, EH?
I BET I COULD DO *TWICE* AS MUCH GOOD AS YOU.
ARE YOU *KIDDING*? YOU'VE GOT NOTHING ON ME WHEN IT COMES TO HELPING PEOPLE.
SHOOT. I'LL HELP MORE PEOPLE IN THE TIME IT TAKES YOU TO GET OUT OF THE BATH AND DRESSED THAN YOU *EVER* WILL.
SQUINT
SQUINT
SQUINNT

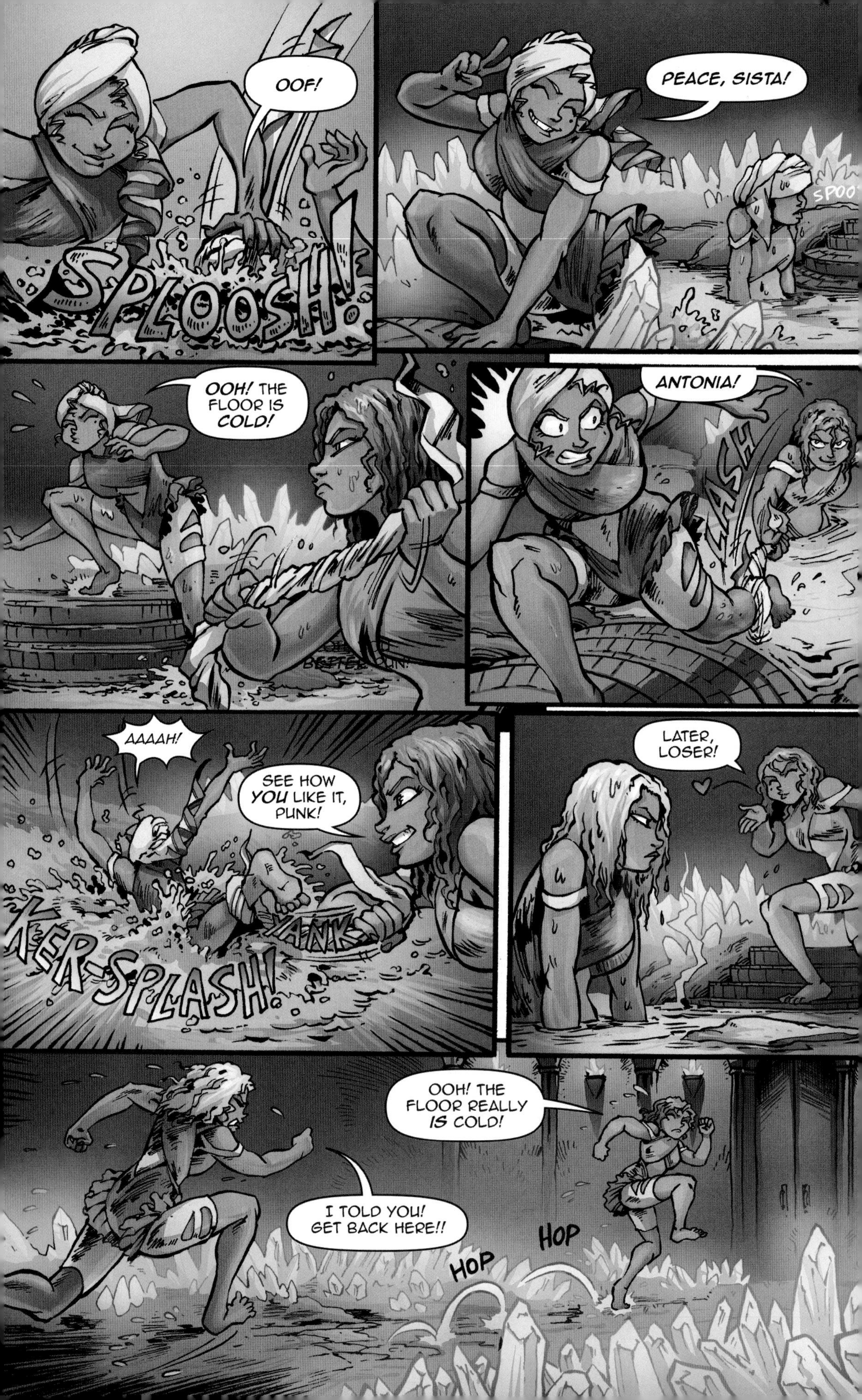
OOF!
SPLOOSH!
PEACE, SISTA!
SPOO
OOH! THE FLOOR IS COLD!
ANTONIA!
SLASH
AAAAH!
SEE HOW YOU LIKE IT, PUNK!
YANK
KER-SPLASH!
LATER, LOSER!
OOH! THE FLOOR REALLY IS COLD!
I TOLD YOU! GET BACK HERE!!
HOP
HOP

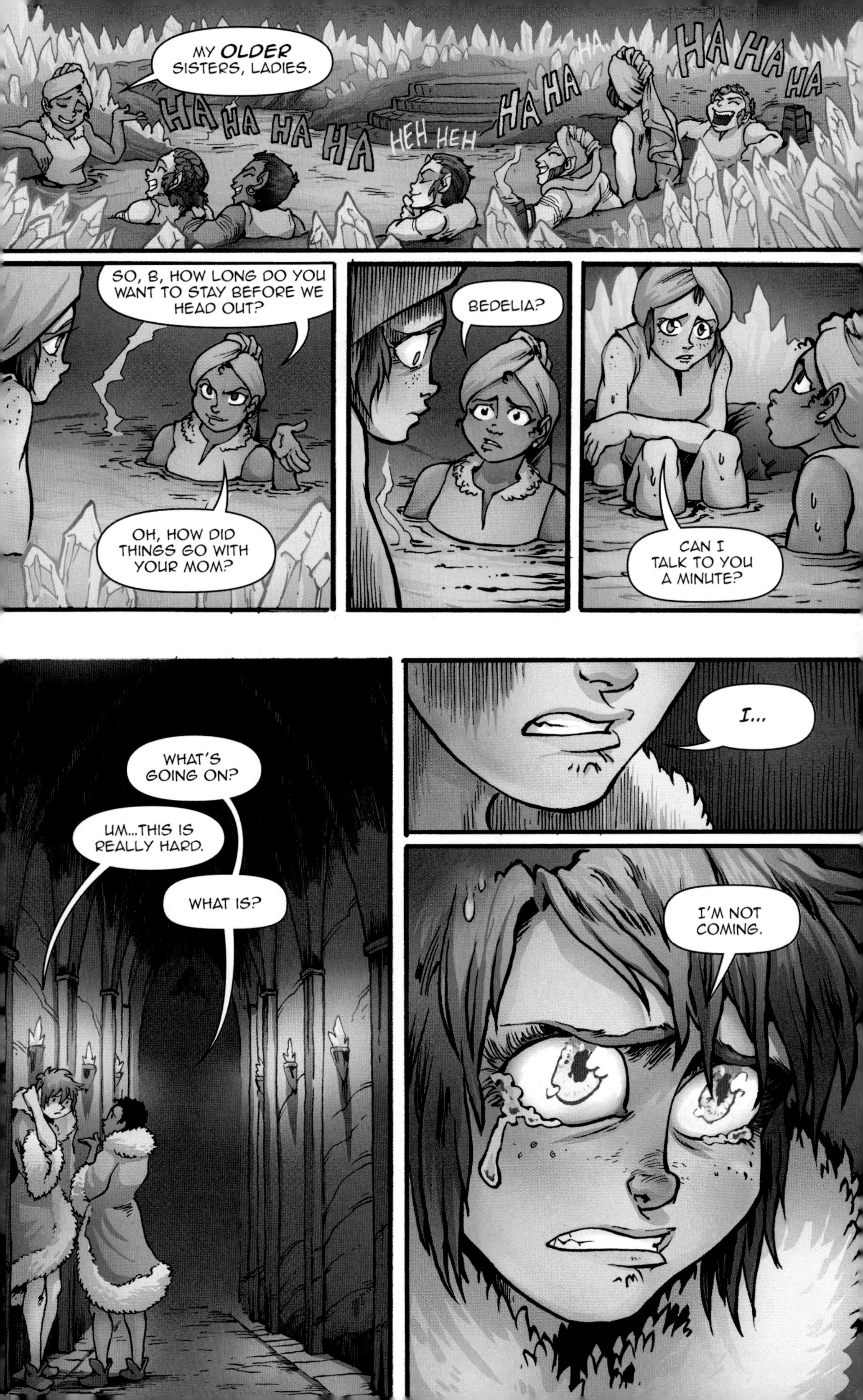

MY **OLDER** SISTERS, LADIES.
HA HA HA HA HA
HEH HEH
HA HA HA
HA HA HA HA
SO, B, HOW LONG DO YOU WANT TO STAY BEFORE WE HEAD OUT?
OH, HOW DID THINGS GO WITH YOUR MOM?
BEDELIA?
CAN I TALK TO YOU A MINUTE?
WHAT'S GOING ON?
UM...THIS IS REALLY HARD.
WHAT IS?
I...
I'M NOT COMING.

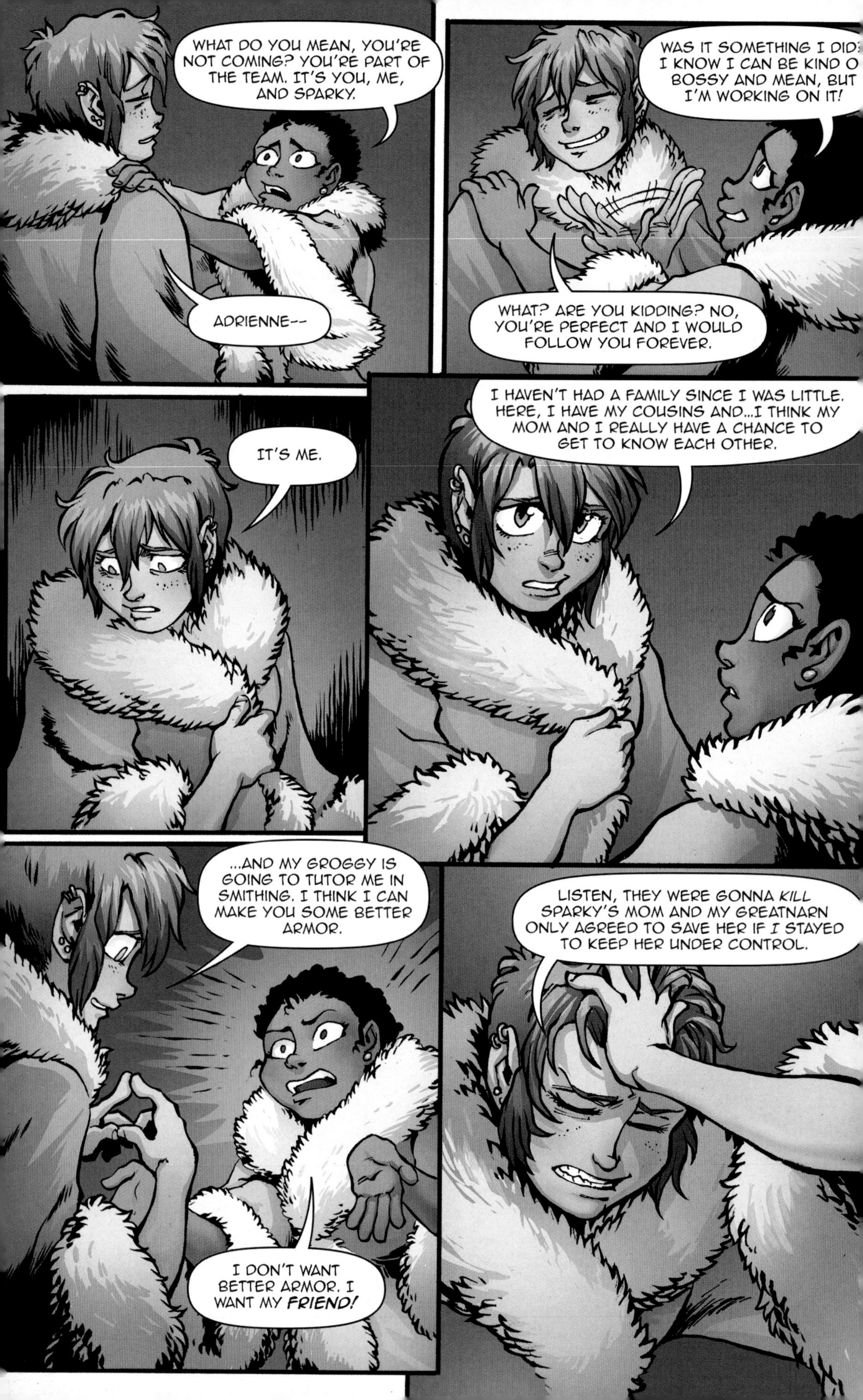
WHAT DO YOU MEAN, YOU'RE NOT COMING? YOU'RE PART OF THE TEAM. IT'S YOU, ME, AND SPARKY.
ADRIENNE--
WAS IT SOMETHING I DID? I KNOW I CAN BE KIND OF BOSSY AND MEAN, BUT I'M WORKING ON IT!
WHAT? ARE YOU KIDDING? NO, YOU'RE PERFECT AND I WOULD FOLLOW YOU FOREVER.
IT'S ME.
I HAVEN'T HAD A FAMILY SINCE I WAS LITTLE. HERE, I HAVE MY COUSINS AND...I THINK MY MOM AND I REALLY HAVE A CHANCE TO GET TO KNOW EACH OTHER.
...AND MY GROGGY IS GOING TO TUTOR ME IN SMITHING. I THINK I CAN MAKE YOU SOME BETTER ARMOR.
I DON'T WANT BETTER ARMOR. I WANT MY ***FRIEND!***
LISTEN, THEY WERE GONNA *KILL* SPARKY'S MOM AND MY GREATNARN ONLY AGREED TO SAVE HER IF *I* STAYED TO KEEP HER UNDER CONTROL.

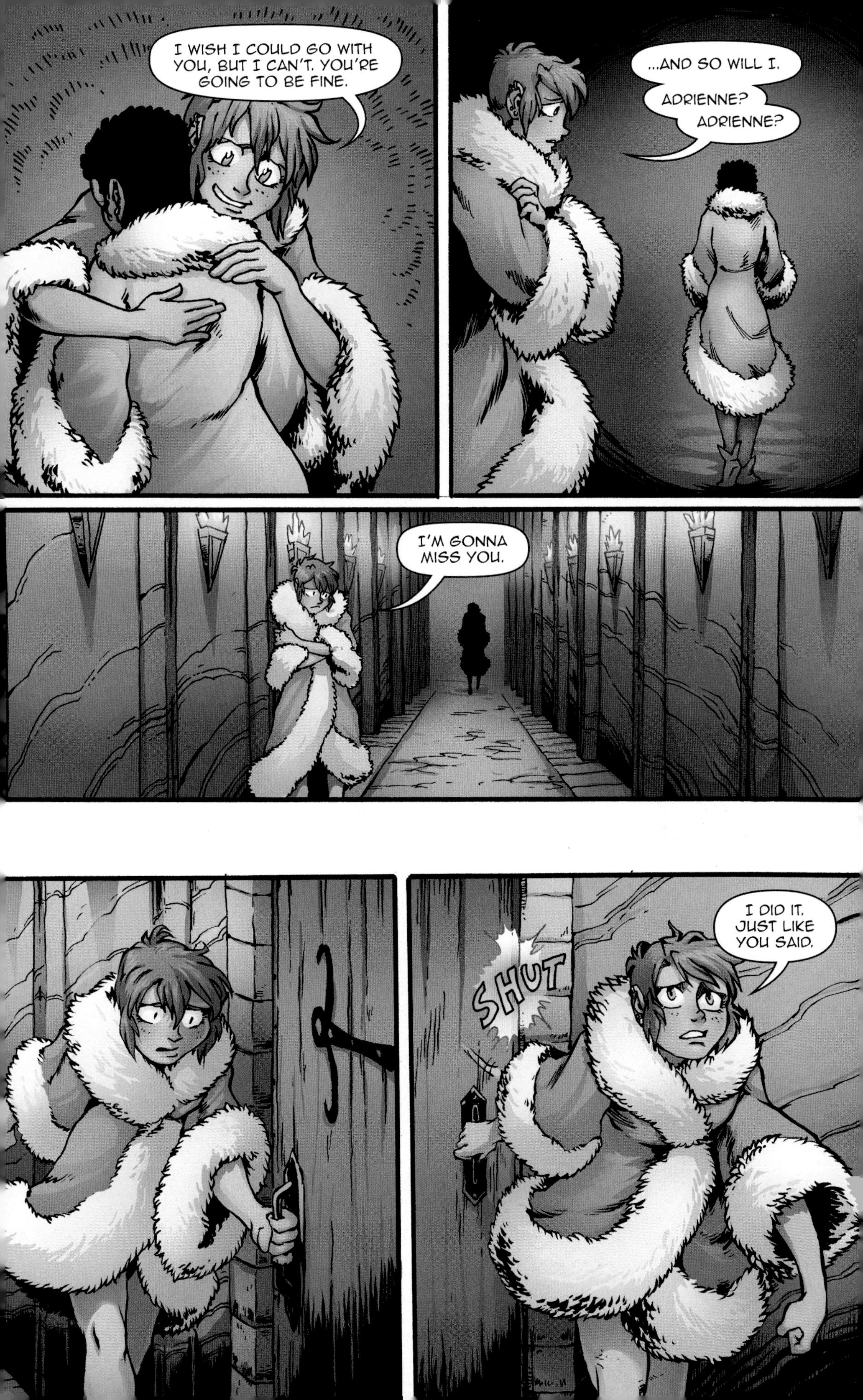
I WISH I COULD GO WITH YOU, BUT I CAN'T. YOU'RE GOING TO BE FINE.
...AND SO WILL I.
ADRIENNE?
ADRIENNE?
I'M GONNA MISS YOU.
SHUT
I DID IT. JUST LIKE YOU SAID.

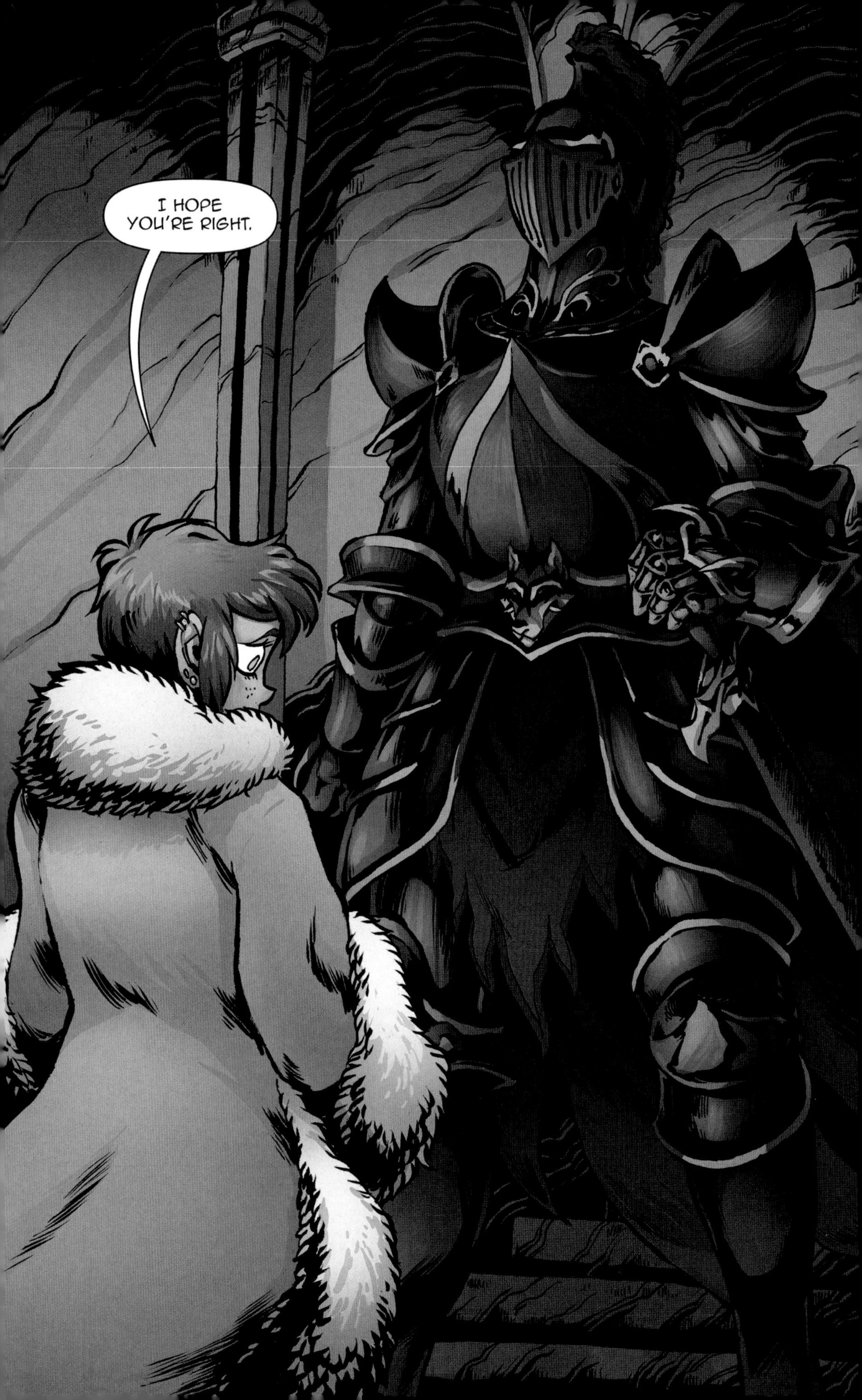
I HOPE YOU'RE RIGHT.

4: Wives (Hunting Day)

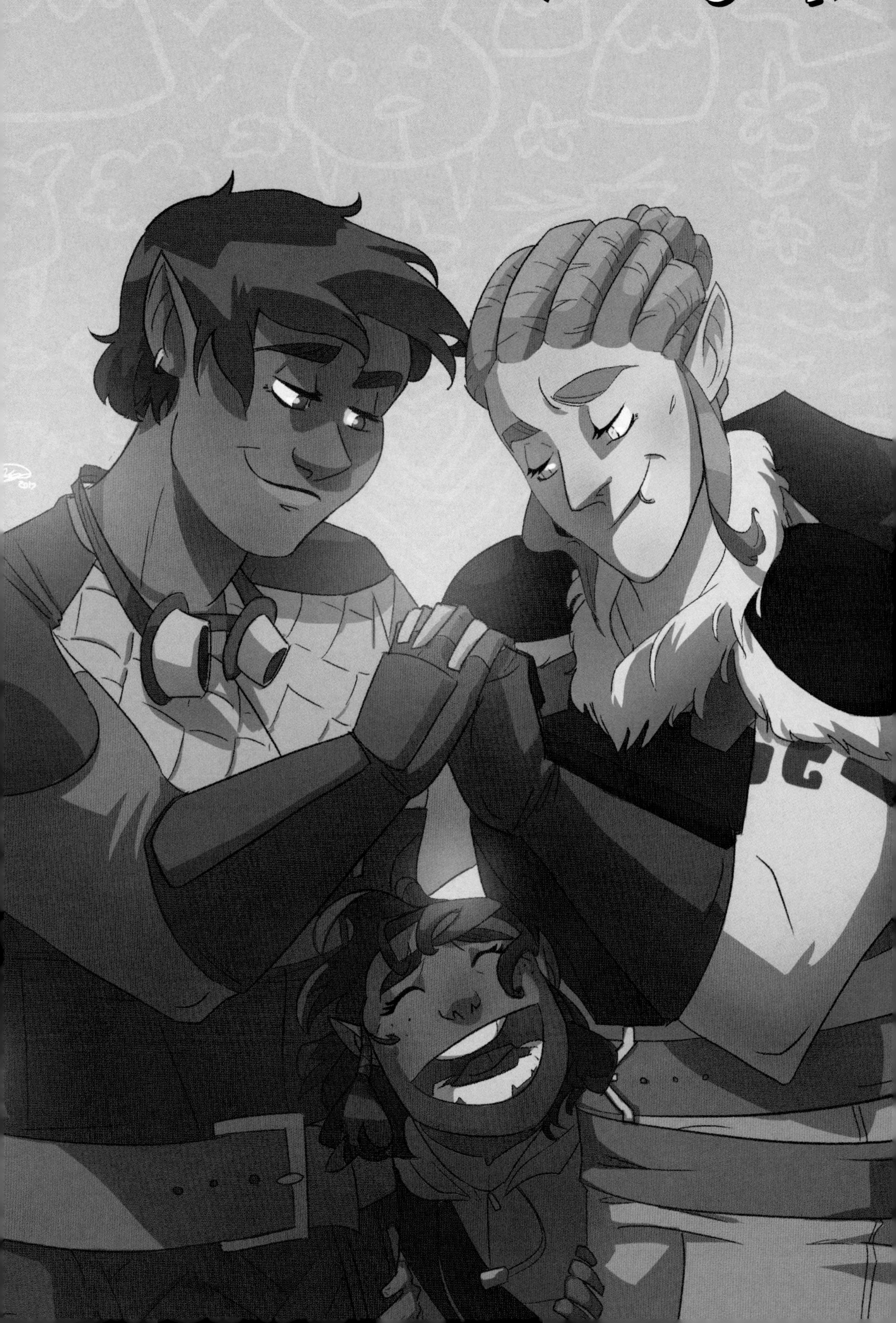

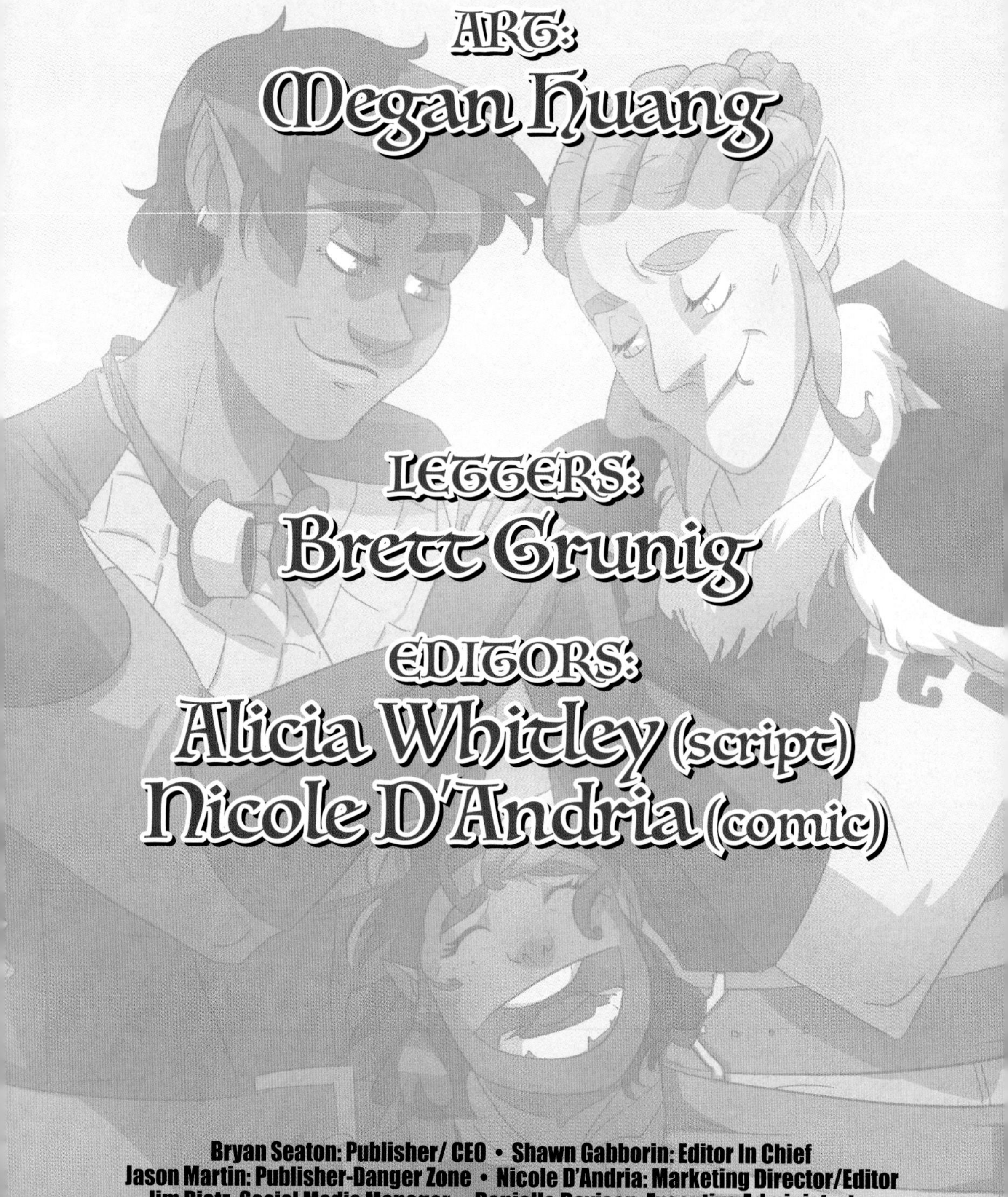

STORY:
Jeremy Whitley

ART:
Megan Huang

LETTERS:
Brett Grunig

EDITORS:
Alicia Whitley (script)
Nicole D'Andria (comic)

Bryan Seaton: Publisher/ CEO • **Shawn Gabborin: Editor In Chief**
Jason Martin: Publisher-Danger Zone • **Nicole D'Andria: Marketing Director/Editor**
Jim Dietz: Social Media Manager • **Danielle Davison: Executive Administrator**
Chad Cicconi: Still Waiting For His Princess • **Shawn Pryor: President of Creator Relations**

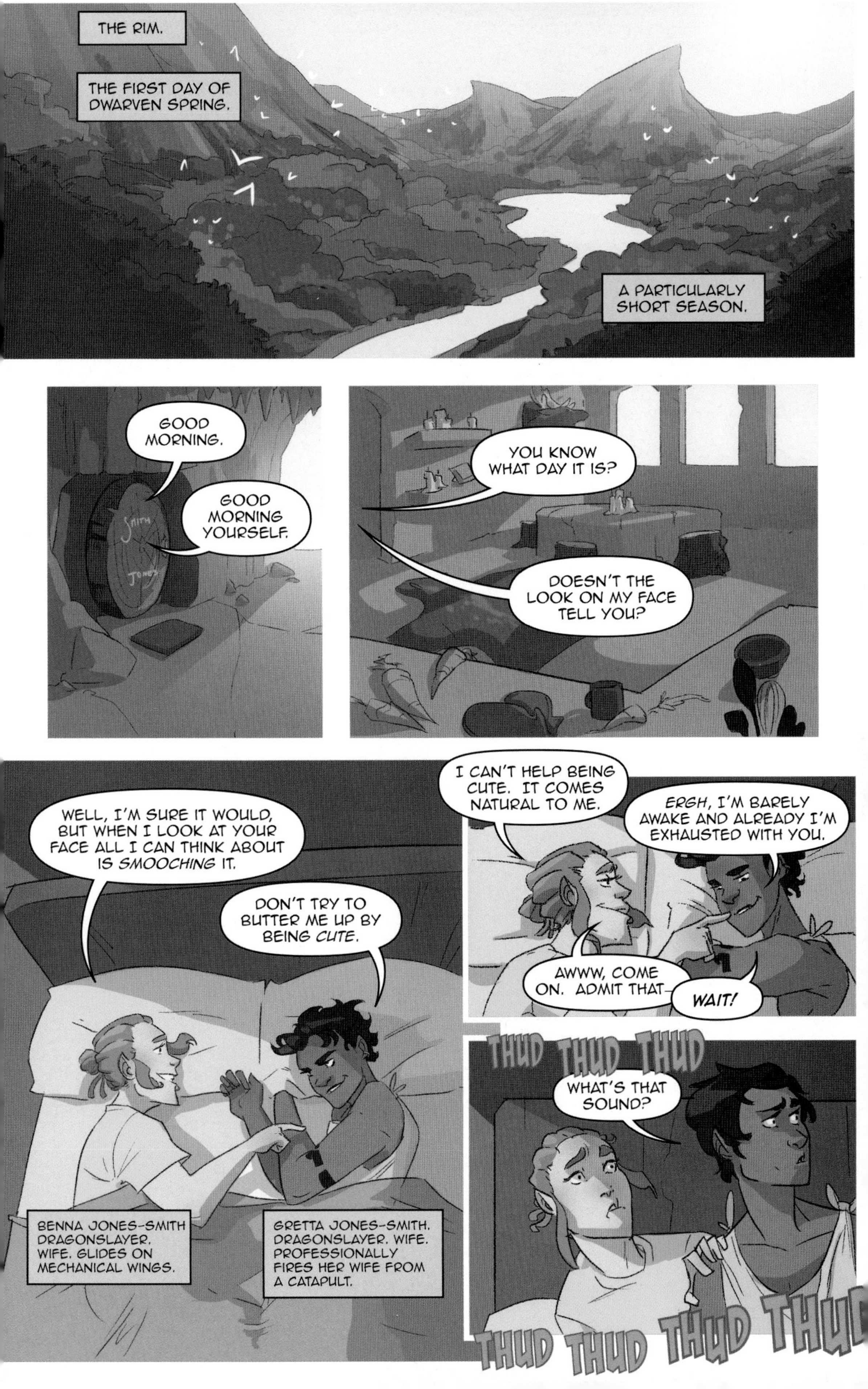
THE RIM.
THE FIRST DAY OF DWARVEN SPRING.
A PARTICULARLY SHORT SEASON.
GOOD MORNING.
GOOD MORNING YOURSELF.
SMITH
JONES
YOU KNOW WHAT DAY IT IS?
DOESN'T THE LOOK ON MY FACE TELL YOU?
WELL, I'M SURE IT WOULD, BUT WHEN I LOOK AT YOUR FACE ALL I CAN THINK ABOUT IS *SMOOCHING* IT.
DON'T TRY TO BUTTER ME UP BY BEING *CUTE*.
BENNA JONES-SMITH DRAGONSLAYER. WIFE. GLIDES ON MECHANICAL WINGS.
GRETTA JONES-SMITH. DRAGONSLAYER. WIFE. PROFESSIONALLY FIRES HER WIFE FROM A CATAPULT.
I CAN'T HELP BEING CUTE. IT COMES NATURAL TO ME.
ERGH, I'M BARELY AWAKE AND ALREADY I'M EXHAUSTED WITH YOU.
AWWW, COME ON. ADMIT THAT—
WAIT!
THUD THUD THUD
WHAT'S THAT SOUND?
THUD THUD THUD THUD

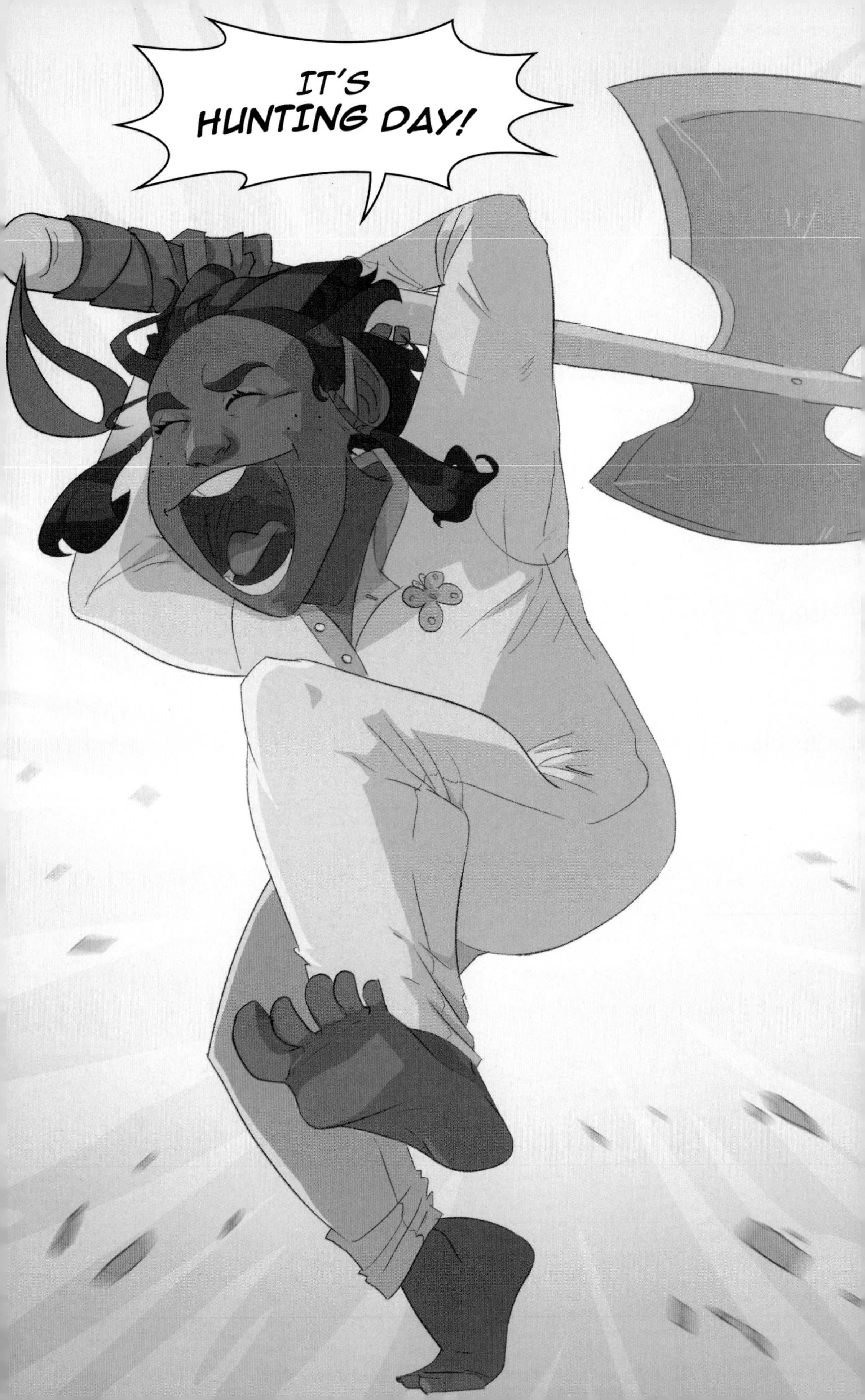
IT'S HUNTING DAY!

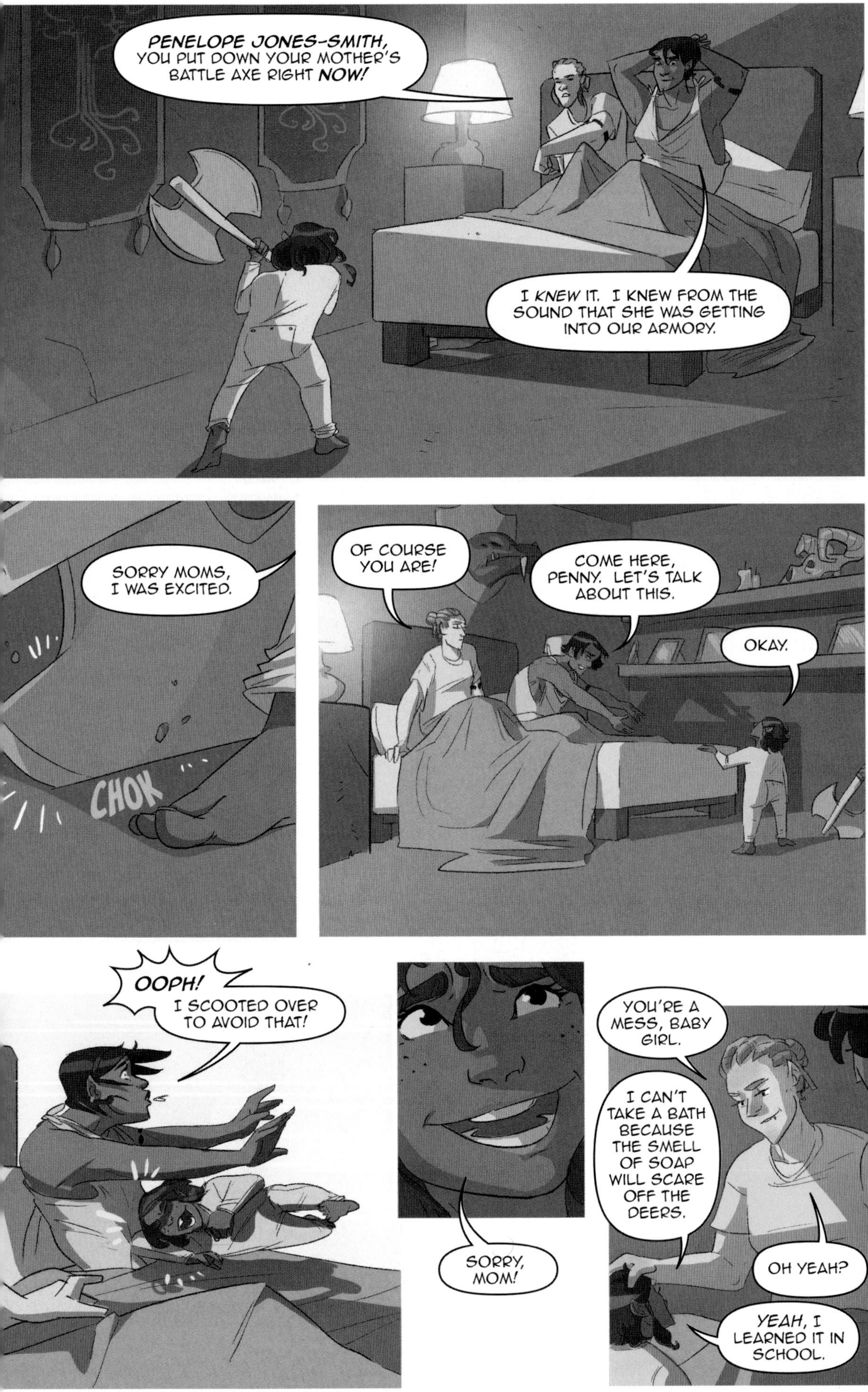

PENELOPE JONES-SMITH, YOU PUT DOWN YOUR MOTHER'S BATTLE AXE RIGHT NOW!
I KNEW IT. I KNEW FROM THE SOUND THAT SHE WAS GETTING INTO OUR ARMORY.
SORRY MOMS, I WAS EXCITED.
CHOK
OF COURSE YOU ARE!
COME HERE, PENNY. LET'S TALK ABOUT THIS.
OKAY.
OOPH!
I SCOOTED OVER TO AVOID THAT!
SORRY, MOM!
YOU'RE A MESS, BABY GIRL.
I CAN'T TAKE A BATH BECAUSE THE SMELL OF SOAP WILL SCARE OFF THE DEERS.
OH YEAH?
YEAH, I LEARNED IT IN SCHOOL.

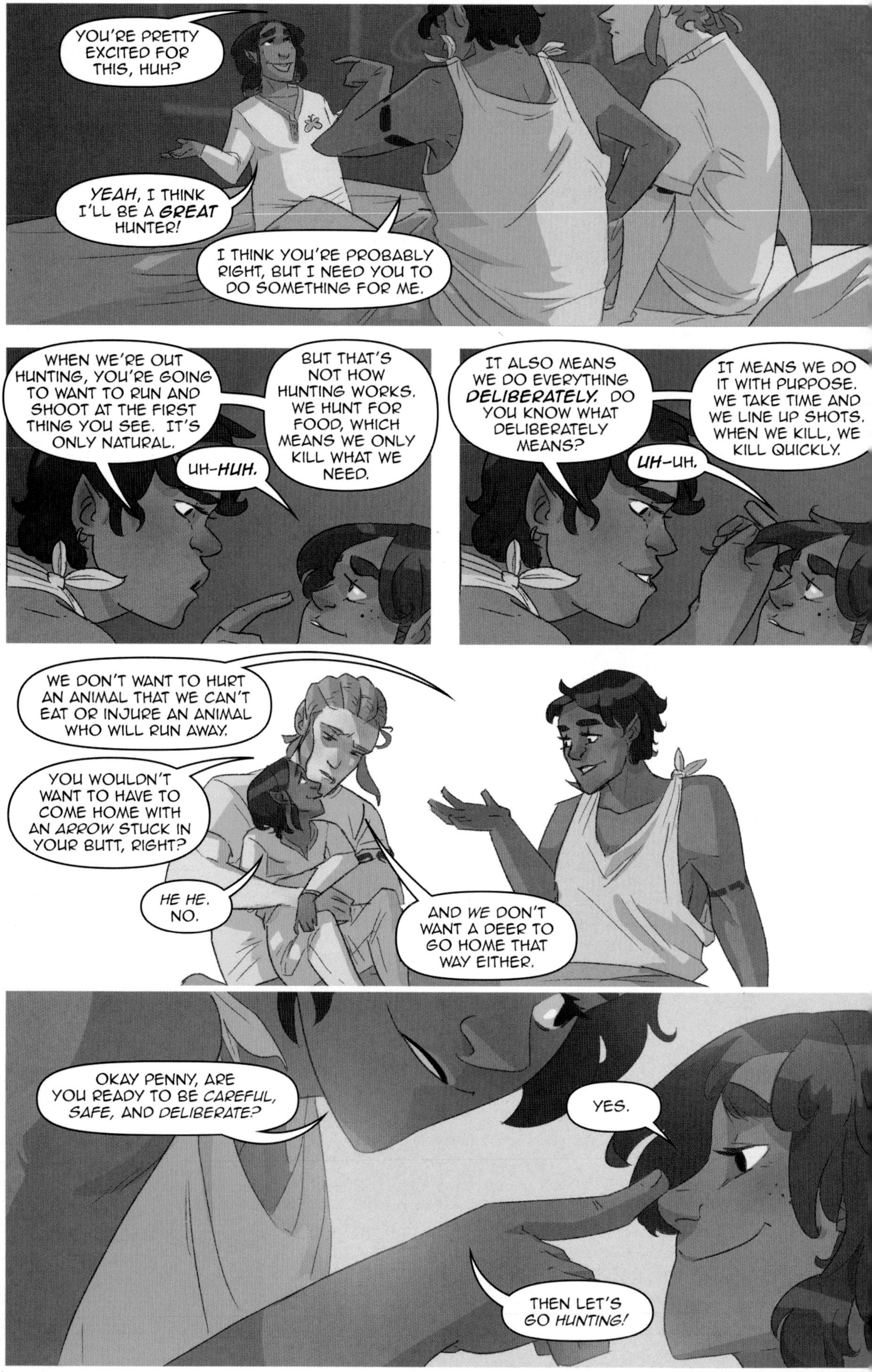
YOU'RE PRETTY EXCITED FOR THIS, HUH?
YEAH, I THINK I'LL BE A GREAT HUNTER!
I THINK YOU'RE PROBABLY RIGHT, BUT I NEED YOU TO DO SOMETHING FOR ME.
WHEN WE'RE OUT HUNTING, YOU'RE GOING TO WANT TO RUN AND SHOOT AT THE FIRST THING YOU SEE. IT'S ONLY NATURAL.
UH-HUH.
BUT THAT'S NOT HOW HUNTING WORKS. WE HUNT FOR FOOD, WHICH MEANS WE ONLY KILL WHAT WE NEED.
IT ALSO MEANS WE DO EVERYTHING DELIBERATELY. DO YOU KNOW WHAT DELIBERATELY MEANS?
UH-UH.
IT MEANS WE DO IT WITH PURPOSE. WE TAKE TIME AND WE LINE UP SHOTS. WHEN WE KILL, WE KILL QUICKLY.
WE DON'T WANT TO HURT AN ANIMAL THAT WE CAN'T EAT OR INJURE AN ANIMAL WHO WILL RUN AWAY.
YOU WOULDN'T WANT TO HAVE TO COME HOME WITH AN ARROW STUCK IN YOUR BUTT, RIGHT?
HE HE. NO.
AND WE DON'T WANT A DEER TO GO HOME THAT WAY EITHER.
OKAY PENNY, ARE YOU READY TO BE CAREFUL, SAFE, AND DELIBERATE?
YES.
THEN LET'S GO HUNTING!

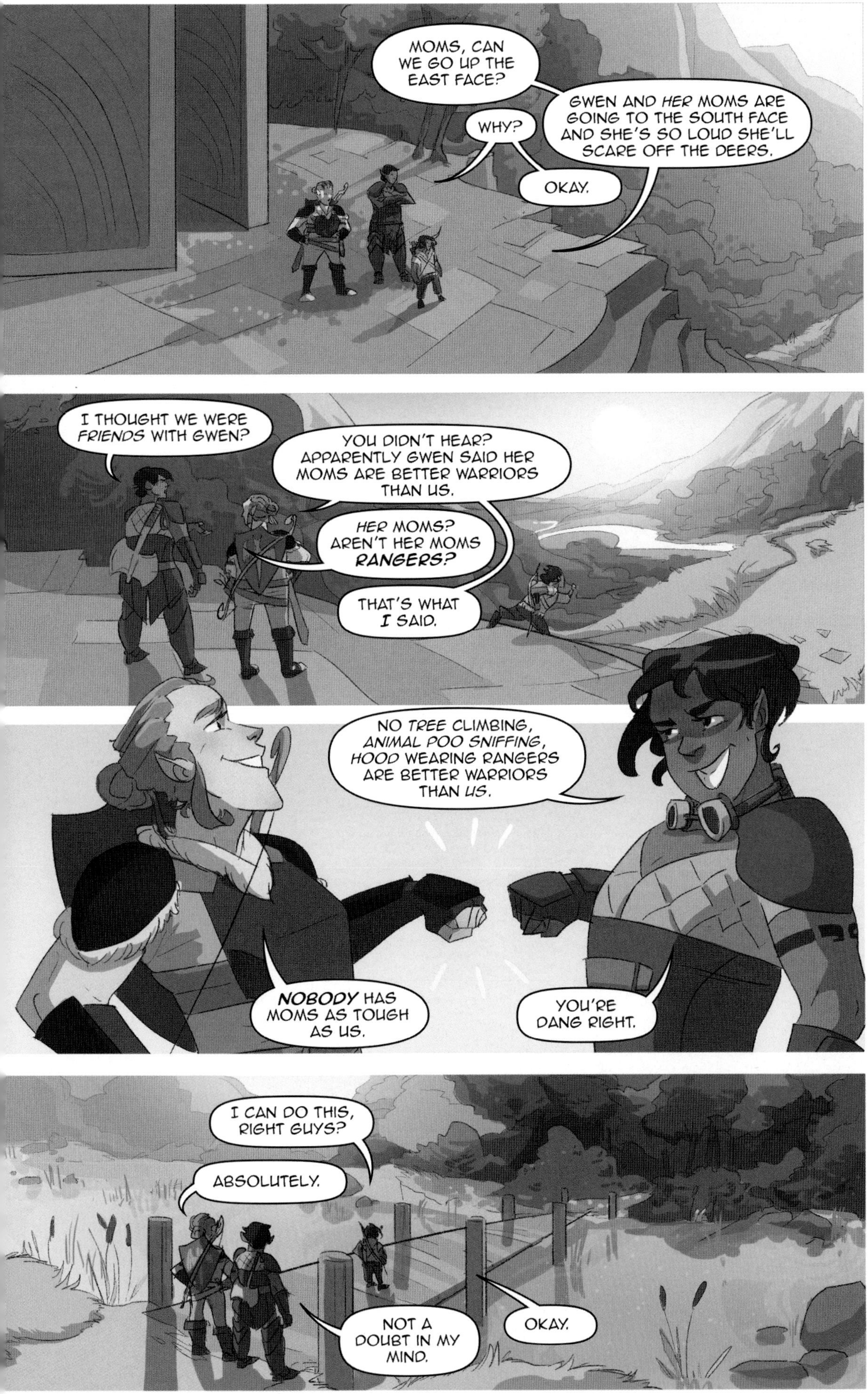
MOMS, CAN WE GO UP THE EAST FACE?
WHY?
GWEN AND HER MOMS ARE GOING TO THE SOUTH FACE AND SHE'S SO LOUD SHE'LL SCARE OFF THE DEERS.
OKAY.
I THOUGHT WE WERE FRIENDS WITH GWEN?
YOU DIDN'T HEAR? APPARENTLY GWEN SAID HER MOMS ARE BETTER WARRIORS THAN US.
HER MOMS? AREN'T HER MOMS RANGERS?
THAT'S WHAT I SAID.
NO TREE CLIMBING, ANIMAL POO SNIFFING, HOOD WEARING RANGERS ARE BETTER WARRIORS THAN US.
NOBODY HAS MOMS AS TOUGH AS US.
YOU'RE DANG RIGHT.
I CAN DO THIS, RIGHT GUYS?
ABSOLUTELY.
NOT A DOUBT IN MY MIND.
OKAY.

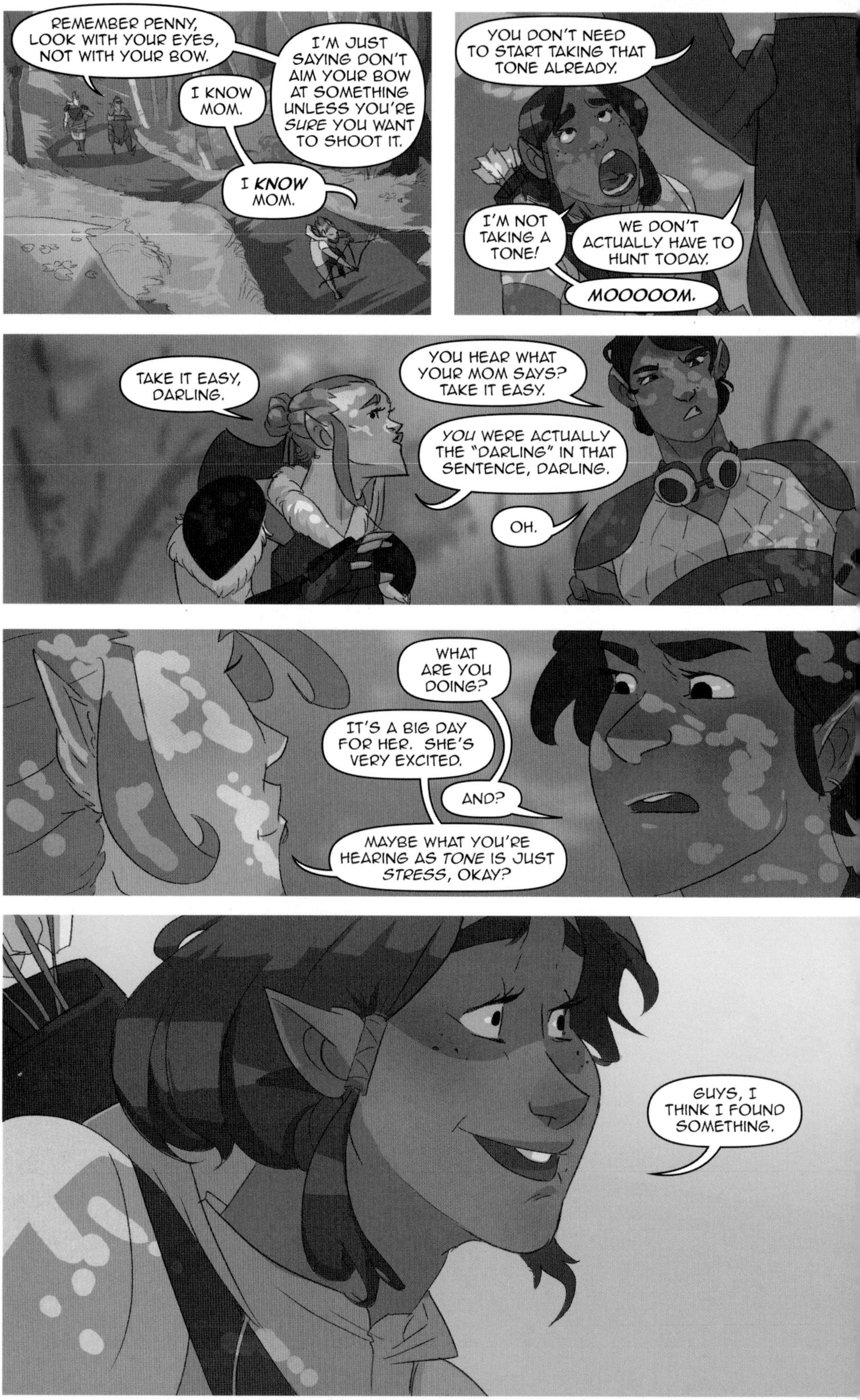
REMEMBER PENNY, LOOK WITH YOUR EYES, NOT WITH YOUR BOW.
I KNOW MOM.
I'M JUST SAYING DON'T AIM YOUR BOW AT SOMETHING UNLESS YOU'RE *SURE* YOU WANT TO SHOOT IT.
I ***KNOW*** MOM.
YOU DON'T NEED TO START TAKING THAT TONE ALREADY.
I'M NOT TAKING A TONE!
WE DON'T ACTUALLY HAVE TO HUNT TODAY.
MOOOOOM.
TAKE IT EASY, DARLING.
YOU HEAR WHAT YOUR MOM SAYS? TAKE IT EASY.
YOU WERE ACTUALLY THE "DARLING" IN THAT SENTENCE, DARLING.
OH.
WHAT ARE YOU DOING?
IT'S A BIG DAY FOR HER. SHE'S VERY EXCITED.
AND?
MAYBE WHAT YOU'RE HEARING AS *TONE* IS JUST *STRESS*, OKAY?
GUYS, I THINK I FOUND SOMETHING.

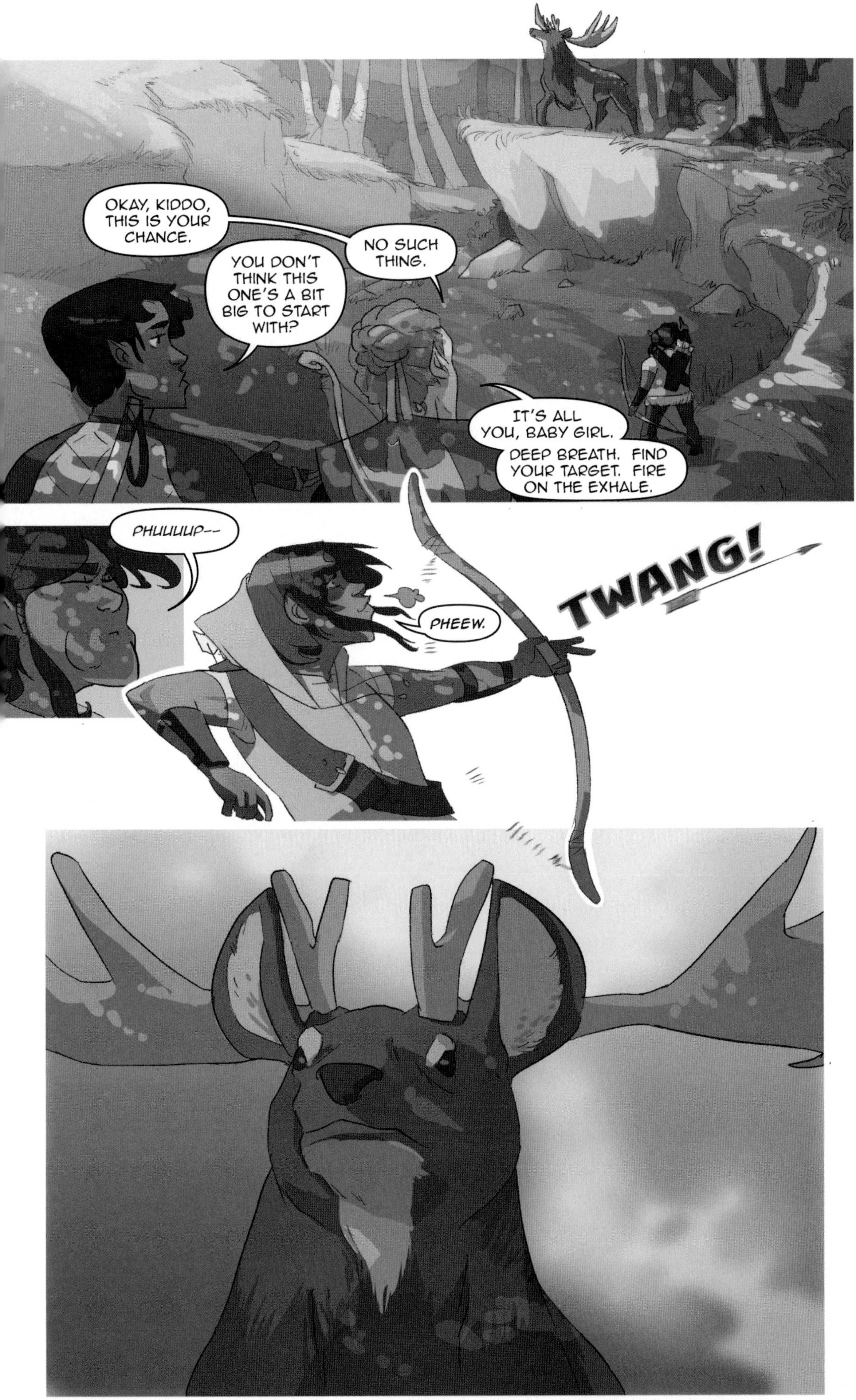
OKAY, KIDDO, THIS IS YOUR CHANCE.
YOU DON'T THINK THIS ONE'S A BIT BIG TO START WITH?
NO SUCH THING.
IT'S ALL YOU, BABY GIRL.
DEEP BREATH. FIND YOUR TARGET. FIRE ON THE EXHALE.
PHUUUUP--
PHEEW.
TWANG!

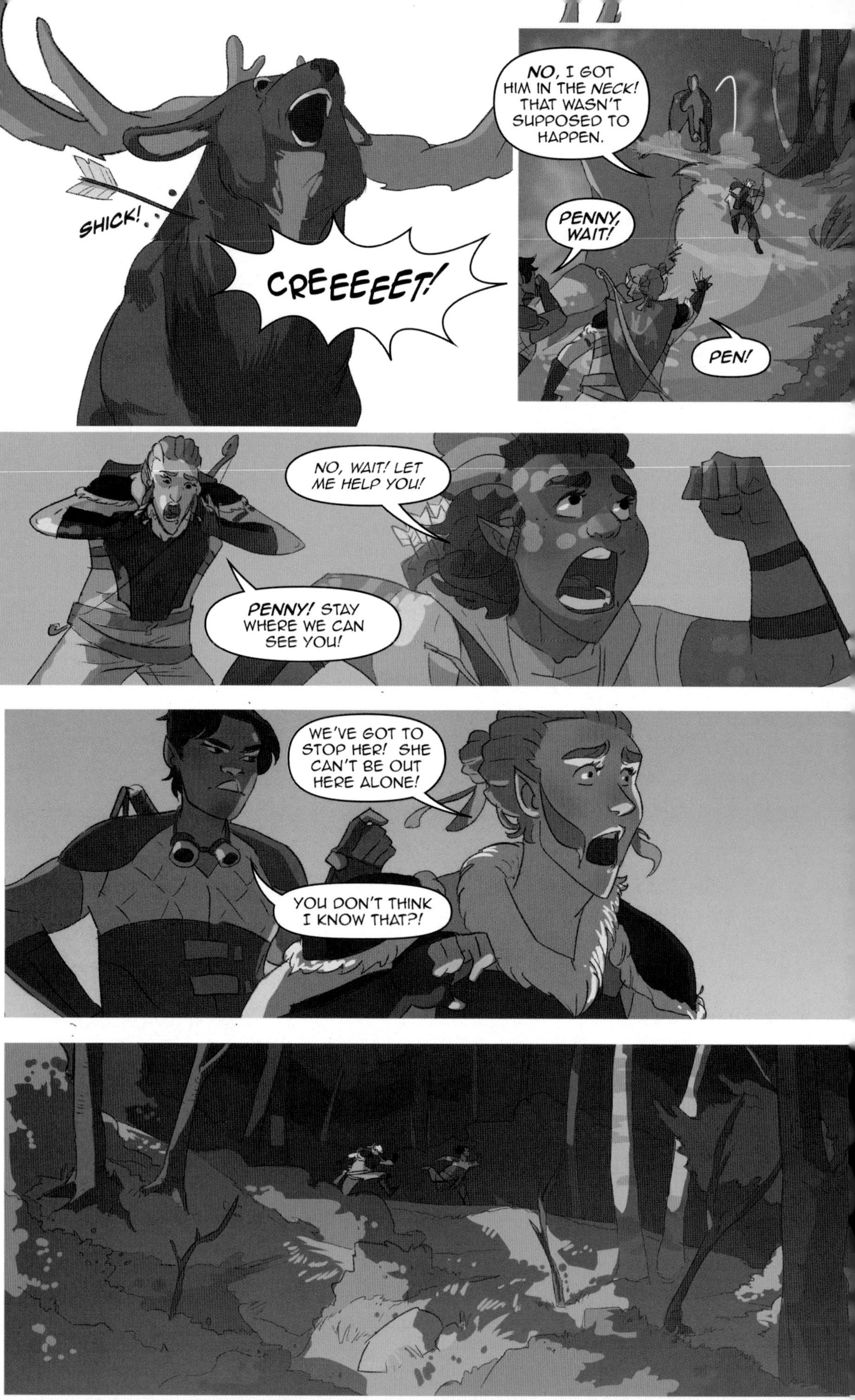

SHICK!
CREEEEET!
NO, I GOT HIM IN THE NECK! THAT WASN'T SUPPOSED TO HAPPEN.
PENNY, WAIT!
PEN!
NO, WAIT! LET ME HELP YOU!
PENNY! STAY WHERE WE CAN SEE YOU!
WE'VE GOT TO STOP HER! SHE CAN'T BE OUT HERE ALONE!
YOU DON'T THINK I KNOW THAT?!

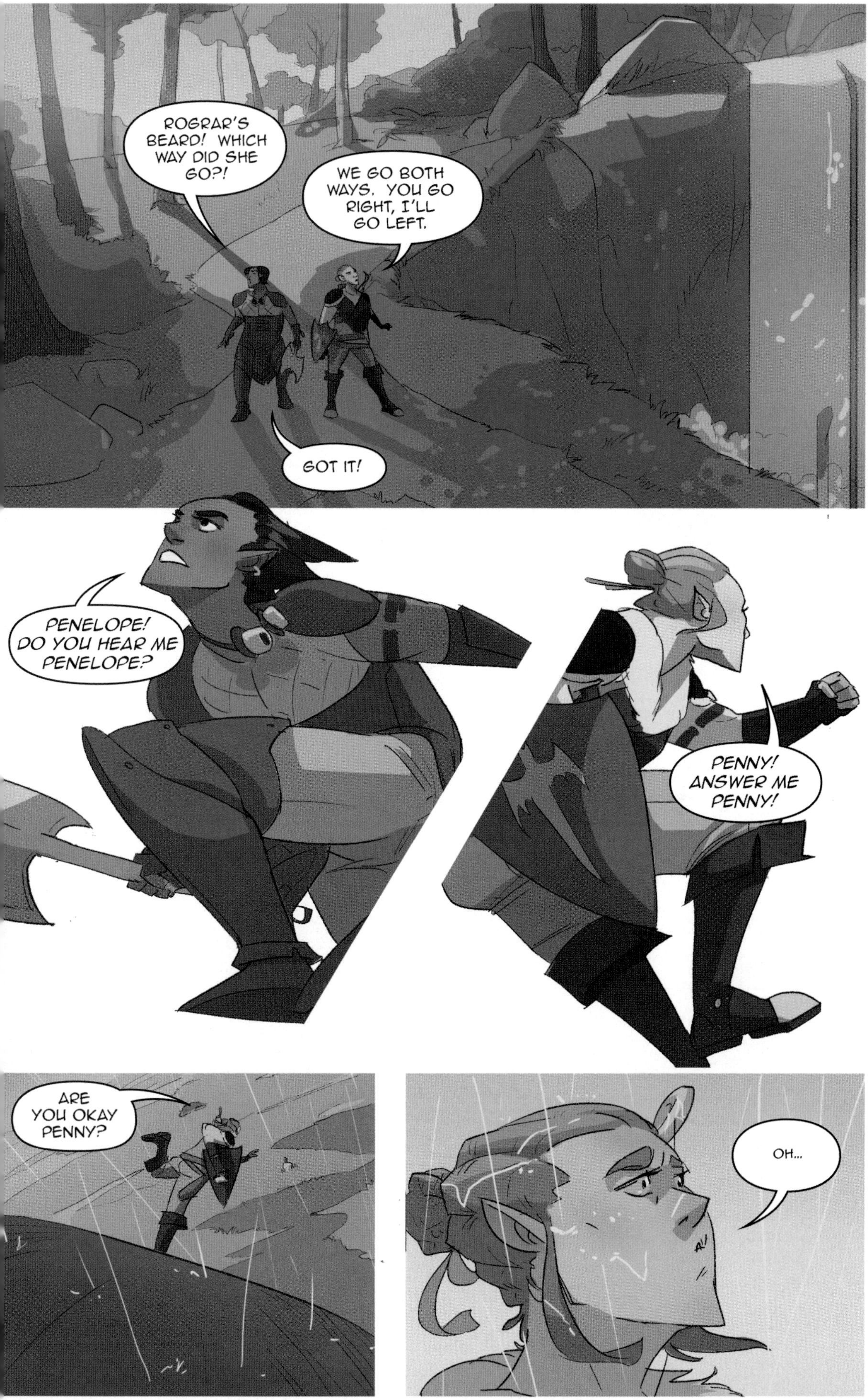
ROGRAR'S BEARD! WHICH WAY DID SHE GO?!
WE GO BOTH WAYS. YOU GO RIGHT, I'LL GO LEFT.
GOT IT!
PENELOPE! DO YOU HEAR ME PENELOPE?
PENNY! ANSWER ME PENNY!
ARE YOU OKAY PENNY?
OH...

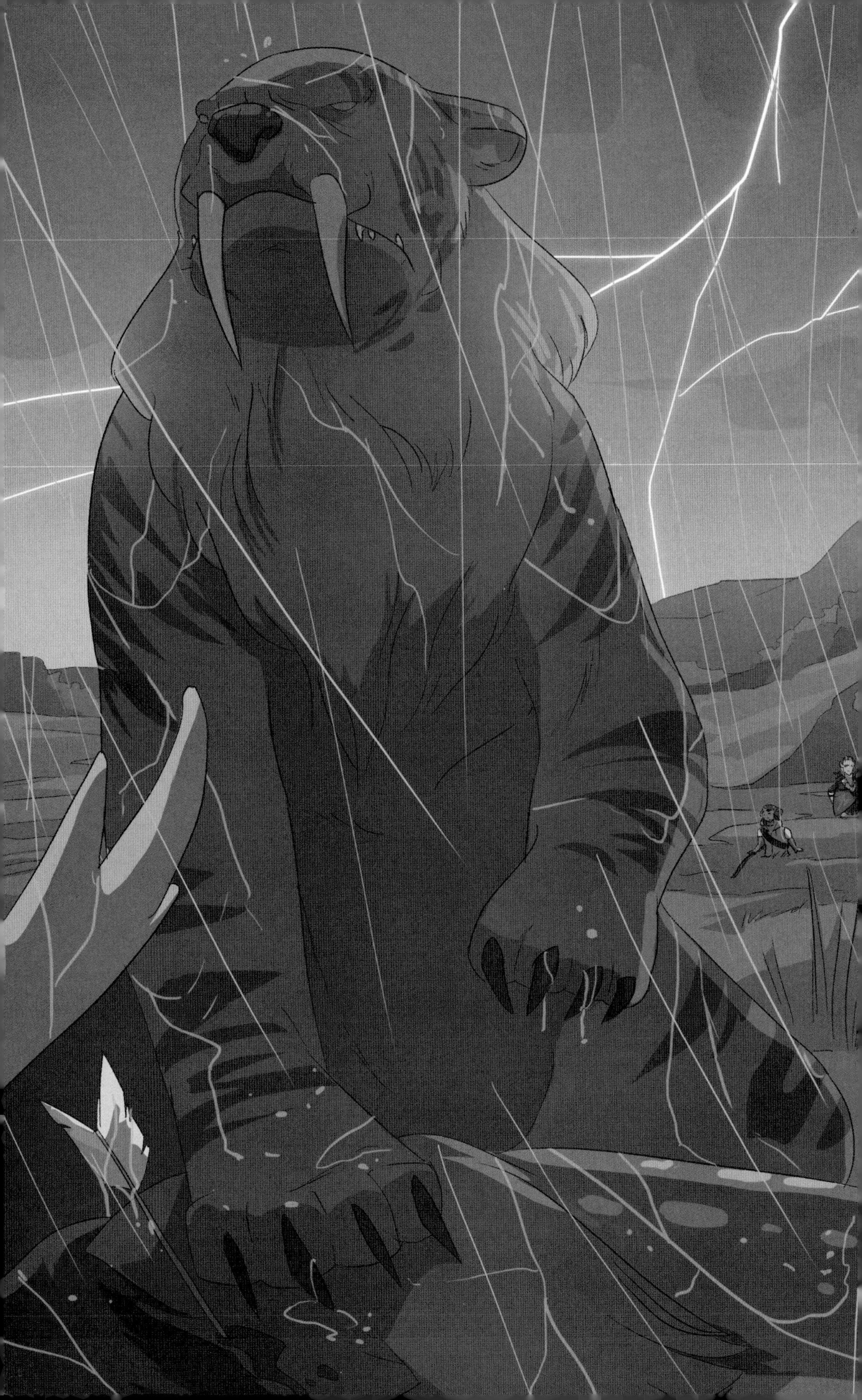

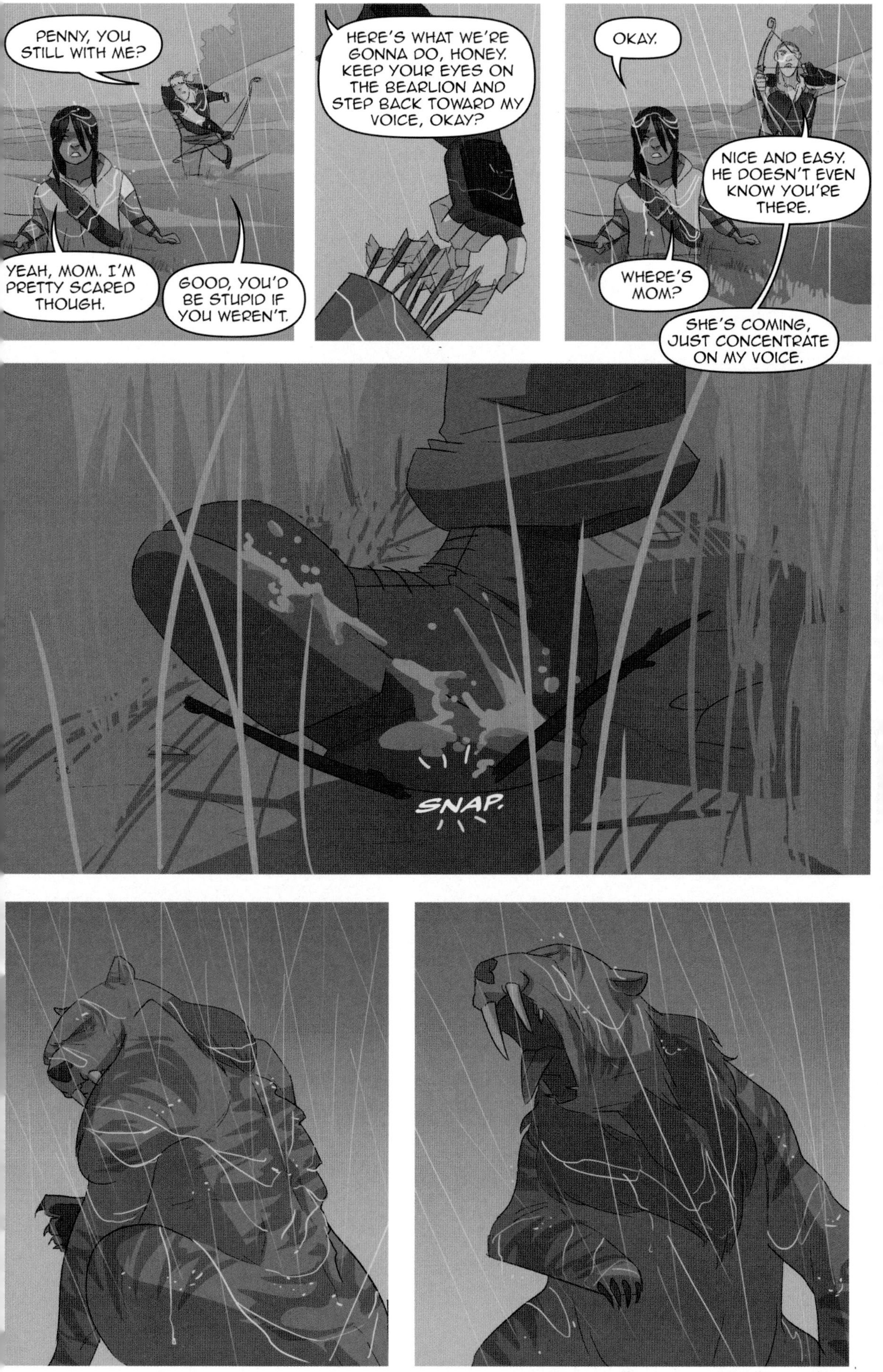
PENNY, YOU STILL WITH ME?
YEAH, MOM. I'M PRETTY SCARED THOUGH.
GOOD, YOU'D BE STUPID IF YOU WEREN'T.
HERE'S WHAT WE'RE GONNA DO, HONEY. KEEP YOUR EYES ON THE BEARLION AND STEP BACK TOWARD MY VOICE, OKAY?
OKAY.
NICE AND EASY. HE DOESN'T EVEN KNOW YOU'RE THERE.
WHERE'S MOM?
SHE'S COMING, JUST CONCENTRATE ON MY VOICE.
SNAP.

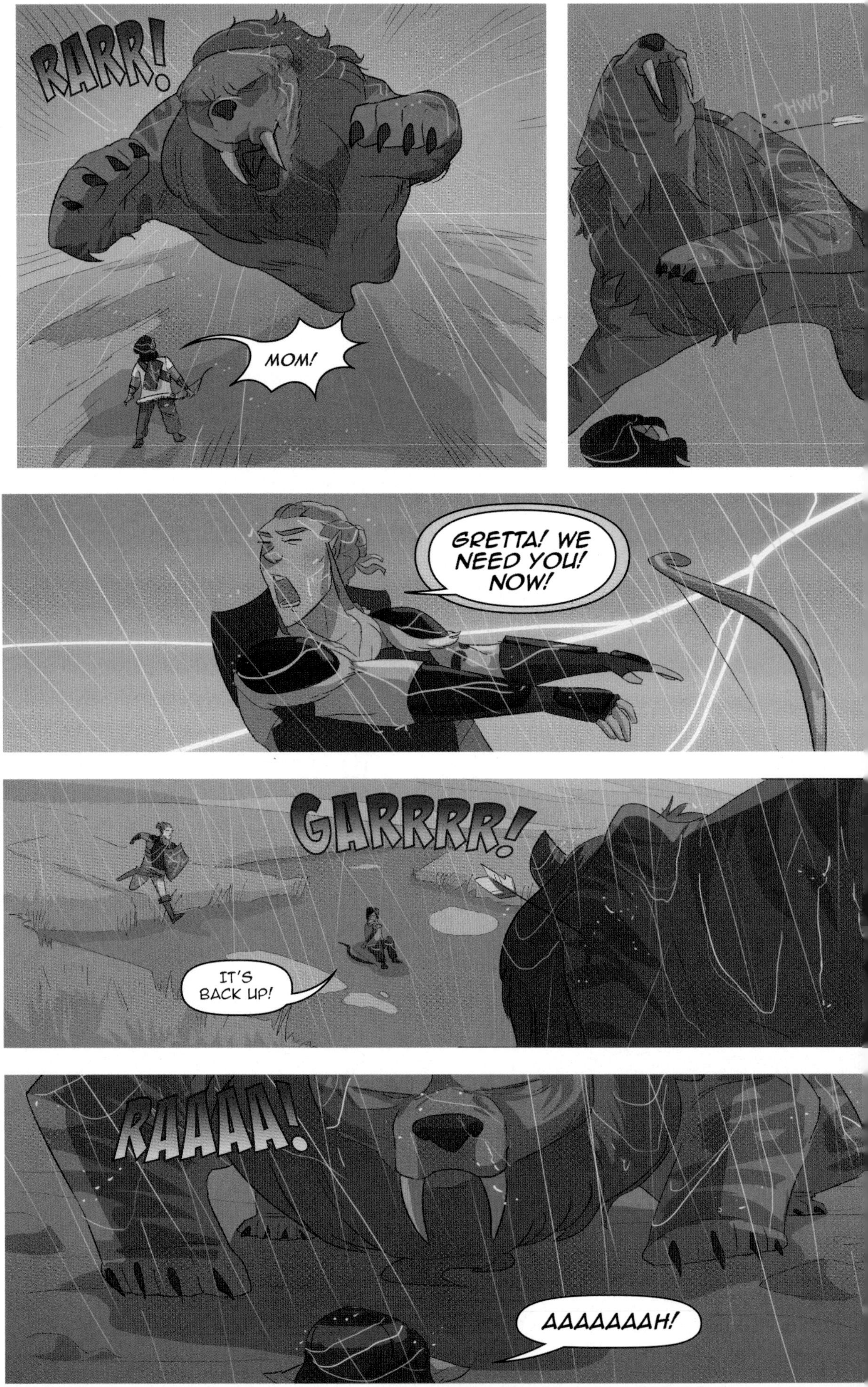
RARR!
MOM!
THWIP!
GRETTA! WE NEED YOU! NOW!
GARRRR!
IT'S BACK UP!
RAAAA!
AAAAAAAH!

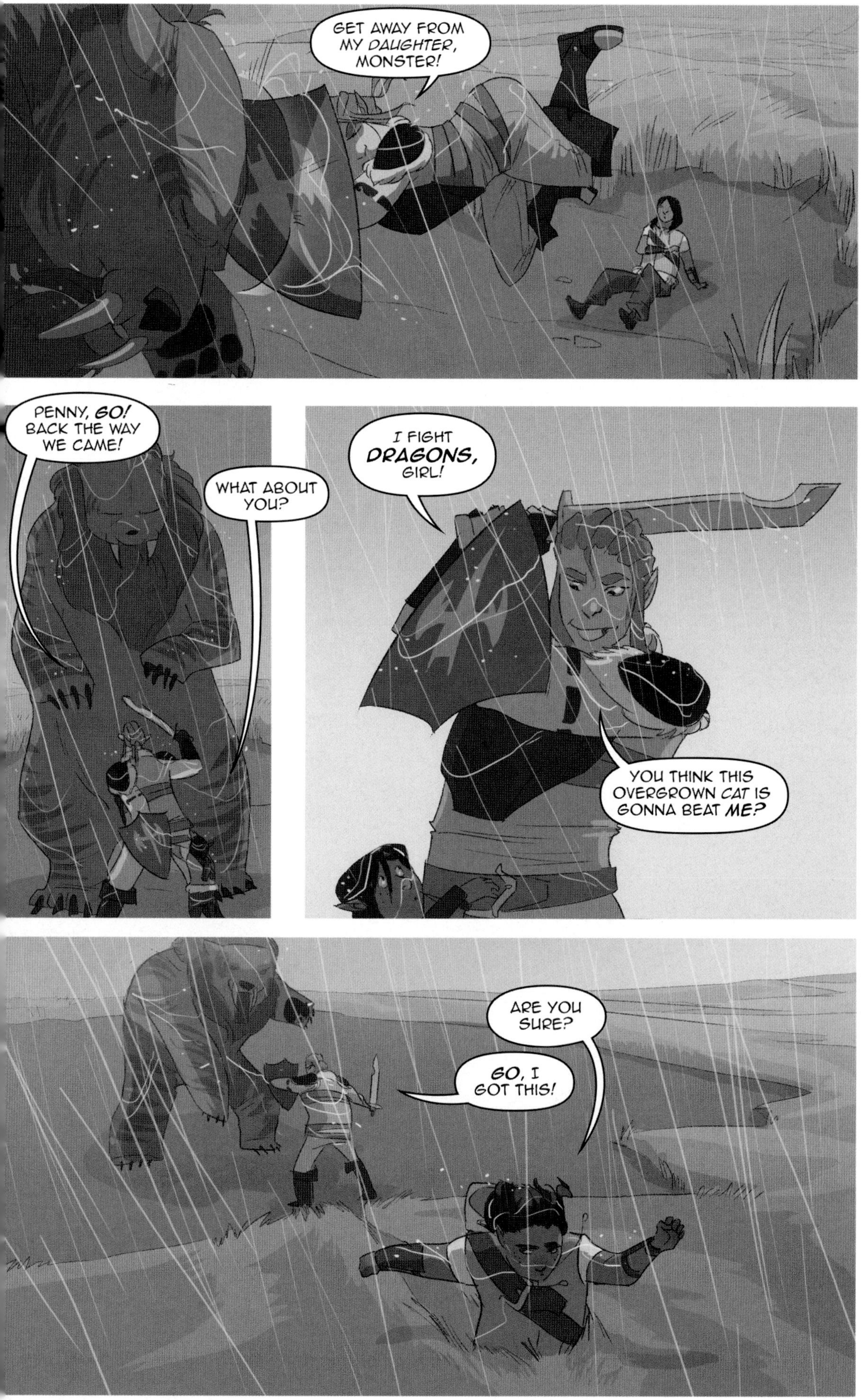
GET AWAY FROM MY DAUGHTER, MONSTER!
PENNY, GO! BACK THE WAY WE CAME!
WHAT ABOUT YOU?
I FIGHT DRAGONS, GIRL!
YOU THINK THIS OVERGROWN CAT IS GONNA BEAT ME?
ARE YOU SURE?
GO, I GOT THIS!

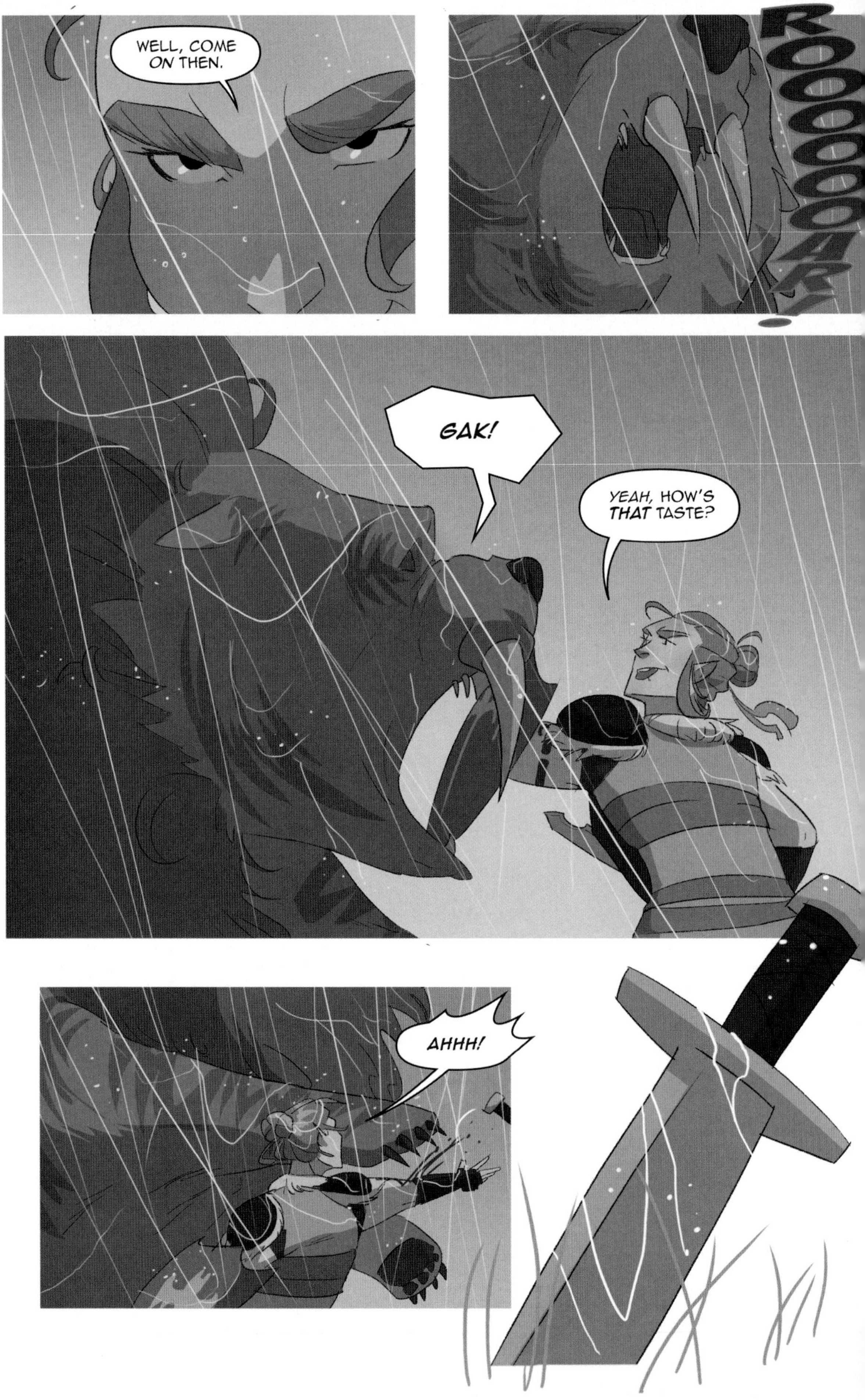
WELL, COME ON THEN.
ROOOOOOAR!
GAK!
YEAH, HOW'S *THAT* TASTE?
AHHH!

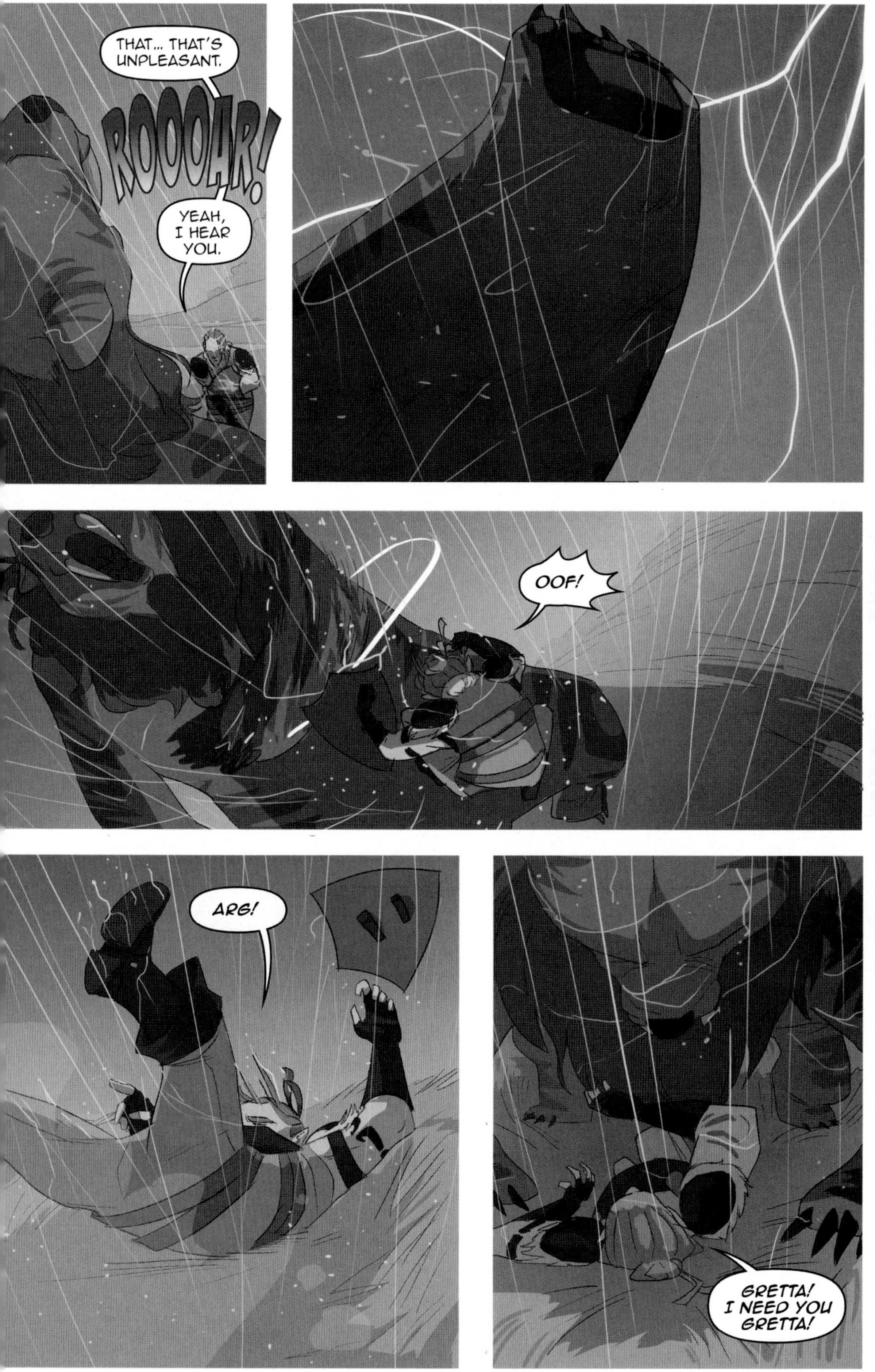
THAT... THAT'S UNPLEASANT.
ROOOAR!
YEAH, I HEAR YOU.
OOF!
ARG!
GRETTA! I NEED YOU GRETTA!

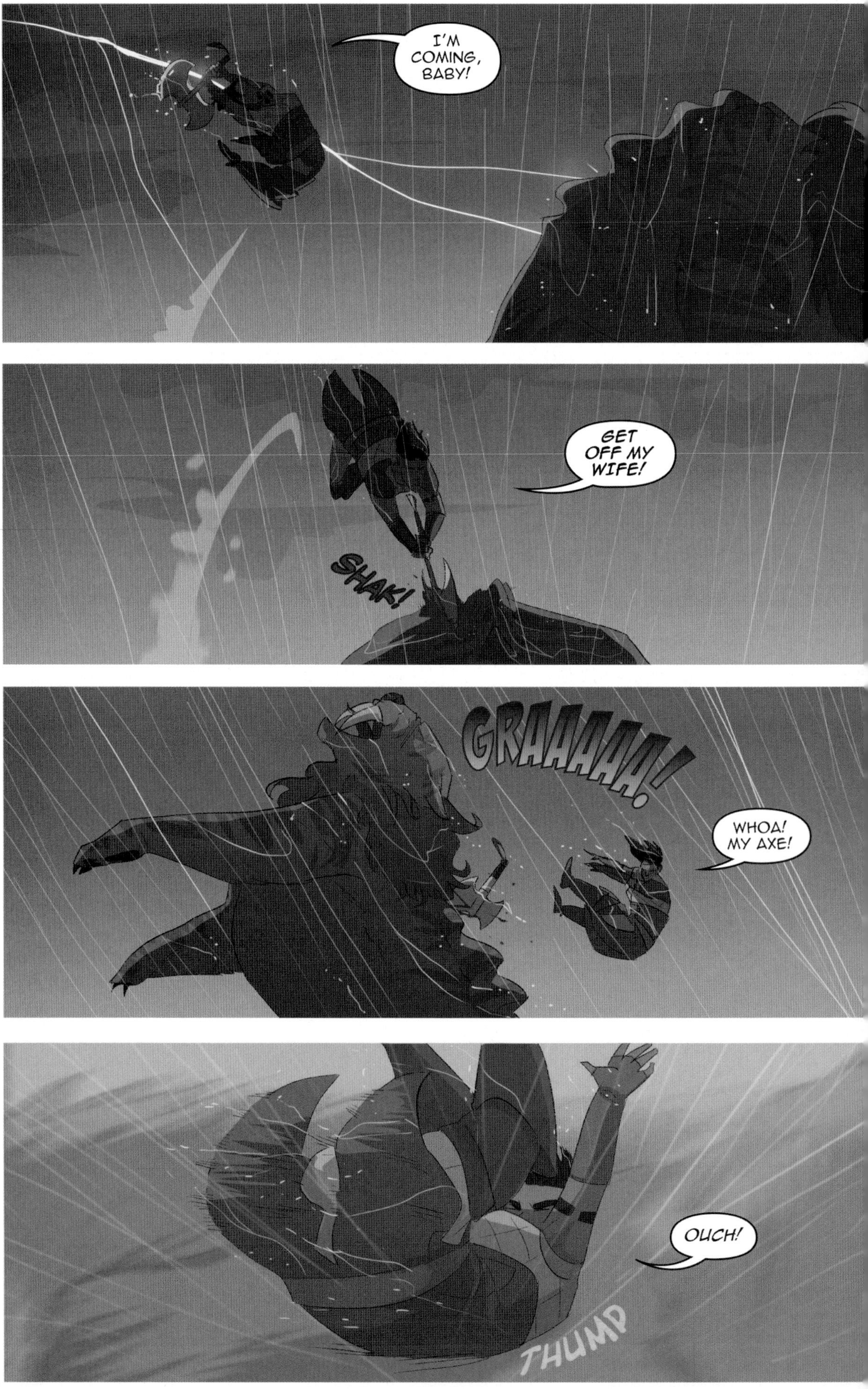
I'M COMING, BABY!
GET OFF MY WIFE!
SHAK!
GRAAAAA!
WHOA! MY AXE!
OUCH!
THUMP

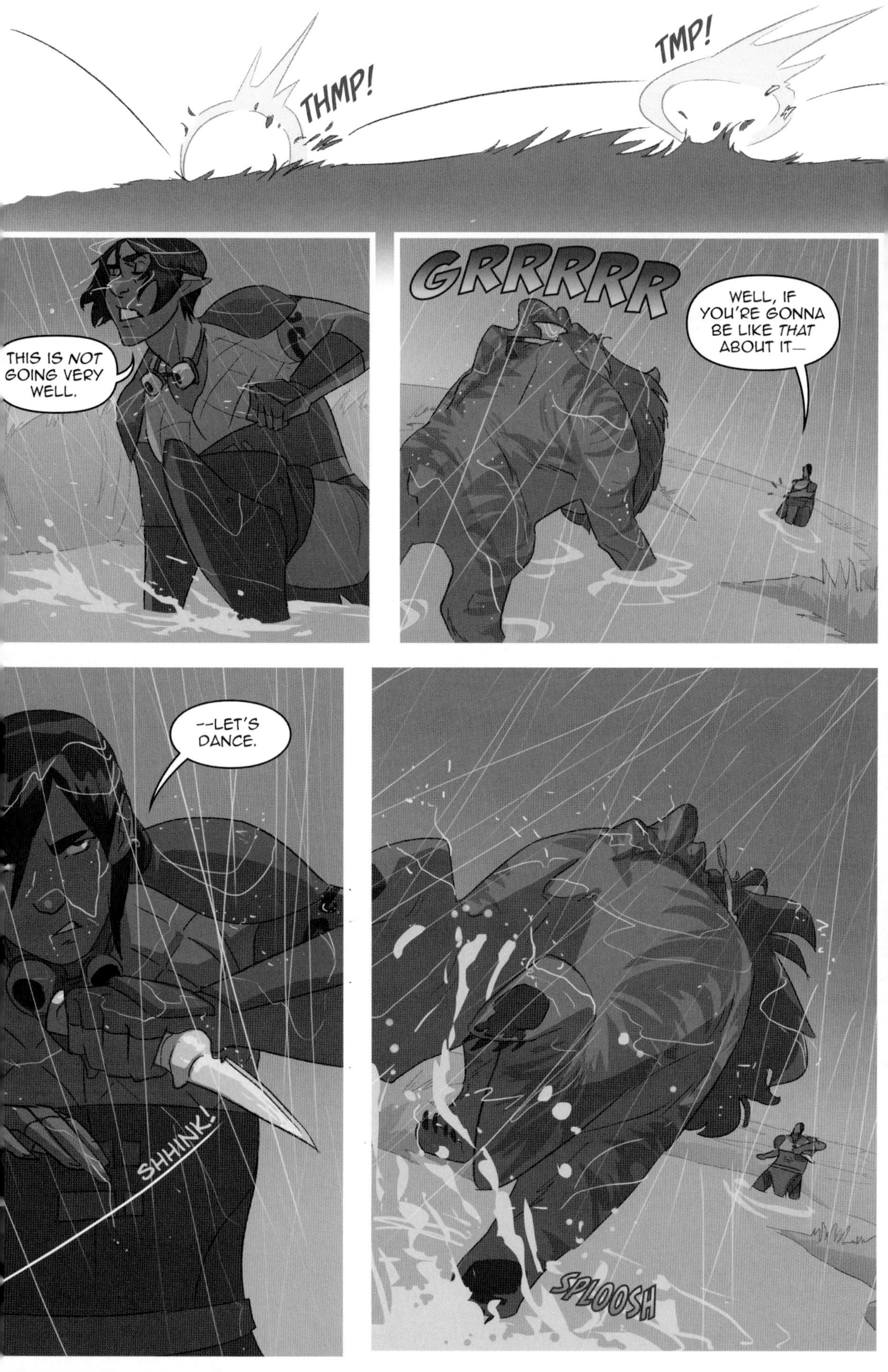
THMP!
TMP!
THIS IS NOT GOING VERY WELL.
GRRRRRR
WELL, IF YOU'RE GONNA BE LIKE THAT ABOUT IT—
--LET'S DANCE.
SHHINK!
SPLOOSH

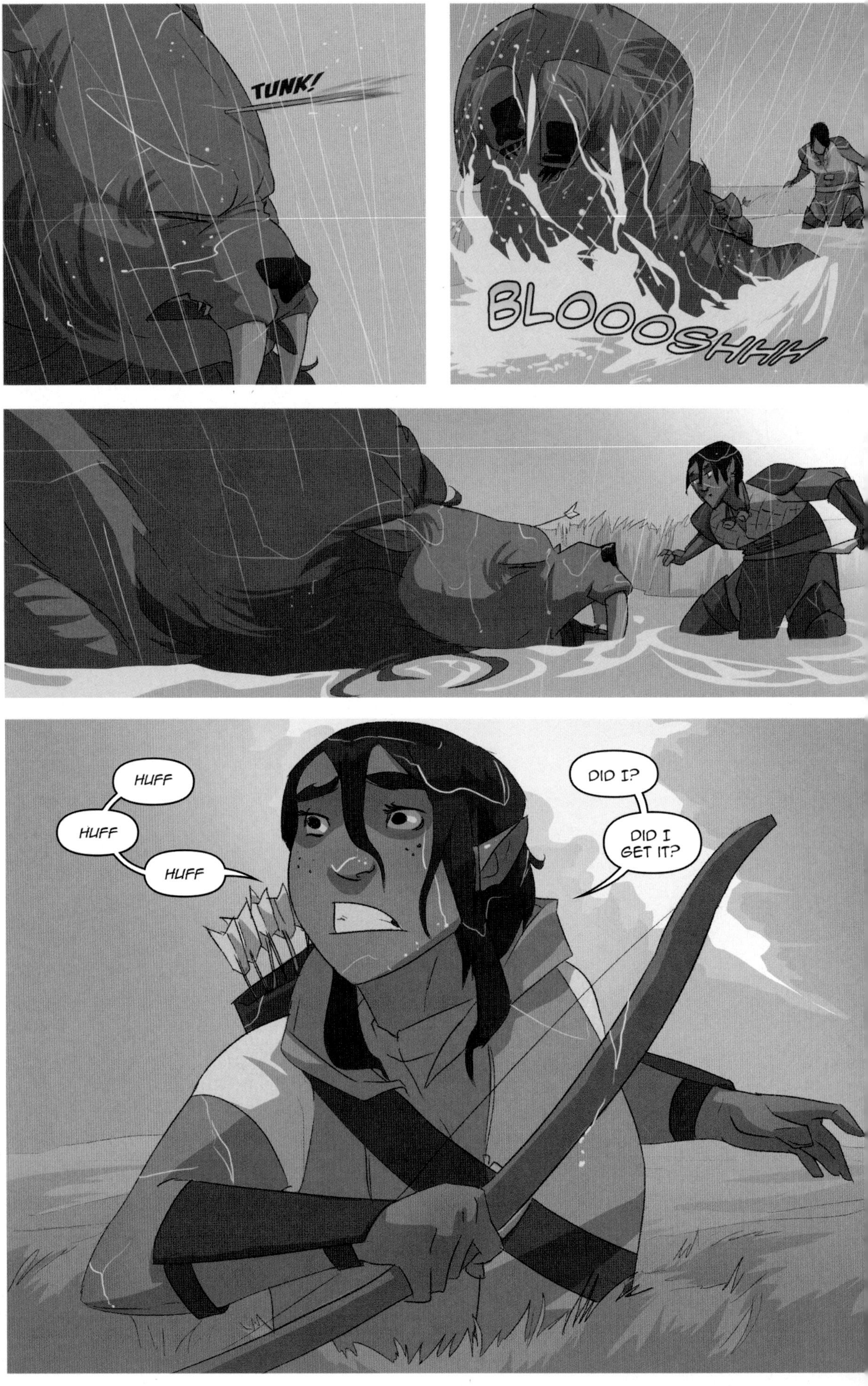
TUNK!
BLOOOSHHH
HUFF
HUFF
HUFF
DID I?
DID I GET IT?

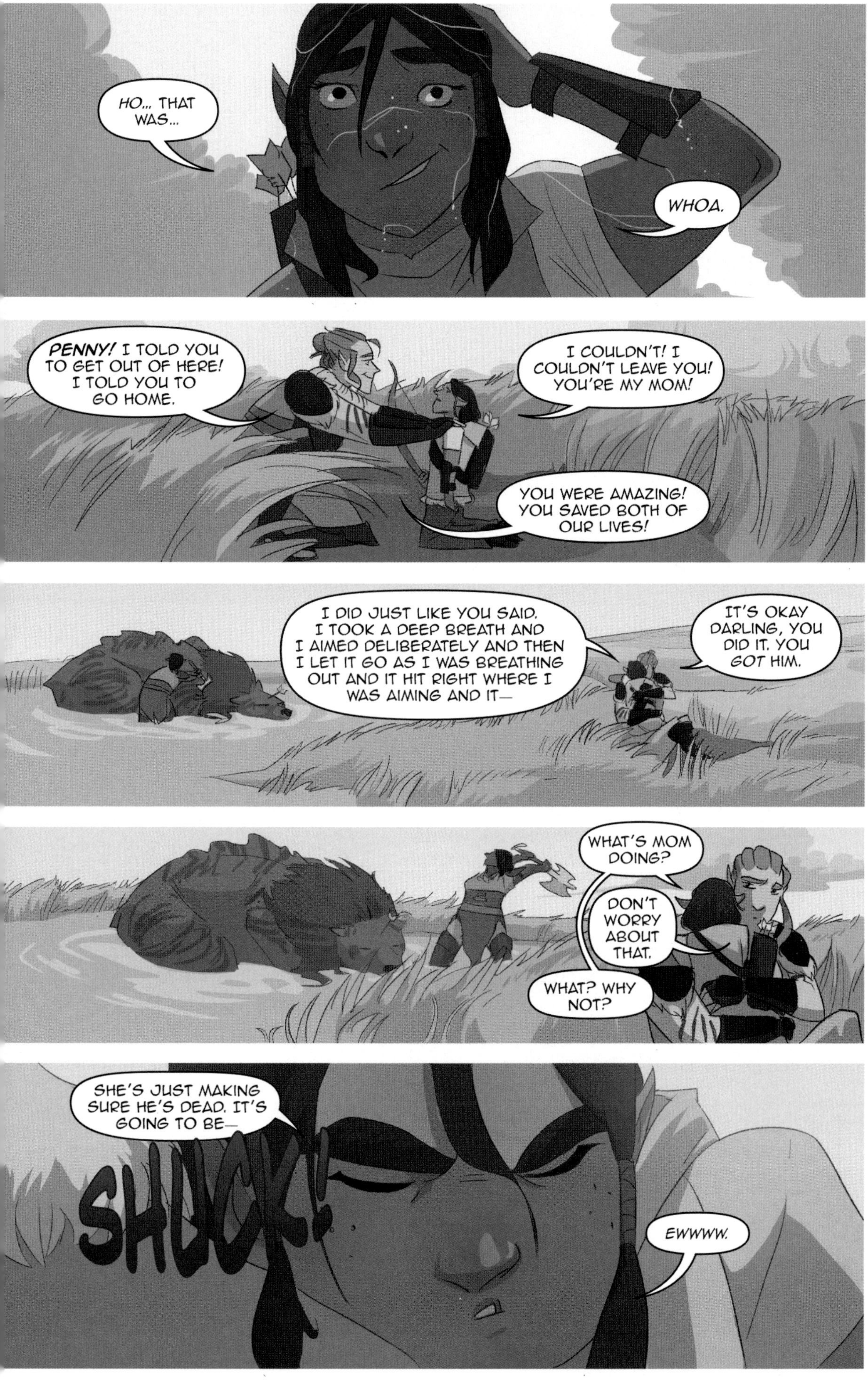
HO... THAT WAS...
WHOA.
PENNY! I TOLD YOU TO GET OUT OF HERE! I TOLD YOU TO GO HOME.
I COULDN'T! I COULDN'T LEAVE YOU! YOU'RE MY MOM!
YOU WERE AMAZING! YOU SAVED BOTH OF OUR LIVES!
I DID JUST LIKE YOU SAID. I TOOK A DEEP BREATH AND I AIMED DELIBERATELY AND THEN I LET IT GO AS I WAS BREATHING OUT AND IT HIT RIGHT WHERE I WAS AIMING AND IT—
IT'S OKAY DARLING, YOU DID IT. YOU GOT HIM.
WHAT'S MOM DOING?
DON'T WORRY ABOUT THAT.
WHAT? WHY NOT?
SHE'S JUST MAKING SURE HE'S DEAD. IT'S GOING TO BE—
SHUCK!
EWWWW.

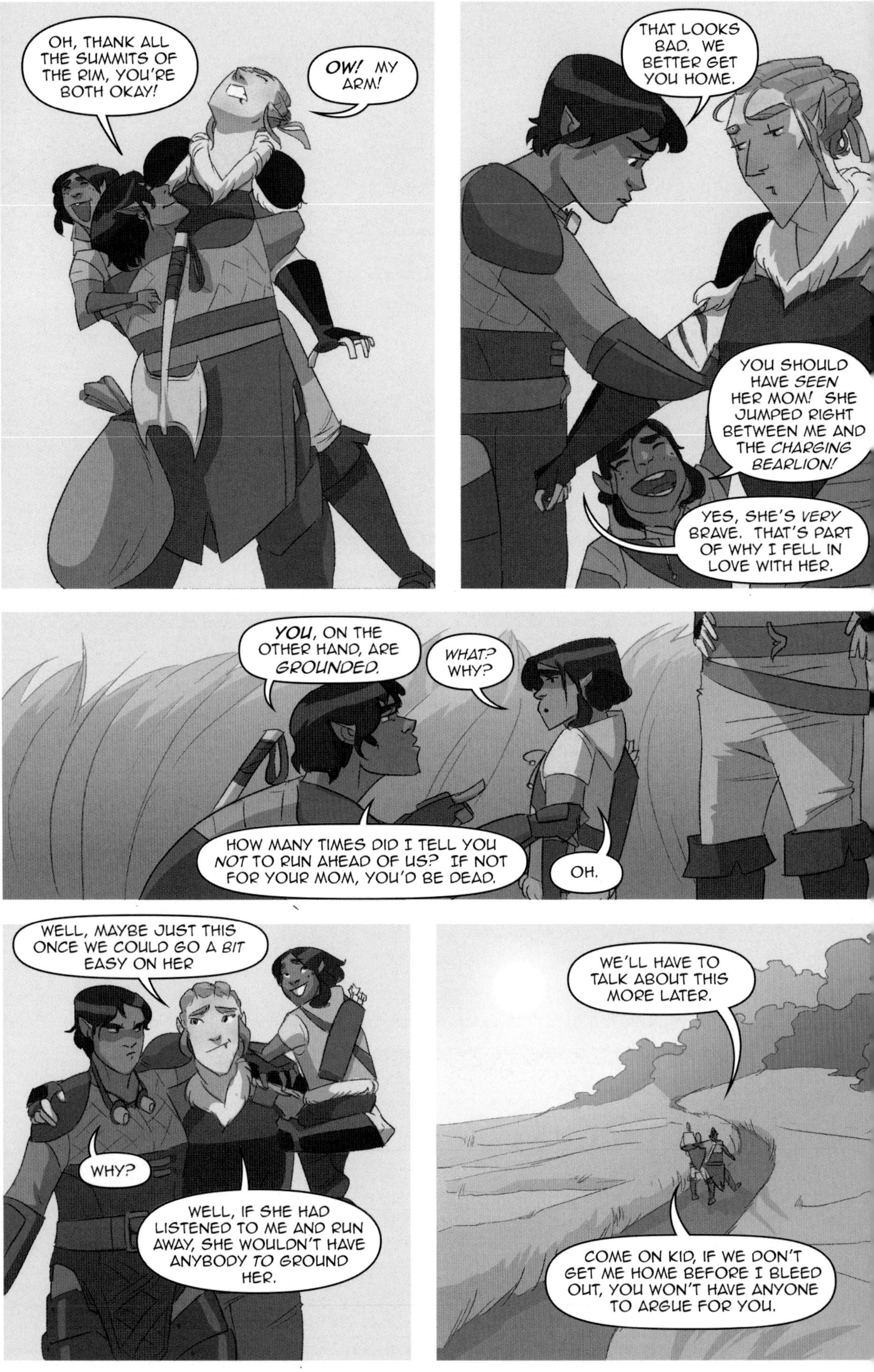
OH, THANK ALL THE SUMMITS OF THE RIM, YOU'RE BOTH OKAY!
OW! MY ARM!
THAT LOOKS BAD. WE BETTER GET YOU HOME.
YOU SHOULD HAVE *SEEN* HER MOM! SHE JUMPED RIGHT BETWEEN ME AND THE *CHARGING BEARLION!*
YES, SHE'S *VERY* BRAVE. THAT'S PART OF WHY I FELL IN LOVE WITH HER.
YOU, ON THE OTHER HAND, ARE *GROUNDED.*
WHAT? WHY?
HOW MANY TIMES DID I TELL YOU *NOT* TO RUN AHEAD OF US? IF NOT FOR YOUR MOM, YOU'D BE DEAD.
OH.
WELL, MAYBE JUST THIS ONCE WE COULD GO A *BIT* EASY ON HER
WHY?
WELL, IF SHE HAD LISTENED TO ME AND RUN AWAY, SHE WOULDN'T HAVE ANYBODY *TO* GROUND HER.
WE'LL HAVE TO TALK ABOUT THIS MORE LATER.
COME ON KID, IF WE DON'T GET ME HOME BEFORE I BLEED OUT, YOU WON'T HAVE ANYONE TO ARGUE FOR YOU.

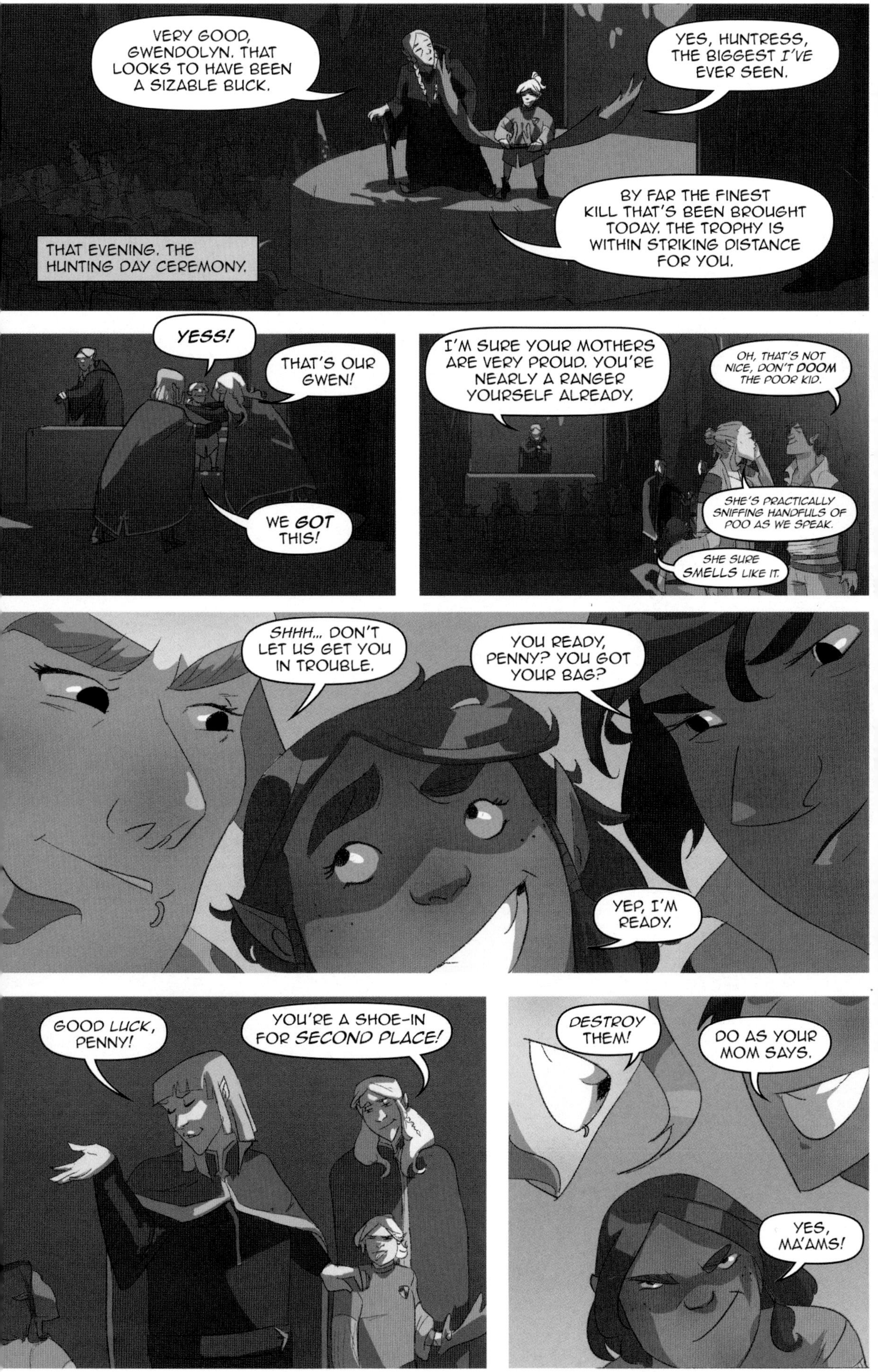

VERY GOOD, GWENDOLYN. THAT LOOKS TO HAVE BEEN A SIZABLE BUCK.
YES, HUNTRESS, THE BIGGEST I'VE EVER SEEN.
THAT EVENING. THE HUNTING DAY CEREMONY.
BY FAR THE FINEST KILL THAT'S BEEN BROUGHT TODAY. THE TROPHY IS WITHIN STRIKING DISTANCE FOR YOU.
YESS!
THAT'S OUR GWEN!
WE GOT THIS!
I'M SURE YOUR MOTHERS ARE VERY PROUD. YOU'RE NEARLY A RANGER YOURSELF ALREADY.
OH, THAT'S NOT NICE, DON'T DOOM THE POOR KID.
SHE'S PRACTICALLY SNIFFING HANDFULS OF POO AS WE SPEAK.
SHE SURE SMELLS LIKE IT.
SHHH... DON'T LET US GET YOU IN TROUBLE.
YOU READY, PENNY? YOU GOT YOUR BAG?
YEP, I'M READY.
GOOD LUCK, PENNY!
YOU'RE A SHOE-IN FOR SECOND PLACE!
DESTROY THEM!
DO AS YOUR MOM SAYS.
YES, MA'AMS!

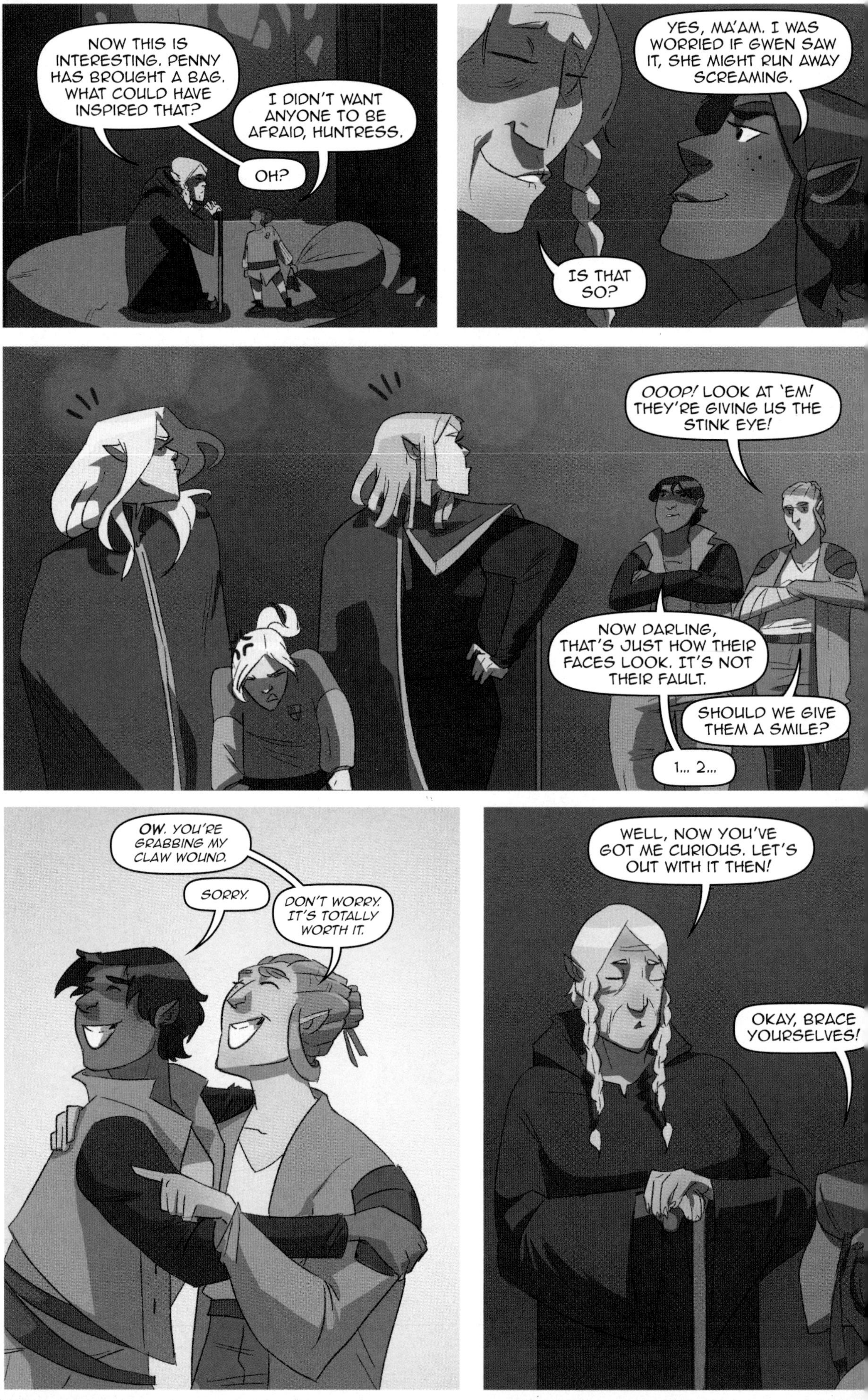
NOW THIS IS INTERESTING. PENNY HAS BROUGHT A BAG. WHAT COULD HAVE INSPIRED THAT?
I DIDN'T WANT ANYONE TO BE AFRAID, HUNTRESS.
OH?
YES, MA'AM. I WAS WORRIED IF GWEN SAW IT, SHE MIGHT RUN AWAY SCREAMING.
IS THAT SO?
OOOP! LOOK AT 'EM! THEY'RE GIVING US THE STINK EYE!
NOW DARLING, THAT'S JUST HOW THEIR FACES LOOK. IT'S NOT THEIR FAULT.
SHOULD WE GIVE THEM A SMILE?
1... 2...
OW. YOU'RE GRABBING MY CLAW WOUND.
SORRY.
DON'T WORRY. IT'S TOTALLY WORTH IT.
WELL, NOW YOU'VE GOT ME CURIOUS. LET'S OUT WITH IT THEN!
OKAY, BRACE YOURSELVES!

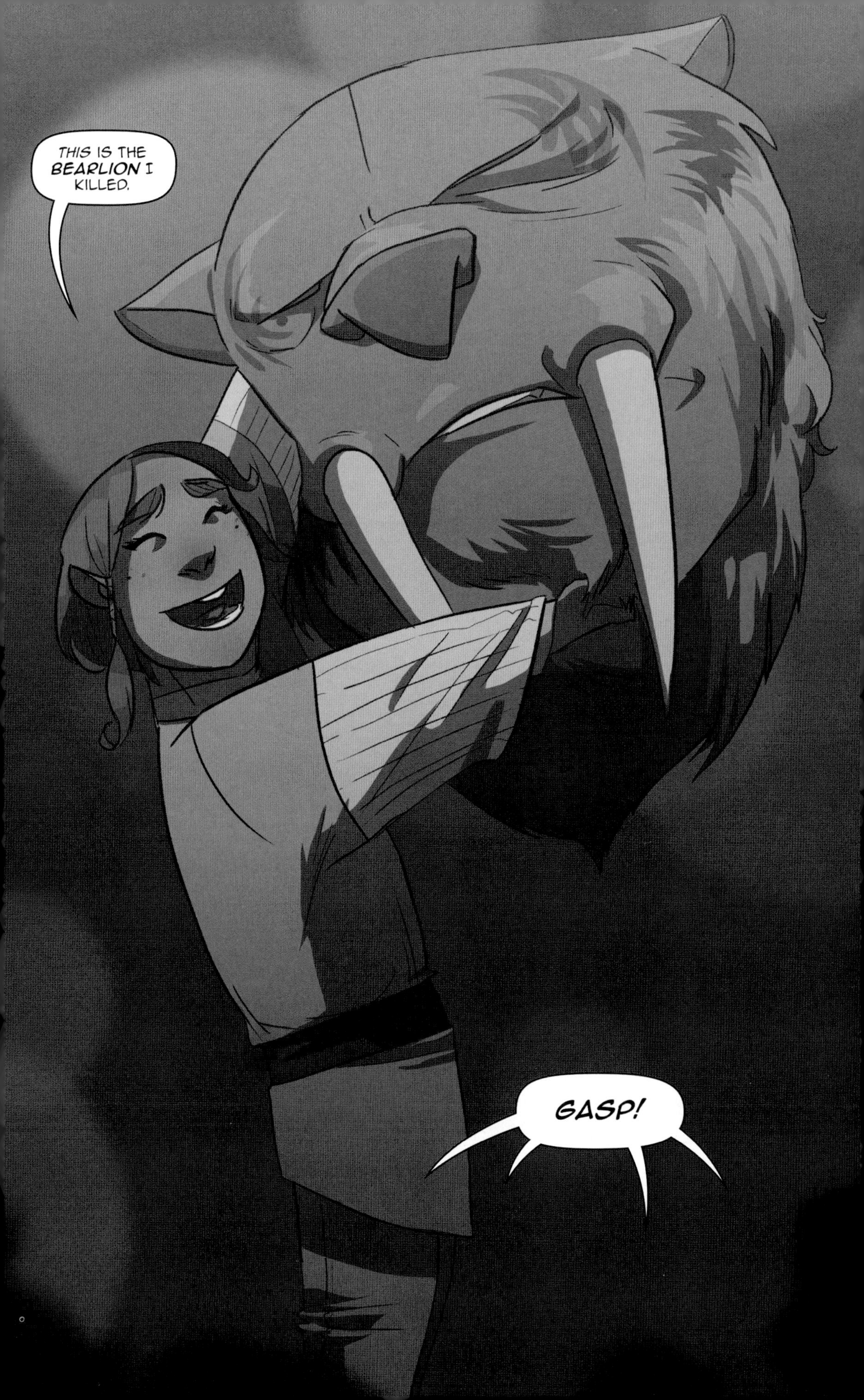
THIS IS THE BEARLION I KILLED.
GASP!

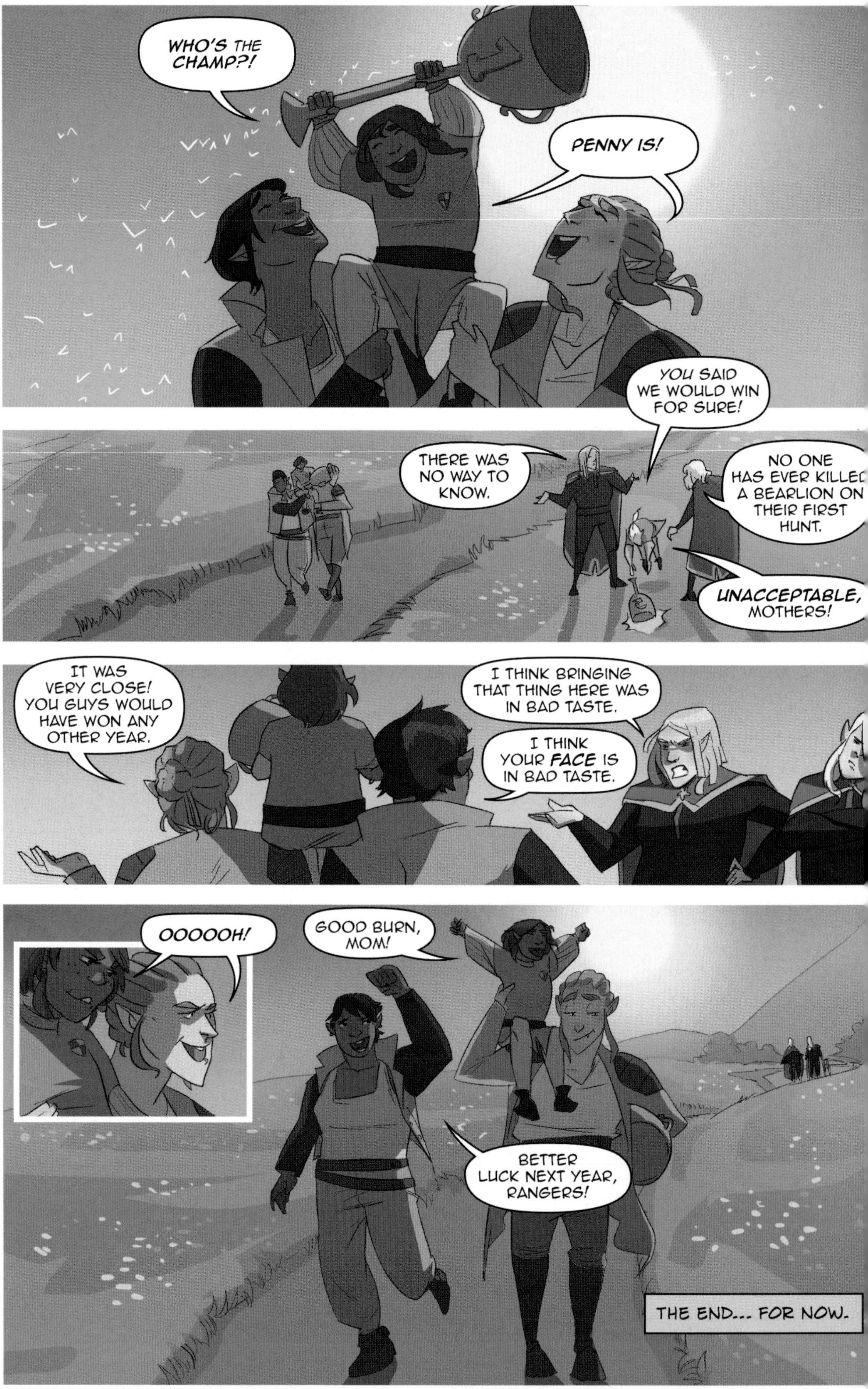
WHO'S THE CHAMP?!
PENNY IS!
YOU SAID WE WOULD WIN FOR SURE!
THERE WAS NO WAY TO KNOW.
NO ONE HAS EVER KILLED A BEARLION ON THEIR FIRST HUNT.
UNACCEPTABLE, MOTHERS!
IT WAS VERY CLOSE! YOU GUYS WOULD HAVE WON ANY OTHER YEAR.
I THINK BRINGING THAT THING HERE WAS IN BAD TASTE.
I THINK YOUR FACE IS IN BAD TASTE.
OOOOOH!
GOOD BURN, MOM!
BETTER LUCK NEXT YEAR, RANGERS!
THE END... FOR NOW.

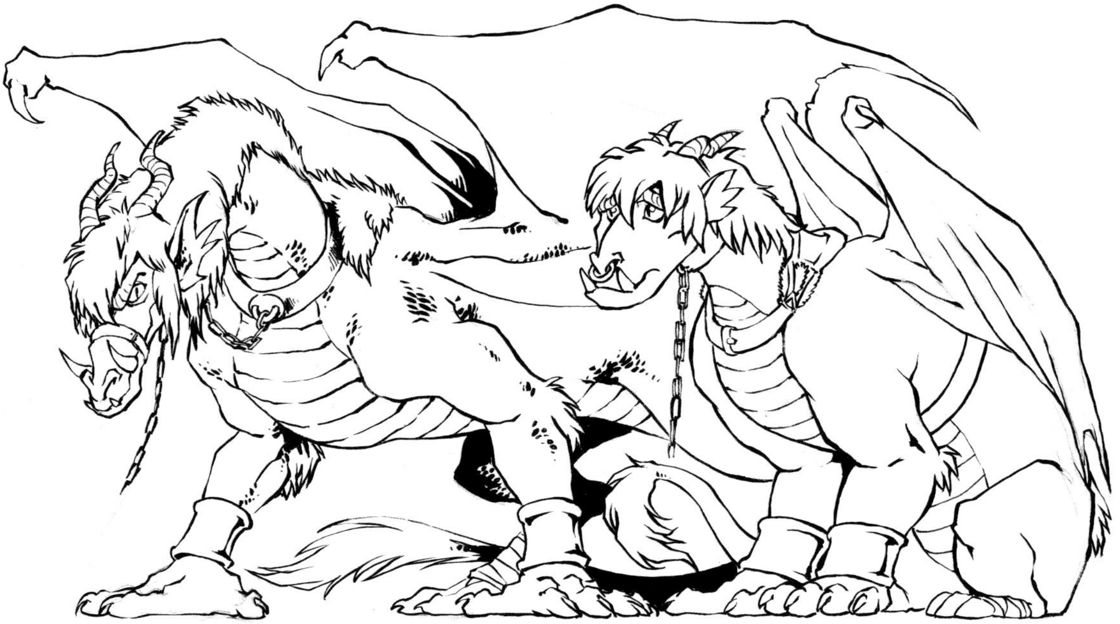

GOLDY AND SPARKY REFERENCE
BY EMILY MARTIN

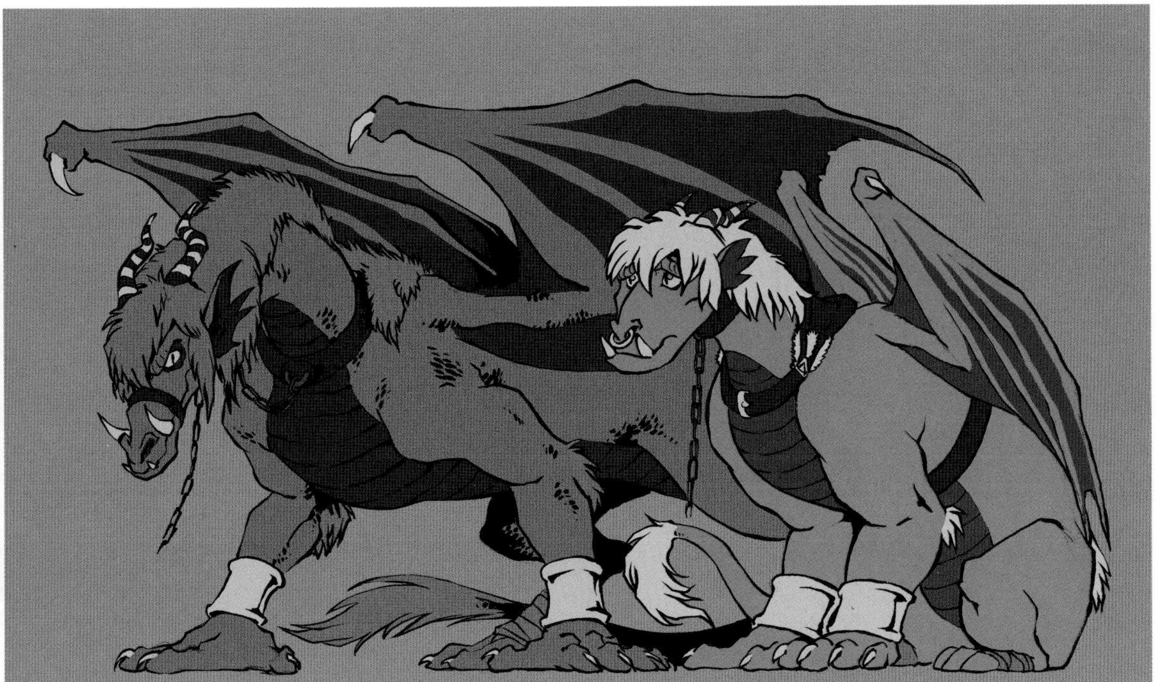

GOLDY AND SPARKY COLOR KEY
COLORS BY BRETT GRUNIG

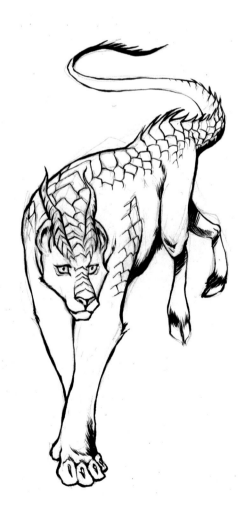

CONNIE CHIMERA AND GRANT GRYPHON
REFERENCE AND SKETCHES WITH ABRAHAM
BY EMILY MARTIN

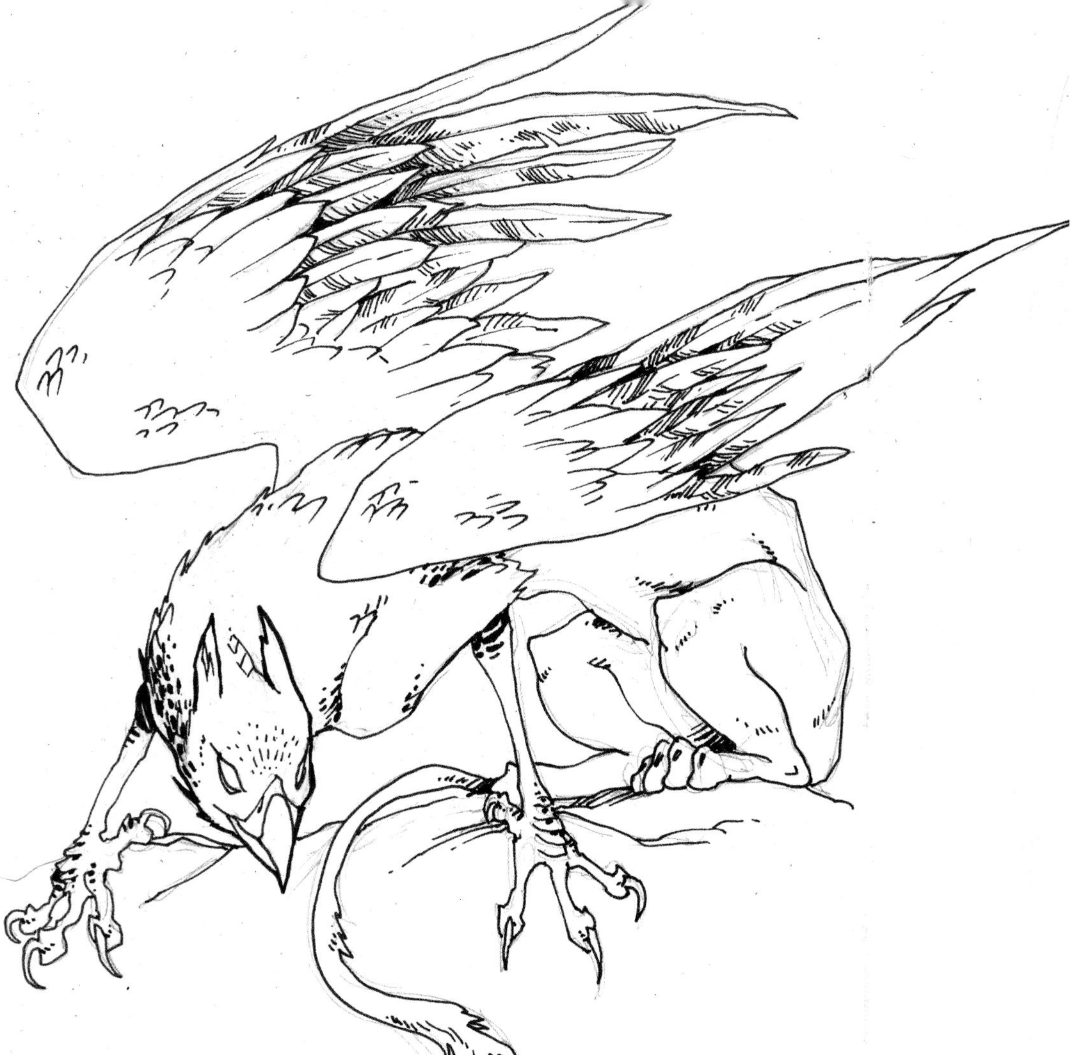

GRANT SKETCH AND ABRAHAM REFERENCE
BY EMILY MARTIN, COLORS BY BRETT GRUNIG

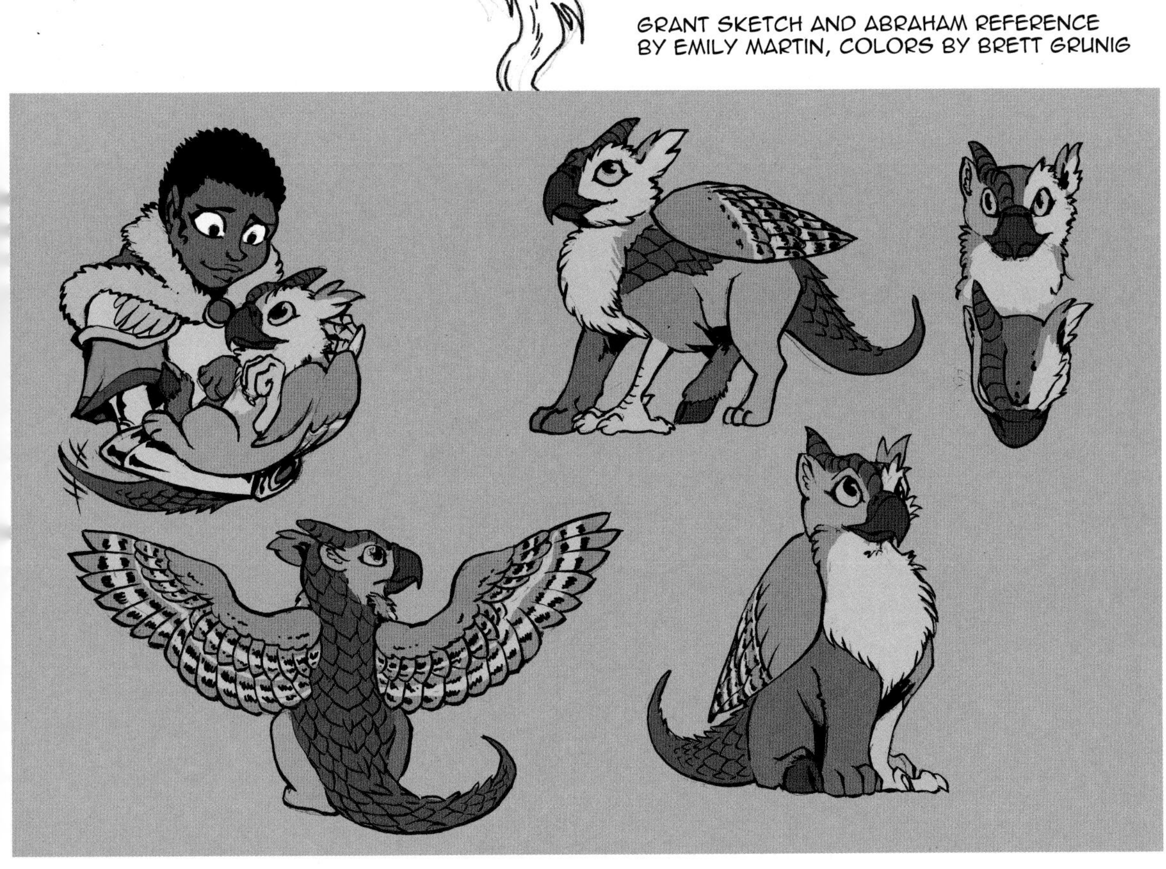

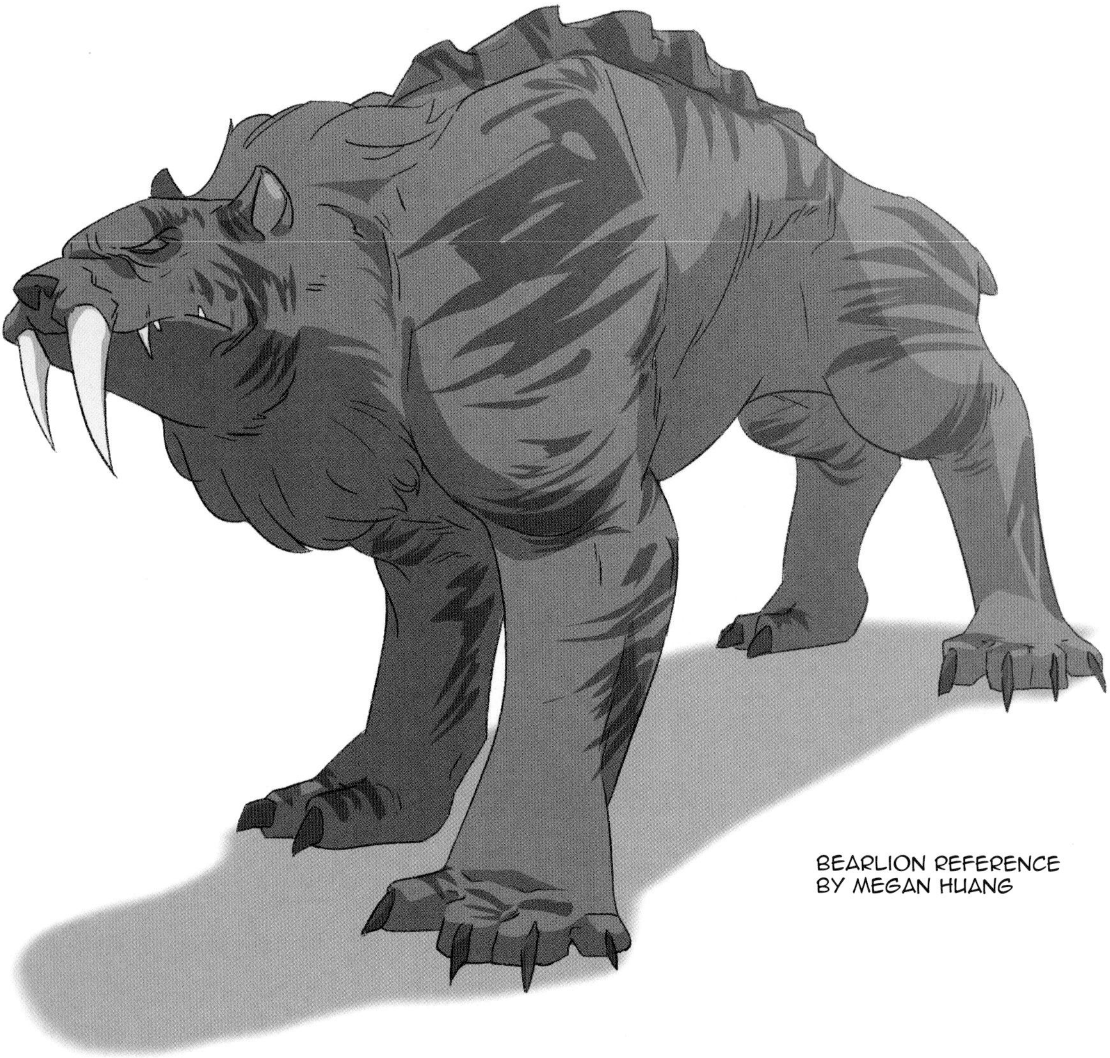

BEARLION REFERENCE
BY MEGAN HUANG

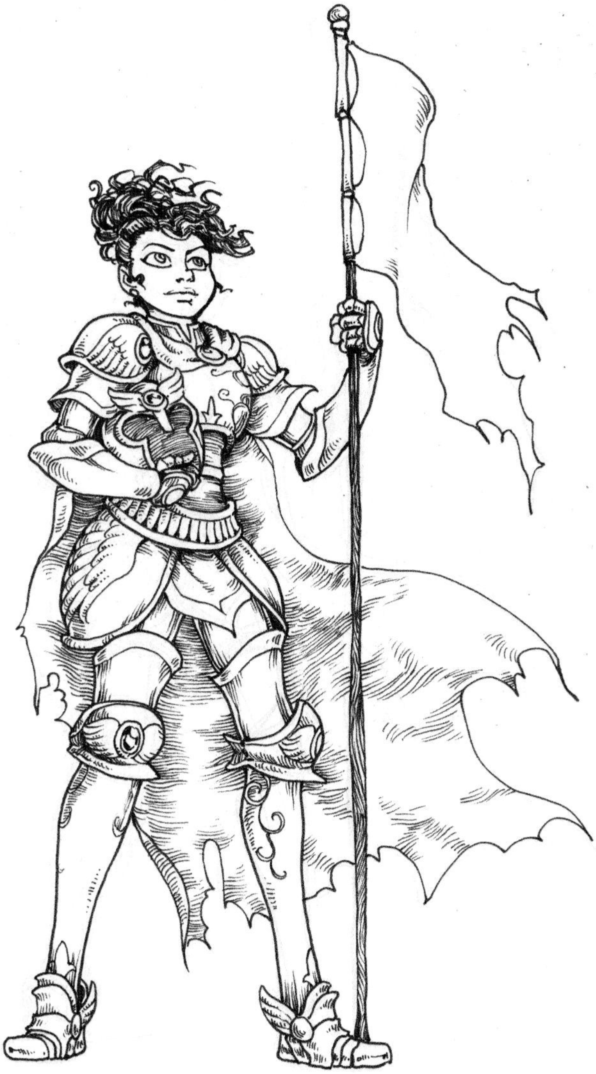

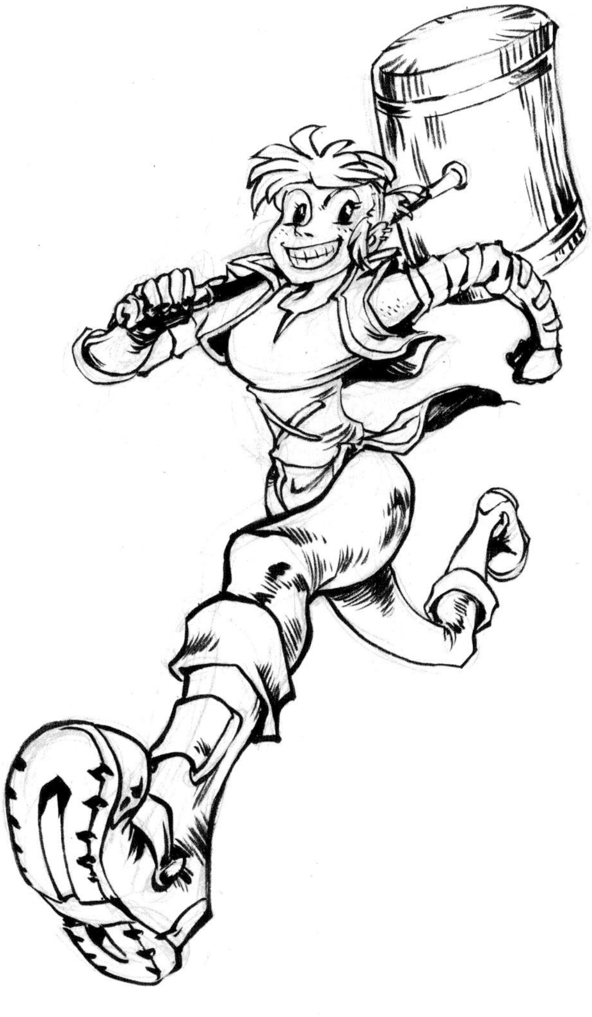

ADRIENNE AND BEDELIA
SKETCHES: INKTOBER 2015
BY EMILY MARTIN

NOTE: CHECK YOUR SOCIAL MEDIA FOR #INKTOBER EVERY OCTOBER FOR ALL THE AMAZING ARTWORK BY ARTISTS PARTICIPATING IN THE INKTOBER ART CHALLENGE!

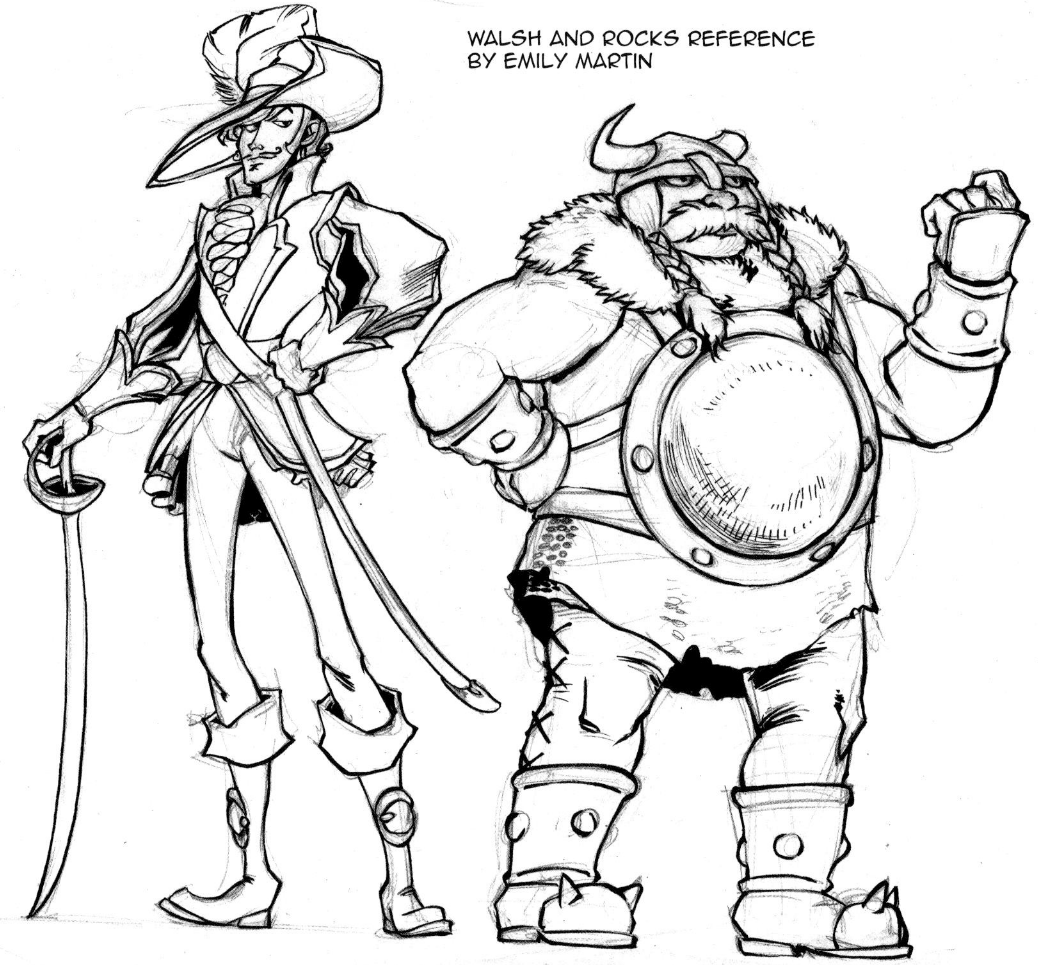

WALSH AND ROCKS REFERENCE
BY EMILY MARTIN

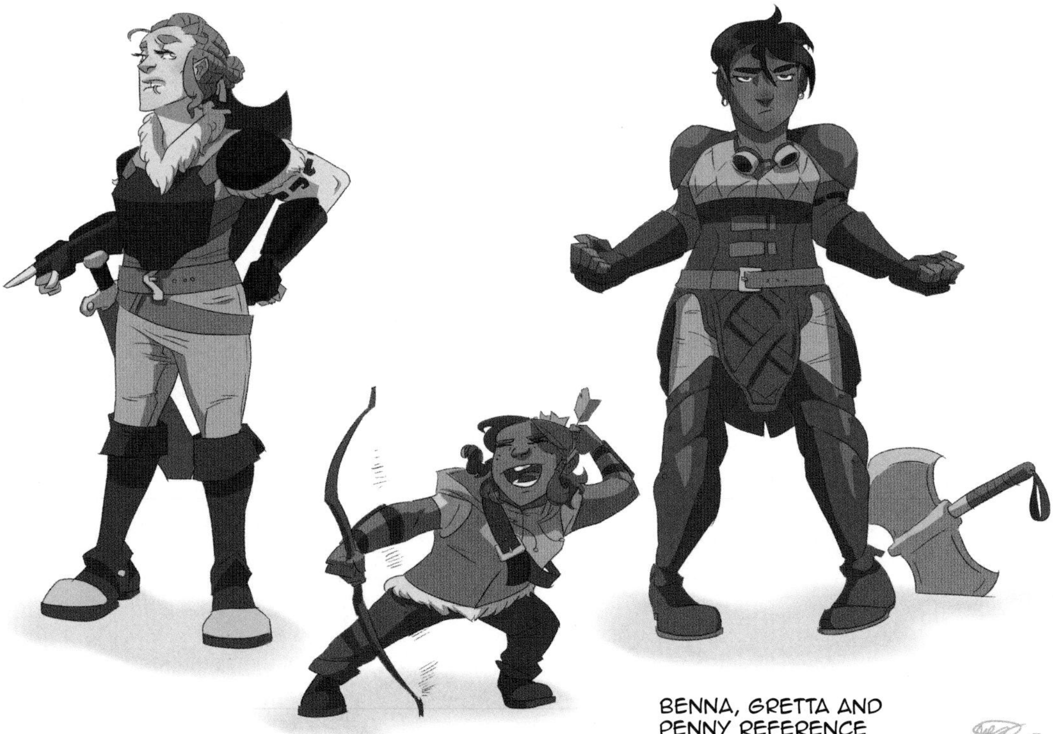

BENNA, GRETTA AND
PENNY REFERENCE
BY MEGAN HUANG

"HUNTING DAY/WIVES"
COVER LAYOUT
BY MEGAN HUANG

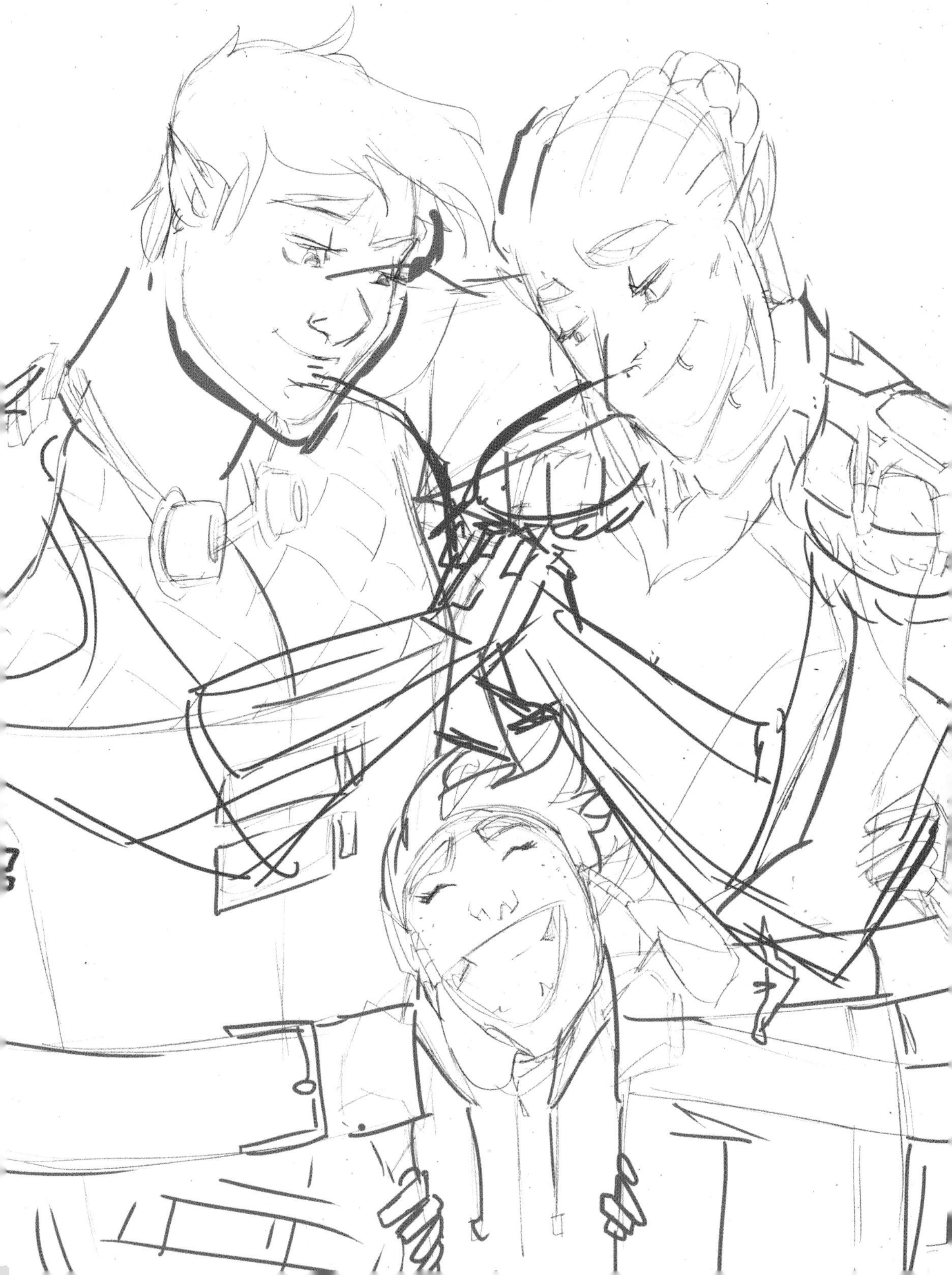

"HUNTING DAY/WIVES"
COVER INKS
BY MEGAN HUANG

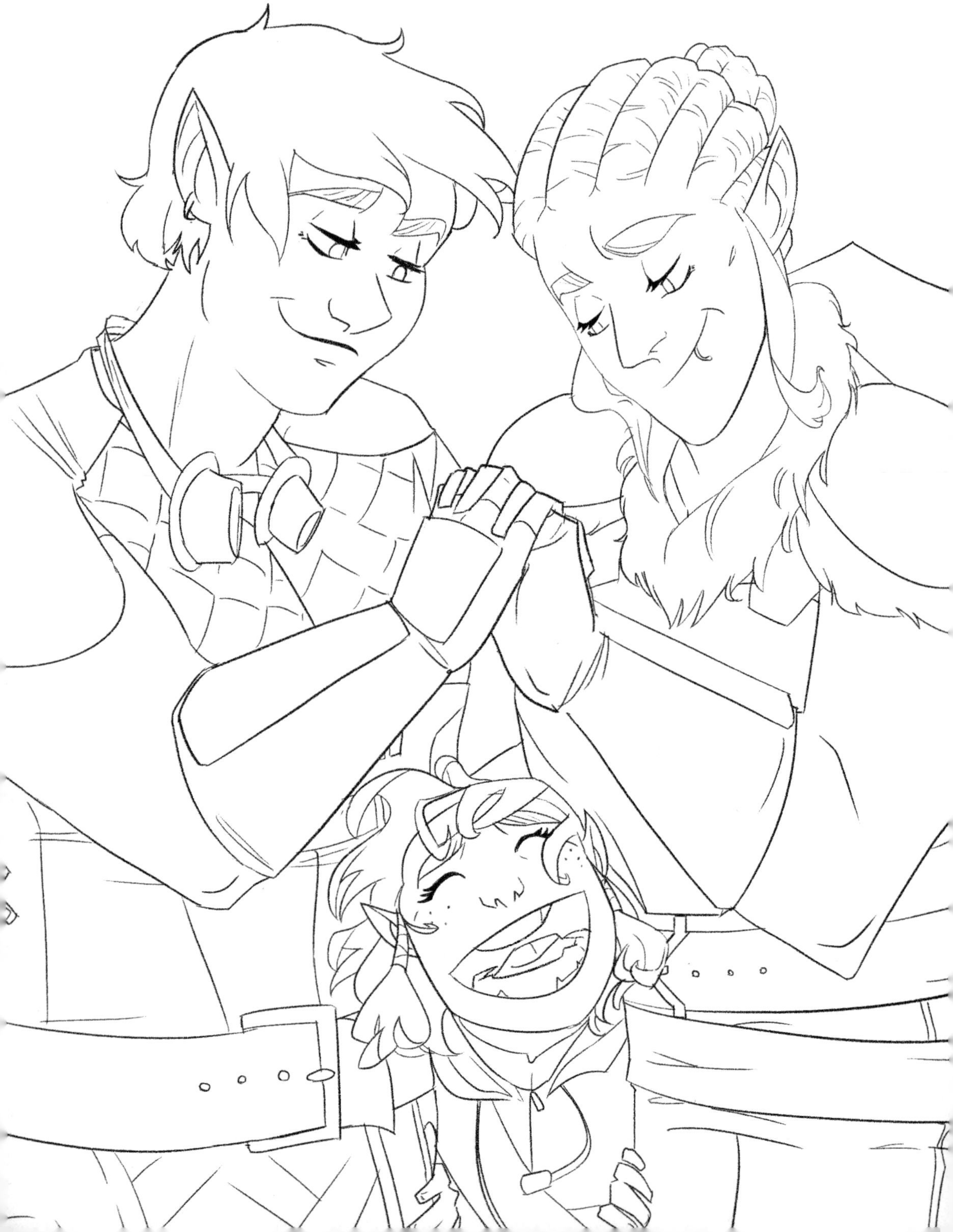

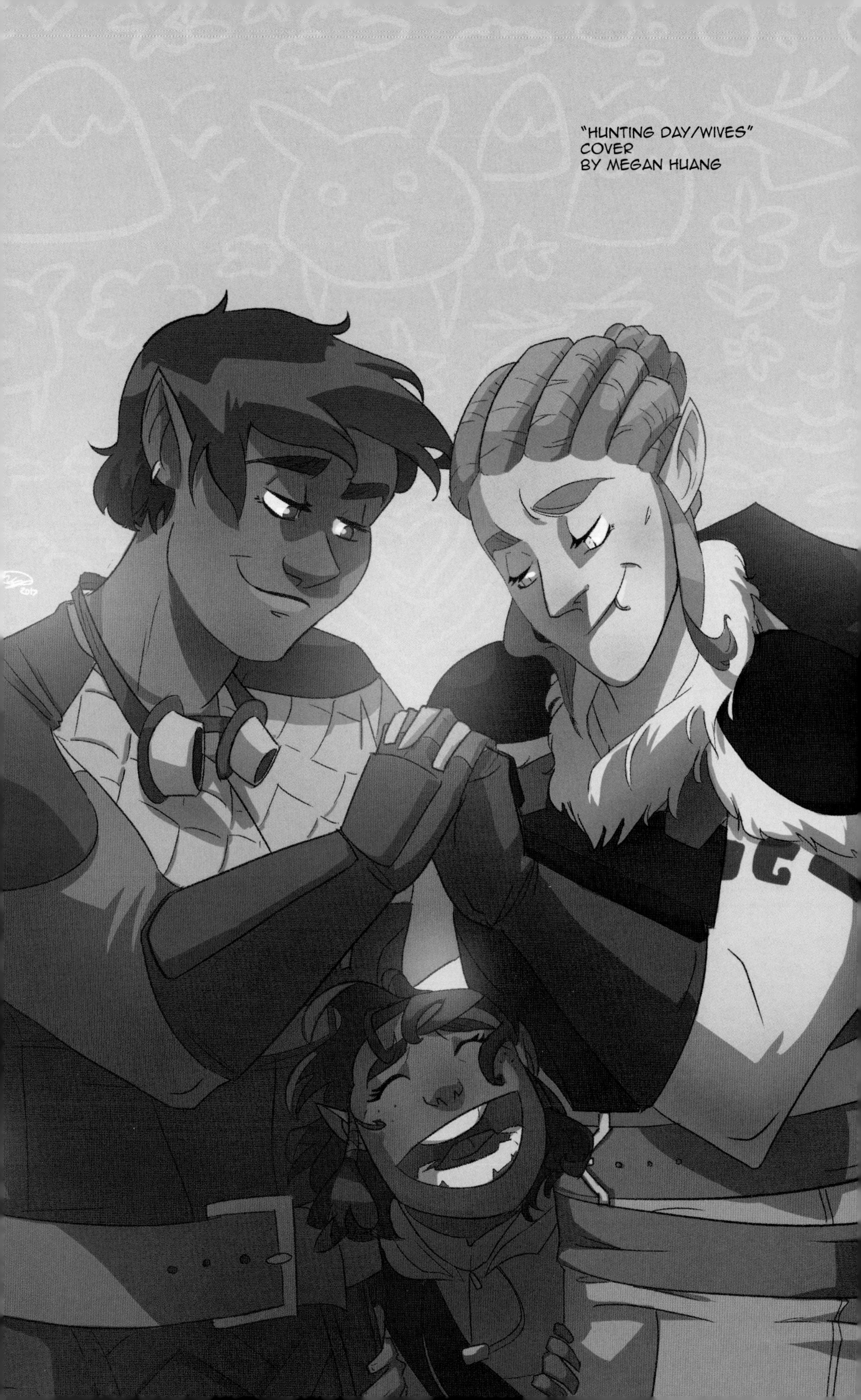

"HUNTING DAY/WIVES"
COVER
BY MEGAN HUANG

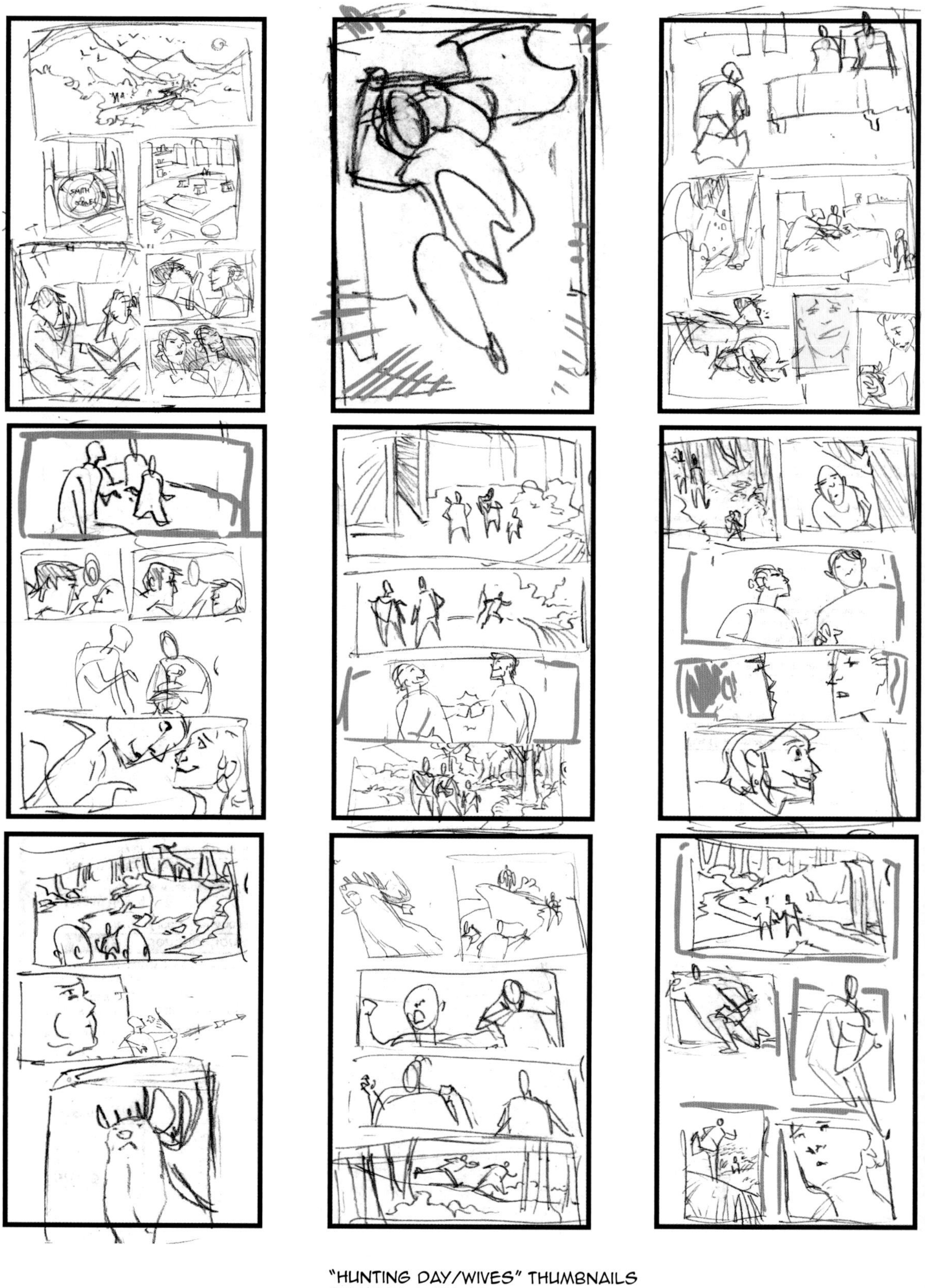

"HUNTING DAY/WIVES" THUMBNAILS
BY MEGAN HUANG

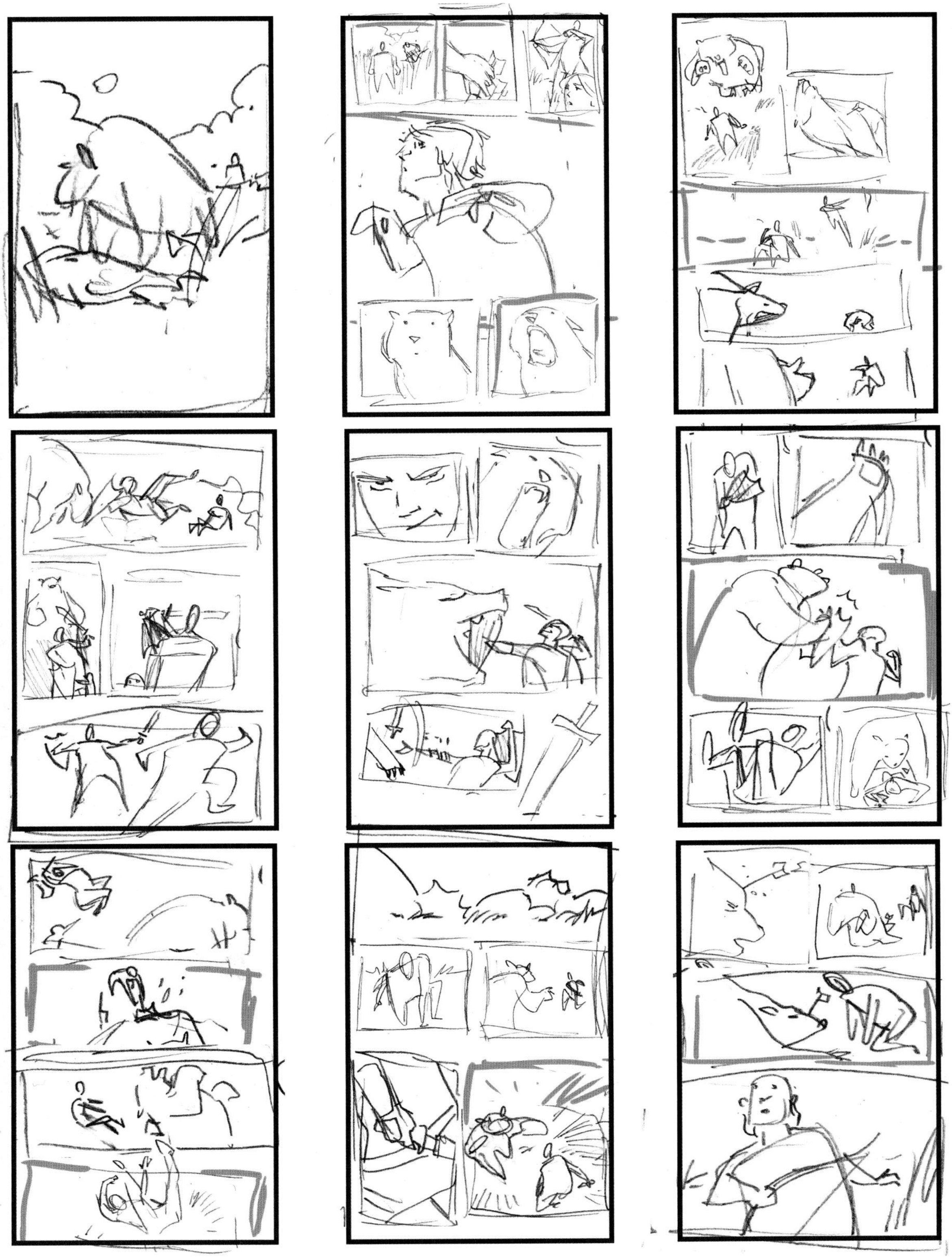

"HUNTING DAY/WIVES" THUMBNAILS
BY MEGAN HUANG

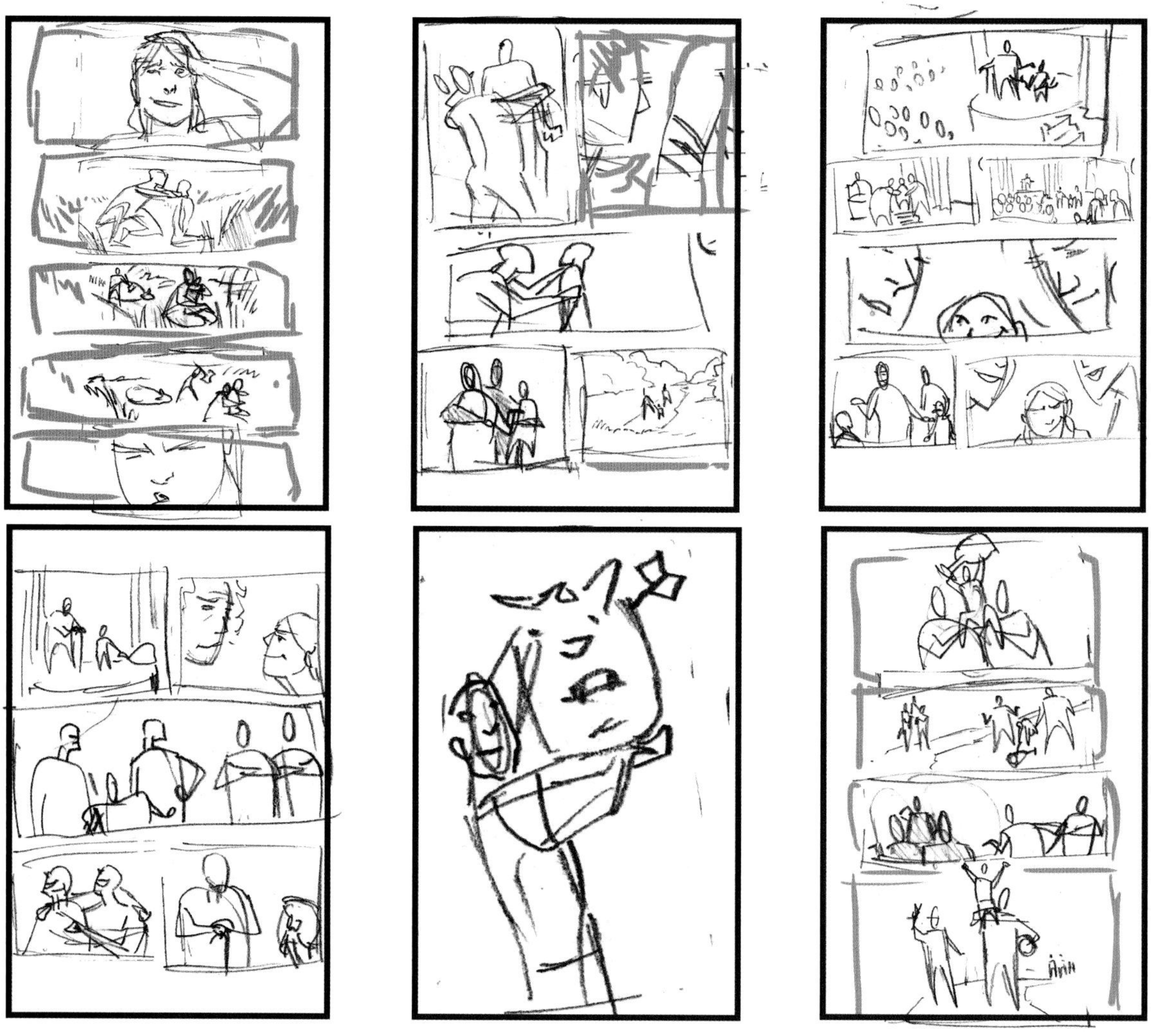

"HUNTING DAY/WIVES" THUMBNAILS
BY MEGAN HUANG

Page 18: (5 panels)

Panel 1: Adrienne talks to Benna, who she thinks is right behind her.

ADRIENNE
You know, I'm thinking maybe we just leave these two. What do you think Benna?

Panel 2: Adrienne turns around.

ADRIENNE
Benna?

Panel 3: Behind Adrienne stands Rocks and Walsh, looking a bit worse for wear. They have Benna tied up. Walsh holds Abraham in his hand.

WALSH
Well hello again, little princess. I can't believe I didn't recognize you before. The hair threw me the first time.

ADRIENNE
Put Abraham down and let them go!

WALSH
Oh, I don't want to hurt the little guy. Not as long as we get what we need.

Panel 4: Adrienne puts her arms out for them to take her.

ADRIENNE
Fine, go ahead, take me! Take me back to my father and claim your reward.

WALSH
Oh, that's a noble move. I didn't expect that from you.

Panel 5: Adrienne looks startled.

ADRIENNE
It was, wasn't it? I didn't even think about it. I was just going to give myself up.

WALSH
Impressive--

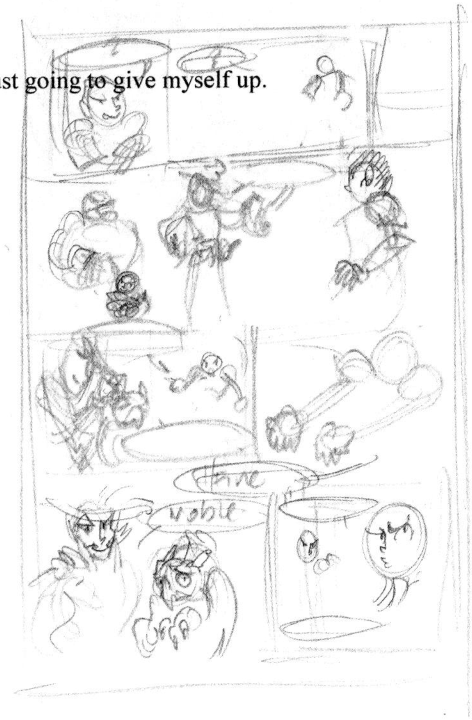
Fine
noble

ARTIST EMILY MARTIN'S NOTES
ON ORIGINAL SCRIPT PAGES
TEXT BY JEREMY WHITLEY

Page 19: (5 panels)

Panel 1: Walsh grins.

WALSH

But I'm afraid it's too late for all that. You see, the reward is dead or alive and killing you is no problem for the greatest swordsman in the world, but the king has no idea who his bounty really is. Should we bring a princess in, who knows what we'd get. Especially if we had to tie her up and drag her there with who knows what injuries.

Panel 2: Walsh points a dagger toward Abraham.

WALSH

Of course. If we brought him the head of the dragon, that might be a different story. Now, that's a more difficult task. But the dragon trusts you. The way I see it—

Panel 3: Abraham bites Walsh's knife hand, pouncing from his other hand.

WALSH
Ow! You little rat!

Panel 4: Walsh throws Abraham down in the snow.

Panel 5: Suddenly both Connie and Grant are ready to attack Walsh.

WALSH
Well this plan fell apart right quick!

ADRIENNE (OFF PANEL)
Wait!

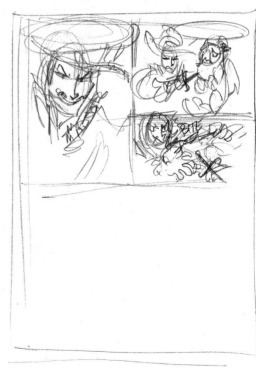

ARTIST EMILY MARTIN'S NOTES
ON ORIGINAL SCRIPT PAGES
TEXT BY JEREMY WHITLEY

Page 20: (5 panels)

Panel 1: Adrienne stands, sword in hand.

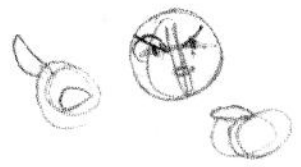

ADRIENNE
Connie and Grant, get Abraham out of here. This one is mine.

GRANT
But what about his friend?

ADRIENNE
Well, surely the greatest swordsman of all time won't object to a one on one duel, will you Sir Walsh?

Panel 2: Walsh stands with his arms out.

WALSH
Not at all, darling. You lose, we get the dragon's head, deal?

ADRIENNE
And if you lose, you leave Ashland forever.

WALSH
Deal.

Panel 3: Adrienne addresses Grant and Connie.

ADRIENNE
Grant Gryphon and Connie Chimera, as Princess of Ashland I relieve you of your post. You are free.

CONNIE
Thank you princess. Kick his butt.

Panel 4: Connie and grant walk away.

Panel 5: Adrienne puts out her sword.

ADRIENNE
Well, shall we?

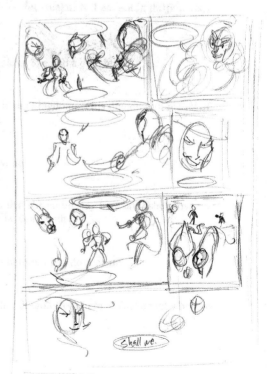

ARTIST EMILY MARTIN'S NOTES
ON ORIGINAL SCRIPT PAGES
TEXT BY JEREMY WHITLEY

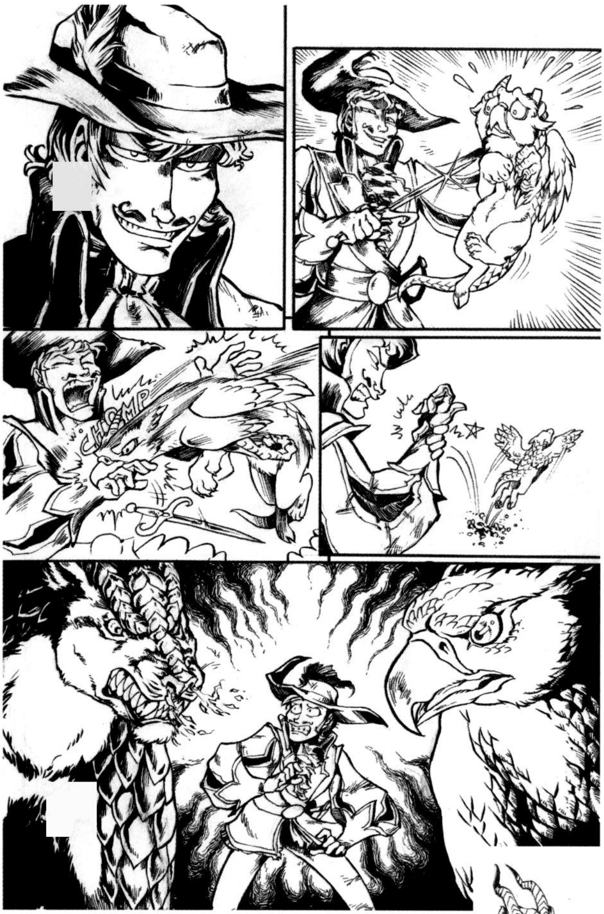
CHOMP

"MAKE YOURSELF: DAUGHTERS"
PAGE 19 INKS
BY EMILY MARTIN

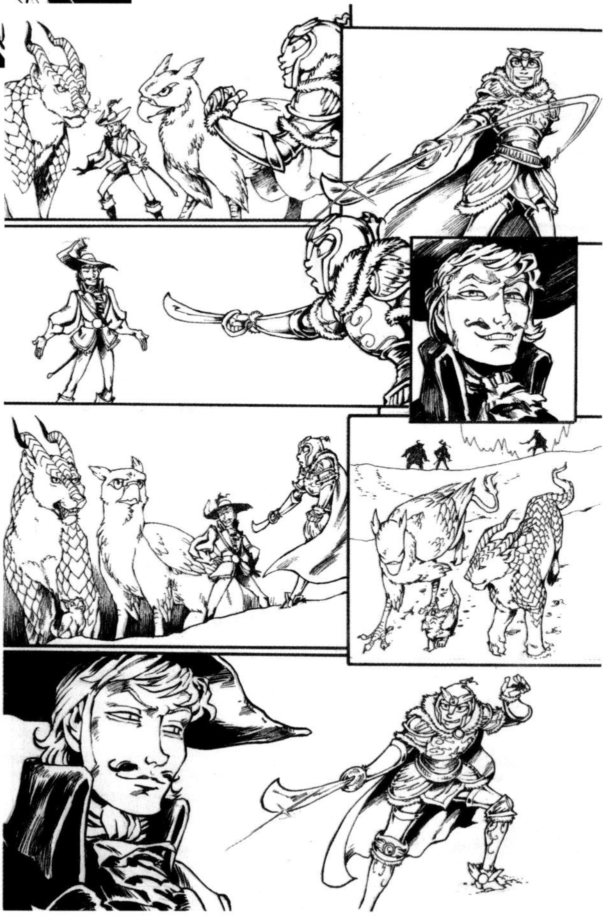

"MAKE YOURSELF: DAUGHTERS"
PAGE 20 INKS
BY EMILY MARTIN

Page 21: (5 panels)

Panel 1: The dwarves push past Bedelia and her mother who stand aside.

BEDELIA
This isn't right! They can't do this!

BEDELIA'S MOM
They can and they will. It's the law.

BEDELIA
But it's not right!

BEDELIA'S MOM
What's right isn't always what happens.

Panel 2: Bedelia runs to catch up with Delia.

BEDELIA
Well if I have anything to say about it, it will!

BEDELIA'S MOM
Bedelia! Come back!

Panel 3: Bedelia puts herself between Delia and the dragon.

BEDELIA
Greatnarn, stop! This isn't right!

DELIA
Bedelia, don't press your luck. Don't take my previous decision for weakness. I am not in the practice of pardoning dragons.

Panel 4: Bedelia tries to explain.

BEDELIA
You can't kill a creature just because it's sick. She ~~had~~ has a daughter.

DELIA
So does your cousin. So do I. So do many of the dwarves in the kingdom. This dragon will put all of their lives at risk.

BEDELIA
But she won't kill anyone!

Panel 5: Delia brushes Bedelia aside.

DELIA
You don't know that. The deal we made with the farm was that she could stay here until she proved a threat. Now she has and must be dealt with.

BEDELIA
But she's not a threat! I calmed her down before, I can do it again.

DELIA
Might I remind you that you just swore an oath to take the other dragon from here. What about when you leave?

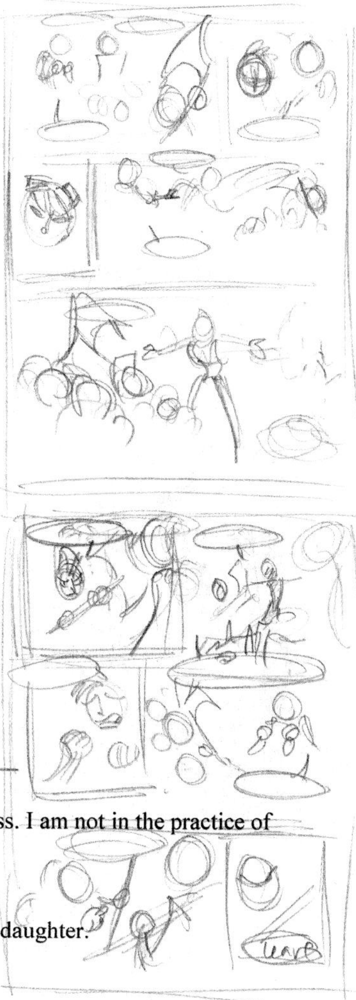
leave

ARTIST EMILY MARTIN'S NOTES
ON ORIGINAL SCRIPT PAGES
TEXT BY JEREMY WHITLEY

23

Page 22: (5 panels)

Panel 1: Delia walks into the destroyed barn. Goldy lies there silently. Bedelia follows her.

BEDELIA
Think about what you're doing. My mother can keep her and watch her when I leave.

DELIA
Your mother has already failed. And she is not part of the Dwarven tribe. Her word means nothing to our law.

Panel 2: Delia lifts her axe.

DELIA
I am sorry that you have to learn it so young, Bedelia, but this is the way things are.

BEDELIA
No!

23
failed
NO
sorry
won't
Take her
stay!

Panel 3: Bedelia puts herself between Goldy and Delia again.

BEDELIA
I won't let you do it!

DELIA
You don't have a choice. Girls, take her away!

Panel 4: Two dwarves grab Bedelia and pull her away yelling.

BEDELIA
This is wrong! You know it's wrong!

DELIA
Not everyone can fly away after each decision they make, Bedelia. Some of us have to stay.

Panel 5: Bedelia yells.

BEDELIA
What if I stay!?

24
Dragon

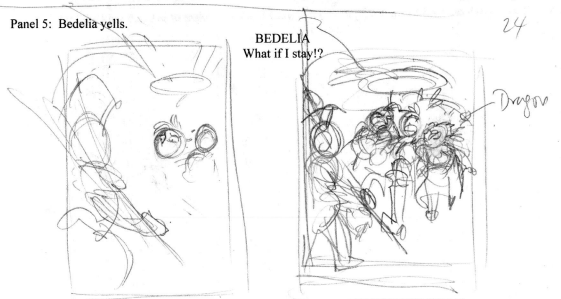

ARTIST EMILY MARTIN'S NOTES
ON ORIGINAL SCRIPT PAGES
TEXT BY JEREMY WHITLEY

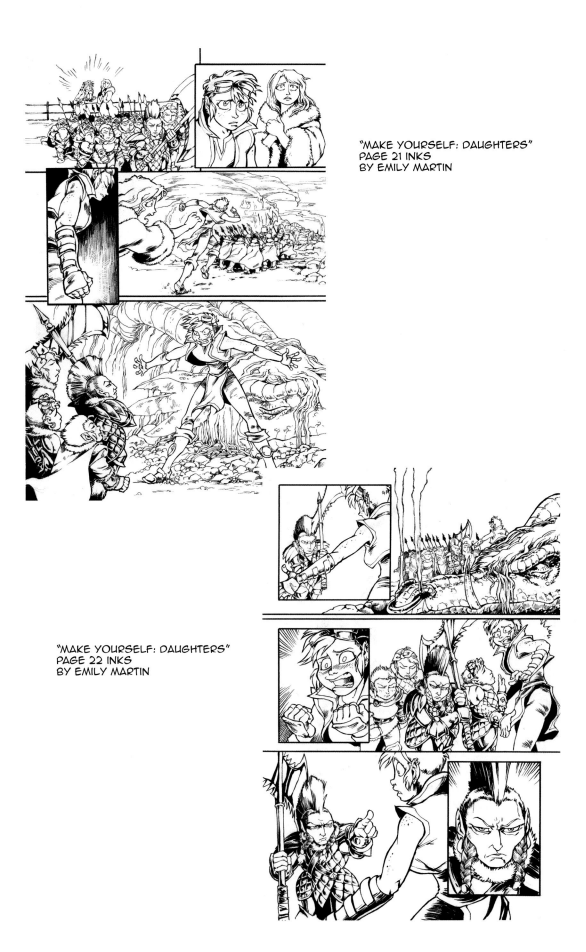

"MAKE YOURSELF: DAUGHTERS"
PAGE 21 INKS
BY EMILY MARTIN

"MAKE YOURSELF: DAUGHTERS"
PAGE 22 INKS
BY EMILY MARTIN

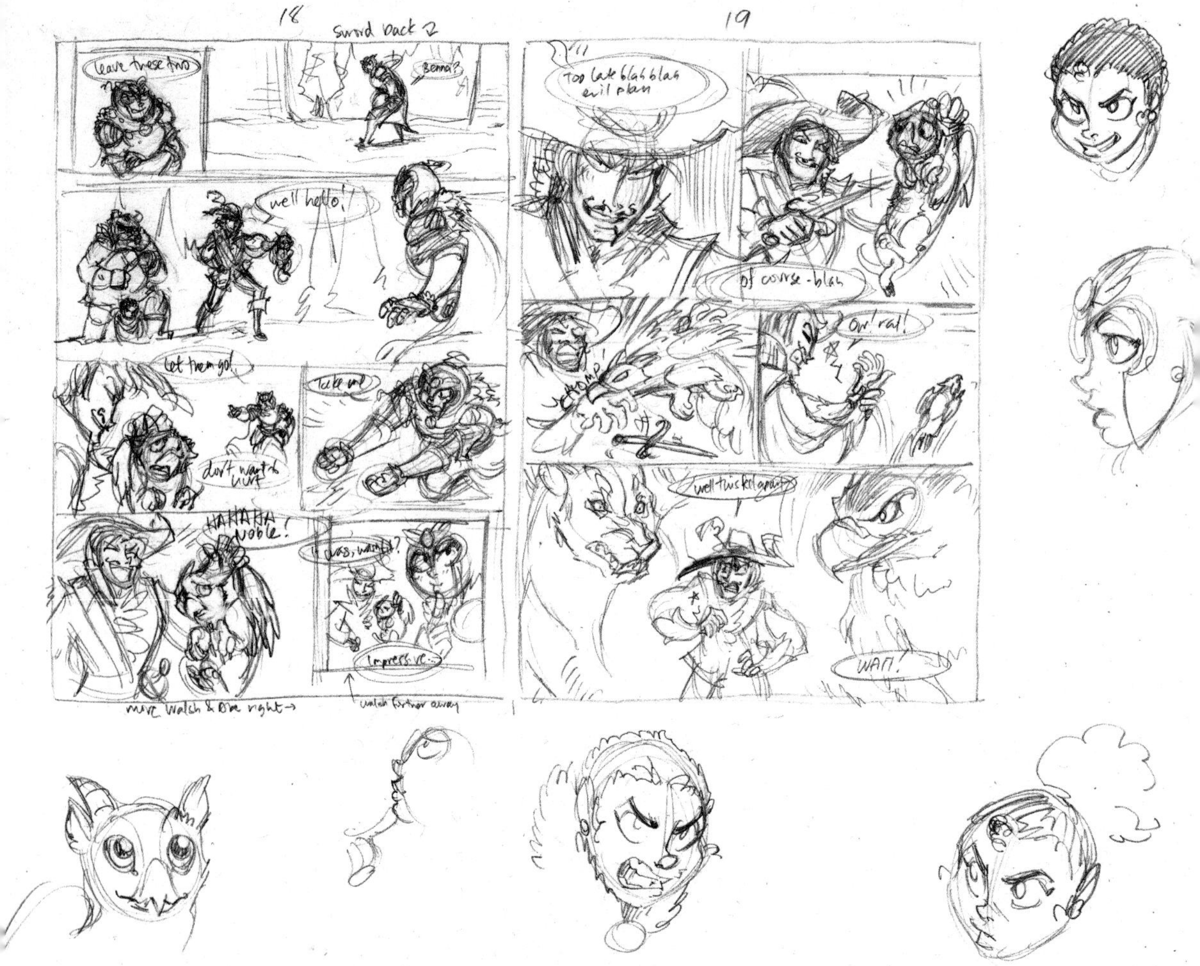
18
Sword back 2
leave these two
Benna?
well hello!
let them go!
Take me!
don't want to hurt
HAHAHA noble!
was, wait!
Impressive...
move Watch & Bree right →
watch further away
19
Too late blah blah evil plan
of course - blah
Ow! rat!
well this fell apart
WAIT!

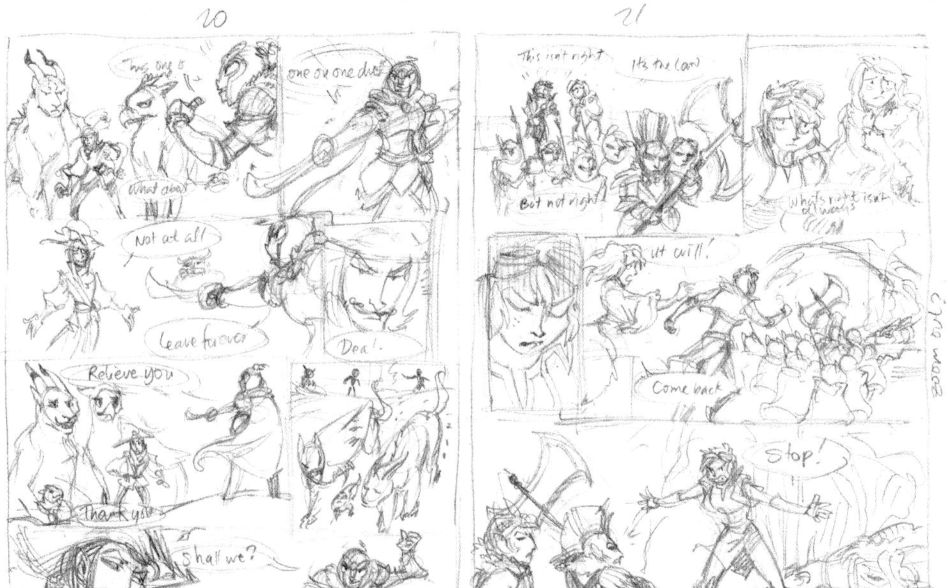
20
one on one duel
what about
Not at all
leave forever
Deal!
Relieve you
Thank you
shall we?
21
This isn't right
It's the law
But not right
what's right isn't always
it will!
Come back
Stop!

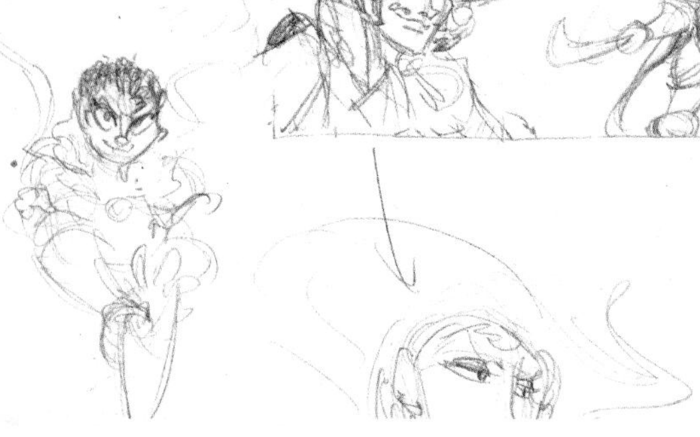

"MAKE YOURSELF: DAUGHTERS"
THUMBNAILS BY EMILY MARTIN

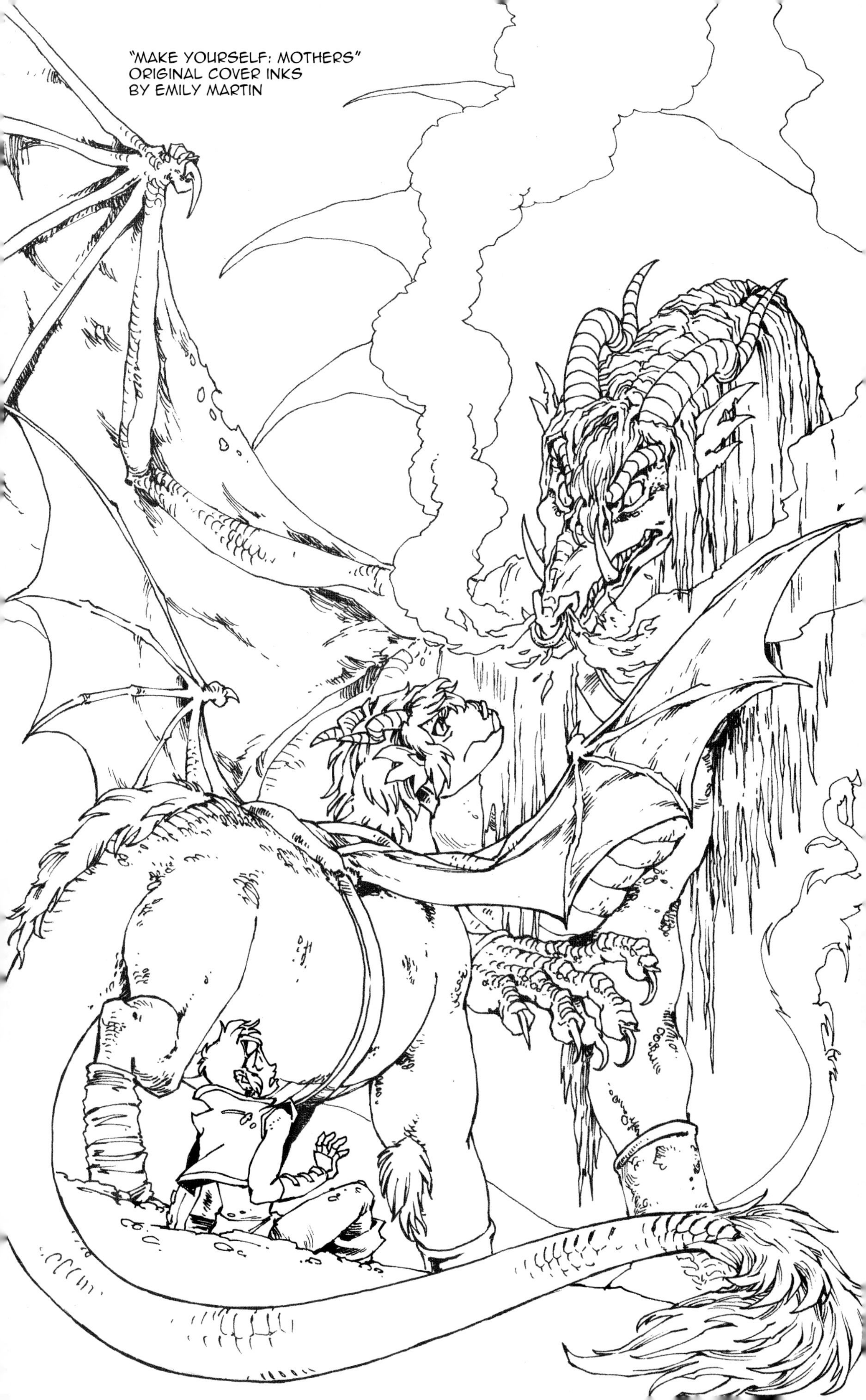

"MAKE YOURSELF: MOTHERS"
ORIGINAL COVER INKS
BY EMILY MARTIN

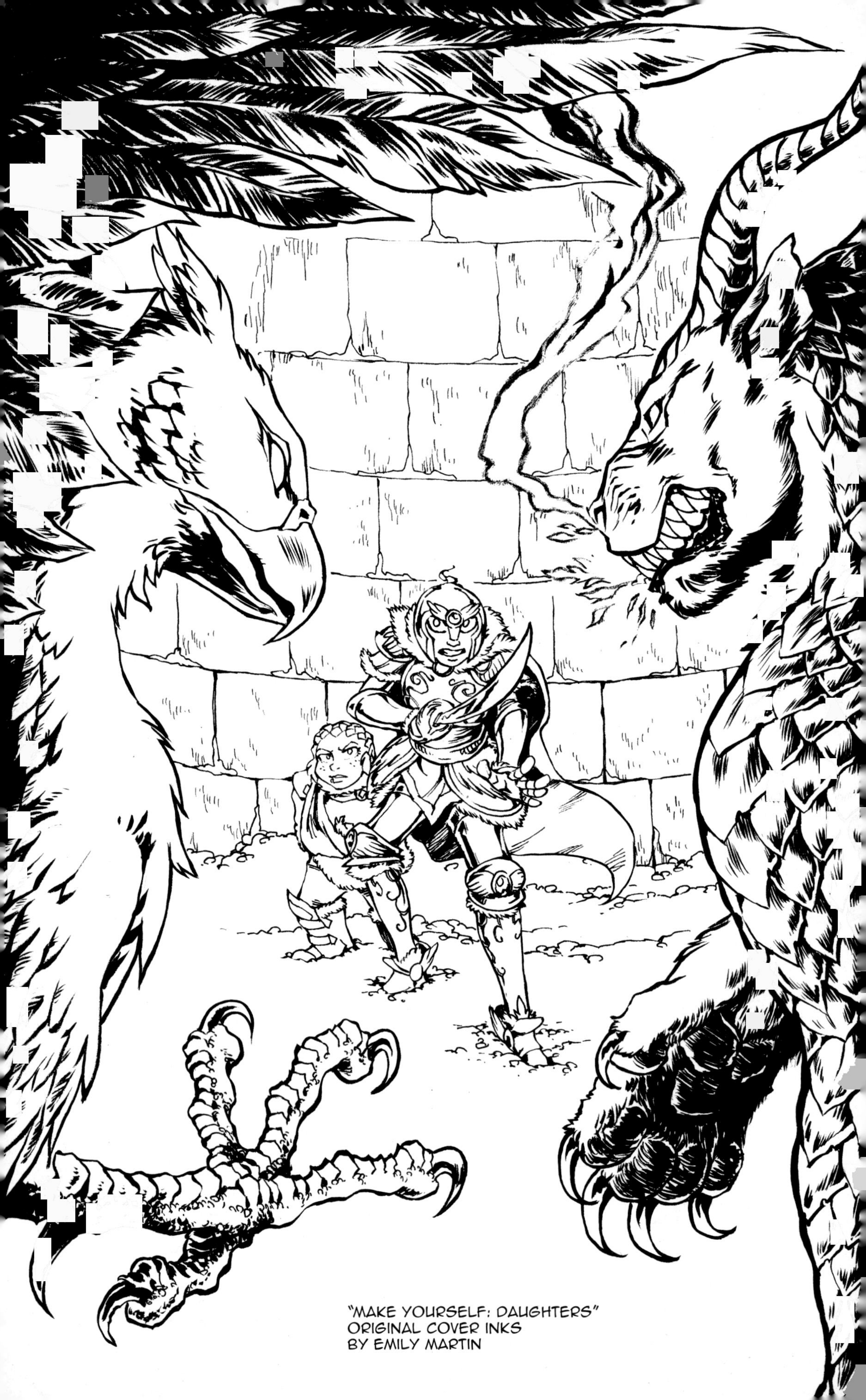

"MAKE YOURSELF: DAUGHTERS"
ORIGINAL COVER INKS
BY EMILY MARTIN

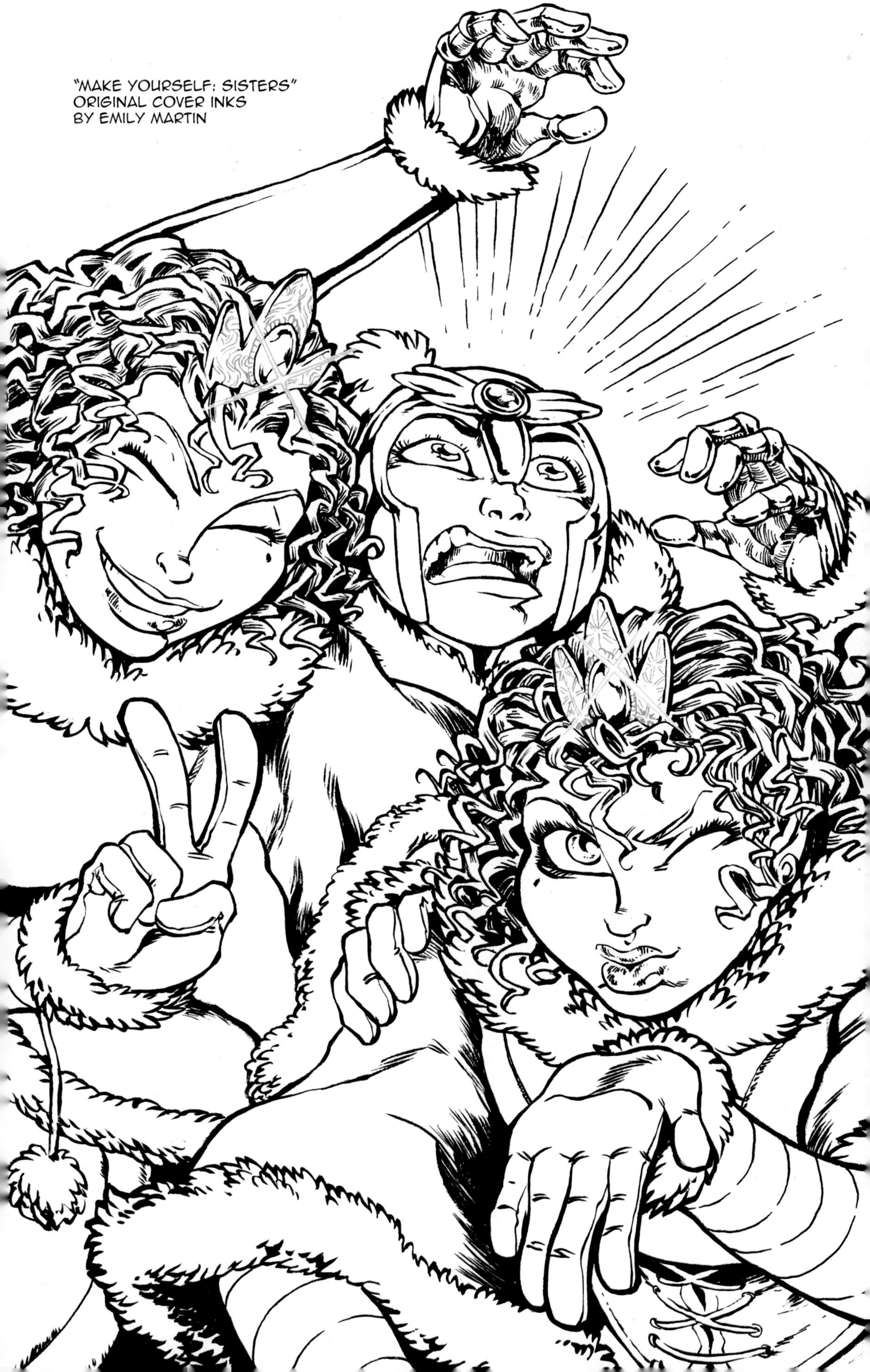

"MAKE YOURSELF: SISTERS"
ORIGINAL COVER INKS
BY EMILY MARTIN

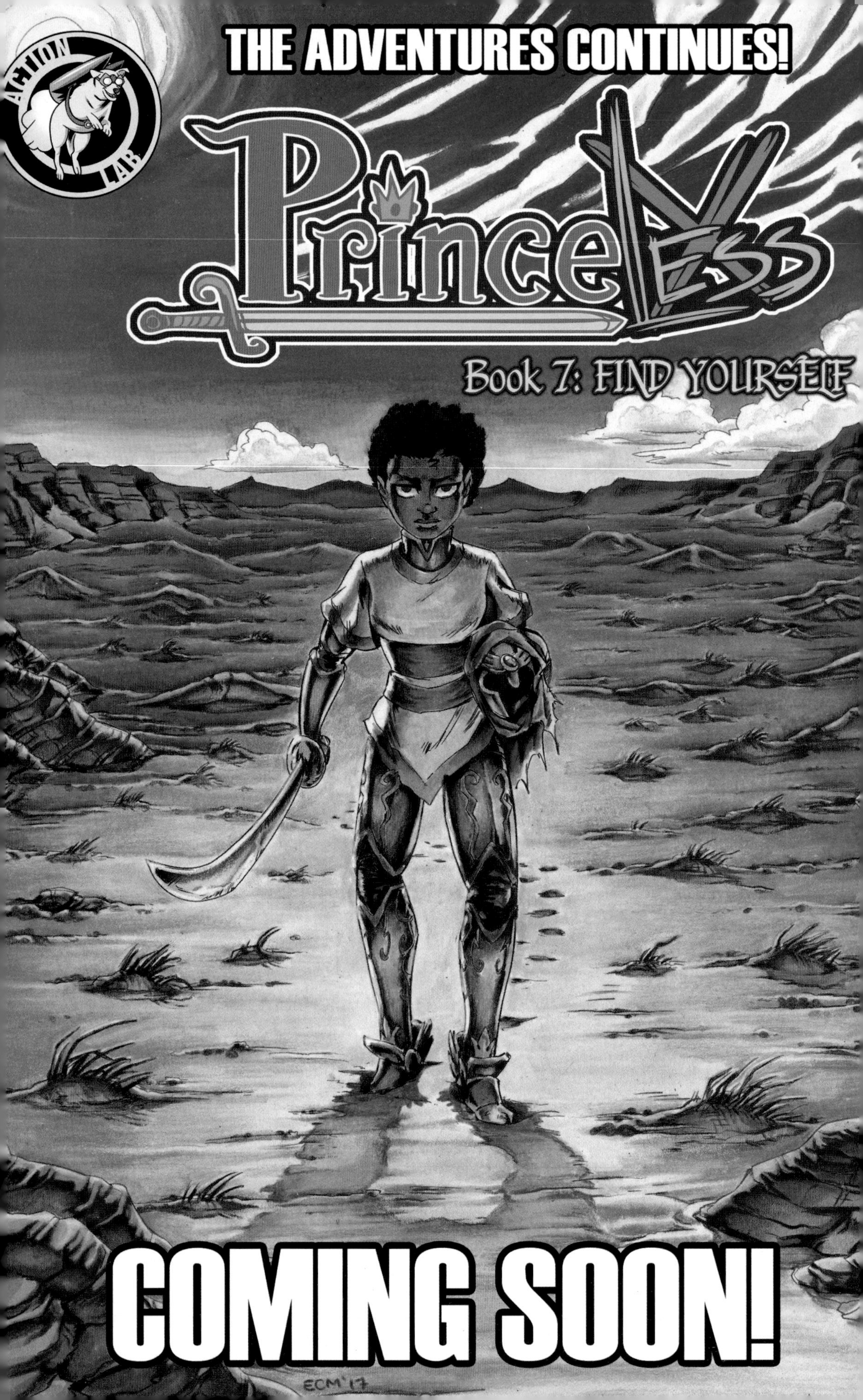

ACTION LAB
THE ADVENTURES CONTINUES!
Princeless
Book 7: FIND YOURSELF
COMING SOON!
ECM '17